TO STEVE

THANKS FOR
YOUR FRIENDSHIP
& SPLENDED WORD
WORK

BEST REGARDS Stewart

RAGE

AN INTERNATIONAL POLITICAL THRILLER

STEWART RAFFILL

This is a work of fiction. Names characters, places, and incidents either are the product of the author's imagination or are used fictitiously, and any resemblance to actual persons living or dead, businesses, companies, events or locals is entirely coincidental.

info@code7books.com
website:StewartRaffill.com

Cover by Kit Foster Design

Interior design by booknook.biz

Manufactured in the United States of America

First Edition: January 2017

Published by Code 7 Books
5776-D Lindero Canyon Road
Suite D-127
Westlake Village, CA 91362-6419

Library of Congress Cataloging-in-Publication Data

ISBN 978-0-9985873-1-8

ACKNOWLEDGEMENTS

I'd like to thank the following people for their assistance in the writing of this novel:

DR. WILLIAM LEWIS, CAPTAIN CHARLIE ANDREWS, & MAJOR ART SMITH JR., special thanks for their technical advice, camaraderie, and encouragement.

KELLY ALBLINGER, my personal assistant, creative foil, and guiding light of perpetual optimism.

DR. MAUREEN HOYT, editor extraordinaire, for her kind support, tireless attention to detail, and insight into the writing process.

JENNIFER BARKOWITZ, my research assistant, whose passion for detail and creative suggestions lightened my burden.

JEANNE DeGATANO and **ANNE HETU**, for their enduring friendship and visceral insights to the characters, plot, and story.

RAGE

CHAPTER 1

MOSHI Ilyche walked down the long airport concourse like a man on a mission. As head of security for a large American airline serving London's Heathrow Airport, late mornings were the busiest time of his day. Hundreds of departing passengers clustered around boarding gates while others sat waiting with bags, bored children, and the spoils of shopping sprees in Europe's trinket world. Airport announcements about departing planes, lost persons, and warnings to keep an eye on all personal belongings overlaid the babble of multiple languages expressing the colors and cultures of the new evolving world.

This was Moshi's domain; these were his charges. It was his job to keep them all safe and alive, which was a daunting task in a world where angry, disenfranchised militant Muslims spent every day of their lives plotting to destroy the vibrant future that so threatened the mores of their ancient beliefs. It was a new clash of cultures encouraged by a militant Islam intent upon forcing its beliefs and values onto a world that had moved beyond it.

Recently married to an English girl, Moshi tried to contain his obsession with work, but it was his angst that kept him focused and alert. Being on defense was a twenty-four hour responsibility. Being on offense was just a chosen moment in time. When he was twenty, Moshi and a fellow enlisted soldier had unwittingly allowed a suicide bomber to cross the border into Israel, his new country. It was a devastating mistake and picking up the still warm pieces of human flesh that had just moments before been vibrant, living people was seared in his brain forever.

The son of Russian immigrants, Moshi had the stocky, muscular build of a weightlifter, which was clearly visible beneath his rumpled suit and open necked shirt. But Moshi didn't try to hide his bear-like presence; he wanted the enemy to know he was there. He wanted them to feel his presence and show a sign - a furtive glance, a flush of cheeks, an effort to look more casual than they really were.

But it was none of these signs that drew his attention to a well-dressed Middle Eastern man casually nursing a coffee as he watched an LA-bound jet pulling away from the terminal building. It was the look of contentment on his face, as he seemed to smile and acknowledge someone on the ground beneath Moshi's line of sight, which caught his attention.

Moshi was a profiler; he remembered every face he'd ever seen in a lifetime of pursuing terrorists. It was an instinct born of pain and sorrow, and as he moved closer to the man, something in his features triggered this instinct and presented a name. *Hassan Mustafa.* Moshi typed the name into an app on his phone and almost immediately received a confirming photo, including a profile of the known terrorist. Ten years earlier Moshi had been in a London court when Mustafa was sentenced to fifteen years in prison for plotting to blow up a synagogue filled with worshippers.

Calling for backup, Moshi walked up behind the man and confronted him. "Hassan. Long time no see."

The man turned and smiled when he saw Moshi's security badge and name. "Very good," he said with a confident smile. "And you're an Israeli."

Moshi ignored his words and continued, "What are you doing here?"

"I'm going to my cousin's wedding in Abu Dhabi."

"And you have a ticket?"

"Of course, I have a ticket." He opened his jacket, reaching for his inside pocket.

But Moshi stopped him and took out the ticket himself. "Qatar Airways…you're in the wrong terminal."

"I was just realizing that when I saw all these big American planes." He glanced out the window at the departing jet, now moving towards the airport runway. It was a moment not missed by Moshi.

"And you're traveling without bags?"

"I'm staying with my mother. She has everything I need. Is that a crime?" He asked almost contemptuously as two uniformed security officers joined them.

"No," said Moshi. "I'm just surprised you're not taking your mother a gift."

"I am her gift. Praise to Allah."

Moshi smiled and turned to the security guards. "Take him to his plane and stay with him until he leaves."

"You have no right to do this. I have a legitimate reason to be here."

"With your record, I can do anything I want." He turned to the guards. "Don't let him out of your sight."

The guards led Mustafa away, and Moshi walked to the window, looking down at the ground crew, already cleaning up the area for the next arriving jet. Nothing seemed amiss, but Moshi's instincts told him something different. Mustafa's behavior just didn't seem right.

With a roar, the LA-bound transatlantic jet raced down the runway and lifted safely into the gray morning sky.

What was it? What was bothering him? Moshi knew better than to ignore his instincts and turned back up the concourse, speaking into his radio.

"Pull up the ground crew camera on Station 5 and back it up to 1157's departure. I'll be there in a minute."

The airline's private operating center was abuzz with activity. Several technicians manned a bank of video screens revealing all of the company's activities in the airport, including its flow of baggage. Keeping everything running on time was a complicated undertaking made even more difficult by the added needs of security.

As Moshi entered, the company's redheaded Chief of Operations, Garrett Miles, looked up from his desk.

"You're holding someone down at Qatar Airways?"

"Yeah."

"Well, he's already complaining. You can't keep him without evidence."

"You'll have your evidence in a minute." He approached Nigel, the company's young video chief sitting in front of his screens. "You get it?"

"Right here." He indicated a screen with the frozen image of the LA-bound jet. "Where do you want to start?"

"Right here's good." He pulled up a chair as Nigel brought the image to life. It was a wide-angle lens, showing the jet being pushed back from the loading zone by the squat, four-wheeled tug vehicle attached to its forward landing gear. At first nothing seemed amiss. Various people moved around in the foreground, but as the jet cleared the area, a fuel pumping truck pulled out and started towards the next gate, its driver barely visible inside.

"Okay, stop there," said Moshi. "Back up five seconds and zoom in on this guy." He pointed to the man in the truck.

With a click of his mouse, Nigel zoomed into the shadowed driver, who for a fleeting moment appeared to look up at the terminal building and raise his hand in a discreet wave. It was barely visible, but to Moshi, it was a revelation.

"That's it. You see that?!"

"What?" asked Garrett, peering at the screen nonplussed.

"He waved. Can you make him any bigger?"

Nigel shook his head, "Not without a pixel enhancement."

"We don't have time for that. Run it again." He videoed the image onto his phone as it played back. "What's his name?"

Elizabeth, a female technician, checked a sheet. "Freddy Coles. Fuel pumper. He topped off 1157 before it left."

"Can I see that?"

Elizabeth turned to Nigel. "Go back ten minutes."

Nigel ran back the video quickly and stopped on a totally different image. The whole area was now a sea of activity. The tug was being attached to the jet's front wheel carriage, cargo hatches were being closed, luggage elevators pulled back from the huge fuselage. The jet's captain circled the aircraft on his pre-flight check, peering into its massive engines, but none of this was of any interest to Moshi, who was honed in on the fuel pumper disconnecting his five inch fuel line from the jet's right wing intake port.

"What are you looking for?" asked Garrett, bored with the images.

"Just a minute," said Moshi, watching the fueler jump down from his truck where he reached into the wing's open wheel housing, pulling out a wire. "What's he doing here?"

"Detaching the static line," said Nigel. "They clip it onto the main frame to prevent static electricity from starting a fuel fire."

"Okay, go back to that again and move in closer."

Nigel zoomed in on the back of the fueler and replayed the image.

"Okay, stop there, and go all the way into here," he indicated the fueler's left hand that appeared to pull a small box from inside his coveralls and place it into the aircraft's wheel well. "He put something in there. You see it?"

Nigel replayed the pixilated image, which Moshi filmed onto his phone.

"What is it?" asked Garrett, moving closer to the screen.

"Looks like a box."

"It's got a clip on it right here, you see?" Liz pointed at the screen.

Moshi cursed and turned to Garrett. "You're going to have to bring it back."

"We don't even know what it is yet."

"Well, it's not a fucking Christmas present for his mother, I can tell you that!"

"I'll have to call New York first."

"You don't have time for that."

"I'm not going to do it without a call."

"They're already climbing out, Garrett. There could be an altitude detonator on that thing."

Garrett cursed and picked up a direct line to the airport control tower. "This is Garrett Miles, Chief of Operations at US West. We've got a possible bomb threat on Flight 1157 and need to bring it back in now."

"Roger that!" said the tower chief, his voice completely unchanged. "We'll have him go to Section 8 and call in the bomb squad."

Section 8 was an isolated area of the airport, and Garrett shook his head, realizing all the problems he was going to have to face. "I hope you're right about this. It's going to cost a fucking fortune."

"I'm right," said Moshi, turning to Liz. "I need to see that fueler, now!"

"He's at Gate 6."

"Tell the ground chief to meet me up at the desk, and have Sid and Mike bring the guy they're watching up to Security and put cuffs on him."

He hurried out of the control center, opening the office door of another security agent.

"We've got a possible ED. Let's go!!"

Matt Ringo, a fit ex-Special Forces Brit with explosive device experience, grabbed his gun and followed Moshi out of the building.

Captain Rusty Bennett was seventy miles out of London and climbing through eight thousand feet when he got the call to return to Heathrow. Bomb threats had become an on-going problem for the airlines, with most of them being call-in pranks. But when the captain received an ACARS communication from corporate headquarters telling him not to increase his altitude returning to London, things seemed a little more ominous.

"Let me see that." He took the printout from his co-pilot and reread the message. "Ask them to clarify the reason for this."

The co-pilot typed in the request, now concerned. "What do you think it is?"

"I don't know, but I have a good idea!" The reply to his request came back almost immediately, and the co-pilot read it out loud.

"New safety procedure. No cause for alarm. See you on the ground."

"Yeah, right!" said the captain, reaching for the aircraft's intercom mic. "This is the captain speaking. We have a small problem with an unsecured cargo door, so we're going to have to return to Heathrow. I'm sorry for the inconvenience, but hopefully, we'll be able to make up the lost time on our flight to LA. Please remain in your seats and stay buckled up until we get to our gate."

His voice had a calming effect on the 389 passengers who accepted his explanation with little concern.

Tom Carney, the middle-aged ground crew chief, was already waiting at the Gate 6 boarding desk when he saw Moshi and Ringo hurrying toward him down the busy concourse. They looked stressed, and he moved away from the crowded waiting area to greet them. "We got a problem?"

Moshi indicated yes and led him into the privacy of the loading ramp, showing him the image of the package on his phone. "You know what this is?"

"No. What is it?"

"Your fueler put it onto 1157, and we think it could be an explosive device."

"No fucking way! I've known Freddy since he was a kid. His dad's been fueling here for twenty years!"

"Well, we need to see him."

"He's down the steps." He led them to an outside staircase descending to the runway below. "This has to be a mistake."

"You know where he's from originally?"

"He's a Cockney!"

"Any kids?"

"No, he just got married. Julie! She's a Cockney as well. They're like a couple of peas in a pod! He's over there in his truck."

They could see Freddy sitting inside his vehicle with the door open, filling out some forms. He was a greasy kid in his mid-twenties with a cherubic complexion. Moshi indicated that Matt should cover the back of the vehicle as he approached the open door with Tom.

"Freddy! Can you come out here and speak with us a minute, please?"

Freddy looked up, surprised. "Sure. What's going on?" He stepped out of the truck still clutching his pen. Moshi didn't waste any time.

"You put a box on 1157. We need to know what was in it."

Freddy feigned confusion. "I don't know what you're talking about."

"We've got a whole movie of you doing it, Freddy, so quit the shit." He flashed the shot of the package on his phone and Freddy paled.

"It's just an isotope that can save people's lives. The Americans won't let it into their country, so they asked me to help get it there."

"Who's 'they'?" said Moshi.

"The doctors."

"What doctors?"

"They got a big posh office down there in Hampstead."

Tommy shook his head, incredulous. "And you just put this thing on the plane?"

"I thought it was a good thing!"

"You're not that fucking stupid, Freddy! What's going on here? There're over 400 people on that plane! Women and kids!"

Freddy finally looked like he was starting to lose it. "I just wanted to help, Tommy. I don't want to hurt anyone. Julie's pregnant. She's having all sorts of problems, so I thought it would be a good thing. They're not terrorists – they're all doctors!"

Moshi held up the picture of Mustafa on his phone. "Is this one of them?"

"Yes, that's Dr. Raymond. He's going to help Julie with her problems."

"Oh, fucking hell!" yelled Tommy. "What have you done?!"

"How much did they give you?" asked Moshi.

Freddy hesitated. Everyone in the area was now watching and waiting.

"Tell the fucking truth!" yelled Tommy.

"Twenty thousand quid."

Tommy shook his head, devastated. "Your dad's going to kill himself! You know that? You just killed your dad!"

"It's not going to be a problem, Tommy. They're good people. We're going to be saving lives all over America."

Moshi suddenly feared the worst. "How many packages did they give you?"

"Three," said Freddy. "I sent one to Frisco, one to Chicago, and this one to LA." Everyone looked incredulous.

"You want me to call them back?" said Ringo.

His words echoed through the madness invading Moshi's mind. "No. Just wait a minute. Wait! Let's see if we can get the one off 1157 first and see what we're dealing with." He called the tower on his radio.

"This is US West security. What's the ETA on 1157?"

"It's on final approach now," replied the tower. "Runway 15R, Heathrow Central."

"That must be him coming in there," said Tommy, pointing to the south.

Less than two miles from Heathrow, Captain Rusty Bennett descended below 2,000 feet and began to feel the weight of fear lifting from his shoulders.

"Five more months of this and I'm getting out!"

His co-pilot grinned, feeling his own measure of relief. "No you're not. You'd be bored to death." He looked out at the green land of England. It seemed like a safe place to live, with its cheery people and enduring history. Then it was all gone in a blazing flash of light, followed by a massive explosion that ripped away the right wing of the aircraft and sent 411 passengers and crew falling to earth in a twisting sea of smoke and screams and rushing air. Mothers tried to console their children. Lovers clasped hands, prayers burst from quivering lips. If it had happened at 35,000 feet, everyone would have been rendered unconscious in a moment. But at 2,000 feet, everyone was alive and aware of the final horror rushing towards them.

"Oh my God! Oh my God!" gasped Tom Carney as he stood with everyone on the tarmac watching 1157 fall to earth. It was like something out of a movie, something in slow motion, until it hit the ground with an explosion that rattled the airport windows and sent shock waves rippling across the land. Black smoke rose into the morning sky forming a mushroom cloud. Freddy couldn't breathe; he gagged for air then fell to his knees, vomiting, uttering pitiful words about lies and betrayal. But he knew in his heart that it was his fault and that life as he knew it was ended.

In his own way, Moshi felt the same sentiments. He had failed, and the only hope he had at redemption was to try and save the lives of the other potential victims, still blithely flying across the Atlantic Ocean.

CHAPTER 2

HASSAN Mustafa sat on a chair, his hands manacled and chained to a table in front of him. He had heard the explosion, felt the joy of his jihadist victory, sent praises to Allah, and now prepared himself for what was to come. Fortunately for Mustafa, he was living in England, where no matter what horrors were inflicted upon its citizenry, they still clung to their sense of a gracious society and its rules of compassionate law. It was an interesting dichotomy for Mustafa to contemplate, but he was lost in the glory of militant Islam, where denial and justification were the mainstays of his life. He was now one with Muhammad, the great warrior, who wrote in his Koran that all lies and deceits perpetrated in the name of holy war were acceptable behaviors, as was the slaughter of all unbelieving infidels.

Moshi could see Mustafa through the one-way glass of the holding room and told Ringo to wait outside and listen to his conversation on the intercom. They needed answers and they needed them now.

Mustafa could literally feel the rage simmering inside of Moshi as he entered the cell and circled behind him. What was he going to do? What could he do? And then he realized it didn't matter anymore. He'd already given his life to Allah, and there was nothing else to lose, nothing else to fear but fear itself. Moshi bent down next to the Arab's face and presented him with a picture on his phone.

"You know who this is?"

Mustafa looked at the picture and nodded. "My mother."

Moshi flipped to another image. "And this one?"

"My sister."

"And this one?"

"My grandparents."

"And you know why I'm showing you these?"

"Because you want revenge."

"No. Because there are hundreds of mothers and brothers and sisters on those two other planes, and we need to save them."

Mustafa smiled. He felt strangely calm and fulfilled. "It's good to finally see that you have feelings. Now you know how my people feel when you drop your bombs on our women and children. But this battle is already over. You lost. And there is nothing you can do to save the others."

"And why is that?"

"Because we have evolved. Our weapons are better and stronger. And you will now have to explain to all those people sitting up there in the sky that they can never come down without dying."

"Altitude detonators?"

"Descending altitude detonators. Ingenious, don't you think?"

"And what altitude are they set for?"

Ringo watched and waited as Mustafa took his time.

"They're all set for different altitudes."

"And why is that?"

"You would have to ask the bomb maker that question, and he lives in his own separate world."

Ringo looked disheartened; they weren't going to get the answers they needed and after a shake of the head from Moshi he left to tell everyone else the news.

"So you have no knowledge of the bombs?"

"No. And as far as my family is concerned, they will be happy to die for the glory of Allah, for a faith that you and your western friends will never understand and never defeat. That is why the future can only be the glorious world of Allah."

"And what will that world look like, Mustafa? Will you be riding camels again, because you and your people have not invented one thing that has improved the world in the last 1,000 years? You're just parasites, living off the glory and inventions of others. You came to this country as a refugee, and they gave you shelter and food and a job and the freedom to worship any god you wanted, and you turned on them like you always turn on each other. That is why you will always be pathetic little people, living in pathetic little countries, while the rest of the world moves on without you."

The airline's control center looked like a war room. Horrific scenes of Flight 1157 exploding into a country village played on several screens connected to news channels. Most of the images were shot on personal phones and sent into the networks. It was like something out of Dante's *Inferno*; burned black naked humans staggering from the flames of what had just been their homes and shops. Several were clutching dead children or dragging those unable to flee themselves.

Airport security agents and a rep from the CIA stood with Ringo and Garrett talking with Jack LeHay, an aeronautical expert sent over from Boeing. The stress was evident on everyone's faces, particularly Garrett's.

"...Is there any way to access the wheel well from the main fuselage?"

"No, they're completely separate areas."

"And what if they lowered the wheels in flight?" said Ringo. "Do you think the rush of air could dislodge this thing?"

"Not if it's clipped on to the main frame. The cowling of the well is designed to minimize turbulence inside even when it's open."

Everyone looked up as Moshi returned.

"Did he give you anything else?" asked Garrett.

"No. We've got people checking out his house and friends. But I don't think any of that is going to help."

"Al Qaeda or ISIL?" questioned the CIA agent.

"Al Qaeda out of Yemen. But they're all the same."

Garrett changed the subject. "Jack thinks we should consider landing both aircraft at Denver International, which is over 5,000 feet high."

"Does the Chicago flight have enough fuel to go that far?"

"We're trying to ascertain that now," said LeHay. "The first device went off at 2,000 feet, which would have brought it down over a busy part of LA. So I imagine the others are set for a similar effect."

Zach Nardi, another Boeing specialist, interrupted them. "Okay, we just did a first run on the Chicago flight's potential fuel range, and we think there's a possibility it could reach Denver. It'll be borderline, but I think it's your best shot."

"Okay," said Garrett. "I'll let them know." He left to call New York as the CIA agent continued speaking.

"So this is all going into our jurisdiction?"

"I don't think there's any other choice," said LeHay.

"And what about the people on the planes? Are you going to tell them the truth?"

"There are no secrets anymore," said Moshi. "They've all got phones and everyone talks."

"Okay, it's a go on Denver," announced Garrett. "Let's all start praying."

It was moving out of Moshi's jurisdiction, and he walked back to the cell window, looking in at the terrorist. He had done his job well, so what should he do now? It would be satisfying to pay him back and kill his family, but Moshi ultimately knew that wasn't in his nature, and he wondered if it was a flaw, a weakness that would someday come back to haunt him and everyone else in the West who felt the same.

Chapter 3

By the time the passengers on the San Francisco and Chicago flights were informed of their change of destination to Denver, most of them had figured out the dilemma facing their lives. The demise of Flight 1157 was already world news, and with speculation running amok about altitude detonators, the airline, working in conjunction with the FBI, decided to tell the passengers the truth and tried to minimize its impact by stressing their belief that a high altitude landing would negate the possibility of an explosion.

Obviously, the news had its most unsettling effect on the children. But in its own strange way, it was the children that united the passengers into a supportive, united front of faith and hope, which upheld everyone as the San Francisco jet started its descent into the Denver airport. People around the world were glued to the news, even Mustafa and his jihadist brothers waited expectantly to celebrate another victory in their war against Western values and societies. But with a breathless expectancy, the San Francisco flight settled safely onto the Denver runway where its passengers and crew were joyously evacuated.

Hearing the news of that successful landing buoyed the spirits of everyone on the Chicago flight, but unbeknownst to them, they faced the added jeopardy of running out of fuel, a fact that only the captain, co-pilot, and chief flight attendant were privy to.

Madeline Grant, better known as Maddie to her friends, was the pilot of the Chicago flight. She was one of the few female pilots flying the company's transatlantic routes, and her credentials were impeccable. Raised in a well-to-do family in South Carolina, Madeline's fighter pilot dad had set her course to the skies when she was just a child, taking her up in his private acrobatics plane, thrilling her with barrel rolls and aerial feats that would have made most grown men cry. But Maddie, like her dad, was a natural born flyer; she got her pilot's license at fourteen, a degree in aeronautical engineering in her twenties, then served fifteen years in the Air Force, flying everything from giant C-150s to jet fighters before turning to the world of commercial aircraft.

Maddie had led an exciting life, but none of it could have prepared her for the final leg of her flight into Denver International Airport. Constantly in contact with Air Traffic Control (ATC) and Captain Greg Mancuso, one of two Air Force F-16 fighter pilots now escorting her, Maddie started her descent into Denver with all of her fuel gauges blinking red and flirting with empty. With the airport still miles away and the aircraft literally flying on fumes, the whole experience began to feel like a surreal dream where prayers and crossed fingers seemed strangely more important than the mechanics of flying. But with 385 human souls dependent upon her skills, Maddie tried to focus on her father's mantra: always expect the worst; always look ahead; and always have an alternative landing place.

It was a clear, sunny afternoon, and Maddie could already see the bright white-pinnacled roofing of Denver Airport at the base of the distant Rocky Mountains. Flying over ranches and bright green circular fields of irrigated alfalfa, she could now see a four-lane highway following her course to Denver and wondered if she could land there in an emergency.

"This is AF-609. Just checking on how you're doing?" It was the Air Force escort pilot on the radio.

"So far, so good," replied Madeline. "Almost empty, but still smiling."

"You're doing good. We've all got our fingers crossed."

Maddie and her co-pilot Roscoe could see Mancuso clearly in his F-16 fighter jet beyond their side window.

"You used to fly one of those, right?"

"Yeah, I wish I was flying it now," said Madeline with a measure of levity.

The door to the cabin opened, and the chief flight attendant peered in. "Would you like some coffee or anything?" She was trying to be supportive.

"No, we're okay right now," said Madeline. "How's everyone doing back there?"

"Pretty good," replied the flight attendant.

"We'll be there soon," assured Maddie.

The flight attendant closed the door and almost immediately the quiet cockpit was besieged with alarms and warning lights as engine #1 ran out of fuel.

"We just lost one," said Roscoe, trying to remain calm.

"Shut those things down!" ordered Maddie, referring to the incessant warnings.

Roscoe switched them off as Maddie got on the radio, "This is US West 723. We just lost engine one. Increasing fuel to number two to maintain air speed."

"Roger that," said ATC Denver. "We've cleared you on runway 27 direct."

"There's no way we're going to make it," said Roscoe. "Everything's on empty."

"Let's try and stay positive, OK?"

But before she could finish her words, another cacophony of alarms invaded the cockpit.

"Number two shutting down!" exclaimed Roscoe, switching off the alarms as the RAM Air Turbine (RAT) deployed beneath the wing supplying emergency electricity to the aircraft's controls.

The plane began to shudder as it lost speed. Maddie pushed the nose down into a controlled dive countering the loss of engine power.

"This is US West 723. We just lost our second engine. Going into a controlled descent, declaring an emergency landing."

Mancuso came in on the emergency frequency. "There's a small air strip two miles to your north. Can you see it?"

"I can't make it that far," said Maddie. She could now hear the distressed passengers in the main cabin and grabbed the mic, trying to be calm. "This is the captain speaking. We just lost power in both engines. Flight crew will now initiate emergency landing procedures. Please follow their instructions." They were now losing altitude rapidly and Maddie's options were shrinking by the second.

"I'm going to try and make the highway."

"There's too many cars," replied Mancuso. He was right, and Maddie looked out the other side of the aircraft. "The only chance you've got is one of the green fields."

"I'm on it," said Maddie, turning the rapidly descending aircraft toward one of the alfalfa fields. "Wheels down!"

Roscoe deployed the landing gear as the ground rushed up to meet them. Time was running out, and Mancuso and his partner pulled out of their following dives as Maddie clipped some trees and yelled a final warning to the flight crew on the intercom.

"Brace! Brace! Brace!!"

They reached the ground, and she pulled back on the stick, lifting the nose of the great aircraft as it plowed into the field at 160 miles per hour. At first, it looked like it might work, but when the nose came down the whole aircraft pitched forward, caught a wing in the muddy field, and flipped over in a cartwheel. It looked like it was all happening in slow motion from Mancuso's jet. The great aircraft exploding into pieces, spewing flames and its human cargo in a trail of death and destruction across the land.

"723 down!! 723 down!!" announced Mancuso, circling the crash zone. "Let's get some help in here! We've got people on the ground!" He was separated from it all in his high performance jet, but Mancuso couldn't help but feel the horror and the loss. He tried to control his emotions. Just eight more minutes of fuel and they would have made it. He began to doubt everything he believed. Is this all there is to life - just the serendipity of being lucky or not?

One thousand miles away, on Bainbridge Island in Washington state, a woman racing home to watch the landing on TV heard the news on her radio and pulled to the side of the road. Monique Besson was beside herself with grief. Madeline was dead; she could feel the loss in her soul, and the permanent separation because she was Maddie's twin sister. In a sea of tears and abject sorrow, Monique pulled a picture of herself and her sister from her purse, observed it for a moment then held it to her heart, sobbing beyond consolation. They had shared their mother's womb together, held hands before they were even born, and now Maddie was gone, gone forever.

CHAPTER 4

SIX months later, the loss of another thousand people and two aircraft was just another statistic in a continuous chain of murder and mayhem perpetrated by militant Islam. It had simply become an accepted part of life in the modern era - a discounting of something that no one could do anything about. Governments tried to apprehend or eliminate militant leaders, but for every one killed, five more rose up from the ever-expanding ranks of disenfranchised Islam. It was a worldwide phenomenon, but most of it centered on the Middle East, where billions of dollars of oil money encouraged and financed the militancy.

But today is a national holiday in America, Veterans Day, when the entire nation pays homage to those who fought and died in defense of their country. A new president placed a wreath on the Tomb of the Unknown Soldier at Arlington Cemetery. Flags decorated the graves of the fallen across the nation and 5,000 miles west of the Capital, Admiral James McCracken, Commander of the U.S. Pacific Command (CDRUSPACOM) peered into the clear waters of Pearl Harbor, observing the remains of the American Pacific Fleet lost to the Japanese in 1942. It was a special place for the 65-year-old admiral whose grandfather had died on that infamous day, and he contemplated the Naval history of his family, reaching back all the way to the First World War. Those were the days of real conflicts when men faced each other in great battles with decisive outcomes. Today's Navy was simply policing the world, keeping open the trade routes, wasting billions of dollars chasing down terrorists and drug dealers with ships and weapons designed for more sophisticated enemies. But a new political correctness had afflicted the world, and even great nations were castrated and manipulated by the seductive notion that everyone was created equal. *Even the assholes of the world,* thought the admiral, almost cracking a smile when he thought of what he'd really like to do to those militant sons of bitches.

It was a perfect Hawaiian day. Veterans and their families lined the harbor watching proudly as the admiral, dressed impeccably in his white uniform festooned with stars and ribbons, placed a commemorative wreath into the harbor water, saluted his fallen comrades then stood at attention as a solitary trumpeter played "Taps."

Not far away, Monique Besson stood watching the ceremony. She was dressed in a simple summer dress that fluttered in the wind and flattered her lithe, perfect female form. She was 37 years old, with light, expressive eyes in which the loss of her sister Madeline still lingered. But there was also something else hidden beneath her calm exterior - a strength of character and purposefulness that seemed almost transcendent.

As a military band began to play a rousing version of *Stars and Stripes Forever*, everyone turned their attention to the harbor channel where an *Ohio*-class Trident nuclear submarine sailed past the gathered crowd. Flanked by a Coast Guard cutter and several smaller Navy patrol boats, the USS Montana was almost two football fields long, 42 feet across her beam, and displaced over 18,000 tons of water when submerged. She was one of the most formidable war machines ever created, with a nuclear arsenal of twenty two Trident D-5 missiles, each one tipped with eight separate, independently targetable nuclear weapons, thirty times more powerful than the bomb that destroyed Hiroshima and killed more than 130,000 people. The Montana was one of fourteen *Ohio*-class submarines continuously prowling the world as the ultimate deterrent against a surprise nuclear attack on the homeland.

As the submarine silently passed, the admiral saluted the crewmembers lining its deck and the captain and his XO (second in command) Garcia perched in the towering wing. It was a proud moment for both Captain John Besson and the admiral, who had once commanded his own nuclear missile submarine. But Besson's attention was not only directed to his commanding officer; he could also see his wife Monique standing in her summer dress, now watching him through a pair of binoculars. There was some unspoken communication between them, some silent understanding that seemed to transcend the moment, and if one looked more closely, they would have seen a tear slide down Monique's cheek and maybe a little moisture gathering in her husband's eyes.

As the flotilla followed the Montana out toward the open sea, the admiral shook hands with several of the last survivors of the attack on Pearl Harbor. It was a touching moment, but Monique kept her binoculars on the Montana, where the assembled deck crew began to break ranks and proceed toward two deck hatches, one forward and one aft of the submarine's towering wing. It was a procedure regularly practiced by the crew. However, when the men approached the hatches, they were confronted by more than a dozen additional crewmen exiting the sub, saying they were being forced out by officers with guns. It was a confusing moment, made even worse when two quartermasters ran to the hatches only to have them slammed shut and locked in their faces.

At first, the quartermasters thought it was a mistake, but when they failed to reopen and the captain and his XO disappeared from the sub's wing, concern began to reign. The submarine had already cleared the harbor entrance and several of the men climbed the thirty-foot wing tower, only to discover the hatch there had also been locked. Fear began to infect the one hundred twenty men on the deck. They were now out in the open sea, and as the sub began to increase its speed, many of them began to panic and leap into the water, swimming for the Coast Guard cutter and other following boats.

"What's going on?" yelled Admiral McCracken, reacting to the confusion beyond the harbor entrance.

"It looks like they're abandoning the boat, sir!" His personal assistant, Lieutenant Lamping, handed him a pair of binoculars. The admiral peered through the glasses and saw more of the sub's crew leaping from its deck.

"What the hell are they doing? Get me a radio and bring my chopper in here NOW!"

Monique Besson stood watching the admiral as he ran through the surprised crowd to an area where a naval helicopter picked him up and roared into the sky. People everywhere were now reacting to the crisis at sea, many of them snapping pictures and shooting videos of the action. Civilian boats joined the sub's flotilla picking up the crewmembers as Admiral McCracken's naval helicopter raced overhead and quickly caught up with the sub, now out in the open sea. It was a noisy ride and the admiral yelled to the chopper's pilot, Barkowitz.

"See if you can reach them on Port Operations!"

"Not responding, sir."

"Try 13-77."

"I already did, sir."

"Try it again!" yelled the admiral.

The sub started to dive, and the few men still clinging to her hull and towering wing were forced to leap into the rising, rushing sea. It Was a chilling sight and Barkowitz shook his head in disbelief.

"Looks like she's going down, sir!"

The admiral could see the ship's crew floundering in the boiling wake of their descending sub. "Get me the captain of that Coast Guard vessel!"

The pilot reached the Coast Guard cutter and asked for the captain.

"Let me speak to him!" said the admiral, pulling on his own headset as the Coast Guard captain came in on the radio.

"This is Coast Guard Captain Lewis, over."

"This is Admiral McCracken. Do you know what the hell's going on down there? Over."

"No, sir. The crew said they were locked out of the hull, and that's all I know. Over."

"Well, you have to stop her and you have to stop her now! Over." The sub's deck was now awash as she sank deeper into the sea.

"And how am I supposed to do that, sir? Over."

"Use your cannon! Put a shell into her wing!"

"That's a billion dollar boat, sir! Over."

"I know how much it's worth, Captain! I helped build the damn thing! She's being hijacked, and you have to stop her NOW!"

The captain of the Coast Guard cutter looked like a cornered rat, but he wasn't going to take any risks. "We'd have to go through chain of command for that, sir."

"I AM THE CHAIN OF COMMAND!" yelled McCracken, almost apoplectic. "And I order you to stop that sub NOW!"

"But I have no proof of who you are, sir."

McCracken turned, yelling to the chopper pilot, "Tell this idiot who I am!"

"This is Captain Barkowitz, pilot of the US Navy Sea Lion. I am confirming that you're speaking with Admiral James McCracken, Senior Commander of the Pacific Fleet. Over."

"I'm sorry sir, but I have no personal knowledge of you or the admiral, and I will not fire on one of our own ships without a chain of command order. Over."

The admiral interceded, furious. "Get Commander Jenson at Coast Guard HQ, NOW!"

Captain Barkowitz got the lieutenant commander on the radio. "Standby for Admiral McCracken, sir. Over." He signaled the admiral that his party was on the line.

"HARRY?!"

"Jack, what's going on?"

"I've got a Captain Lewis on a Coast Guard cutter refusing a direct order from me. So you need to confirm who I am so he can proceed. Over."

"And what is the order, Jack?"

"We've got a runaway sub, and we need to stop it!"

"Russian?"

"No, one of ours!"

As he was speaking, the Montana finally disappeared beneath the surface of the Pacific, and the admiral shook his head and cursed. "Forget it, Harry. It's too late. I'll handle it with my own people. Over and out."

He got off the radio and yelled to Barkowitz. "Take me back to Command and have sea rescue pick up the deck quartermasters and bring them to me."

CHAPTER 5

JACK Anderson stood motionless, barely breathing. He felt like a big cat hunting in the dark forest, every sense focused on his prey. It didn't matter that it was getting dark and beginning to rain, there was still enough light to see the big white-tailed buck drinking at the stream. In just a moment, he would look up, and Jack would immortalize him with a click of his camera.

But Jack wasn't alone in the forest. Two other men armed with guns and wearing earpieces, stood back in the shadows watching him. They were younger and fitter than Jack. But one of them couldn't control an itch in his throat and tried to smother an involuntary cough with his hand. It was just a slight muffled noise but not missed by the buck, which instantly spun away from the stream and bolted into the forest. Embarrassed with himself, the man called out an apology to Jack.

"I'm sorry, sir."

"You need to stop smoking, Lyle."

"I'm already on the patch, sir."

"But you're still cheating, right?"

Lyle lowered his head. "Yes, sir."

"They say cigarettes are harder to quit than heroin. Maybe you need to ask the Lord for a little help. Do you believe in the Lord, Lyle?"

"Sometimes, sir. Sometimes, not."

"Well, welcome to the club."

Jack Anderson was 50-years-old, naturally slender and still

holding on to the physique of a rower that had put him through college and carried him around the world as a documentary filmmaker for the first thirty years of his working life. It had been a rich and colorful experience with lots of lessons learned. But he now had a new profession that had the potential to test all of those skills. He was the first independent President of the United States since George Washington, and like his predecessor, he had a strong sense of self that only comes from surviving extreme difficulties and appreciating the fact that there might be more to life than just fate.

Like Ronald Reagan, Jack came from the world of TV and film. But he wasn't an actor fronting the ideology of conservatism, he was a director and a writer who had spent his life examining and documenting the humanity and inhumanity of the world and forming a much richer, inclusive philosophy of practical conservatism and liberal plurality. Jack, in his own way, was a renaissance man, a throwback to Thoreauvian values for whom personal ambition took a back seat to the simpler things that entertained and purified his mind, like stalking a buck in the forest and feeling the cold rain on his face.

But most of all, Jack was a man of destiny. He made a documentary film about corruption in Washington, a searing indictment of the lobbyists, unions, venal politicians, and the super rich who bought their way into the government and corrupted the entire system. There was no difference between the two parties, Democrats and Republicans. They were all pigs feeding at the bottomless trough of the biggest and richest country in the world. It was a devastating rebuke of the national governance, and after a suspicious attempt on his life and multiple appearances on talk shows and the news, Jack became a national celebrity. He was a refreshingly non-political person, a man of conscience in a sea of moral corruption, and when the national elections were held, people of every party, class, and ethnic background started writing his name on the ballot sheets for president. At first, it was an amusing distraction for the Democratic and Republican parties, but when the groundswell of hope and belief in a new politic reached a frenzy Jack surprised the entire world with his unsolicited election. He was now known as the "Reticent President," the new man of conscience, leading a polyglot nation that no longer had a center, other than the simple wisdom of a people that expected nothing less from their politicians than the same honest day's work they performed themselves.

Seven hours earlier, Jack had placed the traditional wreath on the Tomb of the Unknown Soldier at Arlington Cemetery then fled the city with his wife for a day of rest and rejuvenation in his new favorite haunt, the presidential retreat at Camp David. It was also a favorite place of his wife, Tatiana Bloomford-Anderson, who was engrossed watching the news and doing some stretching exercises when her husband returned to the presidential cabin wet and bedraggled and feeling like a real person again. Like Jack, Tat was an outsider to politics, an independent soul, thrust into a new and unexpected life that still didn't seem real. They had only been married for three months when Jack was elected, and she was both bemused and amused by everything that happened. Tatiana was the beautiful production and research assistant who had become Jack's close friend way before they became lovers, which was a definite change of procedure for Jack, who had spent his previous life in endless trysts based solely on the carnal attraction between men and women. But with Tatiana, Jack had met his match and was surprised to find himself enjoying the more simple and enduring things of life with her. Shared values and shared humor enlivened every day they spent together, and when the physical attraction finally ignited between them, the course of their destinies became inevitable.

"Did I miss anything?" asked the president eyeing both his wife and the TV.

"Yes. They said you're coming to the end of your honeymoon

period."

"Well, I hope that doesn't include our personal lives."

Tatiana grinned. "You're the president now, Jack. You're not allowed to think of such frivolous things."

"You mean sex?"

"Yeah, sex." She gave him a seductive kiss. "I like it when you're all jungled up like this." She grabbed his belt buckle, but he stopped her, looking at the TV that was now showing a special report featuring crewmembers leaping off the Montana, apparently filmed by people on their cell phones.

"What's with the submarine?"

"I don't know."

The president turned up the sound on the TV, listening to a correspondent speaking with a network newscaster from Pearl Harbor. "*...There's been no comment from the Navy yet, but some of the men rescued from the sub said that armed officers locked them out of the ship...*"

"So you think it's some sort of mutiny, Harry?"

"We don't know that yet, but . . ."

The president flipped to the next channel and another reporter. "*...The USS Montana is one of fourteen Ohio-class submarines, each carrying twenty two sea-launched Trident missiles with as many as eight separate independently targetable warheads on each missile.*"

"That's a lot of weapons, Jane."

"Yes it is, and each one of them is over thirty times more powerful than the bomb that destroyed Hiroshima."

Tatiana began to look concerned. "You think this is all for real?"

"I don't know, but we do have those weapons, and as far as I know, I'm the only one that can fire them."

The president's phone rang, and he answered it abruptly. "Yes, I'm already watching it on TV, and I'd like to know how they found out about it before I did...I'll be there in ten minutes."

He hung up the phone irritated and turned to Tat. "NSC meeting. They're warming up the chopper now. I'm going to take a quick shower."

"What did they say?" asked Tat, following him into the bathroom.

"Nothing on the phone," said the president, pulling off his wet clothes and getting into the shower.

"Should I stay here or go with you?"

"Come with me," said the president. "We're not coming back here!"

CHAPTER 6

THE White House was a façade of comfort, an inviting place for the president to live and entertain guests. But, beneath its bucolic exterior lies a fortified maze of reinforced concrete security rooms, communications centers, and three floors beneath the surface, the Situation Room, a heavily guarded soundproofed sanctuary for emergency governance. It was not Jack's favorite place to be, given his tendency towards claustrophobia brought on by a stint in an Iranian prison, but he sucked it up for the nation and started down the narrow steps followed by his Chief of Staff, Gary Brockett. Gary was a savvy Washington pollster who knew his way around the government but had miraculously managed to stay separate from it. He was Jack's roommate from college and despite his Washington roots was one of the few people that Jack knew he could trust, on a personal as well as presidential level. Gary was overweight, had a calming southern accent, and like Tatiana, the ability to lighten the presidential load with humor. Physically, Gary and the president were like Mutt and Jeff and had their own peculiar relationship.

"First major crisis."

"Yeah. Did Tony fill you in on everything?"

"Half of it," said Gary. "He said he'd fill me in on the rest when he got off the elevator."

The president smiled. "You need the exercise."

"What I need is caffeine and sugar to pick me up! You want me to wait down here?"

"Yeah, if I'm going to suffer, you're going to suffer with me!"

They reached the third floor and joined Tony Russo exiting the small elevator. He was the president's sixty-year-old National Security Advisor, an ex-Deputy Secretary of State and a Washington think-tank advisor who had served in two previous administrations. He shared Jack's view that policing the world was no longer a practical and economically feasible reality for a country that had less than five percent of the world's population and growing internal problems of its own. Tony was dressed in an immaculate three-piece suit reflecting his Italian roots. He was easy to be around but reticent with his opinions, which sometimes irritated the president who addressed him less casually than Gary.

"Did you reach the VP?"

"Yes, sir. I just got off the phone with him. I'm going to call him back after the meeting. Everyone wants to know what's going on!"

"Yeah well, that includes me," said the president. "Are there any specific questions we should be asking here?" He indicated the Situation Room with its Marine guards ahead.

"Just clarify all you need to know, sir."

"And jurisdictions?"

"There'll probably be a little push and pull between the DNI and Naval Intelligence, but it's a Naval issue to start with, and they should lead. Tom's also invited the Director of the FBI in case there's a domestic terrorist connection and to help NCIS check out the missing officers' wives and family members."

"How many officers are involved?"

"At least fifteen."

The "Bad" Situation Room, as it was oft times called, was small and plainly decorated with several large TV screens and an oblong table surrounded by the National Security Council members. They included: the Director of National Intelligence (DNI); Air Force

General Tom Pierce, who looked frazzled and older than his 56 years; the Secretary of Defense Robert Gaines, an elegant old timer with two previous administrations under his belt; the FBI Director, Charlotte Ramsey, a smart, risen-through-the-ranks operative with a matter-of-fact manner; Marine General Mack Hayden, a tough, imperious Chairman of the Joint Chiefs of Staff; Air Force General Michael Chiyo and Admiral David Stossel, Chief of Naval Operations (CNO), who was already looking a little uncomfortable. Everyone stood for the president as he entered the room with Russo, leaving Gary waiting outside.

"As you were." The president sat at the long table and everyone joined him. "As you all know, the VP, Secretary of State and General Zant are at the NATO meeting in Brussels. So it's just us today, plus Charlotte, who Tom invited in case there's a domestic connection to any of this. So, who's going first?"

"I will," said Admiral Stossel. "As you've probably seen on the news, at 12:15 Central Pacific Time today, fifteen officers including Captain Besson and his second, Commander Garcia, took over the nuclear missile sub Montana. So far, we have no idea why they did it. ONI (Office of Naval Intelligence) is already interrogating the 120 crewmembers left behind and CDRUSPA's Admiral McCracken is calling in every asset we have in the Pacific to establish a containment perimeter around the Hawaiian Islands in an effort to intercept the Montana."

"And if they do intercept her?" asked the president.

"We'll take her out, sir."

"Without knowing why they did this?"

"We can't risk her falling into the wrong hands, and we haven't had a mutiny on a U.S. vessel since the SS Columbia Eagle in 1970. I believe a swift and unequivocal response is necessary."

"And there isn't any way to communicate with the sub on a radio or something?"

"She does have a VHF SAT COM system. But they're not responding, probably in an effort to avoid detection."

"I understand Admiral McCracken was present when this happened?"

"Yes, sir. He was presiding over the Veteran's Day celebration at Pearl Harbor."

The president looked at his Secretary of Defense. "So we have absolutely no idea why they did this?"

"No, sir. But the good news is you're the only one who can launch the weapons on that sub, and we already changed the launch codes since she went missing."

"And you're absolutely sure about that?" questioned the president, looking at Admiral Stossel.

"Yes, sir, absolutely sure."

The president looked down at some notes. "And what is this D5 Life Extension Program I have a note on?"

"D5-LEP, sir. It's a program to replace obsolete components with commercial hardware that's cheaper and easier to update, and it also includes an upgrade of the missile's re-entry and guidance systems."

"Who performed that work?"

"NIE, sir. National Integrated Electronics. They built and now maintain the electronics on the *Ohios*. It was done at the Groton Naval Yard in Connecticut where the boat was originally built."

"So how long can this thing stay down there?"

"Up to ten years."

The president looked incredulous. "Ten years?!"

"It could stay even longer if they conserve fuel."

"So we could be waiting ten years to resolve this?"

"It's just the way the reactor works, sir."

"Well, we're going to have to assure all of our allies, and that includes the Russians and Chinese, that these weapons are still under our control and cannot be launched. I'm already getting calls from everyone."

The Secretary of Defense tried to be proactive. "We've already initiated that, sir, military to military. But, I'll personally call all the appropriate government ministers with Admiral Stossel and make sure everyone else understands."

General Hayden cleared his throat and interjected. "The Russians have already gone to DEFCON 4, sir. I recommend that we do the same."

"And what does that entail?"

"We start manning up, sir; more staff on hand, more pilots standing by. It's just a first step, in case there's a conflict."

"No. I don't want to do that yet. I've got an important meeting with the Senate tomorrow, and I don't want this thing sucking all the air out of that. How about the NSA surveillance, Tom? Did you see anything on that?"

The DNI shook his head. "No, sir. We did a reach-back on all fifteen officers as soon as this happened but found nothing."

"And how about you, Charlotte? I saw you checking your notes."

"We did get a recent MSS intercept from Beijing requesting information about an employee at the Montana's home base in Kitsap, Washington."

"So you think this could involve the Chinese?"

"I don't know that, sir. It was just a low priority request, but we'll definitely check it out."

"Okay, so the big question still remains: Why would they take a ship if they can't utilize its weapons? I'd like a list of all the possible reasons, and I'd also like the manifest of all the weapons on that sub and what sort of danger they represent."

Chapter 7

It was late afternoon at the Nimitz-MacArthur Pacific Command Center in Hawaii, where Admiral McCracken and his staff were already tightening the containment noose around the islands. They had a lot of assets to deploy, but the *Ohio*-class Trident submarines were the quietest vessels ever made, and in almost all of the simulated search and destroy games the Trident had survived undetected. The admiral was concerned that if the Montana broke out of his encirclement, she could disappear anywhere in the world, including beneath the polar ice caps.

McCracken sat in his office interrogating the two deck quartermasters that had survived the Montana's mutiny. He was tense and frustrated; an officer from NCIS (Naval Criminal Investigative Service) sat in the corner of the room observing the meeting as Lieutenant Lamping stood watchfully at the door.

"...So you had no warning this was going to happen?"

"No, sir," replied the senior quartermaster. "When we left for the deck drill, the armory was locked and secured."

"And prior to that did anyone approach you to join this mutiny?"

"No, sir."

McCracken looked to the second quartermaster, who repeated the same refrain.

"Absolutely not, sir."

"And you heard nothing that might have indicated something like this was going to happen?"

"Nothing, sir."

"A submarine is a very contained environment, gentlemen. There are rarely any secrets. So, are you absolutely certain about that?"

"Yes, sir. We've been with the boat since Groton, and there was no indication at all."

"There is one thing, sir, that could be important," said the second quartermaster. "One of the officers forcing the men out of the sub said they had a new mission."

"And what was that?"

"He said it was for officers only. Code Touché or something."

"Touché?"

"I think it means 'payback' in French."

"I know what it means; the question is, who does it refer to? Who is it threatening?"

"They didn't say anything about that, sir."

"And there's nothing else that happened prior to the mutiny that may shed light on any of this?"

"One of the weapons officers didn't make departure, sir. I don't know if that means anything..."

"And you left without him?"

"Yes, sir. Another officer was promoted to his position."

"What is the name of this missing officer?"

"Lieutenant Chang."

McCracken wrote down the name, "Asian?"

"No, sir, Caucasian."

"And who was the man that took his place?"

"Flynn, sir. Lieutenant Flynn. He was in line for the promotion."

"And how do you know that?"

"It was just general knowledge."

"And did anyone say what happened to Lieutenant Chang?"

"No, sir. They gave us two days R&R on the island, and everyone went their separate ways."

"And what did you do?"

"My girlfriend flew in for the weekend."

"And you?" The admiral looked at the second quartermaster.

"I just hung out with some of the guys."

"Any officers?"

"No, sir. They have their own group."

"Where did they stay?"

"I don't know. Someone said some of them were at The Royal Hawaiian."

"Pretty fancy," offered McCracken.

"Beyond my pay scale, sir."

"Very well, gentlemen. If you remember anything else that may be pertinent to this investigation, contact Lieutenant Darden at NCIS." He indicated the NCIS agent sitting in the room.

"Yes, sir." The two quartermasters saluted McCracken and left the room, leaving the admiral alone with Darden.

"We need to get some more help in here. I want this Lieutenant Chang picked up now, and I want to know everything there is to know about his replacement, Lieutenant Flynn."

"Yes, sir, I'll get right on it."

Darden left and the admiral turned to Lamping. "See if we ever used the code name 'Touché' in any of our missions. And get me a coffee."

"I've got one right here, Jay." Rear Admiral Donald Acker stood in the doorway holding a couple of Red Eye specials. He was the slim, fit, 63-year-old Deputy Commander of the Pacific Fleet and a close personal friend of McCracken's.

"Thought you might need a little pick me up."

"What are you doing here? I thought you were fishing in Alaska?"

"I was, but I came back today. Got a ride on a P8. You've got three of them now."

"So you're up on everything?"

"Yeah, I can't believe it. What the hell are they doing? They can't launch without the president, so what's the point?"

"I wish I knew. Maybe they've figured a way around it. You were at Annapolis; did you ever meet this Besson?"

"Yeah, he was an excellent student, first in class. Great quarterback. We beat Army that year, everyone liked him."

"Predictable?"

"No, that's why he got the promotion."

"Married?"

"Divorced and remarried."

"Kids?"

"None that I know of."

"And Garcia?"

"Married, one boy; always seemed happy. Came in three years after Besson. Best linebacker we ever had."

The admiral lowered his voice, adding gravity to his concerns. "It can't be just them alone, Don. There's no way you're going to get fifteen officers to agree to something like this or even be tricked into it."

"Well, they'd certainly need a cause."

"What kind of cause?"

"Anti-nuke statement? Maybe just a better government."

"You're kidding," said McCracken.

"Why not? It's a pretty useless bunch we've got running things now."

"Democracy is messy."

"And democracies can be bought and paid for, just like everything else."

"So, you think they're going to use this to threaten the government?"

"I don't know. It was just a thought. I'm surprised there weren't any dissenters."

"One of the weapons officers went AWOL. Maybe he didn't want to be part of it."

"So why didn't he step forward?"

"Maybe they got rid of him."

"You don't really think they could break the codes, do you?"

"Not anyone on that boat, but if they're part of something bigger, who knows?"

The admiral took a sip of his coffee. "It's not like the old days, Don. The whole system's melting down. It's the chain of command; there's too many of us. Nobody knows who anyone is anymore! I could have stopped that sub today with a 76 millimeter through its wing, but the Coast Guard captain didn't recognize me, and by the time I convinced him, she was gone."

"Well, you're still going to get her. You've got the Vincent closing from the east, and I understand you're bringing in the Nimitz from the west."

"Yeah. She broke off maneuvers with the Japanese two hours ago."

"How many attack subs?

"Three at the moment, two more on their way."

"That's a lot of assets."

"Yeah, the problem is they already know that. So what're they going to do?"

"I guess that depends on their mission."

"Did you ever hear the word 'Touché' used for any of our operations?"

"No."

"Well, that's what the officers on the Montana are reputedly calling this."

"You're kidding?"

"No."

"That sounds ominous…."

Lieutenant Lamping knocked on the door, interrupting them. "Sorry to disturb you sir, but a P-8 just picked up an unidentified sub off Maui."

Acker grinned as they both stood up and left the room. "I told you they were good."

The Boeing P-8A Poseidon aircraft was the Navy's newest multifaceted anti-sub and surface ship hunter. Fitted with high-resolution radar imaging, anti-ship missiles, depth charges, sonobuoys, and torpedoes, it was a formidable long-range battle platform presently being integrated into the Navy's new force systems.

Admiral McCracken entered the large Nimitz McArthur Pacific Command Center with Acker and approached Fleet Master Peter Yannis standing in front of a large multi-digital screen dominating the room. Over two dozen military technicians manned its high tech equipment.

"What have we got, Pete?"

Yannis indicated the screen. "Unidentified sub, sir, bearing one eight five, 110 miles southeast of Maui. The P-8s are already dropping sonobuoys."

McCracken observed the P-8A's digital position. "Any of ours in the area?"

"No, sir. We've got an SSN-774 on the south flank of the Nimitz group. That's the only sub in the immediate area. The P-8's ready to launch torpedoes if you wish, sir."

McCracken shook his head concerned. "I'll need a positive ID for that. How far is the 774 from the P-8's position?"

The Fleet Chief deferred to one of his technicians who answered, "115 nautical miles, sir."

"Okay, bring her in for a positive ID and bring her with a DDG cruiser for back up and let's get a ST2400 in from the Nimitz in case she starts evasive action."

"Aye, aye sir."

"You think she could be a Russian?" queried Acker.

"I don't know. They don't usually come in this close, but I'd hate to make that mistake."

CHAPTER 8

CAPTAIN Harry Hamasaki was the first Japanese American Commander of a US SSN-774 *Virginia*-class fast-attack nuclear submarine, which was ironic, considering he was presently cruising just southeast of the area where the Japanese Navy and American Navy had fought their greatest World War II battle at Midway. The 774 is the fastest and quietest attack sub in the world - only the *Ohio*-class missile boats are quieter, but nowhere near as agile and fast as the hunter killer *Virginia*-class submarine. Over 370 feet long, the SSN-774s are designed to seek and destroy enemy submarines and surface ships, project power on shore with Tomahawk cruise missiles and Special Operations Forces, and engage in mine warfare.

Cruising on the forward flank of the Nimitz battle group, Commander Hamasaki had just received orders to intercept the fleeing missile sub USS Montana, positively ID her sonar profile with his acoustic array then destroy her. At first, the commander thought the order was a mistake. But after a request for clarification, the order was reaffirmed, and he started the hunt for the Montana as if she were an enemy combatant.

Less than a year earlier, Hamasaki had had a personal encounter with Besson and remembered the commander's intense combative manner as they sparred with each other in a simulated hunt and destroy mission, during which Besson had eluded Hamasaki in a convergence zone (CZ) and theoretically destroyed him and his sub with an MK-48 torpedo. It had been an extended cat-and-mouse game with both subs employing the full range of their technological arsenals of deception, stealth, and destructive power, and the loss of that conflict had scarred the competitive Hamasaki, who now relished the opportunity to redeem himself.

Constantly in communication with the P-8A circling the unidentified sub and a Naval chopper now towing an ST2400 sonar array over the contact zone, Hamasaki had set his course south of the sub's present trajectory, anticipating that Besson would eventually react to the growing array of detection devices directed towards him and retreat to the southeast.

"Message from the P-8, sir." It was the radio operator who handed Hamasaki the readout that brought a smile to his face. The target sub had finally taken evasive action and disappeared behind the ridge of a deep undersea canyon.

The captain handed the readout to his XO Trudeau, "Reduce speed to twenty-five knots."

The helmsman relayed the order to the engine room. "Slow turns for twenty-five knots."

The slower speed put the *Virginia*-class submarine safely inside of her tactical range, which meant she could still be quiet enough to remain undetected, while all of her tracking sonar still functioned at maximum efficiency.

"We should be coming into range now," said Hamasaki.

His XO expected a change of course, but when it didn't come he finally said, "That canyon runs east to west, sir. You want to change course?"

"No, he'll come back to our position."

Trudeau looked doubtful but said nothing more. Submarine warfare was always a chess game, a battle of guile and evolving technologies, played out in a three-dimensional, constantly changing hostile environment where one mistake could result in a very unpleasant end. It was a game Hamasaki had played out in his head a thousand times since his simulated defeat by Besson, but this was a real conflict now, a real life and death struggle, and he felt the pressure stalking every one of his decisions.

"Conn, Sonar light contact bearing one seven three. Designate Sierra One." It was Sonarman Second Class Wallace hunched over his instrument array like a vulture viewing the world ahead. Hamasaki peered over the man's shoulder at the sonar screen.

"She's right here, sir." Wallace indicated the mark of a grease pen on the screen which Hamasaki watched as a ghosting image appeared fleetingly beneath the rotating sonar arm.

"Not much there."

"He's riding the thermocline, sir. But I did get a partial… assessment coming in now." He tore the readout from a computer presenting its assessment of the contact vessel's sonar profile. "Looks like one of ours, sir. *Ohio*-class."

Hamasaki felt a shiver race up his spine; he had been right to hold his course, but he was by nature a cautious man and wasn't taking any chances.

"Double check it on the HP." The HP was a super-computer that dissected every sound into its component parts and identified them separately. Knowing your enemy was almost as important as knowing all of the weapons arrayed against you, and Hamasaki could almost feel Besson's presence. Cruising at 200 feet beneath the surface, the CO turned to Petty Officer Novak, in the weapons control center.

"Do we have a solution yet, Mr. Novak?"

"Still spotty, sir, but I have a range of 5,000-7,000 yards depending on the CZ."

The convergence zone (CZ) was the thermocline line between the relatively warm surface water of the ocean and the colder, deeper, sea. It was a constantly changing phenomenon that played havoc with acoustical conditions and provided submarines with a virtual barrier to hide behind and mask their actions from pursuing vessels. It was a convergence zone that had given Besson the ambush advantage in their earlier conflict, and Hamasaki now anticipated Besson would retreat to the southern coast of the Big Island of Hawaii, which had the largest active volcano on the planet. Mauna Loa rose over 13,000 feet above the ocean and was constantly spewing molten lava into the surrounding seas, creating a veritable layer cake of convergence zones. It was a playground for experienced submariners, a deadly maze in which they could hide like wolves and attack the uninitiated. But this time, Hamasaki was ready. He had spent weeks playing in the convergence zones off the coast until the whole region had become his personal domain.

"Conn, Sonar, aspect change Sierra One. New bearing one-nine-zero, beam on." The target submarine had turned away from the *Virginia*-class sub, directing its towed sonar array directly towards the attack sub in an apparent attempt to maximize its surveillance capabilities.

"You think she ID'd us?" queried the XO.

"I don't know, but she's going blind for the next thirty seconds, so come right to two-nine-zero."

"Aye, aye," said the Conn tower. "Helm ten degrees right, coming to new course two-nine-zero..."

"Down 100 feet to second CZ."

"One hundred feet down!" repeated the helmsman, pushing his yoke forward. "Fifteen degrees down on shearwater planes."

The towed sonar of the target submarine extended one thousand feet beyond the vessel's stern and required at least a minute to realign with the ship's new direction, creating a window of opportunity for Hamasaki.

As Hamasaki's sub descended into the second convergent zone, the commander took advantage of the sonar cover, speaking to the combat control officer. "Load three fish-1, 2, and 4; put a MOSS

(Mobile Submarine Simulator) in 6." The MOSS was a decoy torpedo that simulated the *Virginia*-class submarine's own sonar profile and could be used to lead any incoming enemy torpedoes away from the sub.

As the weapon's officer initiated the order and prepared the torpedoes, the Sonar handed Hamasaki a readout from the HP computer. "It's not a confirmation, sir. There's a discrepancy in the readout."

"What is it?" asked the CO.

Wallace pointed to an asterisk on the digital readout, "It's a pump in the reactor, sir. We discontinued that model two years ago."

Hamasaki's mind raced. Was Besson projecting an old profile? Or was it a Russian sub he was now facing? Besson was definitely devious enough to play such a game, and if that were the case, he had already thrown a delaying caveat into Hamasaki's plans. The commander was tempted to lash the phantom sub with his active sonar, but that would give away his own position without guaranteeing results, so he decided to be patient and wait for his passive sonar to clarify. Sweat began to gather under the CO's arms. The game was on. The stakes were life and death and everyone on the sub could feel the growing tension as the commander was forced to delay his attack and notify command of the identity discrepancy.

Chapter 9

It was almost midnight in the White House when the president finally returned to his living quarters and found his wife sitting cross-legged on their bed, engrossed in her laptop. "Long day?" she said, barely looking up.

"Too long." The president poured himself a scotch and took a sip, as his wife indicated her computer screen.

"This was my favorite moment of the day."

"What is it?"

"You lying to the nation, telling them not to worry about the submarine."

"How do you know I was lying?"

"You were clenching your hand. You always clench when you lie. So do you have anymore secrets you're not supposed to tell me?" She grinned playfully and the president sat on the bed beside her.

"I wonder if all the presidents' wives were as nosy as you are?"

"Of course they were! It's in our genes, along with some very nice things."

"I like those nice things."

"You look tired."

"I just read the report about the weapons on that sub, and I'm shocked we ever made the damn thing!"

"That bad?"

"Worse. Even with the SALT limits, there are enough weapons on that one sub to destroy any country in the world, and we have fourteen of them!"

"And they don't know how to find it?"

"No one sounds that confident."

"You should talk to the crew's wives; they always know what's happening."

"I'm sure they're already doing that," said the president, pensively taking another sip of his drink. "None of it makes sense. There's no way those guys could have taken that sub without other people knowing about it."

"So, you think it's some sort of conspiracy?"

"I don't know, but I looked at all those faces at the NSC meeting today, and I began to wonder who I could trust."

"So who is this Besson?"

The president pulled a picture of the captain from a folder and handed it to his wife. He had fine, masculine features and an aura of confidence and control, dressed in his immaculate officer's uniform.

"Wow!" said Tatiana. "Looks like a movie star."

The president read from his resume. "Top of his class in military school, top of his class at Annapolis. His resume describes him as resourceful, unpredictable in his military skills, and unwaveringly loyal to the Corps. He's also from a military family – three generations."

The phone rang and Jack rolled his eyes, exhausted.

"Don't answer it," said his wife, "just pretend you're asleep".

"And what if it's something important?"

"It'll keep on ringing."

Which is exactly what it did until the president finally picked it up and found himself speaking with Gary Brockett, who apologized for calling so late, but said it was important that he speak to the Commander of Naval Operations, Admiral Stossel.

"What does he want?" the president asked.

"He didn't tell me. I'm just fluff, remember."

"Okay, why don't you patch him through and get up here."

"I'm sorry to call so late," said Admiral Stossel from the Pentagon, "but I thought it important to inform you that we have found what we believe is the Montana and will be initiating action against her presently."

"You believe?" questioned Jack skeptically as Tat let Gary into the room.

"Yes, sir. We're presently confirming the vessel's sonic profile."

"And what does that mean?"

"It's the way we identify the sub, sir. The Russians have been known to broadcast a diversionary profile, so we're eliminating that possibility."

"So it's not an absolute yet?"

"No, sir. But it will be before we fire."

"Well, I don't think we should be risking destroying a Russian sub, Admiral. So why don't I just call the Russian President on the Red Line and ask him directly?"

"I don't think you'll get an honest answer to that, sir."

"Even if he thinks we're about to destroy one of his most expensive weapons?"

"He would be giving away state secrets."

"What state secrets?"

"The disposition of his naval assets, sir."

"Well, at this moment, I don't think that's as important as avoiding an international incident, so I'm going to give him a call, and I'll get right back to you before you do anything, you understand?"

"Yes, sir."

Tatiana looked surprised by her husband's dismissal of the admiral but said nothing as he buttoned up his shirt and turned to Gary.

"See if you can get Bob Gaines over here. I'm going to call the

Russian Prez."

"You'll have to do it in the Oval Office."

"That's fine, but I'm not putting my shoes back on."

He finished off his drink and gave Tat a peck on the cheek.

"I'll be back..."

"Yes sir, Mr. McArthur."

The president left his quarters and started down the hallway with his old friend Gary.

"How are you holding up?"

"Good," said Gary. "But I did think of something when I was getting into bed."

"And what was that?"

"If the missiles on that sub can't be activated, why are the weapons officers still on the ship?"

"That's a very good point," said the president. "Why didn't I think of that?"

"Not enough sugar. You need a donut in the morning."

Chapter 10

WITH all of his nation's problems, the Russian President slept well. Some people said he was ruthless, that he didn't have a conscience, but he was running a country that had been through a decidedly difficult century, and reassembling the pieces was not an easy task particularly in a country where brute force in support of the Rodina, the motherland, was still revered.

Vladimir woke with a groan when an aide knocked on his door, but he quickly went into his office and took Jack's call with a measure of concern. Both presidents spoke German, and the common language had already facilitated a more personal and honest relationship between them.

"Jack, what are you doing up so late?"

"I'm sorry to wake you, Vlad. But I have a problem that I think only you can resolve."

"Well, I hope it doesn't involve that sub you keep telling us not to worry about."

"Actually, it does," said the president. "We think we've tracked it down, but it's displaying a possible Russian sub profile, and I don't want to take action against it unless I'm absolutely sure it's not one of yours."

"So, what do you want me to do?"

"I need to know if you have a sub presently in the area around the Hawaiian Islands."

"Well I don't exactly have that information in front of me, but if you'll give me a few minutes, I can probably have an answer for you."

"I appreciate that. I'll owe you one."

"The only thing you owe me, Jack, is to tell me who else has the launch codes to the weapons on that sub."

"No one else has the codes, Vlad. I already told you that. I'm the only one." The president sounded emphatic, but Vladimir was not convinced.

"So why would they take the sub if they can't use its weapons?"

"I don't know the answer to that. But when I do, you'll be the first to know."

"Well, I hope you remember those words," said the Russian President. "I'll get the information on the sub and call you back."

Jack hung up and turned to Gary and the Secretary of Defense Bob Gaines, now waiting in the Oval Office with him.

"He's calling me back. He doesn't believe they took the sub without knowing the codes."

"He's just fishing," said the Secretary of Defense.

"I think he has a legitimate point."

The Secretary of Defense shook his head frustrated, "No one else has the codes except for you, sir."

"Well, if that's the case, why are the weapons officers still on that sub?" He reiterated Gary's observation, and the secretary flushed with irritation.

"I don't know the answer to that, sir. But I can assure you that no one but you has control of those weapons. We've already changed all of the codes. Did he say when he'd get back to you? A lot of people are waiting for that information."

The president didn't like his pressing tone. "He has to check it out first, Bob! I don't know where our subs are; why would he know where his are?"

Gary could sense the growing tension and intervened with a

question about the Russian. "So, you think you can trust him?"

"I don't see any reason why he would lie… the question is, how do we confirm it if it is a 'yes'?"

"Have him notify the Russian sub to ID itself with three pings. It's something they'll understand," said the secretary.

"Pings?" reiterated the president.

"Sonar pings. They can be directed towards any sea vessel. It's a common means of communication."

"And what if it's not one of theirs?"

"We take her out," said the practical Secretary of Defense. "We have no other choice."

Hamasaki felt like he had betrayed his nation by not clearly identifying Besson's sub and eliminating it. Time was now passing with the phantom sub still drifting free and silent through the convergence zones where it had shut down virtually all of its systems, presenting absolutely no sound to identify it. But in Hamasaki's mind, that's exactly what Besson would do. He was the master of deception and with that constantly playing on his mind, the *Virginia*-class submarine's commander was forced to wait, constantly alert in case the target sub turned like a snake and fired its own weapons toward him.

Only the rhythmic beep of the rotating sonar arm broke the silence in the sub's control room. Every minute seemed like an eternity. Even Admiral McCracken waiting in the Pacific Command Center, and the Joint Chiefs of Staff standing by in Washington, could feel the tension. Then suddenly, like a heralding trumpet, three explosive pings rattled Hamasaki's hull, confirming the presence of a Russian vessel and the disappearance of the Montana.

After responding to the Russian's signal with a three-ping salute of his own, Hamasaki disarmed his torpedoes and rejoined the Nimitz battle group in its continuing search for the Montana, now at-large in a sea that encompassed over one-third of the world's surface. She had become an enigma, a ghost ship with an unknown purpose, and a sense of foreboding descended on everyone.

Naturally, the Joint Chiefs of Staff and Admiral McCracken were not pleased by the president's intervention in their military affairs. But Jack was smart enough to minimize his involvement, even though the Russian President took great pleasure in telling everyone how he was now helping the Americans in their search for the missing Montana.

It was three in the morning before everything was wrapped up for the president, but before retiring to his quarters, he made one last call to the Russian President, thanked him for his help, and presented him with a rhetorical question he had always wanted to explore with his Russian rival.

"Vlad, can I ask you a question? It's something I've always wondered about."

"Sure," said the Russian.

"There are 148 million Russians living on a landmass that is bigger than China and Europe combined. Just how do you intend to protect that much land from the ever growing billions massing at your borders without any allies?"

"What are you suggesting, Jack?"

"I'm suggesting that Russia and its people are basically European in their essence and that Russia should consider returning to its roots and become part of a greater Europe that would make everyone safer and infinitely richer."

"And what about your vaunted NATO?" queried Vladimir with an ironic smile.

"You'd become part of it. . . just a thought. Think about it," the president smiled.

He had made his point and let it sit in the festering ether of reality.

Chapter 11

By the following morning, the disappearance of the nuclear missile submarine Montana dominated the international stage. A veritable blitzkrieg of video images showed the sub escaping Pearl Harbor, Admiral McCracken chasing it in his chopper, and multiple shots of its crewmembers leaping into the sea as it descended into the Pacific Ocean. It was like a theatrical movie shot on multiple cell phones.

Nations around the world, including America's allies, expressed their common concerns while those in conflict with the United States said it was impossible for a technologically evolved country like America to let this happen without the government's knowledge. It was a conspiracy, an effort to threaten the world, and even with all of the president's reassurances that the launch codes were secure, people were not convinced. It was a growing crisis of confidence and the pressure to solve the riddle of the missing sub took precedence over everything in the government, including the president's plans to appear before Congress that very day and present the bedrock of his new plan for governance, a fair and simple flat tax for everyone. Frustrated by the distraction of the sub and a press conference where the tax initiative never even came up, the president returned to his private quarters where even his wife was enthralled by the crisis.

"Did you see that the North Koreans are threatening to launch their own weapons against America if they're attacked by the sub?"

"Yes, I did," said Jack, "but I don't know what the hell they're talking about, because if that sub attacks their piss-ant little fucking country, they won't even exist anymore!"

Tatiana was surprised by his outburst. "You're that upset?"

"Yes, I am! No one's even talking about the tax bill, and if I wasn't a rational person, I'd think this whole thing with the sub is just another distraction to maintain the government status quo."

"So why don't you take all this frustration and use it to light a fire under Congress? You're in a fighting mood, so go fight!"

"Yeah, I'll grab my sword and put on my armor."

"I'm serious."

"I know," said the president. "I'm just venting. You know how many heads of state I had to talk to this morning? Foreign policy's taking up more time than running the nation! I guess that's the way it goes. You come into the White House full of high expectations and it just wears you down."

"Only if you let it," said his wife.

The president smiled. "So we fight on?"

"Yes, we fight on! No compromise. No retreat. And no complaining! Let me hear your speech."

CHAPTER 12

THE FBI was an old-boys club in which Charlotte Ramsey had steadfastly risen through the ranks to become its first female director. She was still young, in her mid 50s, and always stylishly coiffed. It was a by-product of her marriage to a well-known Washington architect and a natural desire to maintain her own feminine identity. But that didn't mean in any way that she was weak or vulnerable in the workplace. Charlotte was a crack shot with a gun, a gifted martial artist, and most of all, a person of ambition, which made her very aware that solving the mystery of the missing Montana was the greatest opportunity she may ever have.

After a conversation with General Tom Pierce, Director of National Intelligence, Charlotte joined forces with the Navy's Criminal Investigative Service (NCIS) and flew overnight to Seattle to oversee the questioning of the wives and fiancés of the Montana's mutinous crew, most of whom resided near the Navy's largest submarine base at Kitsap, near Bremerton, Washington.

Charlotte had always been one of the FBI's best interrogators and wanted to be personally present when the sub captain's wife, Monique Besson, was interviewed. Traveling with her counterpart from the NCIS, a lean, keen, Lieutenant Darryl Silver, she arrived in Seattle early morning and checked into a dockside hotel, where she and the lieutenant were joined by the local FBI chief, Sid Bailey, in the coffee shop. Sid was in his early sixties and was an old friend of Charlotte's.

"Charlotte, welcome to the west!"

"How are you, Sid?"

"Good."

"This is Lieutenant Silver from NCIS; he'll be working with us." The men greeted each other, and Charlotte asked Sid if he wanted to join them for breakfast.

"No, I've already eaten, but I will have a coffee."

"This is a beautiful place," said Silver, looking out at the snowcapped mountains and green islands.

"Yeah, we're lucky, but we also have the highest suicide rate in the nation. Not enough sun."

"You need to take some vitamin D," suggested Silver.

"I'm already on it. So don't worry, I won't be killing myself today."

Charlotte smiled; she had grown up in the agency with Sid. "So what did you find out about the Bessons and the Garcias?"

Sid placed a folder on the table. "Nothing too insightful. They live about fifty miles apart, so they don't spend much time together. Occasional phone calls. I got a federal judge to let me check some of their past conversations on the national database, but there was nothing of significance, just the usual female trivia." He caught himself. "I'm sorry Charlotte."

"It's okay. Did you hear anything between the men that was less trivial?"

Sid got the point. "No, all they talked about was baseball."

"Any financial problems?"

"Nothing. No boyfriends, no girlfriends. The only thing that stood out was that Mrs. Besson lost a sister on the US West flight that went down near Denver six months ago. She was the pilot."

"I remember that," said Charlotte. "What's her maiden name?"

"Grant. Her sister was Madeline Grant."

"Yeah, I heard the cockpit conversation on that. She was a tough lady."

"Yeah and Garcia lost a brother at the Pentagon on 9-11."

"Okay, so that's one possibility to check out. I've already arranged 24-hour surveillance on all of the wives and have permission from a federal judge to tap their phones and watch their internet activities. I understand Mrs. Besson and Mrs. Garcia are coming in on the overnight from Hawaii?"

"Yeah, they should be arriving in about a half an hour," said Sid. "The Garcias live in Bremerton, the Bessons on the back side of that island that you can see out there."

He pointed out to sea.

"Okay. I want to make sure we interview them both at the same time. So why don't you head down to Bremerton, Daryl, and we'll wait for Mrs. Besson."

Chapter 13

MONIQUE Besson arrived in Seattle on the overnight flight with Theresa Garcia and her son Tommy. They all looked tired and gave each other hugs and kisses before going their separate ways. Aware that the authorities had probably placed a GPS tracker on her Jeep Cherokee, Monique drove onto the Bainbridge Ferry casually keeping an eye on everyone around her. Normally, she would have bought a coffee and stood outside on the ferry's deck, breathing in the fresh air, looking out at the pine covered islands, but this time she just sat in her car and did nothing. She could already feel the pressure of being watched, and even though it was something she had anticipated, the concern still played on her mind.

"Monique?!" Someone knocked on the Jeep window startling her. It was Susan Haber, a friend from the real estate office where she worked, and she opened her window with a wan smile.

"Morning, Sue."

"You okay?"

"Yeah, just got off the overnight from Hawaii. I'm just tired."

"I can't believe this whole thing with John. What are you going to do?"

"I don't know. I'm just trying to figure it all out right now."

"Well, if you need a place to hang out, c'mon over to the house. I'll tell the kids to behave themselves."

Monique smiled. "Thank you. You still going to Mexico?"

"Yeah, leaving tomorrow. Can't wait!"

It took Monique twenty minutes to drive across the forested island to her small house perched on a cliff looking out at the distant Olympic Mountains. It was a picturesque place, and she half expected to see FBI agents or members of the Navy's Criminal Investigation Service (NCIS) waiting for her. But there was no one there except Bruce, the family dog, who appeared from a dog door in the house and ran to greet her. He was a large, independent mongrel with the loving instincts of a golden retriever and the underlying strength and courage of a German shepherd that made him a good watchdog.

"You're such a good boy!" said Monique hugging the dog. "I love you so much!" She gave him a kiss, and the dog licked her face.

It was a gray morning, and as she carried her bags to the house, a thousand memories flooded her brain. She had spent the last three years of her life in this home with John, and they had talked about this moment many times: the abject loneliness that would follow their actions, the realization that their lives together had ended forever. But they were warriors now and had given their lives to a cause that transcended their own existence, and Monique forced herself to be strong. Bruce could sense her sadness and whined his concern as she unlocked the house door. But as she opened it, a pickup truck approached up the long wooded driveway, and Bruce ran towards it, barking. It was Sean Lariat, a local lawyer who had helped Monique's husband through a divorce five years prior and had remained friends with him and Monique because of their mutual interest in cross-country bike racing. He was in his early forties, ruggedly handsome, and casually dressed. Monique was pleased to see him and called off the dog, speaking to Sean in a familiar fashion as he walked towards her.

"Mr. Lariat! What brings you out here?"

"I'm sorry to bother you, Moe. But I got a letter from John this morning saying I should come and see you." Monique shook her head and he smiled. "So, you don't know anything about it?"

"No, but I'm not surprised. He probably figured I'd be needing some help."

"Yeah well, looking at the news, I'd say he was right!"

"You want to come in for coffee?"

"Sure, sounds good. I need something to wake me up." He followed Monique into the house with Bruce now regaling him with licks.

"Leave him alone, Bruce!"

"I'd rather be licked than bitten," said Sean, patting the dog as Monique led him into the kitchen where the floor was covered in dog food.

"Sorry about the mess. He's got an automatic feeder that goes crazy sometimes." She put on the coffee maker and got out some cups. "I haven't seen you since the last race."

"Don't remind me; there were 12-year-olds with better times than I got."

Monique smiled; she liked him. She liked his sense of humor, and her husband knew that she did. It was a strange feeling, realizing he had arranged to bring them together. "So, you've obviously heard what happened."

"Me and the whole world," said Sean. "What the hell's going on?"

Monique hesitated, "It's a long story, but I'm not ready to talk about it, yet. But I am going to need a lawyer."

"Well, that's OK. I'm surprised the place isn't filled with them and reporters already!"

"I took the numbers off the mailbox," said Monique smiling as she poured him a coffee. "Milk and sugar?"

"Just a little milk if you've got it."

Monique retrieved a carton from the refrigerator and handed it to him. "I hope it's okay." Sean sniffed the container and made a face. "Oh, I'm sorry."

"I'm just kidding," said Sean. "It's fine." He poured some milk into his cup and took a sip. "So, this is beyond crazy, Moe! The whole world's talking about this. People are frightened."

"Yeah, well maybe they should be. At least the bad guys that want to destroy us."

"So you really think they're going to use those nukes?"

"I didn't say that, and I don't think I should be discussing it any more; at least until you're officially my lawyer. If you still want to be?"

"I want to be."

"Okay, so draw up the papers. How much is it going to cost?"

"It's not going to cost anything. I haven't done anything, yet."

"But when you do . . .?"

"We can discuss that when it happens, okay? You're a friend, I'm here on that basis right now."

"Thank you," she sounded vulnerable. "So what else did John say?"

"He wasn't very specific, he just said I should come and see you and take care of you. Make you happy, take you to the races." Tears began to fill Monique's eyes. "Hey, it's okay. Everything's going to be fine."

"No, it's not. It's never going to be fine again. He's never coming back, and I'm going to have to deal with that."

"You don't know that, Moe."

"Yes, I do. If they catch him they're going to execute him for what he's done, and he's not going to let that happen. He knows that and I know that. That's why he asked you to get involved."

Sean could feel her vulnerability, but there was something else that he couldn't put his finger on. Monique had always fascinated him with her mysterious beauty and physical strength, but now there was something else there, some unspoken secret. But before he could ask any more questions, the dog ran from the house barking at two government sedans and a van pulling up in front of the house.

"You know who they are?" said Sean.

"Someone from the government. I'm surprised they weren't here earlier. They're going to tear this place to pieces."

"They haven't interviewed you, yet?"

"No."

"So it's a good thing I'm here."

"I don't want you here for this, Sean. I haven't done anything wrong, and if I have a lawyer here it'll look like I have. It's better if I just handle it on my own now."

"That's not a good idea, Moe. If you're going to have a lawyer, you need to listen to him and let him help you."

"I need to handle this first meeting on my own, Sean."

"And you're absolutely sure about that?"

"Yes."

"Okay, give me a call."

"I'll come down to your office later."

She kissed him on the cheek and exited the house, calling the dog away from the cars and van. Bruce took a little coaxing before Monique could put him on a chain allowing Sid Bailey and five other agents to step from their vehicles.

"Mrs. Besson?"

"Yes."

"I'm FBI Agent Bailey." He held up his badge and some typed papers. "I have a court order to search your premises, and we'd like to ask you a few questions, if that's all right."

"That's fine," said Monique waving to Sean as he drove away.

"Reporter?"

"No, personal friend."

Bailey signaled his men to the house, causing the dog to lunge and bark again. "Can you just chain him away from the house, please?!"

"I'll put him in the shed."

"No! We're going to search the shed. Put him over there," he pointed to some trees beyond the house where Monique chained him up and calmed him down.

Charlotte Ramsey watched her actions from Sid's sedan. She was surprised by how young Mrs. Besson was, how all-American and innocent she looked, and realized for the first time how young the officers on the sub with all that explosive power really were. With a quick check of herself in the mirror, Charlotte stepped from the car and approached Sid, who introduced her to Monique.

"This is Agent Ramsey; she's going to be monitoring our interview."

Charlotte held out her hand in a respectful way. "It's nice to meet you. Is there anywhere private we can do this?"

"Sure," said Monique. "We can go into the conservatory; it's on the other side of the house." She led Charlotte and Sid to the glassed-in conservatory overlooking the Olympic Mountains.

"Wow! Spectacular view," said Charlotte. "Is that the Hood Canal down there?"

"No, next range over. I used to go there to watch the subs going out to sea."

"Did that include your husband's?"

"Yes."

Charlotte observed several bright colored realist paintings in the conservatory. "Who's the painter?"

"John. He paints most of them when he's at sea. It's all from memory; there's nothing down there but grayness."

Sid changed the conversation, indicating the room. "Okay. This'll be good. If you'll sit right here, we'll set up the camera and put a mic on you."

As Monique sat, Charlotte asked if there was a bathroom close by. "It's down the hallway, third door on the left."

Charlotte walked through the tidy house observing its details. There were pictures of John and Monique enjoying all sorts of outdoor activities, skiing, canoeing, cross country bike racing and pictures of them standing in front the houses of Parliament in London with

Moshi Ilyche and his English wife, Gwen. They obviously had rich lives together, and the FBI chief casually snapped pictures of each photo, like the good detective she was.

Entering the quaint bathroom, Charlotte checked the medicine cabinet looking for prescription drugs or anything else, but there was nothing. Just some aspirins and tummy remedies. Charlotte thought it could be her own bathroom, with its beauty products and perfumes, but when she turned back into the hallway, she saw Monique's purse on the kitchen counter, and checked inside of it. It had the usual clutter of female paraphernalia and a new birth control dispenser that started the previous day. It was a strange discovery, to say the least.

Monique sat in silence as an agent attached a radio mic to her collar then focused his camera on her.

"Okay, we're all set."

"Very good," said Sid. "I'm just going to read your Miranda Rights, and then we can get on with this."

Charlotte returned to the room and stood in the doorway watching Sid read Monique her rights. She had a strong presence, and Monique could feel her prying mind. It was always harder for a female to deceive another female, and she felt distracted and intimidated by her presence.

Finishing with the Miranda Rights, Sid started with his questions. "Okay, state your full name, please?"

"Monique Besson."

"And your maiden name?"

"Monique Grant."

"Can you verify your husband's occupation?"

"He's an officer in the Navy. One of the commanders of the missile submarine Montana."

"When was the last time you saw your husband?"

"Hawaii," said Monique. "He was sailing out of Pearl Harbor on his submarine."

"And have you seen or spoken to him since then?"

Monique smiled, "No."

"And that's funny?"

"It is, considering the circumstances, don't you think?"

"And what circumstances are those?" countered Sid.

"The whole world is aware my husband has disappeared in his submarine."

"And do you know the reason for that?"

"No."

"Your husband never said anything about what he was planning to do?"

"No."

"And he made no last minute preparations for this disappearance?"

"Not that I know of."

"But you went to Hawaii to see him."

"Yes. Most of the wives went. The crew usually leaves on a two month rotation and never come back to the surface, so this was a nice change."

"And what did you do in Hawaii?"

"We stayed at a nice hotel, swam in the sea, went out to dinner, saw a show..."

"And there were no conversations about the future?"

Monique shrugged, "Nothing that meant anything."

"But there was something?"

"We always talked about getting a boat and sailing around the world when John retired."

"And that was it?"

"That's all I can remember."

"And the other crewmembers, did you spend time with them?"

"Just John's XO, Tommy Garcia and his wife, Theresa."

"And what did you talk about?"

"I dunno, everything."

"Everything?" Pressed Sid.

"The weather, Hawaii, Terry's kid, John's mother…"

"What about John's mother?"

"She just remarried for the fourth time, and she's in her seventies, so we thought it was pretty remarkable."

Charlotte watched the whole thing from the doorway then finally spoke, "So what did you think when your husband took the submarine?"

"I couldn't believe it. I thought it was a mistake, some sort of drill or something."

"And when did you realize it wasn't a drill?"

"When the admiral ran to his helicopter and everyone started shouting."

"And what did you do after that?"

"I went back to my hotel room and watched it all on television."

"So would you say you and your husband are a happily married couple?"

"Yes."

"You did everything together?"

"Yes."

"Shared all of your intimate secrets together?"

"Yes."

"And now you're telling me that with all of that intimacy, you had absolutely no idea that your husband was planning to commandeer one of the most powerful weapons in the US military?"

"My husband spends six months of the year under the sea with his men. That's more time than I spend with him. So yes, I suppose there was a breakdown in our communications."

"So how do you feel now that you know he's betrayed you and your country?"

"I guess that will depend on why he did it."

"And the answer to that is?"

"I don't know."

"Would you be willing to take a lie detector test to that fact?"

"No. Everyone knows they're not accurate, particularly when people are upset."

"Did your husband ever mention the fact that only the president can activate the missiles on his sub?"

"No."

"Then he never mentioned the codes and fail-safe systems incorporated into that process?"

"No."

"So you know nothing about that?"

"I think the whole world knows something about it. It's been in at least five films that I can think of."

Charlotte took a deep breath and changed the subject. "I see you and your husband were recently in London."

"Yes."

"Vacation?"

"Something like that."

"And what does that mean?"

"We went to see the trial of the terrorist who killed my sister."

"Hassan Mustafa."

Monique looked surprised. "You know about that?"

"Yes. I heard the cockpit transmissions before your sister's plane went down. She was a very brave lady."

"Yes, she was, and I also went there to thank the man who tried to save her."

"And who was that?"

"Moshi Ilyche. He was head of security for the airline when it happened."

"And did you do anything else while you were in London?"

"We walked by the mosque and saw the imam who encouraged the terrorists that killed my sister."

"And did you speak to him?"

Monique shook her head. "No, he spoke to us. He asked what we were doing there, and when John said we were just passing by, he realized we were Americans and confronted us with his followers."

"And what did he say?"

"He said, 'We don't want Americans in this country' and John said he was sure there were plenty of people there that did."

"And how did that go over?"

"The imam laughed and said, 'The English don't count anymore. They just want to eat their pork pies and get drunk in their pubs. Another generation from now this'll be a Muslim country, and you won't be able to come here anymore. Unless, of course, you're willing to accept Allah as your salvation.'"

"And that was the end of it?"

"Not exactly. They told us to leave, and John said he'd go when he was ready and they beat him up. And not one person on that busy street did anything!"

"And how about the trial? How did that go?"

"The bomber got life in prison and laughed. He killed over one thousand people, including women and children, and said he was just doing the work of Allah and would do it again."

"So you think this may have something to do with your husband taking the submarine?"

"I hope so..."

"You hope so?!"

"Yes."

The head of the FBI was surprised by her cold-blooded answer. "And do you think your husband's XO Lieutenant Garcia feels the same after the loss of his brother on 9-11?"

"I think that anyone who has lost a loved one to religious fanatics feels the same."

"So you think that could be the reason all this is happening?"

"I don't know. I guess we'll have to wait and see about that."

A misting rain descended through the pine trees as Sid drove Charlotte away from the Besson house, leaving the rest of their agents behind still searching the residence. They were both surprised by the interview, particularly Monique's last words, which Charlotte repeated derisively. "I guess we'll have to wait and see about that…this is one twisted lady."

"You think she knows?" said Sid.

"Of course she knows, and she knows we know she knows! She's just playing us. She's up to her neck in it."

"And the other wives?"

"I wouldn't be surprised. We need to run a check and see if any of the other officers have lost relatives or friends to militant Islam."

"I already started that, and I ran a search on the guy who was at the house. He's a local lawyer."

"Of course he's a lawyer!" said Charlotte with a twist of irony.

"So why didn't he stay when we arrived?"

"Because she didn't want him interrupting her game."

"So maybe we should take her in for a day?"

"And do what??" said Charlotte. "She'll have that lawyer there in two minutes and the press there in about five! Let's just give her some rope and see if she'll hang herself."

"They looked like a close couple."

"Yes, but can you tell me why she started taking birth control pills one day after her husband disappeared?"

They were interrupted by Lieutenant Silver calling from Bremerton after his interview with Theresa Garcia.

"How did it go?" asked Charlotte on the speakerphone.

"I think she was totally rehearsed. Short answers, no elaborations and repeated the same answers verbatim when asked again."

"And what did she say about her brother-in-law and 9/11?"

"Just another short answer, 'It was something they had to deal with.' How was Mrs. Besson?"

"A little more forthcoming. I'll email you the transcript."

"Okay, I'll do the same. I just got a call from Darden, our man in Honolulu. He just tracked down Lieutenant Chang, the missing weapons officer. He's on his way to his hotel now."

"Okay, keep me up on that, and I'll call Washington and bring General Pierce up on everything."

CHAPTER 14

THE president stood before Congress with his wife watching proudly from the crowded gallery. It was an important moment and everyone could feel the tension in the air. Jack held up a small bound book with the original tax code, then pointed to the new amended document that stood over four feet high.

"This, ladies and gentlemen, is the original 400-page tax code written in fairness for the whole nation. And this is the present version with over 73,000 pages that have been amended over 4,000 times in just the last ten years by members of this august body. Amendments bestowing privileges on anyone with enough money and power to corrupt the system while the rest of us are stuck with the bill and the debt. Obviously, there will be a lot of opposition to my new flat tax proposal; all of those in the privileged class of tax dodgers will try to stop its passage. There will be lies and cabals of congressmen and women who will faithfully defend the privileges they have bestowed upon themselves and their friends. But, we, the people, are not going to put up with this anymore. There is a new consensus in this nation and that consensus is for change, so I warn all of you gathered in this Congress today that your jobs will be in jeopardy if you don't start serving all the people's needs as you were elected to do."

A cry of agreement and applause erupted from the people's gallery, overriding the complaints and boos of congressmen and women, outraged by the temerity of his assault. It was a rousing event that made the president's wife smile with pride, but when the president left the Senate and faced the press, there was only one question about his tax proposal: What would happen to the 89,000 IRS agents that would no longer have jobs?

"They'll still be working for us," said the president. "It's estimated that over 260 billion dollars are stolen every year from the federal government, so they will now spend their days eliminating that corruption." It was a good point, but that was the last question about the tax bill. Everything else was about the Montana and its mutinous crew, which left the president totally disappointed as he drove back to the White House with his wife and Gary Brockett. Getting anything passed through Congress was going to be a nightmare, and his darkening mood became palpable.

"It's just another storm in a teacup," said Tatiana, trying to cheer him up. "We'll still win in the end."

"The question is, at what price? We'll probably have to trade away a national monument to get anything."

"Well, I suggest the Statue of Liberty," said Gary. "We've already welcomed enough immigrants. It's time to start looking after the ones we have here. And besides, we've already got gridlock in every major city, so what do we want more people for?"

"Capitalism!" said Tatiana. "More people need more stuff, and that means more jobs for everyone!"

"Not if we send all the jobs abroad! And how long do we keep doing this for? We need a new system that's in balance with our needs and the land we live on; I mean, who made the decision to let a million new immigrants into the country every year?"

"I don't know, but I like it when you guys get riled up like this!"

"We're just doing it to distract you," said Tatiana, grinning at Gary. "You got any jokes?"

"Yeah, you know what the government's greatest invention is?"

"The internet," said the president.

"No, term limits. Which means you've only got another 1,360 days to go!"

"You're such a schmuck. You didn't even give me a second term!"

"You're too nice to last two terms."

"Any news on the sub?" said Tat.

"Charlotte Ramsey said they're following up on a possible motive."

"And what's that?"

"Four of the officers on the sub lost family members and friends to Muslim militants, and they haven't even checked the rest yet."

"So they're vigilantes, now?" queried Tat.

"Not if they can't activate the missiles," said the president, "which still doesn't make sense to me."

"Well, I already feel better. It's good to know they may be planning to blow someone else up besides us."

"Maybe they're going to blow us all up," said the president. "They've got enough weapons to do it."

Chapter 15

It was still morning in Honolulu when Lieutenant Darden drove to the Pearl Hotel with five additional NCIS officers to arrest the Montana's missing weapons officer, Tommy Chang. The hotel was an old, rundown four-story building not far from the airport in a poor section of town.

"Okay, this is the guy," said Darden. "Let's memorize it." He passed around a photo of Chang who was a lean, six-foot tall, thirty-five year old Caucasian with attractive, boyish features. "He's in room 305. The front desk's going to give us a key.

"I'll take the stairs with Matt and Carlos. Hayley, you take the elevator and stay with it. Larry, you take the rear entrance with Erin and keep an eye on his window; it's third down from the northeast corner. We can't afford to let this guy get away, so no mistakes. If you have to shoot him, shoot him in the leg."

Darden let Larry and Erin off at the back of the hotel, parked on the side and quickly entered the building with his three other officers. The lobby was old and empty except for a Filipino couple arguing about the value of some Chinese money. Hayley went directly to the elevator as Darden approached the manager, sitting behind a counter, and flashed his badge.

"NCIS. I spoke to you on the phone about 305."

"Right, I've been waitin'. What'd he do?"

"Deserter."

"Wow, he didn't act like no deserter," said the manager handing Darden the room key.

"Is he still here?"

"I haven't seen him leave."

"Ok, let's go," Darden started up the stairs with Carlos and Matt as Hayley took the elevator.

Three flights up the steep staircase, Darden was warmed up and ready for action. Covered by Matt and Carlos with weapons drawn, he quietly turned the key in the lock and opened the door to room 305. It was a small single room with someone lying belly-down on the bed with his head covered by a pillow. He was wearing a Hawaiian shirt and a pair of surfer shorts. Wielding their pistols like extensions of themselves, the three agents quickly checked the room and surrounded the bed where Carlos abruptly pulled away the pillow causing Kerry Mack, a longhaired surfer dude, to rise up ready for action.

"Hey, hey, hey," said Darden, leveling his pistol.

"Hey, hey, hey, yourself!" said Kerry squinting in the morning light. "What the hell are you guys doing!"

"NCIS," said Darden showing his badge. "Where's Lieutenant Chang?"

"Chang? I don't know no Chang."

"So what are you doing in his room?"

"The guy that said I could stay here was Joe Montana."

"Montana?"

"Yeah, that's what he said. He was leaving for three days and gave me the key so I could sleep inside."

"Is this the guy?" said Darden holding up the picture of Chang.

"Yeah, that's him."

"Where'd you meet him?"

"Street outside. He wanted to use the phone, so I gave it to him."

"And who did he call?" asked Darden.

"Some airline."

"You remember which one?"

"Aloha, I think."

"And he left after that?"

"After he gave me the key. His stuff's in the closet over there."

Carlos checked the closet and held up Chang's uniform and shoes.

"What day was this?"

"Two days ago. Friday."

"And the time?"

"I don't know, morning. Maybe ten?"

"And this is everything he left here?" He indicated Chang's possessions.

"Yes."

"Let's see your ID."

Kerry pulled out a beat up wallet and handed his driver's license to Darden as Matt and Carlos finished searching the room.

"How long have you been in Honolulu?"

"Two weeks."

"Doing what?"

"Looking for a gig. You guys need any extra help?"

"No. We're all manned up. So you think this guy's coming back?"

"I don't know; he's still got his stuff here and the room's paid for. You're not going to throw me out, are you?"

"No, but I'm sure the manager will." He handed the kid one of his cards. "If you see this guy again, call me at this number."

"And what do I get?"

"I'll rent you a fucking room!"

After a conversation with Lieutenant Silver and Charlotte in Seattle, Darden left two of his men to watch the hotel and went to the Aloha Airlines office at the Honolulu airport where he spent two hours reviewing all of the surveillance videos saved on a hard drive from the previous Friday. It was a boring task, but he finally found a shot of Chang checking onto a flight to LA. It was a one-way ticket with no additional ticketing, and he quickly called Charlotte, who immediately sent several of her LA-based agents to the Aloha Airlines terminal at LAX to try and track down Chang's movements after he arrived at the airport.

"What name did he travel under?" said Charlotte.

"Jimi Hendricks," said Darden.

"And nobody questioned that?!"

"No, he had a bona fide ID."

"So, what else do we know about this Lieutenant Chang?"

"35-years-old, degree in nuclear physics and computer science from MIT."

"Smart."

"Yeah. Grew up in Bedford, Massachusetts; father deceased."

"From what?"

"Natural causes. He was a professor at MIT, John Chang."

"Chinese?"

"Yeah, both parents were Chinese; they adopted him, but he looks European."

"That must have been weird. Married?"

"No. His friends said he likes to clown around and chase the ladies."

"Where does he live?"

"Seattle. He shares an apartment with a girl, but she hasn't heard from him for six weeks, which isn't unusual, according to her."

"Do they have a relationship?"

"Maybe. But if they do it's pretty casual."

"And his politics?"

"Registered Independent."

"Just like the president," said Charlotte.

It took the agents in Los Angeles less than an hour to find the footage of Tommy Chang leaving the flight from Hawaii. He seemed casual and relaxed and even took time to speak with an airline hostess before disappearing into a crowd outside the airport. Charlotte and Sid observed the airport footage on a large screen in their office as the LA agent made his report.

"The girl he spoke to isn't working today, but I contacted her at home and she couldn't remember the meeting until I texted her the guy's picture, and she called him 'the kid'. Said he just wanted to know where Southwest Airlines was."

"And did he go there?" said Sid.

"No, never showed up."

Charlotte turned to Matt and Sarah, standing with them. "Let's get everything we can on this guy, and I mean everything!"

Matt and Sarah left and Charlotte turned to Sid and Lieutenant Silver. "He doesn't look old enough to drive!"

"He was fast tracked into the officer's corps because of his credentials," said Silver. "Someone must have got to him."

"Yeah well, just spend an evening on the internet, and you'll see all the choices."

Chapter 16

After a very long day the president and his wife retired to their quarters, preparing to sleep. Tatiana busied herself in the bathroom putting on night cream as the president sat on the bed in his pj's, checking some papers, sipping a scotch. Tat could see him through the open doorway in her mirror.

"Did you see the Senate Whip turning purple today?"

"Yeah, we probably started a war there."

"We need a war. They're just a bunch of self-serving bloodsuckers that have institutionalized corruption, and we need to get rid of them!"

"God, you sound like Attila the Hun!"

"I am Attila!"

"Well, I hate to tell you this, but you married a traitor."

"What did you do?"

"I told the Speaker there was some wiggle room."

Tat rolled her eyes. "What did you do that for?!"

"I want a deal! I want it done so I can concentrate on this sub thing! It's driving me crazy!"

"I need a cause!" said Tatiana. "Every First Lady has one."

"How about the national debt we've saddled our kids with?"

"I don't want to get involved with the budget."

"So how about overpopulation? That's the real problem with the world. How can poor countries dig their way out of poverty when there's another 100 million of them to feed, house, and find jobs for every year?"

"You don't have to worry about that anymore. They're all coming here!"

"I'm serious!" said the president.

"I don't want to get into that. I'd rather do something scientific."

"Like?"

"Support global warming."

"Support it?"

"You know what I mean. Support the environment and all that. At least I'd get to travel."

"Travel where?"

"Greenland, Antarctica, the Maldives - you know that whole island chain is disappearing into the sea?"

"Sounds good," said the president. "Maybe you can push up the temperature even more with all that jetting around."

"Cynic!"

"It's the truth!"

"No, you're just being nasty, so I'm not going to give you any of this." She stepped into the doorway and did a pirouette in a sheer negligee.

"Wow!! Where did you get that?"

"Internet."

"I hope you didn't use this address."

"No, I used the VP's."

"You are such a bad thing! Come here." He reached for her, but she spun away.

"Only if I get a concession."

"You sound like Congress!"

"I want to go to Paris with you."

"I'm not going to Paris."

"Well, you're not getting any of this, then." She lifted up her negligee revealing her perfect, inviting form.

"Oh, God! Okay! I'll get on it first thing in the morning!"

"Do it now." She handed him the phone. "I'll give it to you while you're making the arrangements. I like to watch you being presidential. It turns me on."

CHAPTER 17

ADMIRAL McCracken walked into the officer's mess of the Nimitz-MacArthur Pacific Command Center and waved a greeting to the civilian Filipino chef, who quickly left his grill, greeting the admiral with a big smile.

"Afternoon, sir!"

"Afternoon, Arvin. I haven't eaten anything healthy in two days, so what've you got?"

"Oh, good day for healthy, sir! Fresh ono, caught this morning, Maui potatoes, yams fresh from mountain, and organic vegetables!"

"How about garlic?"

"I make you side with grated cheese and olive oil. You eat as much you want."

"You're a good man, Arvin. Better than my doctor! I'll take it with a mixed green salad and bleu cheese."

"Oh, bleu cheese no good too much salt. You need balsamic vinaigrette."

"Okay, I'll take some of that."

"Very good, sir. Coming quickly!"

The admiral walked across the commissary and sat at his table in the officer's section. It had been thirty-six hours since the Montana's disappearance, during which time, she could have traveled as far as one thousand miles in any direction of the compass without encountering a single piece of land. The Hawaiian Islands were the most isolated archipelago on the planet, and every minute the Montana was free, the area of her concealment grew exponentially. It was like looking for a needle in the proverbial haystack, and more importantly, it was a dilemma of McCracken's own making. He had spent literally years of his life eliminating any possible flaw that would lead to the sub's demise, only to become the victim of his own success. He had participated in the creation of a perfect monster that was now his own monster to destroy.

McCracken had always liked mystery novels; they took him out of himself, distracted him from the daily routines of his life, and most of all gave his overactive brain something different to chew on. He liked those little clues that would ultimately unravel a mystery and make its readers feel like they had participated in its resolution.

So when the admiral went to bed after the discovery of the Russian sub, something didn't quite seem right. There was an anomaly in the riddle that he couldn't resolve. How could a P-8A discover a Russian sub so quickly in the vast Pacific Ocean? Was it a matter of luck, serendipity, or was there a reason they came together? And if there was a reason, it could only be for the purpose of a diversion, a sleight of hand that would allow the Montana to slip away into the vast Pacific while everyone was looking in the other direction. And to accomplish that deceit, someone had to know the Russian sub was there, a fact that even he didn't know, Commander of the entire Pacific Command. It was a question that haunted the admiral, so when the pilot of the P-8A that discovered the Russian sub approached his table with a salute, he was anxious to find answers.

"Lieutenant Commander Anik, sir. Sorry to disturb you, but Lieutenant Lamping said you wanted to see me?"

"Ah, yes, Captain. Take a seat. I wanted to congratulate you on your success in locating the Russian missile sub yesterday."

"Thank you, sir."

"I understand you flew in with Vice Admiral Acker?"

"Yes, sir. He joined us in Seattle."

"So how did you come to be in Quadrant S46? I understand you had a different designation?"

"Yes, sir. S49. The vice admiral had told me about the convergent zones along the Big Island's southwest coast and his belief that US and Russian subs were using the area for concealment. So I made that part of my flight plan out to S49."

"So it was just by chance that you went there?"

"Just by chance, sir."

McCracken was surprised to hear that Acker suspected there were Russian subs in the area but chose not to mention it. "Well, it was a good choice, captain. Thank you again. And keep up the good work."

"Yes, sir. Thank you, sir."

The captain stood, saluted, and left the room as Vice Admiral Acker approached, looking somewhat surprised to see the departing airman.

"I was just congratulating your P8 pilot on finding the Russian sub," said McCracken. "We need more men like him."

"Yeah, he's a good kid. Did he tell you he's an Eskimo?"

"No."

"Grew up in Nome eating whale blubber and has absolutely no cholesterol problems."

"Genes. They make us and they break us. I just ordered something healthy for my genes if you want to join me?"

"What are you having?"

"Fresh ono and vegetables."

"Sounds good," said the vice admiral. "Thank you."

McCracken caught the eye of the chef and held up two fingers, pointing at Acker.

"So did you hear the latest from NCIS and the FBI? Four of the officers on the Montana, including the CO and XO, have lost family members to militant Islam, so they think that may be a motivation for this whole thing."

"And you believe that?" said Acker.

"At this point, I've given up speculating."

"Well, I guess Muslim fanatics are better than going after that little psycho running North Korea and starting a conflict with China and Russia."

"I don't think the Russians count anymore," said McCracken with a smile. "Old Vlad's the president's new best friend."

"Yeah, and he can't stop telling everyone about it! Did you find out anything else about the missing weapons officer?"

"He went back to the mainland and disappeared."

"So they didn't kill him?"

"Doesn't' seem that way."

"Well maybe he is one of them."

"Sure as hell looks that way. The FBI's all over it, and now the president wants a list of all the possible reasons they took the sub and what their potential targets could be."

"Long list."

"Yeah, they've got everyone working on it. What would you do to stop militant Muslims if you could break the codes?"

"I don't know, but they do cost us a lot of money and blood."

"Death by a thousand stings! That's what Bin Laden taught."

"Yeah. And they've been pretty successful with it. We've all lost our rights to privacy because of them, flying anywhere has become a pain in the ass, and if you look at a map of the world, ninety percent of all conflicts on the planet involve Muslims killing Muslims, Muslims attacking their neighbors, or militant Muslims terrorizing Western countries who have taken them in as refugees trying to give them a better life. And we're still letting them into the country!"

"Muslim immigrants?"

"Yeah, it's the stupidest thing I ever saw! There are hundreds of millions of people that want to emigrate here who don't want to kill us, so why don't we let them in instead?"

"Political correctness."

"Yeah, and oil money."

"So if it is militant Islam they're going after, where do you think they're going to start?"

"Middle East," said Acker. "That's where most of the radicals and money comes from."

"And if it is the Middle East, where would you put yourself?"

"Sunda subduction zone. Indian Ocean."

"That's what Stossel thinks. He's already deploying assets there from the Atlantic and east Pacific."

"That's logical."

"Yeah, but we're not fighting someone who doesn't already know that, and I can't believe they'd be that predictable."

"Well, every Trident on that sub has a range of over 4,000 miles, so they could attack the Middle East from a lot of different positions."

"Yeah, it's going to be a tough call."

"So what will you do?" said Acker.

McCracken smiled and turned coy. "I haven't decided yet." He wasn't giving away any more information, considering the fact that his friend had virtually led the P-8A to the Russian sub.

Chapter 18

By the following morning, the FBI and NCIS had set up a control center in Seattle to handle the massive amount of data and facts surrounding the missing missile sub and its mutinous crew. Replete with the agency's best analysts and technical equipment, Charlotte Ramsey and her team tried to put all of the pieces together, following up on even the most unlikely possibilities. Every one of the fifteen mutinous officers' wives, friends, and family members were interviewed and followed up with detailed background checks. Charlotte had stuck her neck out at the National Security meeting mentioning the intercept of a message from the Chinese Secret Service (MSS) regarding someone at the Kitsap Submarine Base, and was now stuck with following up on a case that had apparently been dropped because of insufficient evidence. The whole thing looked like a dead end, but in a face-saving effort, Charlotte sent two of her younger agents, Sarah Singh and Matt Weston, to the base to check out the mystery man, Kurt Maldauer.

Matt and Sarah were both recent graduates of the agency's Organized Crime division and had impressed Charlotte with their unraveling of a sophisticated international money-laundering ring. They were both in their mid-twenties, neophytes when it came to physical conflict, which was a potential problem in the wrong circumstances, but the Montana case principally involved collecting information and putting the pieces together.

"So how did it go?" asked Charlotte as the two agents returned to the Seattle control center.

"We found him," said Sarah, "but he didn't work at the base, never had, and was in fact a local police officer who was not very happy about being questioned."

Charlotte smiled. "And what did he say?"

"He said the whole country was going to hell in a hand basket with the government snooping into everybody's business."

"Well, he's probably right about that. Where did you find him?"

"At his house."

"And what was that like?"

"Better than any police officer I've ever seen. And he had a new $60,000 Mercedes Benz."

"Did you ask him about that?"

Sarah glanced at Matt, who smiled. "That's when he got upset. He said it all came from his father, who recently died."

"And what did his father do?"

The young agents looked pleased with themselves. "He was a Marine stationed at the submarine base until he got a dishonorable discharge for assaulting an officer."

"And he left his son $500,000 in cash and gold!" interjected Sarah. "We spoke to his banker."

"Five hundred thousand?!"

"Yes!"

"Is the officer who got assaulted still at the base?"

"He's the Chief of Security," said Matt.

"Okay, I want to go and see him," said Charlotte, finally sensing a possible break. "Good work, guys. Matt, you can drive me. Sarah, I need you to contact ODNI (Office of the Director of National Intelligence) with Lieutenant Silver and find out who exactly handled the MSS intercept."

"We already did that," said Sarah. "It's like the whole thing was scrubbed from the record. There's absolutely nothing there except the note you originally received."

"And Lieutenant Silver helped you?"

"Yes. He's still trying to find out more, but the Director of ODNI said someone mistakenly erased the material after the case was closed."

"Okay," said Charlotte, "why don't you stay on that Sarah while we're at the base."

The drive to Bremerton passed through some of the most spectacular scenery in America. Precipitous hills covered in pines and cedars crowded aquamarine waterways leading to the Pacific Ocean. Charlotte stared out at the vista as Matt drove down the winding road.

"Beautiful place. I understand you grew up here."

"Twenty years."

"And what was that like?"

"I'd rather be in a big city," said Matt.

"Anonymity?"

"Yes, ma'am."

"You don't have to call me 'ma'am'. Charlotte will be fine unless we're with other people."

"Sorry, ma..." He caught himself and smiled. Charlotte Ramsey was an intimidating figure for a neophyte in the agency.

"So how old are you?" asked Charlotte.

"Twenty-eight."

"I wish I was twenty-eight again. So what do you think about this case?"

"I was surprised to see how many weapons those subs carry. Pretty scary."

"Yeah, even more scary in the wrong hands. The most dangerous machines on earth, based in one of its most beautiful."

Matt smiled. He was beginning to relax, and indicated a fishing boat heading out to sea.

"That's my dad's boat out there."

"He's a fisherman?"

"Yep. Salmon season. He'll stay out till he's got a full load."

"And how long will that take?"

"Sometimes a week; sometimes just a day. It's a business of luck."

It was strange for Charlotte to be with someone so young and raw, and she marveled at the ability of each new generation to figure it all out and continue the chain of life. Then she thought about the officers on the submarine. They were just a few years older than Matt, and she wondered what could have possibly compelled them to mutiny. What cause, what lie, what misunderstanding? Or was someone else simply controlling them?

Lieutenant Colonel Ruckman was head of security at the heavily guarded Kitsap Submarine Base. He was a typical Marine: lean, ramrod straight, with intense steely eyes. Lieutenant Silver had already called ahead and informed the lieutenant colonel that FBI agents were stopping by to see him. Matt wondered if the Marine even realized that he was meeting with the director of the agency.

Considering the fact that the lieutenant colonel had one of the most important jobs in the military, guarding almost a quarter of the nuclear weapons in the U.S. arsenal, his office was surprisingly spartan. He did, however, have a commanding view of the base - built along the deep water Hood Canal, with its widely separated submarine sheds.

The lieutenant colonel stood from his desk, greeted Charlotte and Matt with firm handshakes, and invited them to sit down.

"Lieutenant Silver said you were interested in the Maldauer case?"

"Yes," said Charlotte. "I understand you're the officer he assaulted?"

"Tried to assault," said the major dismissively. "He was in a classified area and took umbrage when I insisted upon strip searching him."

"And did he have anything on him?"

"Not that I found. But two years later, we did discover a breach in one of our computers that occurred on that same date and at the same time as the Maldauer incursion."

"And was anything done about that?"

"Yes, we went back and tried to trace who his contacts were, but by that time he was dead, and the few leads we found led nowhere."

"And what about his son? Was he checked out?"

"Yes. He's a cop in town - didn't get on with his father and wanted nothing to do with him. He was raised by his mother."

"And what did Maldauer die of?"

"Cancer of the liver, from what I remember. I pulled a copy of his file if you'd like it?"

He pushed a folder across the desk.

"Thank you," said Charlotte. "Does it state what the nature of the computer breach was?"

"No, that was all classified and beyond my jurisdiction. You'd have to talk to Doctor Goddard about that. He works for the DOD and the NIE here."

"NIE?"

"National Integrated Electronics. They built and maintain the electronics on the *Ohios*."

"And where could I find Doctor Goddard?"

"He has an office on the base. Let me see if I can find him for you."

As the lieutenant colonel placed his call, Charlotte looked out of the window at one of the moored *Ohio*-class missile subs. It was black and ominous, particularly considering everything she now knew about it. In a strange way, it looked like a tomb, a sarcophagus for the ungodly might of men.

"He's in his office now if you'd like to see him," said the lieutenant colonel, interrupting her thoughts.

"That would be good, thank you. Did Maldauer have any other problems on his record?" said Charlotte, standing.

"He was a drinker, so yes. The details are all in the folder."

"Well, thank you for your time," said Charlotte.

"The pleasure's all mine, ma'am." Matt almost smiled at his formal use of "ma'am".

Chapter 19

THE civilian offices of National Integrated Electronics (NIE) were contrastingly modern and comfortable compared to the military installations surrounding it. Doctor Goddard was a scientist working for both the Department of Defense and the civilian company responsible for maintaining the *Ohio* fleet's electronic systems and had a large office lined with bookshelves and miniature replicas of early inventions like the Tesla coil and early computing systems. He was a tall, skinny Bostonian, dressed like a university professor in slacks and a tweed jacket with leather patches at the elbows. The doctor was reserved and reticently charming when his secretary introduced Charlotte and Matt.

"Thank you for seeing us on such short notice," said Charlotte, shaking the doctor's hand, which felt like a floppy fish compared with Lieutenant Colonel Ruckman's firm, forthright greeting.

"Sit down, please." He indicated a sitting area and joined them. "I only have a few minutes, so I hope this won't take too long."

"I'll be as quick as I can," said Charlotte. "As Lieutenant Ruckman mentioned…."

"Lieutenant Colonel Ruckman," he corrected her.

"Right, as Lieutenant Colonel Ruckman mentioned on the phone, we're investigating a possible leak of classified information from your department on…May 17th, two years ago." She referred to Maldauer's folder for the date.

"It wasn't a possible leak," said Goddard, "it was an out and out theft by a foreign government, and Captain Maldauer was responsible for it."

"And you're absolutely sure about that?"

"Yes, but it's too late to do anything about that now. You can't put the genie back in the bottle."

"And what was that genie?" asked Charlotte with a forced smile.

"Classified. I can't even discuss it with you."

"And the means by which you came to realize your system had been breached?"

"Also classified."

Charlotte turned to Matt. "Could you leave us for a minute, please?"

Matt left the room, and Charlotte turned back to the doctor. "We have reason to believe that the information stolen from your facility may be of the utmost importance to the security of our country, so I need you to give me more information about this."

The doctor smiled imperiously. "As I already said, ma'am, that's classified information, and you'd have to get DOD and ODNI clearance for that, plus clearance from Charles Peterson, President of NIE. He's the man I work for and presently have a meeting with."

"May I use your phone for a moment, please?" said Charlotte. "It's a secure line, I presume?"

"Yes, and for that reason I can't let you use that either."

"Even if I'm an FBI agent?"

"Even if you're the head of the FBI."

"All right. We'll do this the hard way, Doctor. You'll remain in your office while I make some calls." She stood up and opened the office door, addressing Matt in the reception room. "Doctor Goddard is to remain in his office until I return. If he tries to leave, you will cuff him and read him his rights."

"Oh come on, you've got to be kidding?" said the incredulous doctor.

"That's only the beginning, Doctor. There's a good chance I'll be taking you into custody as well."

Goddard looked beyond her to his rapidly paling secretary, watching from the adjoining room. "Wendy, would you call Charles and tell him I'm being detained and threatened in my office by the FBI?"

"You can call the President of the United States if you want," said Charlotte dialing a number on her phone, "but you'll still be in this office until I say you can leave."

She exited the building where Matt could see her through the window talking on her phone.

"What is the name of your partner?" asked Goddard, picking up a pen. "This is absolutely ridiculous."

"Charlotte Ramsey."

"And she is?"

"Not someone you want to make an enemy of," said Matt.

The secure phone in the room rang, and Goddard indicated it sarcastically. "May I?"

"Yes."

The doctor saw his boss's name on the phone screen and answered it.

"Charles, thank you for calling. I've got two members of the FBI here and…."

Peterson cut him off. "Just tell them what they want to know, John."

"But it's all classified!"

"I've already received a call from Admiral Stossel, and you have unequivocal clearance. Charlotte Ramsey is the head of the FBI, and you should have known that."

"Oh, I'm so sorry! I…."

"It's okay, just answer her questions. It's all about the Montana.

Use the normal protocols."

"Yes, of course. I'll be at the meeting late." He hung up the phone and turned to Matt. "You should have been more clear in your introductions." Matt had just witnessed the total diminution of the doctor's ego, but before he could respond Charlotte returned to the room, addressing the doctor.

"Did you get a call from your boss yet?"

"Yes I did, Ms. Ramsey. I'm sorry. I owe you an apology."

"That's perfectly all right. You were just obeying the rules. I can appreciate that."

She let him off the hook in a graceful fashion, and the doctor now seemed relieved and anxious to help her.

"We'll need to go to a safe room in order to discuss everything, if that's all right with you?"

"That's fine," said Charlotte.

"And I'm afraid you'll also have to have a pat down from a female Marine. It's just a precaution in case someone has planted a listening device on you."

"No problem," said Charlotte. "Matt, you can wait here with Wendy."

She left and Matt joined the doctor's secretary in the waiting room. She looked relieved at the abatement of hostility and tried to be cordial. "Is your life always like this?"

"No, not normally." He felt obliged to say more, but he was an agent in the field now, and that was not part of his protocol.

The safe room was a small, sound proofed meeting place with a plain table and chairs for six. It was sparse, windowless, and devoid of any decorations. Charlotte felt a surge of claustrophobia as the heavy door closed behind her, and she realized she was in a totally sealed environment.

"No air vents."

"No, but there's plenty of air in here, and I can open the door any time you wish," said Goddard. "Would you like some water?"

"No, I'm good, thank you."

"I'm also required to inform you that everything we discuss in here is considered classified information and cannot be shared with anyone else. Do you understand that?"

"Yes, I do."

"All right. So I told you earlier that a foreign government had stolen information from one of our servers two years ago, but it was in fact the Chinese military. And the reason we know that is because a year after that theft, we hacked into their system and discovered our own classified material. It was obviously a surprise, but the windfall of information we were receiving was so important that everything that might compromise it was scrubbed from the system. That included the entire Maldauer case. Only the head of National Intelligence, Chief of Naval Operations, the Secretary of Defense and the people at ODNI that hacked the system, have this information. Plus of course, you and me and my boss, Charles Peterson. And the only reason I'm party to it is because I reviewed the data and identified the original breach."

"And what sort of information was it they stole?"

"The Trident launch system. All the electronics and circuitry used to activate the *Ohio's* missiles."

"And can they use that against us?"

"Not in a way that could interfere with our launch potential, but it's still a great help in designing their own weapons. In fact, part of the material we retrieved included design details of their own launch system, which is a simplified version of our own."

"Simplified how?" said Charlotte.

"We require four steps to launch: the president, two separate weapons officers and the ship's captain. They only require their head of state and the ship's captain."

"So you've obviously heard about the mutiny on the Montana?"

"Yes."

"And you're well aware that the officers can't launch the ship's weapons without the president's codes?"

"Correct."

"So do you think access to this alternative launch system might change that?"

"No, we've already been through that. You'd still have to reprogram the entire computing system on the sub, and we would know that."

"How would you know it?"

"The system's checked every time they come into base."

"But what if they did it after leaving the base?"

"We did consider that possibility, but a statistical analysis of a failsafe system to counter it came to the conclusion that it would be more dangerous to the ship's mission than the probability of someone gaining all the technical elements and knowledge to achieve it."

Charlotte looked confused.

"Put more simply, any failsafe system runs the risk of falling into enemy hands and being used against it. That's why we never incorporated a self-destruct mechanism into the missiles themselves. Once they're launched, there's no way to stop them."

"So how do you check the ship's system for tampering?"

"I don't think that's something you need to know."

Charlotte smiled, appreciating his logic. "You're right. I'm already nervous I'll be talking in my sleep. So is there anyone else that could have gained knowledge of this whole thing?"

"Only the people I mentioned to you, plus you and me, and one dead person."

"And who was that?"

"Our Chinese translator, John Chang."

Charlotte felt the hairs rise on her skin. "MIT professor John Chang?"

"Yes. You know him?"

"No. But his son was one of the weapons officers on the Montana. He went missing when they reached Hawaii."

The doctor looked shocked. "I didn't even know he was in the service."

"So you think he could have accessed the material?"

"Only if his father took it home with him."

"And he was allowed to do that?"

"No! Absolutely not! But interpreting thousands of documents, most of them irrelevant, is a long and laborious undertaking, and sometimes it happens."

"So if he did access the material, do you think he'd be smart enough to incorporate it into the Montana's launch system?"

The doctor took a deep breath. "Well, he'd still have to strip out the presidential decree code, but I suppose if anyone could do it, it would be someone like Tommy. He was head of his class in computer engineering and nuclear physics."

"So if all that is true, and he did figure it out, why do you think he left their mission in Hawaii and flew back to the mainland?"

"He did that?"

"Yes."

The doctor looked perplexed by the information then seemed to have a revelation. "It's the D5! We replaced a bunch of the sub's electronics before she left Groton, and we had to change some of the codes to facilitate it. He has to go back to the original download to fix it." He looked like a man trying to come to grips with a reality he couldn't accept.

"So the original material he stole didn't work?"

"No, he has to realign the changed codes, and they probably didn't realize that until they tested it."

"So where do you think he's going to get it?"

The doctor turned pale. "I don't know. But if John did take it home with him, maybe it's still there. I imagine Mrs. Chang's still living in the same house."

"Do you know where that is?"

"Massachusetts somewhere...Bedford, I think."

"I need to make a secure call," said Charlotte, no longer hiding her concerns.

"You can use the phone in my office if you wish." It was an irony even the doctor had to smile at.

In less than five minutes, Charlotte had communicated the possible location of Lieutenant Chang to Sid Bailey in the Seattle control center, and East Coast agents were dispatched to investigate. Even though she was not allowed to tell Sid the details of her secret conversation with Goddard, the urgency in her voice made it quite clear that finding Chang was now of absolute importance.

Chapter 20

It was evening on Bainbridge Island when Monique Besson drove to the small township next to the ferry terminal and parked her Jeep in front of the law office of Sean Lariat. She was followed from the house by two FBI agents who had been watching her home since the Evidence Collection Unit had departed, and she felt like waving to them as she entered Pierre's, a small French restaurant located next to Sean's office.

Pierre, the owner of the establishment, greeted her in a friendly fashion and led her to a quiet table where Sean was already waiting for her. She was wearing a skirt and blouse and looked particularly beautiful, considering everything she'd been through.

"You look great!" said Sean.

"That's because I'm starving. It brings the animal out in me!"

"Well maybe I won't feed you then." He grinned playfully, but Monique was not amused.

"That's not funny right now!"

"I'm sorry," said Sean, backing off immediately.

Monique smiled. "Well, don't be too sorry. I'm just under a little stress here." She looked out the window at the FBI agents waiting in their car.

"They're following you now?"

"Yes. Are they allowed to do that?"

"Probably, but if they do anything more, it could be considered harassment."

"So there's nothing I can do about it?"

"You could file a complaint, but I doubt a local judge is going to override the FBI."

"Did you see the female agent that interviewed me?"

"No."

"Well, I just saw her on TV, and she's actually the head of the FBI!"

"The Director?"

"Yes! Charlotte Ramsey."

"Shit! This is a big deal, Moe! The president said he has control of the nuclear launch codes, but if he doesn't, and a lot of people think that's the case, this could become an international crisis."

"It already is a crisis. But there's nothing I can do about it. Did you bring the contract with you?"

"Yes. It's just a one-pager. You sign here."

He gave her the document with a pen, and she signed it without reading. "So you're officially my lawyer now?"

"Correct."

"And everything I say from now on is in absolute confidence?"

"That's what the law says."

"Well that's reassuring." She glanced outside at the agents. "So this is the problem: I think they're going to arrest me because of what my husband has done, and I need you to get me out of that."

"They can't just arrest you for being his wife, Moe. That's not a crime."

"They can under the Patriot Act, from what I understand."

"They'd still need evidence that you're collaborating with him, and you already told me you had no idea what he was doing, right?"

"Right. But what if they contrive something?"

"They'd be in big trouble if we could prove it!"

"But if they did? Could you just tell them they'd be making a big mistake? John could go completely crazy if something like that happened!"

Sean was taken aback by the implication of her statement. "You can't threaten the FBI, Moe. Just suggesting something like that could get you arrested."

Monique looked disheartened, and Sean reached out and touched her hand. "You need to relax. Why don't you eat something? I'm sure we can work it all out. You want some wine?"

Monique took a deep breath and seemed to regain her center. "Is that your professional advice?"

"Yes, it is."

"Well, we always have to do what our lawyers say, right?"

"Absolutely," said Sean, pouring her some chardonnay.

Monique took the glass and touched his glass with her own. "So here's to our new relationship, professional and otherwise." She took a sip. "Mm, I like that."

"It's from Pierre's own vineyard."

"Excellent...Oh, by the way, now that you're my lawyer, I need you to take care of this for me." She handed him a folder.

"What is it?"

"Divorce papers. John served me with them in Hawaii. I guess he knew what he was going to do and wanted to let me off the hook."

Chapter 21

The Chang house was situated in an upper middle class neighborhood in Bedford, Massachusetts. It was forty years old, and stood alone in its own grounds surrounded by a quaint picket fence and well-tended flowerbeds. The FBI field team arrived in two separate vans and quickly surrounded the two-story building where interior lights illuminated the downstairs rooms. There was no ringing of the doorbell, just the sudden bang of a steel door ram slamming into the lock, snapping it open with the sound of splintering wood.

"FBI! FBI!" shouted the lead agent, rushing into the house with his black clad cohorts. They were so quick, and filled with such stealth that even the family's poodle failed to bark a warning, and leapt into Mrs. Chang's arms, terrified.

"Don't move! Keep your hands where I can see them!"

Mrs. Chang was in her late seventies, petite and controlled enough to mute her TV and raise her hands as the agents spread out through her house, yelling and wielding their weapons. Agent Marty Diaz, an old friend of Sid's, followed the lead men into Mrs. Chang's room which had a decidedly Chinese influence, with its faux Ming art and inlaid mother of pearl furnishings.

"Is there anyone else in the house beside yourself, ma'am?" he asked in a calm voice.

"Not that I know of," said Mrs. Chang. "If you're looking for drugs, the only ones I have are some Xanax in the upstairs bathroom!"

"We're not looking for drugs, ma'am. We're looking for your son, Tommy. Is he here?"

"No, he left two days ago. Did he do something wrong?"

Charlotte Ramsey, Sid Bailey, and Lieutenant Silver watched the whole incursion on a large split video screen from their Seattle office. Body cameras attached to the lead agent and a second one on Agent Diaz were filming the images. It was like watching a Hollywood action movie on shaky cameras.

Charlotte shook her head at the mayhem. "A bit overdone, don't you think?"

"Not in my book," said Sid. "If he has the keys to blow up the world, I'm not taking any chances!" Sid was starting to get wound up, which was his modus operandi when things heated up.

"She looks pretty controlled," said Lieutenant Silver, indicating Mrs. Chang.

"She's probably in shock," said Charlotte, watching the lead agent ascend the stairs peering into a small, tidy bedroom.

"This looks like the kid's room."

"Is that a picture of the Kremlin on the wall?" asked Charlotte.

"Yeah. Bunch of pictures from Russia – all with the same couple and a kid in 'em." He panned his camera over several pictures of what appeared to be a young Russian couple with a child. "I'll check all the drawers and cupboards." He started searching the room as Marty Diaz spoke on the second screen.

"Okay, I'm going into what looks like a back office." He switched on a light, illuminating a cluttered room filled with books, racks of computer hard drives, and a cluttered desk with an Apple laptop on it. "This looks promising." He panned his camera around the room. "You want me to bring everything in, or start checking it here?"

"Have the techs check the laptop now and see if it's been used recently," said Charlotte. "And let me speak to Mrs. Chang."

In just a minute, Charlotte was looking at Mrs. Chang on her screen, as Mrs. Chang looked at her on an iPad held before her by Diaz.

"Can you hear me, Mrs. Chang?"

"Yes."

"My name is Agent Ramsey. I'm sorry to disturb you like this, but we're looking for your son on a matter of national security."

"I keep asking what he did," said Mrs. Chang.

"We don't know if he did anything yet," said Charlotte, trying to diminish her concerns. "We just need to ask him a few questions. Do you know where he is?"

"No, I already said he left two days ago."

"And when did he arrive?" said Charlotte.

"The day before he left!"

"And what did he do when he was there?"

"He did what he always does. He gave me a big kiss and took me out to dinner. We had a good time."

"And after that?"

"He spent the night with his girlfriend."

"And what is her name?"

"Joyce. She works at the university in the book department."

"The library?"

"Yes."

"And what's her surname?"

"Bradford, I think. I never use it."

In just a moment, Sid was showing Charlotte a picture of Joyce Bradford on his computer. She was a cute girl in her mid-twenties.

"And after he spent the night with Ms. Bradford," continued Charlotte, "did you see him again?"

"Yes. He took me out for breakfast then spent the rest of the day and night in John's office. I haven't changed it since he passed away."

"And what did he do in the office?"

"Played on those computers. That's all they ever do these days. They'd rather do that than live anymore!"

"And after that what did he do?"

"He slept in his room, then left early the next morning after telling me he loved me."

"Did he say where he was going?"

"He never says where he's going. Probably to see another girl!"

"Who are the people in Russia that he has pictures of in his room?"

"Those are his birth parents. They were killed in a Chechen bomb attack before we adopted him."

Sid typed the words 'more terrorists' onto his computer as Charlotte continued.

"So did you see the president's speech today?"

"No. I never watch the news. What did he say?"

"He's going to try to simplify the tax code."

"Well that's good; I never could understand it anyway."

"Neither could I," said Charlotte, satisfied that Mrs. Chang probably didn't keep up on current events, including the Montana's disappearance. "If your son calls, will you please tell him that we just want to talk to him? The agents there will give you my number."

"What about my broken door?" said Mrs. Chang.

"I'll have them fix it for you." She got off the phone as Sid signaled her.

"You need to see this." He indicated the video screen, now showing a close angle of the Chang's laptop, displaying the words, 'Mission Touché'.

"What is it?"

"It's French."

"I know what it is!" said Charlotte. "Why is he using it?"

"I think he's sending us a message!"

"Pay back?"

"Yes."

"That's pretty brazen!"

"Yeah, I'd say fucking cocky!" said Sid, showing his frustration.

By the following morning, the agents at the Chang house, working in conjunction with Doctor Goddard, now situated in the Seattle control center, had found enough evidence on the house computer and hard drives to confirm that Lieutenant Chang did have access to his father's files from the Chinese hacking and had now acquired the additional information necessary to rewrite the Montana's launch codes to accept the simplified Chinese launch system. It was devastating news, and Charlotte quickly wrapped a cloak of secrecy around the whole discovery and called in her inner circle, which now included Goddard, his boss Charles Peterson, a clean-cut California businessman, plus Sid and Lieutenant Silver.

"So let me clarify this," said Charlotte, "if Lieutenant Chang or someone else helping him is successful in reaching the Montana with these new computer codes, the crew will be able to launch their missiles, which have the potential to destroy any country on earth, including our own?"

"That is correct," agreed Goddard.

"And you're absolutely sure about that?"

"Yes, ma'am."

Peterson reaffirmed his conclusion. "We've spent the last six hours going over everything multiple times, and the conclusion is unequivocal. They'll be able to launch."

"And there's nothing you can do to stop that?"

"Nothing other than destroy the Montana or prevent the codes from reaching her."

"And you said they made copies of these codes?" asked Sid.

"Two copies that we know of. They just go on small drives."

"So they could mail them anywhere?"

"Unfortunately, yes."

Charlotte looked frustrated. “What I don’t understand is if they knew they had the wrong codes, why didn’t they just delay the mission?”

“Probably too late for that,” said Silver. “Too many things set in motion that could expose them.”

“So they’re just going to sit out there and wait for this kid to bring them the correct codes?”

“That’s the way it looks.”

“And they can’t fix it on their own?”

“Not without access to the original material.”

“We need to put out an international arrest warrant for this kid now!” said Sid.

“And what about the president’s assertion that the Montana’s weapons can’t be launched?”

“He’s going to have to retract his position.”

“Well, it’s out of our hands now,” said Charlotte. “I’ll call Pierce and fill him in on everything. He’ll probably call you for clarification.”

“That’s fine,” said Peterson. “I’m also required to inform Admiral Stossel’s office of any breach in security.”

“I’ll have Pierce take care of that for you. It’s his job to coordinate everything. Not a good day to be the president.” She walked over to the picture of Monique, still watching her from the gallery of mutineers. “I bet she knows where everything is.”

Chapter 22

The president walked down the corridor towards the Oval Office with his press secretary, Matilda Graham. He was all business and so was Matilda.

"Fifteen Democratic senators and twelve Republicans have gone on the record saying you're starting a war with Congress."

"It's not me that's going to war," declared the president. "And you can quote me on that; it's the American people. Congress has a lower rating than Richard Nixon had when they impeached him! So I'm not backing down, and neither are the people of the United States."

He arrived at the Oval Office just as General Pierce, the DNI, was leaving.

"We're having an NSC meeting about the Montana in ten minutes, sir."

"Good or bad news?" asked the president.

"Not good."

"Okay, I'll be there." He checked his watch and entered his office where he was scheduled for an informal meeting with his personal staff which included Matilda, Gary Brockett, Maggie Malone, one of his speechwriters and colorful advisors, and several under secretaries from Commerce, Treasury, and the Attorney General's office.

"Okay," said the president. "I've got eight minutes, so let's get on with this. There's over three trillion dollars in foreign banks owned by US corporations who won't bring it home because of the government's business tax, which is the highest in the world. I want to get that money back, so let me hear the issues. Who's going first?"

Gary held up his hand. "I'm the elephant."

Everyone laughed. "And I'm the donkey," said Maggie, covering her ears and wiggling her fingers.

"Okay, Gary you're up."

"I'll have to walk to think."

"I'm surprised you can do both," said the president, introducing his friend, "the peripatetic Mr. Brockett."

"As the president has so eloquently stated, there's money abroad, and he wants it back. So, lower the taxes! Make them competitive with other countries. And make it retroactive as long as the corporations repatriate their cash and pay the new taxes within fourteen days!"

"That's just what the nation needs," said Maggie, "another handout for the rich! Five percent of the population already owns ninety percent of the country's wealth. I say we sue them; put them in jail – make them pay or leave the country!"

"And that's exactly what they're going to do," said Gary. "We're already losing hundreds of factories and thousands of jobs every year. So why should they stay if they can manufacture cheaper abroad?"

"That's because they're using slave labor!" countered Maggie, fervently. "We should charge them import duties on everything made abroad and level the playing field."

"And what will you do when other countries start charging us import duties?"

"They already do! There are taxes and restrictions on everything we send abroad, including Europe!"

"So you want to start a trade war?"

"We're already in a trade war! The Chinese sell half a trillion dollars more goods to us every year than we sell to them. It's time to level the playing field in trade and in sharing the national wealth!"

"The wealthy already pay over 80% of all federal income taxes," said Gary, "and even if we took all the money they have and all the profits of all the corporations, it still wouldn't pay the interest on the national debt for a year..."

"Okay, okay!" said the president. "I get the point, so let's do an analysis. Tell me how much money we'll lose reducing the tax rate, and what we'll make with new laws enforcing the present one. Let's get this money back in the country, guys! And let's do it quick, because after this I'm going to deal with the shame of our nation, which puts more of its citizens in prison than any other country in the world, including the worst dictatorships! And on another subject, I want to know who makes the decision to let a million more immigrants and refugees into our country every year when we can't even look after the people we've got here. Why do we need more people when we already have gridlock in every major city? Change, change, change! I want change! Did you get all that?"

Everyone looked confused, except for Gary, who checked his notes. "I got everything except the fourth point!"

"Yeah, right!" said the president. "We've got a lot to do, so let's get on it!"

Two minutes later, the president was in the Situation Room with his NSC members, talking to Charlotte Ramsey, Dr. Goddard, and his boss, John Peterson, on a secure video line from the Seattle office. The FBI director described all the twists and turns of the previous two days that led them to the conclusion that Lieutenant Chang now had the codes necessary to launch the Montana's missiles. It was shocking news to everyone, particularly considering all the failsafe systems set in place to avoid such a calamity.

"So let me get this straight," said the president. "The Chinese military stole our missile launch design, we hacked their system, found our own launch material, and a simplified version of it, which the Chinese have created to launch their own weapons. And now this kid…" He glanced at his notes. "This Lieutenant Chang, has figured out how to use the Chinese system, which he stole from his father's computer, to subvert our own codes so that he and his friends can launch the Montana's missiles for themselves? Correct?"

"Yes, sir," said Peterson on the video.

"And I can't say anything about any of this because it will reveal the fact that we've hacked the Chinese military?"

"Yes, sir."

"So what the hell am I supposed to do? I've already assured the whole world that the Montana launch codes are safe in my hands."

"We have to put every asset we have into finding this kid NOW!" exclaimed Marine General Hayden, Chairman of the Joint Chiefs.

"And does that include going public? Do I now have to tell the whole world that some thirty year old kid has stolen the nation's most important secret?"

The Secretary of Defense interceded. "The Washington Post already knows that Lieutenant Chang is the code breaker, sir. They found out his father worked for the DOD on the Trident launch system and put it all together."

"And how the hell did they find that out?"

"Someone leaked it."

"So why haven't they printed it?"

"Because I asked them not to, sir. National security reasons."

"And how did you find out about the article?"

"They called me in for a clarifying comment…."

"There's no way we're going to keep all this secret," said Tony Russo, the president's personal National Security Advisor. "We should just tell the truth. Lieutenant Chang stole the codes, and we need to stop him! We'll get a lot more international help with that statement than anything else."

"We'll look like a bunch of idiots!" snarled General Hayden.

"We are a bunch of idiots!" agreed the president. "We let fifteen young men steal the most formidable killing machine we ever made! Not just five nuclear weapons, not ten, not twenty, not fifty, not one hundred and fifty – one hundred and seventy six nuclear fucking weapons, each one thirty times bigger than the bombs that destroyed Hiroshima and Nagasaki! Who the hell would build such a thing?! What were they thinking?!"

General Hayden tried to justify the strategy. "It's from the Cold War, sir."

"There is no Cold War anymore! We spend every damn day of our lives chasing third world Islamic terrorists." He caught himself and turned to Admiral Stossel. "I have a question for you, David. If the missiles on the Montana are directed to their targets by GPS satellites, why don't we just shut them down until this is over?"

"They're not directed by satellites anymore," said the admiral. "They're directed by a star-sighting system – Astro Guidance. We changed it all when our satellites became vulnerable to attack."

"And there's no way we can shoot these missiles down if they're launched?"

"If we knew where they were coming from, maybe, but the main purpose of the Tridents is a quick strike. They launch from under the sea, hit their targets before anyone can respond, and disappear."

"Did you ever read Tom Clancy's *Red October*?"

"Yes, sir. Great book."

"So you're aware that the Russians always place a hidden political officer on their missile subs?"

"A *zampolit*, sir."

"Right. So do we have anyone like that on our missile subs?"

"No, sir. We thought about it, but who is a reliable political officer in America? A Democrat? A Republican? A white man? A black man? A Christian? An atheist? We couldn't answer that, so we didn't do it. Russia is a closed, homogenous society that has always been ruled from the top down."

"So we never spy on our men?"

"Not without cause, sir. There was a time when we thought about wiring the *Ohio*'s with hidden mics, but that had First Amendment issues, and the information gathered could only be accessed after the sub returned to base."

"So there's no one on that sub that's likely to step forward and help us?"

"Not that I know of, sir."

"Can fifteen men really run a sub like this?"

"It would be a lot of work, but if they get tired, they can always sit on the bottom or the surface in some isolated place and take a rest."

"And the nukes? Do they have to be refueled like the reactor?"

"Yes, sir. But they can go for a long time without doing it."

"How long?"

"That's classified, sir. I don't even know the answer to that."

The president took a deep breath. "So Charlotte, is there any possible way we can still handle this internally? Maybe with help from some of our allies?"

"We can try, sir, but without help from the public, and with the likelihood that Lieutenant Chang will flee abroad, it's going to be very difficult. He's not your normal kid, and we still don't know if he's part of a larger conspiracy."

"Do you have any evidence to support that possibility?"

"No, sir. But we don't have any evidence to support the idea that they're doing this on their own either."

The president finally realized he had no other choice. "Okay. So I guess we go public. INTERPOL and the whole works, right?"

"Yes, sir. I think it's the right decision," agreed Charlotte.

"And what about the captain's wife?" He glanced at his notes. "Monique Besson? She hasn't told you anything?"

"No, but she did express the hope that her husband would go after militant Muslims for killing her sister."

"She wants to blow up the world to avenge her sister?"

"And a few other people."

"So you think she knows more than she's saying?"

"I'm certain of it."

"Because?"

"Instinct. How she is."

"And how is that?"

"She's disciplined, like a soldier on a mission. And everything she did in her life was with her husband, so I can't imagine that he kept any of this secret from her."

"Then you think she's actually involved?"

"Yes, I do."

"So why don't you bring her here?" asked the president, surprising everyone.

"To the White House?"

"Yes. I'd like to talk to her myself. Maybe I can change her mind about things."

Chapter 23

A LIGHT fog drifted in from the Pacific Ocean as Monique moved through her house systematically, finding all the listening devices hidden there by the FBI. She was more amused than offended by their presence and chose to leave most of them in place, destroying only the most obvious, which she assumed were planted there to be discovered.

Since returning home, Monique had left the televisions in the house continuously playing cable news channels in an effort to keep current with everything involving her husband and the missing Montana. It was an endless parade of colorful prognostications and absorbing possibilities that kept the world's citizens glued to their TVs and the networks raking in millions. Monique kept a casual eye on the repetitive babble of "experts" and the president assuring the world that the launch codes were safe. But when a breaking news flash with multiple pictures of Thomas Chang lit up the screen, her demeanor changed. It was not something expected, and she looked concerned.

"The FBI has issued an international warrant for the arrest of Lieutenant Thomas Chang, one of the weapons officers from the missing nuclear submarine Montana. Lieutenant Chang, who is a graduate of MIT, was last seen in Bedford, Massachusetts last night and may be trying to leave the country. The FBI is offering a reward of twenty-five million dollars for anyone providing information that leads to his arrest. The Washington Post has released a statement from unconfirmed

sources that Lieutenant Chang is in possession of the launch codes that would enable the Montana's mutinous crew to fire her nuclear missiles. President Anderson has called for a press conference in one hour, in which he is expected to clarify Lieutenant Chang's involvement in stealing the Montana's launch codes, which he previously assured the world were in his safekeeping. Reaction to the news has been swift around the world. North Korea has already stated it will launch its own weapons at U.S. forces if it is attacked, and even friendly nations, like Pakistan, have threatened similar reactions."

Monique was surprised by the details of Chang's involvement in the mutiny, and hurried into the bedroom, retrieving a pre-paid (burn) phone taped to the back of a drawer. The entire operation was in jeopardy, and she quickly dialed a number, listening to the recorded message of a male voice, *"I'll be there tonight. Second location. 11:00 pm."* Monique looked relieved and switched off the phone, as the landline rang, and she saw Sean Lariat's name on the caller ID.

"Hello?"

"Are you sitting down?" asked Sean.

"No. What?"

"I just got a call from your friend, Charlotte Ramsey, informing me that the President of the United States wants to see you for a private meeting at the White House."

"I don't want to meet the president," said Monique. "I'm not interested in getting involved with all of this. I've already got the press all over me, including some idiot who climbed the gate and got bit by Bruce!"

"He actually bit someone??"

"Yes! Blood and the whole works!"

"Well, this may be a good thing for you, Moe. At least you can express your innocence and clear your name."

"I don't like the president, and I don't like the people in his government. Why should I help them? They put microphones all over my house, they're spying on everything I do, and they're probably listening to this conversation we're having right now!"

"So what do you want me to do, Moe? I already told the head of the FBI I'd get right back to her!"

"Tell her I'll sleep on it."

Charlotte Ramsey, was listening to the conversation in her Seattle office, and turned to Sid, frustrated.

"She doesn't want to meet the president and he's expecting to see her tomorrow!"

"Pick her up and force the issue."

"Yeah, I can see the president sitting down for a meeting with somebody in handcuffs. Maybe we can get an orange jumpsuit as well."

"You could talk to the Attorney General and see if he'd make a plea bargain with her."

"For what? Taking a meeting?"

"You want me to call her lawyer and put some pressure on him?"

Charlotte shook her head, calming herself. "No. I'll just wait until tomorrow. Maybe we'll get Chang by then and have more leverage."

"Oh, by the way," said Sid, "I heard from Diaz in Bedford. He checked out Chang's friends at MIT, and besides a bunch of very pretty ladies, he spent most of his time with a fellow classmate, Harlan Flynn." He raised his eyebrows speculatively.

"And I'm supposed to know who that is?"

"He's the weapons officer who replaced Chang on the Montana."

"Did you tell Daryl that?"

"Yes. He called Admiral McCracken in Hawaii, and he said it was Captain Besson who promoted Flynn to replace Chang, with permission from his superior officer, Vice Admiral Acker. He said everything was by the book."

"Does Flynn have the same credentials as Chang?"

"I don't know about that, but they do have one thing in common: Flynn's parents were killed in the bombing of the American Embassy in Nairobi."

"So you think someone's going around selecting victims of militant Islam to start a war or something?"

"I think it's beginning to look that way."

Sarah Singh and Matt Weston peered into the office interrupting them.

"Do you have a minute?"

"Sure, what have you got?" said Charlotte.

"We were doing background checks on the officers' wives and families and found every one of them had taken their 401k's and personal savings and given them to an investment broker in London."

"For what purpose?"

"To purchase high risk short-term puts on the international oil market."

"Which means?"

"They're betting the price of oil is going to go up in the next two weeks," said Matt. "If they're right, they stand to make millions."

"Mutiny for money?" said Sid.

"It can't be just that," mused Charlotte. "They're not going to give up their whole lives just to make a buck."

"It's more than a buck, and who's to say there aren't a bunch of others doing the same thing?"

Charlotte paused. "Well, that's a good point. Can we do a search and see who else has purchased the same futures?"

"Its all classified information, as far as the banks and brokers are concerned," said Sarah, "but we could try to access it by other means."

"And what means are those?" asked Charlotte. "We can't start hacking banks and brokerage firms."

"No, I know that. But there are people who do it all the time, and we could check with one of them."

"And who are they?" said Charlotte, sensing dangerous ground.

"Other brokers, they spy on each other all the time."

"Do you have someone in mind?"

"Yes, my brother."

"Okay, so why don't you try that? But as far as the agency's concerned, you're doing it on your own. Do you understand?"

"Yes, ma'am."

"All right. Thank you. Excellent work."

The two young agents mumbled their thanks and started out of the room when Charlotte stopped them with a question. "How long did you say those oil puts take to mature?"

"Two weeks," said Sarah.

"Okay, thank you." The agents left and Charlotte turned back to Sid. "So they're going to blow up the Middle East in the next two weeks?"

"Or make it look that way," said Sid.

Chapter 24

The Pacific fog had now reached Bainbridge Island drifting through the pines surrounding the Besson house. It was almost evening and the moody, isolating weather added a strange melancholy to Monique's state of mind as she closed the bedroom curtains and changed into a tight fitting cycling outfit. Night was quickly approaching and after checking her watch, she found a hidden thread of fishing line and pulled a semi-automatic Benelli pistol from deep inside an air vent. The weapon was well kept, and she expertly popped out its cartridge, checked its load then reassembled it, snapping one of its hollow point bullets into the chamber before setting the safety. She was obviously well acquainted with the weapon, and placed it in a small backpack along with a change of clothes, her wallet, and the burn phone. She was preparing for some kind of mission, and lifted a picture of her and her sister posing together in happier times.

Most people get over such losses by acceptance and forgiveness, but for Monique the loss of her sister was an outrage she couldn't put aside, and in her nihilistic state, only one emotion remained – the desire to wreak revenge and a crushing, unimaginable defeat upon the murderers of her sister.

Over half a dozen press vehicles, including vans with satellite dishes, lined the country road in front of Monique's house, which was hidden in trees down a long, private driveway. The whole world wanted to know about Captain John Besson and his fellow officers, and Monique was quickly becoming one of the centers of that international obsession. Two FBI agents, Siebert and Kelly, observed the spectacle from a black sedan parked next to the closed gates of the house. They were both dressed in dark suits, and kept a continuous eye on an iPad, displaying video pictures of the front and back of the Besson house from cameras strategically placed in trees by the agency.

Doris, a pretty production assistant for one of the newscasters, approached the agents, clutching a couple of coffees. She had a curvaceous figure and a seductive walk that quickly caught Kelly's eye.

"Wish I was a newscaster!"

"Yeah, not bad, eh?" Siebert covered the iPad screen as Doris peered into the car.

"You guys want some coffee?"

"No, we're good, thank you," said Kelly.

"You think she's still here?"

"I hope so, or we'll be in big trouble! How's the guy who got bit in the ass?"

Doris grinned. "He had to get a rabies shot! You sure you don't want these?"

"No, we don't drink on the job."

"You can't drink coffee?" asked Doris amused; but before the FBI agent could respond Monique suddenly soared over the fence on her bike. It was a spectacular leap that caught everyone off guard as she bounced on the gravel shoulder and raced away down the road in the opposite direction to the one all the vehicles were facing.

"Is that her?!" yelled Siebert, turning in his seat, watching Monique disappear around a bend.

"That's her!" shouted Kelly, starting the engine, backing down the road, pulling a 180 as he fishtailed after Monique.

It was like the beginning of a Grand Prix, with Doris and all the newscasters leaping into their vehicles, desperately trying to turn around and join the chase. Kelly's high performance sedan raced down the road, sliding into the bend as he yelled to Siebert.

"You didn't see her on the screen?"

"No! It was covered over."

"It's okay – there she is!"

They cleared the bend and raced toward Monique, quickly approaching another bend.

"What do we do?"

"Just keep her in sight!"

Monique looked back at the rapidly approaching FBI agents and swerved across the road, soaring out of view over a roadside berm.

"What the hell is she doing??" Kelly followed her across the road where he nearly hit a truck passing in the opposite direction.

"We don't need to die for this!" yelled Siebert over the blasting horn of the truck.

Kelly cursed and hit his brakes, skidding to a stop next to the berm in a cloud of dust through which he could see Monique racing away down a narrow dirt trail.

"I'm going after her! See if you can circle around in front of her!" He leapt from the car and slid down the steep embankment chasing Monique as the procession of press vehicles arrived on the road above him. It was like a traveling circus, and Siebert yelled to a news van blocking his way.

"Get out of there!!" He blasted his siren, forcing the vehicles to clear his path as other news members grabbed their cameras and chased after Monique and Kelly on foot.

There was a river rushing down a deep crevasse, spanned by a large fallen tree. It was a scary place, but Monique didn't even hesitate as she raced her bike over the fallen pine, her tires ripping bark from its surface. It was like something from a movie, and Kelly stopped on the rim of the crevasse, weighing his odds as the first cameraman caught up with him.

"I got that shot! Can you believe that?!"

Kelly ignored him, stepping onto the log, realizing he had no alternative but to continue the chase with all the press approaching.

"Wait! Wait!" yelled the cameraman, checking his focus. "Let me get this!"

"Fuck you!" said Kelly, his words lost in the roar of the rapids as he advanced across the gorge. It was a terrifying place. The river churned, wind ruffled his hair, his legs began to wobble then a branch snagged his foot, and he fell forward, clutching the tree like a baby holding its mother.

"Keep going! You're looking good!" yelled the cameraman, joined by another film crew that ran to the base of the fallen tree, shooting a different angle. Kelly realized he was going out "live" to the nation and the sheer humiliation of failing in public gave him the courage to rise back to his feet and run, teetering across the chasm to the opposite side. It was a miraculous event, and the news crews cheered as Kelly took a bow and continued the chase. He was a celebrity now, and so was Monique, although she didn't know that yet.

Chapter 25

THE president's news conference was filled with reporters from around the world. After making a brief statement, confirming that a member of the Montana's crew now had possession of the launch codes, he started answering questions.

"Why are they doing this?" asked a reporter from Reuter's. "What's the purpose of their mutiny?"

"We don't know the answer to that yet," said the president. "So far they haven't made a statement about their intentions."

"And Lieutenant Chang? Does he have any history or affiliations that would suggest a reason?"

"None that we've discovered. But obviously there's an ongoing investigation into all of the officers involved." He pointed to another reporter. "Joe?"

"Is it true that some of the Montana's crew, including the captain and his first officer, have lost close family members to militant Islam?"

"Yes, we've identified five crew members so far that have suffered such losses. But that doesn't mean to say that is the reason for the mutiny."

Two thousand miles away, Charlotte Ramsey and Sid sat in their Seattle office watching the president's speech.

"And here begins the dance," said Sid.

"He's not going to stick his neck out."

Sid was interrupted by a call from Agents Siebert and Kelly informing him that Monique had escaped their surveillance. Charlotte could hear the frustration in his voice and muted the TV.

"She took off cross country on a bike?"

"Yes, sir."

"And you couldn't follow her?"

"No way! She jumped a six-foot fence then went across a river on a fallen tree! She's like a maniac on that thing!"

As they were speaking, Charlotte pointed to the muted television now showing a clip of Monique racing across the river chasm, followed by Kelly's less than heroic pursuit.

"All right, I get the point," said Sid. "We're watching it on the TV now."

Kelly rolled his eyes. "It's already on the news?"

"Yeah, you're a hero…or close to it." The TV cut back to the president's news conference as Sid continued. "You'd better call in the local police; I'll have the night crew stay at the ferry and see if she goes there."

"Are there any airports on the island?" inquired Charlotte.

"There's a small one for private planes," said Siebert, "but the whole area's fogged in; there's no way to fly out now."

"How about the bridge to the peninsula?"

"Already got two local officers there watching for her."

"Are you still monitoring the house on the videos?" said Sid.

"Yeah, she hasn't returned, yet, but we're on our way back there in case she does."

"Okay, keep us informed." Sid got off the phone as Charlotte looked out the window, where the fog was now drifting over the city.

"You think she could have taken a boat?"

"I don't know. Looks pretty bad out there."

Lieutenant Silver joined them, handing Charlotte a folder. "This is a recent picture of Lieutenant Flynn and his resume. Looks like he has the credentials to do everything Chang could do. They both went to MIT."

"And what about the hard drives that Chang made?"

"He's either got them with him, or he mailed them to someone else."

"Can we check that out?"

"That's a long shot," said Sid, "He could have mailed it from anywhere, and we don't even know where it's going."

"Let me see what I can do," said Silver leaving the room.

Charlotte looked at Monique's picture on the wall. "You think she's making a run for it?"

"I dunno. Where would she go?"

"Maybe to see her husband?"

Monique's business associate, Sue Haber, lived in a modest house with a spectacular view of the island's coastline, but you could see none of that through the drifting fog. It was an eerie night, and Monique hid her bike in some trees and approached the house, knowing its occupants had left for a Mexican vacation. She'd obviously been there before and quickly found a hidden key in a fern pot, letting herself into the cedar home. There were several pictures of Sue with her sons and boat-loving husband, but Monique didn't hesitate. She went straight into the kitchen, grabbed some keys hanging next to the back door, and let herself out onto a deck with a wooden causeway leading to a boathouse.

It was a short walk to the quaint building that housed a thirty-foot Grady White fishing boat with two large outboard engines. Monique had been out on the boat many times, and after checking the fuel tanks were full, she opened the boathouse doors, which slid around the wall on iron tracks.

Visibility beyond the shed was no more than fifty feet, but Monique was on a mission and quickly pushed the boat outside, closed the sliding doors, and started the two Yamaha engines, which roared to life then quickly quieted down as she engaged the propellers and pulled away from the house.

It was almost pitch black on the open sea, and Monique carefully followed her progress on the boat's GPS system. Five hundred yards off the coast, she slowly increased fuel to the powerful engines until the boat rose from the sea like a living form and skimmed across the surface at forty knots per hour.

Chapter 26

ADMIRAL McCracken was as shocked as everyone when he heard that Lieutenant Chang now had the codes to launch the Montana's missiles. At first, he didn't believe it was possible, but when he spoke to Admiral Stossel on a secure line and heard about the China connection, it all made sense. It was devastating news, but there was some good in it. The codes were not yet on the Montana, and to get them, she would have to come back to the surface and reveal herself.

It was still light in Hawaii, and the admiral sat in his office at the Nimitz McArthur Pacific Command Center contemplating what opportunities this new information might present. Where would the transfer take place? Would Chang be the carrier, or would it be someone else? Who had the most obstacles to overcome – man or boat? People usually prefer places they know, places they can get in and out of safely. He spun the world globe on his desk and stopped it abruptly with his finger. It pointed at the northwest coast of Washington state and western Canada. Was that a sign? An insight from the gods? Or just serendipity pulling his chain?

The old admiral ran all the permutations through his mind and came to the conclusion they would basically have to meet there. How would Chang get out of the country with the whole world looking for him?

So what could he do to be ready for that? It was like hunting a smart animal that knew exactly what you were thinking; how could he foil that? What he needed was someone who knew more about the Montana's mutinous crew than he did. And that person was someone he no longer had confidence in.

Vice Admiral Acker arrived at McCracken's office and announced his presence with a knock on the open door. "Julie said you were looking for me?"

"Yeah, come in. Close the door. Take a seat." He opened a folder on his desk as Acker sat.

"So how you holding up, Jay?"

"I've had better days. You've obviously heard about Chang and the codes."

"Yeah, I just watched the president's speech. Pretty humbling."

"Very humbling."

"It's not your fault, Jay. The whole system failed. Chang's father helped him, right?"

"That's what they say."

"So you think there's a China connection?"

"No, the old Chang died over a year ago. I think this is more homespun. You want a bottle of water or something?"

"No, I'm good."

The admiral grabbed a bottle for himself and looked down at his folder. "So I did a little archival search of Navy records looking for the word *Touché*, and the only use recorded anywhere was on February 24, 1995 at a class in Annapolis where you taught the art of modern warfare and the defeat of terrorism under the title, 'Touché to the Rescue'."

"Wow, I'd forgotten about that."

"So as a matter of interest, and considering the fact that Captain Besson and several of his officers attended that class, I downloaded the lecture…and I quote, 'Terrorism is a successful form of warfare particularly against modern democracies who instinctively try to apply their values of deduction, psychoanalysis, secularism and the belief that everyone is ultimately redeemable. And to achieve this nirvana of social engineering, they try to win the hearts and minds of their enemies by limiting their response to any aggression solely to the front line aggressor, leaving his support team, his family, friends, and covert benefactors unaffected by their actions. It's like castrating a horse before a race and for what reason; the stupefying deceit that the enemy will give up his values and beliefs for the magnificence and inclusivity of Western culture. But what really happens is they laugh at that notion, hide behind its hubris, and continue their low cost war ad infinitum…fighting limited wars simply does not work.' That's pretty incendiary, Don."

Acker smiled. "It's just a simple lesson in contemporary history, Jay."

"So you're advocating total war? Kill them all – mothers, sisters, uncles and aunts?"

"That's precisely what they're doing to us."

"So we become like them?"

"Exactly like them. That's the only thing they understand. It's a reaction they expect but never get, so they continue to chip away at us until they eventually get nuclear weapons, and then they win because they're willing to do anything for their cause and we're not."

"We did nuke Hiroshima and Nagasaki."

"And we won that war."

McCracken had to smile. "So do you still see these kids that you taught?"

Acker smiled. "What are you suggesting, Jay? That I coerced them into doing this? I know you questioned Lieutenant Anik about my helping him find the Russian sub."

"Yeah, I was wondering how you did that? Even I didn't have that information."

"It was just a general conversation about CZ zones, Jay. I didn't know that sub was going to be there, and I didn't know what Lieutenant Anik's deployment would be when he got here. You're barking up the wrong tree. We're both on the same side."

"And what side is that, Don? Total war? Or the limited actions the president has prescribed?"

"I work for the president, and I work for you. And that's the way it's always been. But that doesn't mean to say I can't have my own opinions."

McCracken felt a measure of relief in their clearing conversation and returned to the more pressing issue of the Montana's crew. "So with your more personal knowledge of the Montana's crew, where do you think Chang will try to meet them with his codes?"

Acker smiled. "You should have read my lecture on global reach. Terrorists live local. They don't have the means or the infrastructure to reach further. The crew are mostly from the northwest; that's where they live, that's what they know, and that's most probably where they'll meet."

"That's pretty predictable."

"They're terrorists now. They don't have a lot of choices."

McCracken felt vindicated that he had come to the same conclusion, but he still had the nagging feeling that it could be something else.

"And what if Chang mailed the codes to someone else? Someone in a foreign country?"

"Then all bets are off, and we're in for a wild goose chase!"

Chapter 27

Less than a mile from the FBI's Seattle control center a Chevy sedan appeared from the thick coastal fog and drove to the end of a jetty, providing access to a marina filled with private boats and yachts. The hazy lights of the city could be seen through the drifting mist, but it was a cold, uninviting night, and the place was deserted.

A phone rang, and the young man driving the car answered it. He appeared to be Latino, with his long black hair pulled back into a ponytail.

"You here?"

"Yep. Just pulling in," said Monique, speaking from the helm of the Grady White on her burn phone.

"I'm at the end of the dock. Green Chevy."

"I see you. Come on down. You got everything?"

"Yeah." He grabbed a small satchel from the parked car and walked down a floating ramp, joining Monique as she tied her boat to the dock.

"Tommy!" She gave him a hug and a kiss on the cheek. "I would never have recognized you!"

"Tanning cream and a wig!"

"Is that it?" She indicated the satchel.

"Yeah." He handed it to her. "I sent the other one to the address you gave me."

"That's good." She checked the drive in the satchel and placed it on the boat. "Does it work this time?"

"Yeah. I already ran it against the new system. It's perfect."

Monique detected a distraction in his voice. "So how you doing?"

"Not so good."

"What happened?"

"I got made."

"By who?"

Tommy rolled his eyes, belying his guilt. "A girl I gave a ride to."

"Are you kidding me?!" exclaimed Monique.

"No. I picked her up at the airport in Spokane when I got the car."

"Shit, Tommy! Where is she now?"

"In the trunk. She recognized me from TV and tried to call the police. I didn't know they were going to figure everything out that quick!"

"Is she still alive?"

"Yes."

"And you said she had a cell phone?"

"Yeah. I threw it onto a truck going in a different direction."

Monique took a deep breath and pushed back her hair, contemplating their options, but there was only one that made sense. "Okay, we'll just have to deal with it." She reached into her backpack and pulled out the Benelli pistol.

Tommy looked horrified. "Are you serious?"

"You got a better idea?"

"I don't know…I never hurt anyone before!"

"Well, she won't feel much, I can tell you that!" She started up the ramp to the car with Tommy following.

"Can't we just leave her in the car?"

"She knows where you are, Tommy; she'll bring everyone here! And God knows what else you told her!"

"I didn't tell her anything!"

Monique approached the car and lowered her voice. "Is she tied up?"

"Yes."

"Gagged?"

"Yes."

"Okay, open it."

Tommy hesitated. "We'll be gone before anyone finds her, Moe. Can't we just let it go?"

Monique's temper flared. "We're going to kill millions of people, Tommy. This is just one person. Open the fucking trunk!"

Tommy obeyed, and a pretty Latin girl in her twenties looked up at them with frightened, doe-like eyes.

"Turn around so I can get your hands," said Monique. The girl looked relieved and turned in the trunk. Tommy couldn't bear to watch and looked away as Monique depressed the safety on her pistol and shot the girl in the back of the head. The noise of the exploding gun echoed through the marina, and Monique looked around concerned, but the noise quickly dissipated into the sounds of the nearby city. Tommy looked at the dead girl and started to throw up. Monique shook her head and closed the trunk.

"It's all your fault, Tommy. You shouldn't have picked her up. You were told not to do that. You jeopardized the whole operation." She peered into the sea beneath the causeway. "Is there anything in the car that can ID you?"

"No."

"And the girl?"

"Just her bag."

"Give it to me." Tommy retrieved the bag. "Okay, put it in neutral and we'll push it off the dock."

Tommy was in a state of shock and obeyed her like an automaton.

With a splash, the green Chevy plunged into the dark sea and disappeared beneath the surface. It was closure for Monique, but Tommy couldn't deal with it.

"I can't do this anymore. I just can't."

"We're at war, Tommy. You made a commitment!"

"She didn't do anything. She was just an innocent person!"

"There were over 350 innocent people on my sister's plane, three thousand in the Twin Towers, and over two hundred when your parents were killed in Russia! They're killing our people every day. That's what we're fighting for! An eye for an eye. You have to put it behind you."

"I already did my part, Moe. You've got the codes. I can't do it anymore. I'm out of here!" He started walking up the causeway. Monique cursed and followed after him.

"Where are you going?!"

"I'm going to turn myself in."

"You can't do that, Tommy. You're just upset. You'll get over it."

"I'm not a soldier, Moe. I'm a computer nerd. I write code; I don't kill people!"

"You already killed someone, Tommy. The only reason she's dead is because of your stupidity! Now you want to turn us all in?"

"I'm not going to tell anyone anything, Moe. You can still go ahead and do what you want."

"Tommy, I beg you, please!" She grabbed his arm, stopping him. "Look at me! We've all committed our lives to this! To right a wrong, to stop an injustice that will go on and on forever unless we do this! You can't stop believing now!"

Tommy shook his head. "It's not who I am, Moe! I'm not like you. Just get in your boat and go! I won't say anything. I'm sorry." He continued towards the city.

"You're going to kill us all, Tommy, for nothing!!"

But Tommy had made up his mind and didn't look back. Monique watched him go for a moment, then stepped forward, leveled her pistol, and shot him in the back. Tommy went down, then rose up on his arms like a bewildered child until Monique finished him with a second shot.

It was a brutal execution, but Monique couldn't afford to feel anything. She already knew that Tommy was the weak link in the terror cell they had formed. He was a spoiled playboy, and ultimately lacked the discipline, obsession, and mental outrage to complete the mission. Fortunately, there appeared to be no blood spilling onto the causeway, and Monique quickly grabbed a two-wheeled cart used for carrying things down the narrow ramps to the boats and lifted Tommy onto it. It was just a short walk back to the ramp leading to the Grady White, but as she reached the floating dock beneath it she heard a noise that stopped her in her tracks. It was the chatter of a police car radio approaching down the causeway. Caught off guard by the vehicle's appearance, Monique quickly turned the cart upside down, covering Tommy's body with it and ducked beneath the causeway as the patrol car stopped above her. The cops were just feet away and shone their searchlight up and down the rows of boats moored at the marina.

"You see anything?" said the car's driver.

"Just a lot of boats! You think we should go down there?"

"No, there's not going to be anyone here in this shit!"

"Two different people reported it."

"Two people in the city. It could have come from anywhere."

"Okay. I'm just going to take a pee."

Monique heard him get out of the car and saw Tommy's hand sticking out from under the cart. It was clearly visible, and she quickly pushed it out of sight as the cop appeared above her. He was so close she could hear him pull down his zipper then a stream of urine descended in front of her, splattering onto the dock and the upturned cart.

"How much you reckon these boats cost out here?"

"Hundreds of thousands. Bob Roberts had one and said it cost him fifteen grand a year just to keep it here."

"I'd rather go to Hawaii..."

A few minutes later, the police were gone and Monique was racing away from the marina, tears cascading down her face. She'd never killed anyone before, never truly considered the emotional ramifications of such an act, and she looked back at Tommy sitting in the wheel well of the boat next to the bloodstained cart. His eyes were still open, and he bobbled back and forth like a living marionette as the boat rode up and down over the choppy sea. "It's your fault! You made me do it!"

Chapter 28

It was past midnight on the East Coast, and the president's wife walked down to the Oval Office to check on her husband. His secretary, Betty, was busy on her computer as Tat peered inside.

"You guys still at it?"

"Hi, Tat! Yeah, he's still on the phone, but this is his last one. He said you should go in. He's talking to the Prime Minister of Pakistan."

"I'll just wait out here."

"No, he wants you to go in. He's looking for an excuse to leave!"

"Okay." Tatiana knocked on the Oval Office door and peered inside where the president indicated for her to join him. He was talking on a speakerphone as Gary, Bob Gaines, the DNI, Tom Pierce, and his National Security Advisor, Tony Russo, sat listening to the conversation. Gary waved her over to the couch beside him. Everyone looked tired but pleased to see her and nodded their greetings. The Prime Minister of Pakistan was speaking and sounded upset.

"...Nobody in my entire country, including our military leaders, believes that this mutiny could possibly happen in America without people in your government knowing about it."

"Well, it's interesting you say that," said the president, "because for the last twenty years people in my country have said the same thing about your people. That you have encouraged, supported, and provided sanctuary for multiple terrorist groups that have continuously attacked the people of Afghanistan, India, and America. So I suggest you don't judge others by your own actions."

"That is totally ridiculous!" said the Prime Minster. "And I can tell you right now, sir, if your submarine attacks any city in our country, we will hold you responsible and respond with our own nuclear capability."

"And I can assure you, Mr. Prime Minister, that if you so much as point a weapon in the direction of America, you and your country will cease to exist, guaranteed. And that is all I have to say tonight."

The others in the room looked shocked as he hung up the phone.

"Well, that went well," said Gary.

"Yeah, fifteen heads of state and over half of them think we did this on purpose!"

"For what reason?" said Tatiana.

"To have our own terrorist organization so we can kill anyone we want and not worry about culpability or political correctness...okay gentlemen, I think that's enough for one night. Does anyone have any last insights? Bob?"

"No, I think you said the right thing. I've been wanting to say that for over a decade!"

"You should have reminded him they hid Osama bin Laden as well!" said Russo.

"I'll mention that next time." He opened the door and spoke to Betty. "Is there anything else I have to deal with tonight?"

"No, you're all done," said Betty.

"And the Montana?"

"Nothing more."

"Okay. I'm going to bed. 'Night everyone! Come on, baby. Thank God, we don't have to drive home." He put his arm around his wife, and they walked away from the office.

"Do you really think they could send a nuclear weapon here?"

"Not on a rocket," said the president, "but they could hide it on a ship or something."

"That's pretty scary."

"That's what we're facing. Tit for tat until the whole world's blown up. And for what? A difference of opinion about how to worship God? It makes you wonder if there is one."

CHAPTER 29

THE single story house stood on a bluff, one side facing the open Pacific, the other an inland waterway. The fog had dissipated and a rising moon gave Monique a clear view of the house and a dock at the base of the bluff. It was an isolated location, and she shut down the Grady White's engines, drifting silently up to the dock where she tied the boat, which no longer had Tommy Chang and the blood stained cart on board.

Checking the load in her pistol, Monique grabbed Tommy's satchel and started up the stairs. It was just a short hike to the house, and she approached it, pistol in hand, like an advancing soldier.

There was a light on in the main building, and a solitary van parked in front of it. Monique looked down the empty driveway, then out at the Pacific Ocean, stretching almost 5,000 miles to Asia with only the Hawaiian Islands in its vastness. It was a reassuring presence, and she rang the doorbell, hiding the pistol in the pocket of her jacket. A dog barked then a bright light illuminated her as she looked up at a camera on the porch wall.

"It's me!"

"Come in! Door's open."

Monique smiled, relieved to hear a familiar voice, and entered the house where a friendly Golden Lab greeted her.

"Hey, Babu, how you doing?" She greeted the dog and looked into a large living room with a man in a wheelchair sitting next to a VHF radio transmitter on a table. Staley Combs was about forty years old, legless, with a ruddy shrapnel scarred face and a strong upper body that still heralded the fit soldier he used to be.

"Staley! How's my favorite soldier?"

"Better now you're here!" said Staley. "I was beginning to worry."

"Everything's good. Give me a hug."

She bent down and hugged him. They were obviously pleased to see each other.

"So you finally went ahead and did it!"

"Paybacks are hell!"

"Hallelujah!" said Staley, holding up his hand for a slap. "How about a little celebration?"

"Sounds good to me!" said Monique.

Staley poured a couple of shots from a tequila bottle. "So do we have a problem with this Chang kid and the codes?"

"Not anymore. He fixed them, and we got them back. This is the one for the kid." She handed him Tommy's satchel. "When are you seeing him?"

"First thing in the morning."

"And you're still sure about him?"

"Yeah, he's good. Looking forward to his vacation." He held up his iPhone revealing a picture of a surfer kid smiling with his board, then handed her one of the shot glasses. "Here's to the cause!"

"Touché!" said Monique knocking back the tequila, catching her breath. "Did you hear from Hawaii?"

"Yeah. Second location." He glanced at his watch. "John's set to call in two minutes, you ready?"

"Yes." She sounded vulnerable.

"You've got the worst of it, kid."

"No worse than everyone else. How you doing?"

"I'm ready to die for it. Can't think of nothing better." It was a powerful statement, and Monique reached out and held his hand.

"You still watching the Ayatollah?"

"Every Friday. Death to America! Death to America! He's been preaching that shit for twenty years. I'm looking forward to changing his tune."

A phone rang and Staley pulled a burner phone from a drawer, checking the incoming number. "Okay, this is him. You want to take it?"

Monique indicated yes and took the phone, looking tense, as she held back her feelings.

John Besson stood on a narrow dock in front of a hotel, where a group of vacationing guests were dining and dancing on a large patio. At the end of the dock, barely visible in the shadows, a small, motorized rubber dinghy waited with two of Besson's crewmembers crouched inside. All of the men were wearing light civilian clothes in the tropical location.

Like Monique, John was tense and sitting on his emotions when he heard his wife's sweet voice.

"Hi."

"Hi. How are you?"

"Good...well, good as can be expected. And you?"

"I miss you."

"I miss you, too." Staley felt the emotion and excused himself, indicating he was going to the kitchen to make coffee. "Is that music I hear in the background?"

"Yeah. Some people are having a party. Did you get the money from the accountant?"

"Yes. Two checks. I put one in the B of A and one in Wells Fargo. If you're going to write a check, you should use the B of A account first."

"Okay, B of A. I'll be sure and remember that. How was the accountant?"

"Not good. I had to let him go."

John looked surprised. "You let him go?"

"Yes. But he finished everything he had to do first."

"He was that bad?"

"Really bad. Indiscreet. Said he didn't want to work with us anymore. Changed his mind."

"So he's gone forever?"

"Yes."

John was surprised by her calmness. "I'm sorry you had to deal with that. You going to be okay?"

"It's my job. I put the second check into the Wells Fargo Bank. It goes out tomorrow."

"Okay, that's good. Did you see Sean?"

Monique looked even more distressed; it was a subject she didn't want to discuss. "Yes, twice."

"And how did that go?"

"It was fine."

"Fine isn't good enough, Moe. I'm not coming back. I need to know you've moved on. It'll make it easier for me, and it'll make it easier for you."

"I'm not a machine, John."

"We have to be machines," said her husband emphatically. "That's the choice we made. We have to live up to it now. You hear me?"

"Yes."

"You're a soldier now."

"I know what I am, John." Her words hung in the air.

"You can't afford to have feelings anymore."

"I don't. I'm killing them all, one by one."

John felt drained by her apathy. "I did this for you, Moe. You and Maddie and the cause."

"I know, I'm just having a bad day."

"Okay. I think we should release the memorandum tomorrow."

"Before you've cashed the check?"

"It'll make things easier. They'll think we already have it."

"You sure about that?"

"Yes."

"Okay, I'll tell Staley."

"Let me speak to him."

Monique turned to the kitchen. "Staley! He wants to speak to you!"

Staley rejoined her and took the phone. "Hey man, how's it going?"

"Good. Everything's going well. How about you?"

"Excellent. So we're moving on?"

"Yeah. I'm going to release the memorandum tomorrow. So we'll keep to the same routine."

"Okay. Good luck, man. Here's your wife."

Monique took the phone back. She wanted to say so much. She wanted to reach out and touch him one last time, but she knew she never would again, and simply said, "Bye."

"Be strong."

"I will."

She switched off the phone and turned to Staley. "Can I have another shot?" She indicated the tequila.

"Sure." Staley refilled her glass, which she emptied in a gulp.

"I have to look like I fell off a bicycle, so I need you to hit me with this." She lifted a fire log from the hearth and handed it to him.

Staley hesitated. "You sure about this?"

"Yes. Do it hard," she kneeled next to him and presented her shoulder. "See if you can rip the jacket as well."

"I don't feel good about this, Moe.

"Just do it!"

Staley slammed the log into her shoulder, raking it downward, ripping the jacket and her flesh beneath it. Monique caught her breath, absorbing the pain.

Staley shared her grief and even the dog whined his concern. "You okay?"

"I'm good." She took back the log and smashed the side of her head into it.

Staley shuddered at the impact. "Oh my God, girl! You're bleeding!"

"I want to bleed." She returned the log to the fireplace, letting the blood from the wound run down her face and drip onto her clothes unrestrained. "You know what bothers me the most? I can't pray to my God anymore. He wouldn't condone this."

"I still pray to mine," said Staley. "We're just killing infidels. Isn't that what they say about us?"

Monique smiled. "It would be nice if it were that simple."

"It is that simple. Either they win or we win. And if they win, say goodbye to all your freedoms as a woman. You see these guys here?" He pointed at two soldiers in a picture of his platoon from Afghanistan. "They were with me when we dispersed a crowd on the outskirts of a village and found a woman buried up to her neck, stoned to death because her husband said she cheated on him. And that wasn't the end of it! The woman wasn't dead. She tried to say something, her whole face caved in by her family and neighbors, and the captain told us to move on. It was their Sharia law, and we weren't there to change it. That's what the Taliban and all these fanatics believe in. And that's what they want to inflict upon us."

"So do you still believe in God after all that?"

"No. I just pray in case I'm wrong." He grinned, and Monique clasped his face and kissed him affectionately.

"You're crazy, you know that? Thank you for everything."

Staley watched her leave. "You're a soldier now. Don't forget it."

"Don't worry about that. I've got my own scores to settle."

John Besson switched off his cell, drained by the conversation with his wife. They had discussed it all before, thought of every possible emotional caveat that would endanger their mission, but destroying their love for the greater cause ripped his heart out. It was the ultimate sacrifice, and he now knew the depth of the emotional roller coaster he would live until his inevitable end. But as all those thoughts swirled in his mind, an unexpected female voice snapped him back to reality.

"It's a beautiful night."

John turned and saw an attractive American woman from the hotel joining him. She was Monique's age and obviously looking for some company.

"Yes, it is," said John, mirroring her friendly manner, trying to hide his true emotions.

"Are you staying at the hotel?"

"No, I'm just visiting a friend."

"Well, lucky friend. Where are you from?"

"Los Angeles."

"I'm from Santa Monica," said the girl with a grin.

"Nice place."

"Yeah, very nice…anyway, you have a good night."

"You too. Thank you."

The woman started away, then looked back. "My name's Hilda. I'm in Room 324 if your friend doesn't work out."

John matched her smile. "324. I'll remember that."

"Okay…see you."

She walked away with the ornamented stride of a temptress.

John took a deep breath and exhaled slowly. He never imagined that being a terrorist would present such a mix of conflicting emotions, and he quickly rejoined his shipmates in the dinghy.

"What did she want?" said Jones, the sub's navigator.

"Just trying to be friendly."

Jones grinned. "We're going to have to keep you on the boat, Captain! Did they fix the codes?"

"Yes. We're picking them up in Sydney."

They pulled away from the dock, and John looked back at the hotel, where he could see Hilda watching him go. It reminded him of how great life used to be then he quickly shut down his wandering thoughts. Those days were over.

Chapter 30

It was midnight by the time Monique arrived back on Bainbridge Island. The fog had lifted, and she quickly returned the Grady White to its boathouse, refueled it from a large tank and rode her bike to her lawyer's house. The rustic home was in an upper class neighborhood where most of the inhabitants were currently fast asleep in their plush beds. With surprising ease, Monique used the narrow fork of a tree to twist the front forks of her bike then kicked out several spokes, simulating the collision that had supposedly caused her present condition.

Exhausted by the night's activities, Monique took one last moment to contemplate if she had forgotten anything that could incriminate her. Tommy Chang was tied to an anchor at the bottom of the sea. Her Benelli pistol and burn phone were disposed of in a similar fashion, and the Grady White was back home and refueled. Was there anything she had forgotten? Her wounds! She had been running on adrenaline for hours, which had distracted her from the pain of her injuries.

It took Sean almost a minute to respond to the ringing doorbell and appear in the doorway wearing his PJ bottoms and a t-shirt. He looked as though he had just awoken from a deep sleep.

"Moe? What happened? Are you okay?"

"I came off my bike, and it must have knocked me out."

"Oh my God! Come in! Sit over here." He led her into the living room and put on the lights. "I'll get some peroxide. Are you sure you didn't break anything?"

"No, I'm fine. I already walked for hours before I found a road and realized it was near your house."

Sean returned with the peroxide and a bowl filled with bandages and gauze. "Let's get your head first."

"Any chance I can have a shot before you do that?"

"Sure. Good idea." He opened his liquor cabinet. "Scotch or tequila?"

"Tequila."

Sean filled a shot glass, and Monique knocked it back, quickly absorbing its benefits.

"Okay, doctor, I'm all yours."

Sean poured peroxide directly onto the head wound and wiped away the dried blood.

"Wow, this is a bad gash! I wonder if you got a concussion?"

"I don't think so. I feel fine."

"Let me see your shoulder."

Monique carefully removed her jacket and pulled down her bloodstained blouse revealing a large bruise and torn skin.

"You really did beat yourself up!" He cleaned the wound and Monique observed him close-up. He had handsome masculine features and a kind manner.

"You should've become a doctor."

"Then I wouldn't have met you, and you wouldn't be here right now."

Monique smiled. "So do I still have attorney/client privileges now that you're my doctor as well?"

"Yes, you do. You can tell me anything, and I can do the same."

"So what's my diagnosis, Doc?"

"I think you should spend the night so I can take care of you."

"It's that serious?"

"I'm afraid so."

"Okay. I guess I'll just have to do what my doctor tells me."

The hot shower was like a catharsis for Monique, washing away all of the anxiety and fears invading her mind. She felt safe in Sean's presence, and when he knocked on the bathroom door and said, "You want me to get you something to eat?" she realized how hungry she was.

"What do you have?"

"How about some chicken alfredo?"

"Sounds great!"

"Okay, get into bed and I'll bring it to you."

Monique turned off the shower, wrapped herself in a towel, and walked into his bedroom. It was warm and inviting and she slipped into a t-shirt he had placed on the bed and slid beneath the sheets. She was in another man's bed, and she felt good about it.

It took Sean less than five minutes to heat up the Alfredo and pour some wine, but by the time he returned to the bedroom Monique was fast asleep. Sean smiled at her angelic face and turned out the bedroom light.

"Come and sleep next to me," whispered Monique in a sleepy voice.

She was more beautiful than Sean had ever imagined, and he slid under the covers next to her. He wanted to reach out and touch her, wake her with a kiss, melt into her being, but he did none of those things. The simple pleasure of just lying next to her was enough. And when she turned and placed her head on his shoulder, snuggling up to him, he felt like a young boy in love again.

CHAPTER 31

THE Montana Memorandum exploded onto the internet the following morning, quickly covered by every news organization in the world. At first Gary Brockett contemplated letting the president finish his sleep before confronting him with the news, but the outcry from around the world quickly forced the issue.

"I'm sorry to wake you up early, but we finally heard from the Montana, and it's something that's going to require your attention."

"What is it?" said the president, trying to clear his head.

"Can I come in? I'm in the hallway."

"What do you do? Sleep out there?"

"Feels like it."

"Okay, come in."

Gary let himself into the presidential quarters where his boss, still wearing PJs, joined him in an anteroom.

"So what are they saying?"

"It's a whole memorandum. I've got it on my computer." He opened his laptop and sat on a couch with the president. "It's already on every news channel in the world, and we're getting calls from everyone." He pushed play on his computer, and the memorandum lit up the screen. It was a compelling, professionally produced video showing graphic scenes of militant Muslim attacks around the world with a well-spoken narrator adding credence and drama to the disturbing images.

There were shots of Christians and journalists being graphically beheaded, old British ladies slaughtered on a beach in Tripoli. The embassies in Nairobi and Dar es Salaam being blown to pieces, a Russian passenger jet destroyed in Egypt, planes flown into the Pentagon and a field outside of Pittsburgh. The London plane bombing, the Denver crash with Monique's sister, a Nairobi shopping mall and university under siege, Paris under attack, a Russian school and theater invaded. The Paris Underground, London Underground and Moscow Underground attacked. The Charlie Hebdo studio shooting. India's Mumbai City under siege, Spanish trains blown up. A London bus attacked, the Fort Hood massacre, Australian restaurant attack, Chinese train station attack, Nice truck massacre. Attacks in the Philippines, Chad, Bali, and Thailand. Three hundred Nigerian schoolgirls kidnapped. Thousands killed by suicide bombers around the world, some perpetrated by girls as young as twelve, all in the name of Allah. The Boston Marathon bombings. San Bernardino office attack. Florida nightclub shooting. Two hijacked planes slamming into the Twin Towers. Civilians leaping from the burning buildings as people cheered in the Middle East. And superimposed over the carnage, John Besson's silhouette.

"My name is John Besson. I'm one of the fifteen officers that have commandeered the nuclear missile submarine USS Montana. Like ISIS, Al Qaeda, Boca Haram, and the Taliban, we are a new terrorist organization, but our mission is not to destroy Western civilization in the name of Allah. Our purpose is to retaliate and destroy militant Islamists and their supporters around the world. Over ninety percent of all conflicts on the planet today involve Muslims killing Muslims, Muslims waging war on their neighbors, or Muslims terrorizing Western nations who have generously taken them in as immigrants and refugees. This is a religious war being inflicted upon the world by a fanaticism not seen since the Dark Ages. It can only be stopped by the same terrorist tactics used by its jihadist followers. There are

1.5 billion Muslims in the world today. We represent the other five billion people who are not interested in joining their archaic religion or being subjected to its barbaric laws. We are here to counter this terror inflicted upon our people and will respond to any more attacks with attacks of our own." A nuclear explosion appeared on the screen, punctuating his final statement.

The president stared at the screen in shock. "My God, it's like a Hollywood movie!"

"You want to see it again?" asked Gary.

"NO. Does this mean they've got the codes?"

"I asked Russo and Stossel the same question, and neither knew the answer."

"So we still don't have anything new on the sub?"

"Not that I know of. General Pierce has called for an NSC meeting in an hour, subject to your confirmation."

"Okay, let's do it."

Gary left, and the president walked back into his bedroom where his wife was already watching the news and the worldwide reaction to the memorandum. Muslims around the world were outraged and blaming America for opening a new war against them while governments everywhere unanimously denounced the memorandum, playing their parts in global political correctness. But while the politicians did their dance and the mullahs issued new fatwas, tens of millions of non-Muslims around the world were silently enthralled with the idea of a counter-offensive against a militant religious order that was imperiling all of their futures.

"This is going to be a big mess," said Tatiana. "What are you going to do?"

"I don't know. I'm going to try talking to the captain's wife, and see if she can help."

"And if that fails?"

"I'm going to start praying that some angry militant kid doesn't do something stupid and piss off the men on that sub."

Five thousand miles away, the Grand Ayatollah of Iran contemplated the same dilemma as the president but with different concerns. Should he now continue chanting his twenty-year lament "Death to America" and "Death to Israel" at his Friday prayers and risk the wrath of the Montana's mutineers or start praying for his own salvation? There was no global consensus of political correctness to save him from a terrorist organization so the Ayatollah did what he had not done for years. He turned away from politics and back to God, beseeching Him to intervene and save him and his minions from a terrorist organization just like the ones he had so lovingly created against Israel and the West.

But ironically, he didn't wonder about the hypocrisy of his prayers or the fact that God in His celestial wisdom might find his entreaties a sanctimonious pharisaism, or more plainly put, a bullshit request from a self-serving religious poser. So in that new state of hypocritical denial, the Ayatollah summoned his ambassadors to the United States and the United Nations and sent them forth to excoriate the Great Satan that had created this new ungodly terror.

Chapter 32

MONIQUE awakened in the warm safety of Sean's bed. It was already morning and she sat up, trying to keep her mind on the pleasantness of the moment and hold at bay everything that had happened the previous night.

She liked Sean even more than she thought she would and felt a sense of freedom in the knowledge that her husband had told her to be there with him.

"Here you go, sleepyhead." Sean walked into the room with a couple of coffees. He was still wearing his pj's and t-shirt and looked boyishly handsome. "I brought you some coffee. Double mocha."

Monique sat up trying to clear her head. "Wow! That shot knocked me out last night. I don't remember anything. You didn't take advantage of me, did you?"

Sean smiled boyishly. "No, you went straight to sleep."

"And that was it? Not even a goodnight kiss?"

"No."

"So I guess I owe you one?"

"Yes you do...." He kissed her on the lips.

"That was nice."

Monique didn't know why she was doing this. She couldn't accept the idea of being with him twelve hours earlier, but John had forced the issue, pushing her away, and there was a measure of anger and need in her new disposition. A need for someone else to be emotionally close to, someone she could trust, someone she found attractive and someone that would be protective.

Sean kissed her again, and after a moment, they fell back onto the bed together. Monique was living on the edge, a sea of fomenting emotions held tenuously at bay, but when Sean slipped off her t-shirt and their bodies entwined and became one, those feelings shuddered to the surface, and she gasped with pleasure as every part of her being erupted with joy.

Charlotte Ramsey and Sid Bailey watched the Montana Memorandum multiple times, well aware that such internet releases often contained hidden messages for their adherents. The release of the memorandum took precedence over everything else on their agenda, but when Charlotte received a message from the Director of National Intelligence informing her of a National Security Council meeting in half an hour, the emphasis turned back to Monique. Where the hell was she? Charlotte didn't want to have to tell the president and all the NSC members that a suspect in her care had disappeared.

"Did you call Mrs. Besson's lawyer this morning?"

"Several times," said Sid, "but he hasn't responded."

Charlotte cursed. "I've got an NSC meeting in half an hour, and I'm pretty sure the president's going to ask me about her."

"Let me check again," Sid got on the phone, and Charlotte realized she needed something else to present at the NSC meeting: some new information. She signaled Sarah and Matt Weston into the office.

"Any luck with that list of investors you were checking on?"

"We got almost a hundred from the London broker," said Sarah, "but we haven't checked them all out, yet." She handed Charlotte a list.

"Any Americans?"

"About thirty. Most of them professional traders. Just one civilian."

"Civilian?"

"Non-professional," said Matt.

"And what's his name?"

"It's a female. Angelina Kurtz. Married with three kids."

Sarah checked her notes. "Lives in London. Husband's a banker."

"What's her maiden name?"

"Acker." It was not a name that Charlotte knew, but Sid caught it immediately.

"Wait a minute. I know that name." He quickly found Acker on his computer. "Vice Admiral Don Acker, Deputy Commander of the Pacific Fleet. Right under Admiral McCracken."

"That's an interesting find," said Charlotte, turning to Sarah. "When was that investment made?"

Sarah checked her notes. "Five days ago."

"Okay, let's keep this strictly to ourselves and see what else you can find. And you'd better double check that Mrs. Kurtz really is Acker's daughter."

Sarah agreed and left with Matt.

"This is a big deal," said Charlotte.

"If it's true."

"So who do we trust now?"

"I don't know, but if you're wrong you're going to piss off a lot of people!"

"I have to pass it on to someone."

"How about the president directly?"

"How about Admiral McCracken?" said Charlotte. "He tried to stop the sub and the whole thing in Hawaii. He wouldn't have done that if he was involved."

"Still pretty dangerous."

"So why don't you do it?" She smiled mischievously. "Its just part of the larger investigation, and you thought he should know about it."

"Okay, I guess I could do that," said Sid, not missing her slyness.

"Just make sure he understands your concern about a greater

conspiracy."

"And how do I do that?"

"Tell him you haven't told anyone else because of it."

Sid got a call from Siebert on Bainbridge Island and turned back to Charlotte.

"Mrs. Besson just returned to her house with her lawyer. Siebert said she had a bandage on her arm, and her bike appeared to be damaged in the back of his pick-up truck."

"Did he speak to either of them?"

"No, they just went straight in. There's still a lot of press there."

"So she spent the night with her lawyer?"

"Apparently."

"Okay, I'll try and reach her through him."

Monique Besson carried a bowl of food out of the house and gave it to Bruce, now chained to a tree in the yard. He was happy to see her, and she made a fuss of him until Sean called her from the house.

"You need to come and see this!"

"What is it?"

"John and his crew just released a statement about attacking the Middle East. I can't believe he'd do this to you!"

"He did it for me," said Moe, watching the TV lowering her voice.

"So you knew about this?"

"They killed my sister, Sean, and they keep killing people, so John decided to do something about it."

"They're going to put you away for life if you admit to knowing that Moe."

"That's why I have a new lawyer."

"I can't save you if you talk about it."

"You're right. I'll be more careful."

Sean's phone rang, and he answered it, frustrated. "Hello?"

"This is Charlotte Ramsey. May I speak with Mrs. Besson, please?"

"Sure. Just a moment." He handed the phone to Monique. "It's the Director of the FBI. She probably wants your answer about meeting the president."

Monique took the phone and answered it in a calm voice that surprised Sean. "This is Monique."

"Good morning," said Charlotte. "I was calling to see if you had made a decision about seeing the president?"

"I don't want to go to Washington. But if he wants to come here, that would be fine with me."

Her statement startled both Charlotte and Sean.

"The president's a very busy man, Mrs. Besson. It would not be practical for him to come here when he's running a whole country."

"Well, that's his decision to make."

"Even if we send you on a private jet and arrange for your lawyer to go with you?"

Monique was intrigued by the offer. "Would the jet bring us back here afterward?"

"Yes."

"And when would we do this?"

"I can arrange for you to leave this afternoon if you wish."

"How about tomorrow?"

"Tomorrow would be fine," said Charlotte.

"Just a minute." Monique turned to Sean. "You want to go to Washington and meet the president?"

Sean looked confounded but quickly recovered. "Sure."

"Okay." She turned back to Charlotte. "Tomorrow will be fine. But we're not paying for anything while we're there. And you'll have to pay my lawyer's fees for the trip."

Charlotte rolled her eyes, frustrated but kept her cool, "That'll be fine. I'll arrange a car to pick you up."

"Thank you," said Monique, enjoying her small victory.

"Thank you," said Charlotte, knowing she'd just been bested.

"We're leaving tomorrow," said Monique, hanging up the phone. "And they agreed to pay your fees for the trip."

"You're kidding!" said Sean.

"No. I'm your new manager." She grinned and gave him a kiss.

Charlotte hung up the phone, frustrated by her conversation with Monique.

"She's going?" asked Sid.

"Yeah! In a private jet, and we're paying for everything, including her lawyer!"

They were interrupted by Lieutenant Silver entering the room. He looked energized. "Okay, I think we've finally got something!" He placed his computer on Charlotte's desk and fired it up. "At six o'clock this morning a local pier fisherman saw a car under the sea at the end of the Mayview Jetty. When they pulled it out, there was a girl bound and gagged in the trunk with a bullet in her head." He showed them police pictures of the car and the girl. "The coroner estimates she died sometime last night, so we tracked the car to Spokane Airport, where it was rented two days ago by Carlos Rivera. This is his fake driver's license and a video of him getting the car." He showed them pictures and footage from the car rental security cameras. "So I ran this picture through Face Recognition, and BINGO! This Latin boy is in fact Lieutenant Thomas Chang, wearing dark makeup and a black wig!" He displayed the Biometrics rendering on his computer.

"Are you sure about this?" asked Charlotte.

"Ran it three times and had two experts confirm it."

"So who's the girl?

"We don't know. No prints in the database. We're checking Missing Persons now."

"So you think Chang's back here in Seattle?" queried Sid.

"I think it's a very good possibility. And last night Mrs. Besson went missing?"

"So you think they met up?"

"Why else would he come here?"

"Did you do a search of him arriving in Spokane with this new ID?" queried Charlotte.

"Came in from Boston eleven a.m. Monday."

"Anyone else with him?"

"No."

"Okay, this is good!" said Charlotte. "Why don't we use this same photograph and run a check of all the post offices and shipping companies in the Bedford and Boston airport areas and see if he mailed anything two days ago."

"And how about the Spokane area?"

"If he was going to mail it, I think he'd do it before he got on a plane, but let's check it out anyway."

"Okay, I'm on it!"

He left and Charlotte turned to Sid. "So what's Chang doing here?"

"Maybe the sub's coming here."

"And why did he kill the girl?"

"She recognized him, figured something out…or maybe Mrs. Besson did it."

"We can't afford to lose her again, Sid, so let's double up on her surveillance."

"And the Acker thing? We still going ahead with that?"

"Yes."

Chapter 33

THE White House Situation Room was a sea of concerned faces and subdued conversation as the president entered with General Pierce and everyone stood up.

"Be seated, gentlemen." Everyone sat, and the president looked up at Charlotte on one of the video screens. "Can you hear us, Charlotte?"

"Yes, sir."

"Okay, everyone has obviously seen the memorandum, which finally clarifies their motive so what we're facing now is a potential nuclear attack on the Middle East if we fail to stop Lieutenant Chang from reaching the Montana. I understand that you have some news on this, Charlotte?"

"Yes, sir. We have reason to believe that Lieutenant Chang returned to the Seattle area last night via Spokane. He's changed his appearance and ID, but we've been able to track his journey from Massachusetts and are presently checking every post office and shipping company he's been close to, to see if he mailed anything."

"So why do you think he's in Seattle?"

"We don't know. He could be en route to the sub or giving someone else the codes."

"How does that fit in with your information, David?" He looked at Stossel.

"It's a possibility, but if the sub's target is the Middle East, Seattle's in the wrong direction, and we've just received a credible report that

Captain Besson was seen on a hotel dock in Fiji with two other men in a motorized dinghy that fits the description of a dinghy on the Montana."

"And when did this happen?" asked the president, surprised.

"Last night."

"Fiji's a long way from Seattle."

"Yes it is, sir."

"So who did this report come from?"

"An American woman via the consulate in Fiji. She actually spoke to Besson and didn't see the other men with him until they left in the dinghy."

"Did you speak to her personally?"

"Yes, sir. She was absolutely confident it was Besson, and ID'd him correctly from a series of pictures."

"Why would he do this? Why risk coming ashore?"

"He was on a phone, so he probably needed to be in a service area and clear of the sub to avoid detection."

The president looked to General Pierce. "Can we trace that call?"

"No, sir. Foreign phone services don't keep data like we do."

"So we still don't have anything we can share with the public…?"

The silence was deafening, but before the president could speak again, Charlotte received a text and spoke up. "I just received a message from Lieutenant Silver with NCIS informing me that Lieutenant Chang mailed a package from Boston, Massachusetts, to an address in Sydney, Australia, two days ago. I believe this would substantiate Admiral Stossel's Fiji contact."

"What's the recipient's name?"

"I don't have that yet, sir, but I'll get it to General Pierce as soon as I receive it."

"Okay, well that at least sounds positive. Did you contact Mrs. Besson about coming to see me?"

"Yes, sir," said Charlotte. "But she can't leave for another day. She fell off her bike."

"Her bike?"

"Yes, sir."

"Okay, so is there anything else you need from me? I unfortunately have a United Nations Security Council meeting to deal with and twenty heads of state to placate."

No one responded, and the president stood and gathered his notes. "I hope you all realize that if there is a nuclear attack on the Middle East, we will all be held personally responsible for it."

Marine General Mack Hayden, Chairman of the Joint Chiefs, shook his head. "With all due respect, sir, it's their own fault. They have clerics and ashrams teaching religious hatred and violence against non-believers around the world. How long did they think they'd keep getting away with that before someone on our side started behaving like they do?"

"It doesn't matter who started it, Mack. People expect more from us."

"Well, saints don't win wars, sir."

"And they don't start them either, General. I know there are millions of people in our country that agree with your point of view, and I'm well aware of the frustration that generates it. But frustration is not a good generator of judgment when you're running a country."

He left the room agitated, and everyone stood up respectfully until he was gone.

"Okay everyone, I've just received more information on the Australian code connection" said the DNI checking his email. "I guess it's you, right Charlotte?"

"Yes. We now have the specific name and address of the recipient in Sydney."

"Shouldn't we bring in the CIA on that? It's in their jurisdiction now," questioned the Secretary of Defense.

"I've kept them up on everything," said Pierce, "but I think it'll be easier if we continue to work through one entity on this, particularly with a foreign government." He looked at Admiral Stossel. "I understand our naval attaché in Canberra has good connections there?"

"Lieutenant Olkowski," said Stossel. "He has direct access to the Australian defense forces and the Prime Minister's office. I'll contact him immediately."

"And what about our naval assets?" said Hayden. "Are we going to move them into the area?"

"We've already increased our forces in that direction," said Stossel. "But if the Montana is definitely going there, we can certainly double up and bring in the Aussies. The problem is, there are two sets of codes, so Admiral McCracken and I have tried to keep our options open."

"Well, we need to get on this right away," said Charlotte. "The package has a two-day delivery guarantee and should be arriving in the next few hours."

General Pierce realized the urgency and quickly brought the meeting to a close. "Okay, so let's try to pull all of this together as quick as we can, and I'll keep the president informed."

The meeting was over, and everyone quickly dispersed, including Charlotte, who left the Seattle safe room returning to her office, where Sid and Lieutenant Silver were waiting.

"Did you get the details on the delivery address?" said Silver.

"Yes. We should have a direct liaison with the Australians as soon as Admiral Stossel speaks with our naval attaché there. The question is, do we grab the package right away, or wait and see who comes to get it?"

"Do we know what it looks like?" asked Sid.

"I don't know."

"Neither do they," said Silver. "So why don't we intercept it, replace it with a double, and see what happens after that? It'll take the risk out of it."

"Good idea." said Charlotte calling Matt Weston into the office. "Call the tech who checked out the Chang computer in Bedford, and see if he knows what kind of drives the codes were put on. And do it quickly." Matt left in a hurry. "This isn't going to be easy. We don't know one person down there that we're going to be working with."

"Well, at least they speak English!" said Sid.

CHAPTER 34

THE release of the Montana Memorandum was like a deathblow to Admiral McCracken's self-confidence. He had created a weapon that was now threatening humanity, a monster so elusive that even he couldn't find it or destroy it. There had to be a flaw in the system - some technical mistake he could exploit. But what could it be? And would his brain that had dedicated decades of its existence to perfecting his masterpiece aid in its destruction?

The admiral was having all sorts of crazy thoughts, but when he heard of Besson's appearance in Fiji and the mailing address of the launch codes to Sydney, he felt a glimmer of hope. There was now a specific area to focus his attention and all the formidable naval assets at his disposal. As Commander of the Pacific forces, he had control of the largest navy on earth. But there was also another factor reignited in his mind by the memorandum. Many of the words and ideas expressed in it were the exact words and ideas expressed by Vice Admiral Acker in their earlier conversations. 'Look at the world! Over ninety percent of all conflicts on the planet today involve Muslims killing Muslims, Muslims waging war on their neighbors, or militant Muslims terrorizing Western nations who have generously taken them in as immigrants and refugees.'

Once again, they were just words, but Acker had also steered McCracken in the wrong direction in his search for the Montana. He was personally responsible for the discovery and distraction of the

Russian sub, the originator of the codename *Touché*, and the teacher of the Montana's mutinous crew. When he received a call from Sid Bailey informing him of the investment portfolios in oil futures purchased by the crew's families and Acker's own daughter, his concern about his old friend's involvement in the mutiny piqued. Even though it was circumstantial, there was now enough evidence for him to take action.

The news of the codes being mailed to Sydney was still limited to a small circle of people, but it would become apparent to Acker the moment McCracken redeployed his forces to Australia and the southwest Pacific. So could he set a trap? It wasn't even daylight in Hawaii, so he still had time.

Lieutenant Darden was head of NCIS operations in the central Pacific, and McCracken had him come directly to his house before their morning briefing at the Nimitz McArthur Command Center. The admiral had been working with Darden on the mutiny, and they had become well acquainted with each other.

"Lieutenant, come in, take a seat." He directed Darden into the living room of his large bungalow, looking out at the lights of Pearl Harbor and the ensuing dawn. "I'm having coffee; would you like some?"

"I'm good, thank you, sir."

McCracken ordered one for himself from his Filipino housekeeper and joined Darden. "I'll cut straight to the chase, Lieutenant. What I discuss with you here is in the strictest confidence and may not be discussed with anyone else besides my superiors, who are Admiral Stossel, the Secretary of Defense, and the President of the United States. You understand that?"

"Yes, sir."

The admiral paused as the housekeeper brought his coffee and retreated. "I have reason to believe that Vice Admiral Acker may be involved with the mutinous crew of the Montana, and because of classified information I have just received, I suspect he may try to reach the captain of that vessel as soon as he receives the same information. Obviously, this is a delicate matter, and I could be wrong. But if I'm not, it is of the utmost importance that we reveal his involvement."

Lieutenant Darden was remarkably calm as he took in the information. He was obviously a disciplined soldier at the top of his game. "How do you think he'll try to contact them, sir?"

"I don't know. But I suspect he'll try to reach someone with a VHF transmitter, who will signal the sub and bring Captain Besson ashore, where he can be reached on a phone."

"What time do you think he'll become aware of this classified information?" asked Darden, now taking notes.

"After our closed meeting this morning."

"At the Nimitz Command Center?"

"Yes."

"Does he have his own vehicle or a driver?"

"His own vehicle. A silver Lexus SUV."

"I'll have to put a recorder in it."

"That's fine," said the admiral, handing him a piece of paper. "This is his address, phone number, the license of his Lexus, and his office number. I can't tell you how critical this is to national security, Lieutenant. And how important it is that no one else knows what we're doing. If I'm wrong, and I certainly hope that I am, only you and I will know about this."

"I understand, sir."

"Okay, well, good luck." The admiral stood. "I included my private cell number and the landline here at the house on the paper."

"I appreciate your confidence, sir." The lieutenant saluted and left. Admiral McCracken knew he was treading on dangerous ground, but he had faith in Darden's discretion and was confident he himself was not involved in any grander conspiracy.

Chapter 35

FIFTEEN minutes after the NSC meeting, Charlotte Ramsey received a call from Julian Fenwick, Deputy Commissioner of the Australian Federal Police (AFP) in Sydney. Speaking from the safe room in Seattle, Charlotte, Sid, and Lieutenant Silver quickly filled in the commissioner on the missing codes and their belief that one of the sets was presently on its way to Dalton Murray, an unknown citizen of Australia, living in Port Douglas, Queensland, but presently staying at the Menzies Hotel in downtown Sydney.

Matt Weston had already identified the type of hard drive the codes were on, and Fenwick quickly agreed to intercept the Fed Ex package and replace it with a duplicate, which he believed could be best achieved before the package left Australian customs.

It was a complicated plan and following the duplicate would require considerable coordination, particularly if they intended to track it all the way to the Montana. But Charlotte quickly gained confidence in her Australian counterpart who called in a drone, with help from the Prime Minister's office, and set about preparing the trap, utilizing relays of watchers in addition to the ever-present drone and a tracking device inserted into the hard drive.

Fenwick and the Australian Prime Minister were both informed of the hard drive's potential to launch the Montana's missiles, which added even more focus to their mission as they worked with the U.S. Naval attaché setting up a liaison with the Australian defense forces and an American P-8A anti-submarine aircraft, already dispatched to the area by Admiral McCracken from a base in Guam. The P-8A, with its multifaceted weapons and tracking systems, had presidential authority to use its arsenal of torpedoes and depth charges to destroy the Montana once she had been located and positively identified.

"Well, it's all in their hands now," said Charlotte. "That was a clever idea to put a tracking device into the hard drive."

"This is a shot of Fenwick and his bio," said Silver, indicating his computer. "He was involved with forming the first Australian anti-terrorist force after the Jemaah Islamiyah bombings in Bali. It was his job to bring home what was left of eighty-eight Australians killed in the attack. He's now a deputy commissioner in the Australian Federal Police."

Fenwick was a slim, fit sixty-year-old, and you could definitely sense his focus and dedication as he organized his surveillance team in a large office set aside for the investigation. The room had several video screens including one showing the drone's aerial view of a Fed Ex van working its way through the city, and another with the GPS tracking signal overlaid on a map. Fenwick observed the van on the drone screen and spoke to his second in command, Senior Sergeant Karras.

"Does the driver know what's going on?"

"No, the only ones that know are the two customs agents who helped us find the package and rewrap it after switching out the hard drive."

"And how many people are on the ground following the van?"

"Two relays."

"Let me speak to the drone's operator."

Karras quickly introduced the Deputy Commissioner to the Australian naval officer operating the drone on a two-way video screen.

"It's going to be dark in an hour. Do you have an infrared camera to follow the action after that?"

"Yes, sir."

"And what's the drone's altitude now?"

"Two thousand feet. It's hard to see at that height."

"How close can you get with the camera?"

"I can fill the screen with the van if you want." He zoomed into the vehicle with no loss of clarity.

"That's good," said Fenwick. "You know to follow the GPS signal when it separates from the van?"

"Yes, sir."

Fenwick turned back to Karras. "How long before he reaches the hotel?"

"He should be there in just a few minutes. We have three vehicles parked around the building, two agents in the lobby, two in the underground parking, and one in the hotel's security center monitoring the surveillance system."

"Do we have that feed yet?"

"It's just coming up now," said a video technician indicating a bank of screens. "This is the lobby, elevators, third floor corridor where Murray's room is, and the underground parking."

"Is Murray in his room now?"

"No, he's still at the boat show. This is his bio."

Dalton Murray was a 40-year-old boat salesman and tour operator from Queensland. He had no previous police record, was apparently happily married, and had served four years in the Australian armed forces with a year's deployment in Afghanistan.

Murray was reputedly in Sydney for the annual boat show, which all seemed surprisingly normal to Fenwick as he reviewed the man's background.

"Does he come to the boat show every year?"

"He was here last year, according to the hotel's records."

Fenwick shook his head. "Doesn't look like someone involved with international terrorism."

The Menzies Hotel was in the downtown section of Sydney with a restaurant and bar situated next to its main entrance and lobby. It was early evening and the bar area was already busy with noisy patrons and early diners, including a bald-headed man with jowly cheeks and a fat belly chowing down on a large burger. He didn't seem different than anyone else in the establishment, but if someone looked closer, through his tinted glasses, they would see a pair of intense blue eyes observing everything around him. They were the eyes of someone we had seen before, someone with an intensity now disguised beneath his new persona. It was Moshi Ilyche, ex-head of security for the American airline flying out of London's Heathrow Airport.

But this time, Moshi had a different mission. This time he was a terrorist himself, and in his new life as an independent warrior for Western values, he was well aware of the forces of established law and political correctness arrayed against him. They could be anywhere, and as the Fed Ex van arrived at the hotel and its driver carried several packages to the front desk, Moshi placed his attention on the people around him, including a young couple at the bar who seemed less interested in each other than in the people surrounding them. It was a discreet difference, but when Moshi paid his bill and walked to the hotel's elevator, he observed the couple watching him in the reflection of a mirror and felt a growing unease.

Room 323 was pristine except for a small suitcase on a stand with some clothes hanging out of it. Moshi entered using a plastic hotel key and quickly approached the locked door of an adjoining room that he easily picked and entered. Room 325 was the abode of Dalton Murray, replete with stacks of colorful boat brochures and other promotional items. But Moshi was not interested in any of that as he lifted the phone and dialed the front desk, speaking with a disguised Australian accent.

"This is Mr. Murray in 325? I was expecting a package from Fed Ex?"

"Let me check that for you, sir." The desk clerk was gone for a moment then came back on the line. "Yes, sir, we have it here. Would you like me to send it up?"

"That would be great, thank you." Moshi hung up and walked to the window, watching the sun descend over the darkening city. He was calm, but you could sense his relief when someone knocked on the door, and he saw a bellboy through the peephole.

"Fed Ex package, sir."

"Thank you, mate. Here you go." He gave the boy a tip and closed the door, quickly returning to his own room, where he opened the sealed padded envelope and pulled out the hard drive. It was wrapped in a boat brochure with a note that read, *Don't buy any more boats until you check out this new, low draft, all purpose skiff we're coming out with next month! Best wishes, Brandon.*

Moshi observed the hard drive. It was small and innocuous, and he marveled at its potential to counter the forces of terror emanating from the Middle East. He was living in a strange new world, and quickly pocketed the device, double checked his hotel room then left, leaving his decoy suitcase and clothes behind.

The GPS tracking device embedded in the hard drive was small but effective, and Julian Fenwick and his crew could clearly see its movement as Moshi carried it down the third floor corridor, out of the elevator, and through the lobby.

"Who is he?" said Fenwick, observing Moshi exiting the building on a hotel surveillance camera.

"Room 325. We're checking him out now," said Karras as another detective chimed in.

"Joachim Stone, sir. Checked in yesterday. Danish citizen."

"Okay, let's check that out and see if we can get a good still of him off the video."

The evening traffic was heavy outside the hotel, and Moshi had to wait as the doorman flagged down a taxi and opened its door for him.

"You have a good evening, sir."

"Thank you," said Moshi, tipping the man as the young Indian taxi driver started away, speaking with a singsong accent.

"Where would you like to go, sir?"

"Railway station, please."

"Very good, sir." It was a tense departure for Moshi, but everything seemed normal until the taxi pulled onto the street, and he looked back into the hotel lobby, where he saw the young man from the bar couple glance at him again. It was hardly noticeable, but Moshi's senses were elevated, and he turned to his driver.

"Turn left at the next street, please."

"That is not the way to the station, sir."

"I know. I just want to see something on the way."

"Oh, very good, sir."

They turned onto a quiet side street with less traffic, and after several blocks and a couple of additional turns, Moshi was convinced they were not being followed, and turned back to the driver. "Okay, that's good, thank you. You can go to the station now."

The taxi's strange series of turns quickly alerted Fenwick. "What the hell's he doing?"

"Just being cautious," said Karras.

"No, he saw something. Tell everyone to back off. We can't afford to spook this guy."

Moshi finally began to relax as they continued through the busy city. He was living a different life now, a reversal of roles that placed him in a continuous state of danger and caution, and he began to worry if the taxi driver was a plant? It seemed unlikely, but he had to check it out.

"How long you been driving taxis?"

"Just two years, sir. I've only been in the country recently."

"And how do you like it?"

"I like it very good! Very clean. But there are no people. India has lots of people!"

Moshi had to smile. "So are you going to stay?"

"Oh yes! I have a new girlfriend now. She says the future is in countries with less people!"

Moshi's phone buzzed with an incoming text that made his heart skip a beat. *ABORT MISSION. THEY'RE FOLLOWING PACKAGE. CODES COMPROMISED. RESET.*

For a moment Moshi felt like leaping out of the taxi and running for his life, but he knew better than that. *Keep calm, figure it out!* exhorted his military training. *Why hadn't they already arrested him?* Obviously, they want to find the sub, so he still had time. *But how were they following him?* He pulled out the hard drive and shook it, listening to see if there was anything loose inside. He saw it had a seam that had recently been opened, and quickly pried it apart with a penknife, revealing its electronic innards and a small, separate tracking device taped to its plastic side. *GPS marker, shit!* They were following him from a satellite, and he immediately looked up at the sky through the back window. There must be a drone, but he couldn't see it.

His actions caught the interest of the driver, who quickly averted his eyes from the mirror when Moshi looked back at him.

"How much longer to the station?"

"Oh, just five more minutes, sir."

Moshi carefully removed the GPS marker from the drive and placed it in his pocket. He was being hunted, and he took a deep breath, calming himself for the chase.

Only he knew where the Montana was; only he could complete the mission. It was all in his hands now, and he reread the text and its final words: *CODES COMPROMISED. RESET.* He had to move on to the second plan and the second set of codes. But first he had to get rid of his pursuers.

Fenwick and his entire team watched the taxi's progress through the city on the drone's camera and the GPS tracking monitor.

"It looks like he's heading for the station." Karras had grown up in the city and knew it better than Fenwick.

"How long to get there?"

"Two minutes."

"Okay, let's get some agents in there and tell them to use the side entrance."

Karras got on the phone giving the orders as Fenwick continued to another assistant, "Does everyone in the field have this guy's picture now?"

"Yes, sir. And this is a picture of the real Joachim Stone. He's presently in a Copenhagen hospital fighting cancer. He didn't even know his passport was missing."

"Does he have a record with the local police or INTERPOL?"

"No, sir. Not that I can see."

Karras interrupted the conversation, pointing to the drone's camera. "He's coming up on the station now."

"How about our own people?" said Fenwick.

"They'll be there in about a minute."

"Okay, I want that taxi driver picked up the moment he leaves the area and brought in here for questioning.

Moshi took one last look behind the taxi as they arrived at the crowded station. He knew he was probably being watched as well as followed by the GPS marker, so he would have to avoid looking around after he exited the taxi.

"Good luck with your new life," said Moshi paying the driver.

"Oh, thank you, sir. Very kind."

Moshi pushed the hard drive under the front seat with his foot and exited the taxi. There were a lot of people arriving and departing, and he felt less vulnerable in the crowd, knowing he would be inside the station in just a moment and invisible to any more aerial surveillance.

Two thousand feet in the sky, the drone's cameras zoomed into a close angle of Moshi as he entered the station and disappeared.

"Do you still have him on the GPS monitor?" said Fenwick to the drone's operator.

"Yes, sir. I'll pull back wide and cover the whole area until he comes back out."

Karras got off the phone and turned to Fenwick. "We have two officers entering the station now. One's going to the ticket counters, the other to the trains in case he already has a ticket."

Moshi saw the two agents entering the side door of the station. They were both flushed from hurrying, and after twenty years in the surveillance business, he could literally see the guns hidden beneath their jackets. But the detectives were too late. Moshi was already stepping onto an overnight train to Melbourne with a ticket he'd purchased two days before.

The station's PA system announced the imminent departure of the train. People hurried to their seats as Moshi moved down the narrow corridor, where he slipped the small GPS monitor into the pocket of an old, gray haired man passing in the opposite direction. Time was running out, and he quickly stepped into a bathroom. It was small and cramped, but in just a moment, he pulled two plastic molds from his mouth, removing his jowly cheeks, peeled fake skin coverings from his fingertips and palms, then unhitched a stomach pad from his waist, inside of which was a folded jacket, hat and white shirt.

In less than a minute Moshi reappeared from the bathroom looking like the old Moshi from London, now wearing a baseball hat. It was time for the train to leave. The PA system announced its departure, but Moshi took time to help an old lady to her seat with her bags before exiting the train as it started to pull away from the platform.

Marissa James, one of Fenwick's detectives, saw the train leaving and had to make a quick decision. Neither she nor her partner had seen Moshi in the station, and at the last minute she ran and leapt onto the departing train, passing Moshi as he waved to the old lady he had helped.

Once again, the GPS marker was on the move, and the drone operator followed the train out of the station, to the consternation of Fenwick and his crew.

"He's on the fucking train!" exclaimed Fenwick. But before he could say anything else, Karras received a call from Marissa, saying she had made it onto the train herself, and Fenwick relaxed a little.

"Is that GPS marker accurate enough to identify which part of the train the marker's on?"

"Looks like he's near the middle, sir."

Fenwick looked at the drone's view of the train, now bathed in a red hue from the infrared camera filming the action. "Let me speak to the officer on the train."

Karras quickly got Marissa on the phone with Fenwick, who

asked, "Where are you on the train?"

"I'm moving towards the middle, trying to check each car as I go…just a minute." She paused, nodding a greeting to an old, gray haired man passing her in the corridor. It was the same man Moshi had placed the GPS marker on.

"Sorry, I just passed someone in the corridor. There's hardly room for one person here…" But before she could say anything else, the technician monitoring the GPS system interrupted them.

"The marker's on the move, sir. Heading toward the back of the train!"

Fenwick quickly turned back to Marissa. "Who was it that just passed you?"

"An old man."

"Does he look anything like Murray's picture?"

"No, he's in his seventies; skinny as a rail."

Fenwick turned back to the GPS technician. "Is the marker still moving?"

"Yes, sir. Almost at the back of the train now."

Fenwick cursed. He knew he'd been bested and turned back to Marissa.

"Go and catch up with the old man that passed you and check his pockets. He's got the GPS marker in one of them."

"On my way," said Marissa.

"You don't think he's still on the train?" said Karras.

"Not if he knows the marker's there! Get me all the security videos from the station starting with the time the taxi arrived. And how are we doing with the taxi driver?"

"Just arrived," said Karras. "They found the false hard drive under the front seat of his car."

"Bring him into my office."

Fenwick started away but Karras called him back. "You want to speak with Marissa? She's got the old man."

"Does he have the marker on him?"

Karras relayed the question to Marissa and replied, "It was in his pocket. He doesn't know how it got there."

Fenwick shook his head and started away. "Get the taxi driver."

Chapter 36

Admiral McCracken was in the Pacific Command Center reviewing the deployment of his anti-submarine forces along the southeast coast of Australia when he heard about the AFP's failure to follow the fake hard drive to the Montana. At first he felt angry with his counterparts, but after discussing the matter with Fenwick and reviewing what had happened, both men were convinced that someone had tipped off the code carrier and caused him to flee. It was disappointing news, but they did now have one of the two launch codes safe in their possession, and McCracken was finally convinced of a larger conspiracy involving people in his Pacific command. If the code carrier really did believe he was carrying the Montana's launch system, he would never have left it in the back of a taxi, even if it was compromised by the GPS marker. So someone must have told him it was fake.

McCracken began to think he had made a mistake not arresting Vice Admiral Acker before the Australian deployment, but he still didn't have enough hard evidence to support his theory and arranged to meet Lieutenant Darden at his house.

It was late afternoon when the lieutenant arrived at McCracken's home and joined him in the living room with its spectacular view of Pearl Harbor.

"Sit down, Lieutenant," said the admiral, indicating a large couch. "I wouldn't normally do this, but I'm having a drink. Would you like to join me?"

"Yes, sir, thank you."

"Scotch and water?"

"Sounds good."

McCracken poured the drinks and joined the lieutenant on the couch, where he had set up his laptop computer on a low table.

"So how did you do? I saw the vice admiral leaving after our morning meeting."

"Yes, sir. He left at twelve twenty-five and went to a Japanese restaurant for an early lunch."

"Did he speak to anyone on the way?"

"Just his wife. He invited her to join him at the restaurant, but she was at the hair salon and told him to pick up some clothes from the laundry for a dinner they're going to."

"So what happened at the restaurant?"

"He ordered a sashimi plate from a waitress and went into the restroom where the agent had already placed a video camera. But all he did was take a pee and wash his hands."

"That was it?" said McCracken, getting frustrated by the minutiae.

"Apparently, but just one minute after he left the restroom, the sushi chef came in and retrieved what appears to be a piece of paper stuck to the wall beneath the towel holder." He showed the hidden video image on his laptop. "After that he took the paper into the cubicle and made a phone call, apparently reading what was on it. You can just see the top of it in his hand here." He pointed back to the screen.

"Did you see the admiral putting this paper where it was?"

"No, sir. It was hidden by his body."

"So what did the chef say? I couldn't understand him."

"It's not audible. The camera was too far away, and there was some electronic interference with the signal. So I spoke to Lieutenant Silver in Seattle, and he got a federal judge to let me listen to the chef's call from the NSA's data bank, but it was encrypted."

"Encrypted?"

"Yes, sir. But we did manage to retrieve the number he called. It belongs to Staley Combs, an army vet wounded in Afghanistan. He lives on the coast north of Seattle and does appear to have a VHF transmitter."

"How do you know that?"

"Google Earth. He lives in an isolated area, and you can actually see a large antenna next to the house."

"What kind of wounds does he have?" asked McCracken, disappointed by the news.

"Lost both his legs to an Iranian IED."

The admiral took a deep breath. He felt like he was descending into hell, spying on his old friend, and now a wounded vet, but then again, what they were apparently doing was beyond the pale of treason.

Chapter 37

CHARLOTTE Ramsey spent the second part of her day intensifying the search for Tommy Chang and the second set of launch codes. Utilizing the same methods that had found the first codes, the agency began a search of all post offices and private shipping companies along the presumed three hundred mile drive that Chang had taken from Spokane to Seattle. It was a mammoth undertaking involving dozens of agents, but stopping the codes from reaching the Montana was the agency's most pressing objective. It was an objective made even more important by a call from Julian Fenwick informing Charlotte of the failed attempt to follow the fake codes to the Montana. Charlotte was understandably frustrated by the news, but before she could follow up on all the details, she received an urgent call from Admiral McCracken and arranged to call Fenwick back later.

Admiral McCracken quickly filled in Charlotte on everything that had happened in Australia, including his and Fenwick's conclusion that someone had warned the code carrier of their surveillance. Up until this moment, McCracken had kept his concerns about Vice Admiral Acker to himself. But with the additional information from Charlotte about the vice admiral's daughter's investment in oil futures and all the other circumstantial evidence he had gathered, including the sushi chef's encrypted call, the admiral felt compelled to tell

Charlotte everything. He was now aware that she and Sid had their own concerns of a greater conspiracy and felt comfortable sharing his information with them.

Charlotte was, to say the least, surprised by all the evidence the admiral had collected on Acker, but the information about the chef's encrypted phone call immediately caught her attention. Getting a lead on how the sub's crew communicated with their supporters could be the break they were all looking for but keeping it secret was the first consideration.

Both Charlotte and the admiral knew they had to share this new information with their superiors, but which ones could they trust? McCracken had known Admiral Stossel and his family for decades and was confident in his loyalty and ability to handle the information discreetly, so they decided to speak with him first. As Chief of Naval Operations, he also had ultimate control of NCIS and direct access to the president if needed. As far as Acker and the army vet were concerned, it was decided that McCracken and Lieutenant Darden would increase their surveillance of the vice admiral and the sushi chef while Charlotte and her team investigated the vet.

Everything was picking up speed, and Charlotte quickly told Sid and Lieutenant Silver the details of her conversation with McCracken, including his concern not to spook the vet before they could listen in on his VHF transmissions.

"We don't have time for that!" shouted Lieutenant Silver. "The second set of codes are already on their way to the Montana!"

"I think he's right," said Sid. "We need to take him down now. We can't afford the time, and we still have the possibility of someone on the inside tipping him off."

"That's fine," said Charlotte, "but what do we do about the VHF transmissions?"

"It doesn't matter," said Silver. "Even if we intercept them, it's not going to tell us where they are. This has all been set up ahead of time.

They're not going to reveal their position on a radio call. At least, this vet may know where the second set of codes are going."

"Okay," said Charlotte, "why don't you set it up while I inform McCracken why we're going ahead now? And by the way, what happened to the first set of codes?"

"On their way to the base at Kitsap," said Silver. "They're going to have to redesign the whole launch system so this doesn't happen again." Charlotte left and Sid turned to Silver.

"So what does this vet look like?"

The lieutenant held up his computer displaying a couple of pictures of Staley Combs. "Before and after." In the first shot he was a strapping young man; in the second, the disfigured vet in a wheelchair.

Sid shook his head. "I can see why McCracken didn't want to take him down."

Chapter 38

STALEY Combs couldn't sleep. An old dream came drifting back into his mind like a ghost from the past. It wasn't an unpleasant dream, just a series of strange, repetitive images of other people's lives. The first time it happened was as a child with a friend he went to school with. The next time was with his mother, and the last time was in Afghanistan, where images of his three comrades in arms kept drifting in and out of his dream like some haunting documentary. Then they were all gone, dead forever. His childhood friend drowned in a lake beneath winter ice, his mother tumbling down stairs stricken by a massive stroke, and his three comrades in arms blown to pieces in a Humvee - his own legs scattered in the fleshy carnage of their dismembered parts.

Some would say precognition was a blessing, but in reality, it was a curse that couldn't be changed or diminished, and now this last dream was a retrospective of his own life - the joys of his childhood, the pleasures of teenage love, the glory of battle, and now the realization that his own death was imminent.

A couple of times during the night, Staley drifted out of his dream and reached out, touching the dog sleeping next to him. Babu's calm energy and loving presence was always an antidote to what troubled Staley. But the dream persisted until dawn when a growl from the dog brought him back to reality.

There was something outside, and the dog's hackles rose up,

heralding the danger. The power in the house went off, and Staley knew they were coming to get him. He had planned for this occasion with all the precision of his Army training and switched on a battery-operated security camera, which revealed a group of black clad FBI agents quickly approaching the house with bulletproof shields. "It's okay, Babu, they're not going to hurt you!" He slid his legless torso off the bed onto his wheelchair, and grabbed a pistol from under his pillow. The FBI agents were closing fast and Staley wheeled himself to the house entrance where he lifted a dog door and ushered the dog outside.

"You have to go, Babu!" But the dog sensed the end coming and backed away, barking his defiance.

Sid Bailey, advancing with his men, heard the dog and realized their surprise intrusion was over. "He's got a dog; let's get in there now!!"

The agents ran for the house as Staley grabbed Babu by the scruff of his neck and forced him, whining, outside. It was a devastating moment, but the dog quickly regained his courage and ran barking towards the advancing FBI officers. For a moment, the agents didn't know what to do as the dog ran up and down their ranks, barking and growling, until a female officer knelt down and pulled off her helmet, speaking to him in a gentle voice.

"It's okay, baby, come here…come here. We're not going to hurt you." Her voice was calm and seductive, and the dog finally went to her, accepting her friendship.

Staley was pleased to see Babu greeted in a friendly fashion, but when a voice on a megaphone called out his name demanding he surrender, the Army vet went into battle mode.

There were sealed Mason jars set around the living room, which he quickly shattered with his pistol, flooding the floor with gasoline. Time was running out. The agents were now banging on the door, demanding he give up. But in one last act of defiance, Staley cranked up his VHF radio and sent out a final signal. "This is Cyclops One, Rudy Meadow, shutting down. Station compromised. God be with you, guys. Out."

The lead agent could hear Staley talking through the door and yelled to Bailey, "He's on the radio!"

"Knock it down!" commanded Sid, wanting it over as quickly as possible.

The door shattered inward and Staley ignited the gasoline, yelling to the lead agent, "Look after my dog! He served two tours in Afghanistan!"

The agent looked through the leaping flames and saw the vet placing his pistol into his mouth. "Put the gun down!" he yelled.

But Staley had lived long enough, and finally honored his premonition.

Babu instinctively knew what the gunshot represented. He whined pathetically to the agent holding him then lifted his head to the heavens, howling a final farewell to his departed friend.

The whole fiasco was a nightmare for Sid Bailey. They had anticipated the vet may try to take his life and destroy any evidence, but the dog had warned him before they were close enough to intervene. And now everything was lost in the inferno except for an iPhone, which fell from Staley's pocket as the lead agent made a valiant effort to pull him from the flames.

Charlotte Ramsey and Lieutenant Silver watched the entire assault on Staley's home from a helicopter. They could hear bits of everything that happened through Sid and the lead agent's microphones, including Staley's gunshot, the dog's pathetic howl and the agent's voice yelling for a medic and fire engines. Silver shook his head, yelling above the sound of the chopper.

"Did they say he was on the radio?"

"Yes," said Charlotte turning to the pilot. "Let's get down there! Land as close as you can."

As the fire engines arrived and started knocking down the flames, Charlotte landed in the chopper and joined Sid with Lieutenant Silver. The old FBI agent was visibly upset by everything that had happened.

"The dog gave us away!"

"I heard it," said Charlotte, moving away from the noisy chopper. "Did anyone hear what he said on the radio?"

"No. Just something about shutting down the station, and that was it."

"Is that his van over there?"

"Yeah, we're checking it out now."

"So did we get anything?" questioned Charlotte.

"The lead agent grabbed this before everything went up in flames." He held up Staley's iPhone with a picture of the surfer dude frozen on its cracked screen.

"Who is he?"

"We don't know."

"Anything else on it?"

"No, it's frozen. Probably encrypted."

"Let me get a shot of it," said Charlotte, snapping a picture of the screen with her own iPhone, noting a degraded inscription on it. "What does it say here?"

"Looks like 'Ready for the road'," said Sid.

"Okay, let's check this guy out. He could be the new carrier." She turned to Matt, passing by. "Are there any surfing beaches around here?"

"Lots of them."

"How about this one here?" She held up her cell and Matt checked out the seascape behind the surfer.

"Looks like Half Moon Bay."

"How far from here?"

"Twenty minutes in the chopper."

Charlotte turned to Sid and Lieutenant Silver. "Okay, why don't you guys wrap things up here and see if anyone knows this guy locally. Matt and I'll check out the surfing area."

"You want to do anything with the dog?" inquired Sid. "The agent that grabbed him wants to keep him."

"It's fine with me as long as no one in the family wants him."

CHAPTER 39

PRESIDENT Anderson sat in his private quarters at the White House eating a quick lunch, watching the international news with all of its disturbing ramifications. Another Christian school was attacked in Nigeria by Boko Haram, the Taliban were resurgent in southern Afghanistan, ISIS, Al Qaeda and many other Islamic terrorist organizations were all stating their contempt for the fifteen Americans on the submarine, and warning of more attacks against the West.

But Muslims everywhere were now facing their own terrorist threat and experiencing all of the same fears and frustrations the rest of the world had been subjected to by their militant Islamists. Huge crowds demonstrated in front of American embassies chanting, "Death to America!" It was an escalating conflict that should have been dealt with decades ago, but how do you stop people who believe their jihadist war against all non-believers is their God-given right and religious duty? And how did you now stop an equally nihilistic group of Westerners from ending it all by their own insane methods?

The president watched himself speaking to the world, assuring everyone that the launch codes would be found and the submarine destroyed. It was now a global effort, and he thanked all the nations for their generous assistance, but beneath his confident demeanor, he was slowly losing hope.

"Are you still watching that stuff?" said his wife entering the room, dressed for a meeting, still putting on her jewelry.

"It's my job, unfortunately." He switched off the TV. "Now ISIS and Al Qaeda are making fun of the officers on the sub. I don't think they realize how serious all this is."

"Maybe they don't care. Seventy-two virgins is a big deal for young men living in a repressive theocracy. How did things go in Australia?"

"They got the first set of codes back, but the person picking them up got away."

"So, that's good, no? One down, one to go!"

"Yeah, I guess you could say that. But the one that's left can still blow up the fucking world!"

"So what else happened?" queried Tat, sensing his frustration.

"General Pierce just informed me that the head of the FBI and the Commander of the Pacific Fleet both believe there's a larger conspiracy than just the fifteen officers on the submarine."

"Did they say who?"

"They have some ideas, but they're still checking it out."

"People in the government?"

"Military by the sounds of it. And what's even worse, some of the people involved appear to have bet a lot of money on oil futures."

"They're doing this for money?!"

"We're still trying to figure that out."

"Aren't you supposed to see the captain's wife today?"

"No, she fell off her bike and had to delay."

"Well I know this sounds crazy, but do you want to try praying?"

"I've already been praying," said the president, "but what do I say? 'Dear God, please kill all the militant Muslims who want to kill me and my country in the glory of your name'? Can you imagine how He feels listening to all this crap?"

"So maybe you should just thank Him for everything He's done for you."

"What good is that going to do?!"

"It'll remind you of the good things in your life and make you more positive."

The president finally smiled. "Okay…I like that."

"Well, there you go; on your knees. I've got to go."

"Where you going?"

"Women in Business Awards. I'm a presenter. The only one there that's never run anything!"

"You run me!"

"That's not a job. That's a pleasure! You're going to be fine." She kissed him on the cheek and left as Gary Brockett arrived at the door.

"If it's bad news, go away," said the president.

"It's good news. The Senate just agreed to put your flat tax plan up for a vote."

"What brought that on?"

"People across the country are threatening to throw them all out of office if they don't start cooperating. You can smile if you want."

The president forced a grin. "And what are they saying about the Montana?"

"Everyone's glued to their TVs, but I don't think anyone really believes they're going to do anything."

"Why is that?" asked the president.

"They think we're too civilized, and so do the Muslims!"

"Well, I hope they're right about that!"

CHAPTER 40

HALF Moon Bay, Washington, has some of the best surfing waves in America. It doesn't happen every day, but when it does, the best surfers in the world show up to demonstrate their skills.

It was one of those days when Charlotte's helicopter swept in over the rugged bay and landed at a helipad where the local police chief and a young deputy greeted her and Matt. Charlotte had already informed the chief by phone of the surfer they were looking for but hadn't shown him the picture yet.

"Welcome to Big Wave Country!" yelled the chief, above the noise of the helicopter.

"They are big!" exclaimed Charlotte, moving away from the chopper with Matt, looking at the waves. "Thank you for meeting us."

"Pleasure's all mine, ma'am. Hank here's a surfer himself, so I brought him along in case you need some help identifying this fellow."

"I appreciate that," said Charlotte, holding up her iPhone photograph. "Do you recognize this person?"

"Randy Rails," said Hank without hesitation. "My brother sold him that board he's holding."

"When did he do that?"

"Last weekend. My brother and I own a surf shop together."

"Does he come in often?"

"No, he just wanted something smaller and lighter than the boards we normally ride here. Said he was going south for a while."

"South where?"

"Didn't say."

"Do you know if he left yet?"

"No, you'd have to ask Maggie June. He rents a room in the back of her place."

"Is that far from here?"

"Nothing's far in a town like this," said the chief, "we can be there in five minutes." One of the surfers caught a massive wave and raced down its precipitous face, narrowly missing the crushing cauldron of its collapsing curl.

Maggie June was an old retired councilwoman that the chief knew well. She had a pinched face and piercing eyes which recognized Charlotte before the chief could even finish introducing her.

"You're Charlotte Ramsey right? I saw you on CSPAN. All those misogynistic senators asking you inappropriate questions?"

"That's right," said Charlotte, remembering the grueling she went through when she was nominated. "I understand you rent a room to Randy Rails?"

"Actually, his real name is Randall Roberts. But he's not here now. Left a couple of days ago. Did he do something wrong?"

"No, I just wanted to ask him some questions. Do you know where he went?"

"No, he said it was a big secret. Said he was going to bring back pictures and tell me all about some new place he'd found on the planet."

"Did he say where it was?"

"Nope. Randall's lean on words. PTSD and all that stuff."

"He's a vet?"

"Yeah, two tours in Afghanistan. The only person he ever talks to beside myself is Staley Combs. He's a fellow vet living up north of here. He took Randall to the airport. Maybe he knows where he was going."

"Is there any chance I could look in his room?"

"Do you have a search warrant?"

"No, but I could get one."

Maggie hesitated for a moment then acquiesced. "Okay...but if you find anything in there that's against the law I don't know anything about it!"

Randall's room was surprisingly clean and tidy, and Charlotte remembered a psychologist once telling her that people living troubled lives often feel solace in orderly surroundings.

"How long has he been living here?" inquired Charlotte, checking out the room with Matt.

"Just a few months."

"This was his first trip away?"

"Yes, I think he was looking forward to the change."

Randall was obviously an avid surfer and had lots of magazines and pictures of beaches and surfers around the world. He was also an avid pot user, evidenced by a large bong pipe and other drug paraphernalia that Charlotte found but chose to ignore.

"Was he in Afghanistan with his friend Staley?"

"Yes, but I don't think they served together."

Matt saw a writing pad on a desk with the indentation of something written on a previous page. It was a silly little clue, but he took a pencil and ran it back and forth over the clean sheet until it magically revealed the words, "Tandjung Sari".

"What have you got?" asked Charlotte, looking over his shoulder.

Matt showed her the sheet.

"Tandjung Sari? You know what it means?"

"No, but it sounds Indian or something."

Charlotte showed the words to Maggie June. "Do you have any idea what this means?"

"No."

"And what's this here?" said Charlotte, pointing to another indentation on the sheet.

Matt quickly rubbed his pencil over the new mark and revealed the letters 'FLT 3887'.

"Airline flight number."

Charlotte grinned. "Good work, Matt. Call Sarah and have her track that flight and see if Randall Roberts was on board two days ago. And check his military record as well."

She turned back to Maggie as Matt left. "Did Randall ever talk about his time in Afghanistan?"

"No."

"Any pet peeves, strong political opinions?"

"Never expressed any to me."

"And how about a phone or a vehicle?"

"He's got a phone and bike and that's it."

Charlotte saw a zipper toggle hanging down beneath a padded footstool and discovered a loaded snub-nosed revolver tucked into the zipped padding.

"Did you know he had this?" said Charlotte.

"No. And if I knew, he wouldn't be staying here!"

CHAPTER 41

MONIQUE Besson saw Staley's house burn to the ground on the local news. No one had survived the fire except the dog, and even though the FBI was not mentioned by the newscaster, Monique was confident of the agency's involvement. Staley had always said he'd never be taken alive, and Monique was sure that he had destroyed himself and the house to preserve the secrecy of their cause.

The pictures of Staley and his dog displayed on the television were devastating images for Monique, who felt an all-compelling need to rescue the dog but was well aware that such a move would be disastrous to their cause.

Prior to the mutiny, multiple redundancies had been built into the communication systems with the Montana, and now that primary connection had been destroyed, Monique followed pre-arranged procedures and retrieved another hidden phone containing encrypted software and sent a text to her contact in Hawaii. *"Cyclops One and Rudy Meadow destroyed. Did Alpha One receive Phase Two contact info? Do you know how this breach occurred?"* It took less than five minutes for the secure answer to come back. *"Alpha One has new coordinates and schedule. Breach came from our end - reordering system."*

The loss of Staley weighed heavy on Monique's mind. It reminded her of his unwavering courage and commitment to their cause, which rekindled her own passion and need to succeed. Once again she looked at the pictures of her sister, reinvigorating her own desire for revenge and redemption against a militant religious order that had created in her an enemy as relentless as they were. It was an ironic twist of fate that misogynistic militant Islam was now going to be terrorized, not by the Great Satan America, or the detested State of Israel, but by a mere woman.

Chapter 42

LESS than an hour after their journey to Half Moon Bay, Washington, Charlotte and Matt arrived back at the Seattle control room and checked in with Sarah Singh working on her computer.

"Did you get anything yet?"

"Just got a confirmation now," said Sarah. "Flight 3887 was a direct from LAX to Singapore. It arrived there two hours ago, and Randall Roberts was on the passenger list."

"Any connecting flight?"

"None that I can find. I spoke to an airline official in Singapore, and he couldn't find anything either."

Charlotte turned to Matt. "How far is Singapore from Sydney, Australia?"

"Just under four thousand miles," said Sarah, having already checked. "That would take the sub at least five or six days to get there."

"So he must be making a connection somewhere?"

"Singapore is a hub," said Sarah.

"Okay, so let's get this kid's picture and passport information out on INTERPOL. Just a general request and don't mention the Montana connection; we don't need to show our hand here. And let's get a liaison in Singapore to check every flight out of there with the guy's picture. He's probably using another ID by now." Sid and Lieutenant Silver arrived, hearing the end of her conversation. "He arrived in Singapore two hours ago," reiterated Charlotte. "No apparent connecting flight.

I'm going to call McCracken and bring him up to speed. Why don't you see who we have in Singapore, and let's all remember someone tipped off the carrier last time. I don't want it happening again!!"

CHAPTER 43

DEPUTY Commissioner Fenwick stayed up all night after the first code carrier escaped his surveillance in Sydney. He hated failure, particularly in front of the Prime Minister and their most important ally, America. The Indian taxi driver had confirmed his belief that the code carrier had received a warning of their surveillance of him by text but was vague on details about the man's features, age, or accent.

With that lack of evidence, most people would have given up. But Fenwick was an insatiable hunter and spent the next twenty-four hours reviewing all the Sydney station security cameras. It was a laborious job, but he eventually came to the conclusion that the man exiting the train in a white shirt and black jacket was the code carrier, now wearing a different disguise. With his face covered by the bill of a baseball cap, there were no close angles of his features, except for one fleeting moment when he glanced into the sky as he exited the station. It was a blurred image, but enough to reveal his oval, Slavic origins, and approximate age of forty.

For several hours, the commissioner watched the images of the code carrier walking through the station, studying his gait and deportment. He was well muscled and walked with his legs slightly apart, like a weightlifter with over-developed thigh muscles. And his left shoulder was clearly lower than his right, indicating that he was left-handed.

With this minimal information, Fenwick started reviewing

Sydney airport security cameras until he finally saw what appeared to be the code carrier boarding a flight to Singapore the morning after the Sydney station incident. It was now twelve hours since that plane had departed, and even though Fenwick was able to obtain the aircraft's passenger manifest, there was no way of identifying which of the 140 people on board was the code carrier, a fact made even more apparent by Fenwick's growing realization that he was now dealing with a professional who took pride in avoiding being caught. It was a frustrating time for the commissioner. But while he was contemplating his options, he received an unexpected call from Charlotte Ramsey, sounding infinitely more gracious than in their previous conversation.

"Julian, I'm so sorry to call you at this hour, but we just identified the second code carrier, and he's already in Asia."

"Which part of Asia?" said Fenwick.

"Singapore. He arrived there two hours ago. I know it's not exactly your jurisdiction, but Admiral McCracken said it was unlikely he would try and meet the sub in such a busy shipping area. Have you had any luck following up on the first carrier?"

Fenwick could hardly restrain a smile at the change of circumstance and quickly filled her in on the evidence he had collected on the first carrier and his subsequent flight to Singapore.

"So that could be a good meeting place for them?" said Charlotte, intrigued by the new information.

"Them, but not the sub," said Fenwick. "I agree with the admiral. It's too busy for any sea transfer in that area. Is he traveling on his own passport?"

"So far, yes. But he's probably got multiple IDs. Do the words 'Tandjung Sari' mean anything to you?"

Fenwick felt goose pimples rush up his spine when he heard the question. "Yes. It's Hindu. It means 'Cape of Flowers'. Where did you get that?"

"It was written on a phone pad next to the flight information of the suspect."

Suddenly, everything began to make sense to Fenwick, who stated with absolute confidence, "They're going to meet in Bali."

Charlotte was surprised by his declaration. "Bali, Indonesia?"

"Yes. It's the name of a hotel there. I spent six months living next door to it after the Jemaah Islamiyah restaurant bombings."

"I thought the people in Indonesia were Muslim?"

"Most of them are, but the people in Bali are predominantly Hindu. That's one of the reasons I think Jemaah Islamiyah chose to bomb there."

"And how far is Bali from Sydney?"

"Twenty eight hundred miles. But the carrier was on his way to Perth when we lost him, which could put the sub anywhere on the west coast, much closer to the island."

"Do they have any surfing beaches there?"

"Some of the best," said Fenwick.

"How about flights from Singapore?"

"One direct a day. Should be leaving any time now. Why don't I check the passenger list and see if anything pops?"

"Okay, that sounds good. I'll get right back to you."

It was a lot of circumstantial information, but the specific name of the hotel added credence to everything, and Charlotte decided to run it by McCracken before making a definitive decision.

Fenwick hung up the phone and took a deep breath. Apprehending the first code carrier had become a personal obsession with him, and he wondered how that had become even more important than destroying the submarine. Had his competitive ego really become that big, or was there something else lurking in his subconscious, some unexpressed empathy for the Montana mutineers who had decided to wage their own war against militant Islam?

Chapter 44

Admiral McCracken walked back into the Nimitz-McArthur Command Center after a private conversation with his commanding officer, Admiral Stossel, who was now sending additional anti-submarine units from the Atlantic command into the south Indian Ocean in an effort to counter the Montana's apparent move into that region. It was a busy time and coordinating that effort was becoming a distraction to everything else McCracken was trying to solve.

Charlotte Ramsey had already informed him of the second set of codes arriving in Singapore, and he was now trying to decide where the Montana would most likely meet up with the new carrier. So far he had not told anyone on his staff of this new information except for Lieutenant Darden, who was presently expanding his surveillance of Vice Admiral Acker and the sushi chef.

McCracken could see the vice admiral in the submarine deployment section of the control room and wondered who else could be involved with him in the mutiny. Even with the video of Acker in the Japanese restaurant, the sushi chef's encrypted phone call to Staley Combs, and the subsequent discovery of the surfer Randall Roberts, there was still not enough conclusive evidence to arrest the vice admiral who still had the potential to lead them to other conspirators. McCracken also knew that any redeployment of assets to the Singapore region would be an immediate red flag to the vice admiral, who he now noted was keeping a sharp eye on everything he did. It was a conundrum with few options, made even more difficult when he received another call from Charlotte Ramsey informing him of Fenwick's new information on the Bali connection.

"So this whole thing is based on the name of a hotel in Bali, and your belief that the two code carriers are now in Singapore?"

"I know it's all circumstantial," said Charlotte, "but when you add up all the pieces I believe the information is sufficient to act upon."

McCracken hated indefinites, but when he considered Bali's isolated geographic position from major shipping lines, its relative closeness to Australia and the Java Trench, he also began to see the validity of Charlotte's position.

"So how do you want to handle this?"

"Well, first of all, how long would it take for the Montana to get to Bali from the west coast of Australia?"

"Depending on where and when they start, they could probably be there in as little as two days."

"Putting them there late tonight?"

"Potentially," said McCracken. "But do we really have enough evidence to commit our resources to this?"

"It's all I've got right now," said Charlotte. "The flight from Singapore arrives in Bali in less than five hours, and I believe there's a very good chance the second code carrier will be on it."

"Well if that's the case, the only hard asset I could get there would be a P8."

"Which is?" said Charlotte.

"An anti-submarine aircraft. But without surface support or detailed information on the sub's location, it would be a difficult mission. And it also presents another problem we're dealing with: if I deploy anything into that area, we run the risk of tipping our hand to the informants."

"Can't we just arrest them?"

"We don't even know who they are," said McCracken. "And if we miss one, the whole game's over."

"So what do you want to do?" asked Charlotte, frustrated.

"The Montana can't launch without the codes, so if we could interdict them without notifying our forces here the game would be over. Do you have any people on the ground that can do that?"

Charlotte had over thirty thousand agents at her disposal, but the FBI's mandate limited their activities to the United States and its territories. Everything beyond that was the domain of the CIA, and even their budget had been cut back in the Indonesian region.

"The DCI (Director of Central Intelligence) said he has two agents in Jakarta, but they're a husband and wife team with no field experience."

"How about Fenwick?" said McCracken. "We could get him there in time. At least he knows the area and the first carrier's profile."

"The question is, can we trust him?"

"You have doubts about that?"

"He's not one of ours," said Charlotte. "His first allegiance is to another country."

"Which shares our same interests," said McCracken, frustrated. "Don't we have any CIA agents in Australia that can go with him?"

"We don't have time for that!" countered Charlotte, no longer hiding her concern. "We need someone on a plane in the next thirty minutes. How about your naval attaché?"

"Olkowski? He's a good man, but he's not a field agent."

"How old?"

"Forties."

"Fit?"

"Was when he left here."

"Can you reach him without letting everyone else know about it?"

"Yeah, I can do that."

"And how about the P8, just in case we get lucky?"

"I'll look into it," said McCracken, submitting to her persistence. "But we can't just go around blowing up submarines without ID'ing them. We nearly did that already."

"Okay, why don't you fill in Olkowski, and I'll set it up with Fenwick and arrange transportation."

Chapter 45

Lieutenant Olkowski ran for a small corporate jet already warming up in front of a private airport terminal. The naval attaché was, as McCracken had described, a fit, smart forty year old dressed in shorts and a t-shirt, carrying a surfboard. Fenwick appeared in the jet's doorway as Olkowski arrived at the boarding steps, yelling above the noise of its two engines.

"Commissioner Fenwick?" The commissioner signaled him up the stairs and the naval attaché introduced himself. "Lieutenant Olkowski."

"Not anymore," said Fenwick, handing him an Australian passport. "That's your new ID. I'll take your picture and attach it on the plane."

"Sounds good," said the naval attaché, passing him onto the jet with his surfboard. "I brought this in case we need some cover."

"You've got to be kidding," said Fenwick with a measure of sarcasm.

"Actually, no," said Olkowski, "but I can leave it on the runway if you want." He had as much attitude as the commissioner, who quickly backed down.

"No, we don't have time for that; we've got to go!" He signaled the co-pilot who pulled up the jet's steps and locked the door, shutting out the noise as he spoke.

"We're going straight out, so fasten your seatbelts." The jet began to move, and the naval attaché and Fenwick strapped themselves into seats on opposite sides of the jet. Fenwick knew Olkowski was there just to keep an eye on him, and Olkowski ultimately knew his position was subordinate and rejoined the dialogue observing his new passport.

"Who's Jesse Fenwick?"

"My son. It was the best I could do in the time allotted. There's a bio on him so you can brush up on your history."

"Is he a surfer?" asked Olkowski with a touch of humor.

"He is, actually." Fenwick reached into his backpack. "We're not allowed to take weapons into a foreign country, but we do get these." He handed the naval attaché a cellphone. "It's encrypted, and your access code is 3331. Remember it. If you input it wrong twice, it'll erase everything on it. My number's already in there. You also have a direct number to Admiral McCracken in Hawaii, Charlotte Ramsey, head of the FBI, and Admiral Stossel, Chief of Naval Operations. Obviously you only contact them in an emergency or to pass on specific information about the sub. If you have to make any personal calls, use your own phone.

"So what do I call you, 'Dad'?"

Fenwick had to smile. "Yeah, that'll be fine."

"And the purpose of our trip?"

"Pleasure and a break from your troubled marriage."

"Is that for real?"

"They're all troubled," said Fenwick, revealing some darker personal story. "Can you do an Australian accent?"

"Put a couple of shrimp on the barbie, mate!"

Fenwick rolled his eyes. "Just say your mother's an American, and you grew up in San Diego." He showed him a picture of Randall Roberts on his iPhone. "This is the guy we're looking for."

"The surfer dude."

"Yeah, he'll probably look different now, and this is the first carrier that got away. You can't see much, just his general appearance."

"And you think he'll be there as well?"

"I don't know, but it's a possibility. When we get there and go into the Arrivals building, we should split up and communicate by text. We'll cover more ground that way and remember, we're going there to do just one thing! Get the hard drive and get out. The plane'll stand by on the island until tomorrow."

"And what about the sub?"

"If we get the codes, I doubt they'll show. But if they do, you still get on that plane and get out of there! These people have given their lives for a cause, so don't kid yourself they won't kill you for the same reason. This is what the hard drive looks like." He showed a picture of it on his phone.

"How big is that?"

"About the size of this phone but thicker. It's got a seam around the middle and the model number here."

"And it has enough information on it to blow up the world?"

"That's what they say."

Olkowski shook his head at the madness. "So how far are we allowed to go to get these codes?"

"If we can grab it and leave, that'll be best. If it requires more, we do what we have to do. But remember, we'll be in a foreign country with its own laws and regulations, and I can tell you from experience they take them seriously. Neither your government nor mine'll be able to help us if something goes wrong. You're booked into the Hotel Tandjung Sari, which is where we think Roberts is staying, and I'm up the road at The Islander. It's all on your phone. This is $5,000 in Aussie dollars and a couple of credit cards with your new name, which you need to sign. Let me take your picture." He pulled a small camera from his backpack.

"You got a printer for that?"

"Plane does. Say cheese!" Olkowski grinned and Fenwick snapped his picture.

CHAPTER 46

SEVERAL photographs of Osama bin Laden, Hassan Mustafa, and other jihadist warriors lined the walls of a stark, musty concrete room hidden three floors beneath a towering high-rise building in Dubai. It was the secret workshop of Ghalib Farsoun, a Yemeni bomb maker educated in chemistry at a prestigious German university. Safe from American drones beneath the towering edifice, Farsoun assisted an old Arab lady dressed in black, sewing the silk lining back into an expensive Dior suit jacket. Beside them, another Arab woman painstakingly applied nail varnish to an attractive twenty-three-year-old Palestinian girl dressed in an elegant blouse and the matching skirt of the Dior jacket.

Time was running out and Farsoun checked his watch, agitated.

"All right. This is good enough. You can go now!"

He ushered the old ladies out of the room and turned to the young girl, Ayisha, holding up the sewn jacket. "Let's put this on."

Ayisha stood and slipped on the jacket, observing several recent photographs of three other well-dressed girls adorning the walls of the room. They were all wearing silk headscarves like Ayisha, but everything else about them was stylishly Western. Expensive high heels, fitted jackets and skirts, all adorned with trendy jewelry.

"Are these my sisters?"

"Yes," said the bomb maker. "They are all soldiers of God like you." He handed her a ballpoint pen. "You remember how to use this?"

"Yes."

"Just place it in the putty, turn it to the right and push, and you will be with God."

Ayisha smiled. "I hope that is true."

"You have doubts?"

Ayisha shrugged. "I have no life, so it doesn't matter. I just do it for money."

"You went to school in Lebanon?"

"Yes."

"And who paid for that?"

"The same rich man that is paying you for what you do. Now, he will be paying my family."

Farsoun looked at the fitted jacket and smiled. "Well, you look like a real European now." He indicated an old mirror in which Ayisha observed her new, flattering image.

"You can't see anything."

"That's right. A completely new system. Just take your time and all will be well. Allah Akbar."

"Allah Akbar," repeated Ayisha, less enthusiastically.

Dubai Airport is an architectural wonder - a modern, air-conditioned world of glass and marble defying the stark desert lands surrounding it. Rows of jets from countries around the world line the concourses where colorful international travelers mingle with Arabic people still wearing their traditional gowns, many of them women covered completely in black burkas.

Ayisha, now perfectly coiffed in her Parisian clothes and accoutrements, passed easily through the security gate where the x-ray technician was more interested in observing her than in the contents of her purse. With a measure of relief, unseen on her casual countenance, Ayisha walked down the long concourse to her boarding gate, towing a Louis Vuitton carry-on bag like a woman of means. She had never felt that emancipated and feminine before. It was her culture to hide everything that she was, and lifting those restrictions filled her with a strange feeling of exhilaration and guilt as she now felt the eyes of men everywhere appreciating her natural beauty. In this state of existential guilt and delight, Ayisha boarded the plane where a solicitous stewardess smiled a greeting and directed her to a seat in the sumptuous first class cabin.

Sitting back into the comfort of her leather seat, Ayisha tried to avoid eye contact with an old lady sitting next to her but to no avail.

"Are you going to London?" said the lady.

"Yes."

"I feel like I've been on this plane for a lifetime already. Melbourne has to be the end of the earth. Did they tell you how much longer it's going to be?"

"Seven hours," said Ayisha, taking a glass of water from the stewardess as the old lady continued.

"I'm Irene."

"Ayisha."

"You're a Muslim, right?"

"Yes."

"I'm Jewish. Well, used to be. There aren't many Jews in Australia, so I ended up marrying a Greek Orthodox. Nice people. They all wear those funny hats. Do you ever get fed up wearing those scarves on your head?"

"No, you get used to it."

"Well, at least you don't have to worry about your hair, right?"

A voice on the PA system interrupted them, announcing the imminent departure of the plane.

"Okay, here we go," said Irene, pulling a packet of chewing gum from her purse. "You want some? It'll stop your ears from hurting."

Ayisha smiled. "No, I'm good. Thank you." She looked at the other passengers surrounding her. They were the enemy, and she reminded herself it would be fatal to think of them otherwise.

Ghalib Farsoun sat in his car at the end of the airport runway watching Ayisha's jet soar into the night sky. This was his third try at bringing down Western jets, but this time, he was confident it would work. He had tested his new device several times out in the desert without a single failure. The only caveat now was the bomb carriers themselves - all beautiful girls, all Sisters of God, all praised and prepared for their missions by jihadist handlers filling their minds with religious fervor and the glory of life in the hereafter.

But Farsoun also knew it was the training, the mechanics of the mission, that people fell back on when that final fear rose up inside of them. It was that rote, mechanical conditioning that distracted them from their true reality and turned them into perfect, unthinking suicide bombers.

Ayisha had been warned not to keep looking at her watch as the time ticked down to the moment of her annihilation. Normal people on planes simply didn't do that. But as she sat waiting, thumbing through magazines, a thousand thoughts began to invade her mind. All the things she hadn't done in her life. All the things she could have done. All the things she should have done. It was like some form of madness growing inside of her. Life was ending, and everything in her being was beginning to rebel against it. 'Change your thoughts. Control your mind. Focus on your task. God is with you' came the haunting words of her handler. And like the good soldier she had been trained to be, Ayisha turned her mind back to the crushing violence of her existence, the endless conflicts of her people, and all of the injustice and pain that she was now going to inflict upon her enemies. All those hateful thoughts that justified her actions and made them seem reasonable and acceptable to the God she believed in.

But Farsoun had moved beyond all of those festering thoughts and the only redemption he sought was the personal glory of victory, of seeing four great jets synchronously fall from the sky, spewing their human cargoes back to the earth they had defiled as enemies of his people and non-believers of his perfect God. It was something he had dedicated his life to, and at the exact, pre-determined time to accomplish his end, Ayisha stood from her chair and walked down the aisle toward the bathroom. She had become a machine, just like Farsoun had predicted, a perfect soldier lost in her mission, oblivious to the other 394 passengers and crew on the plane. She passed a newborn baby looking serenely into his mother's eyes as she showered him with love. She passed an old couple, holding hands as they slept peacefully together, and she passed a smiling stewardess who graciously opened the bathroom door and let her inside.

The training and conditioning were now in full effect, and Ayisha calmly removed her jacket and ripped out the lining, revealing a large sheet of putty-like explosive material, held together by a mesh of strong, fine threads. Taking hold of the top corners of the quarter inch thick sheet, Ayisha lifted it from her jacket and stuck it to the bathroom mirror. It was fifteen inches wide and two feet long, and she carefully took hold of the bottom edge and rolled it up like a pastry, into a thickened cylinder, which she doubled over several times and pressed into a tight ball of deadly explosive material. It was all very simple, but when Ayisha took the ballpoint pen from her purse, she saw herself in the mirror and paused. It was the moment of truth, and her living body tried to resist its ultimate end, spewing out vomit and restricting her breathing. But in her mind, Ayisha knew she had no other choice, nothing else worth living for. And in angry rebellion against all that had brought her to this moment, she jammed the pen into the explosive putty, turned it to the right, and pushed the detonator button.

The last thing Ayisha saw was a flash of bright light, the glorious light of God she thought, then it all faded to black, because God was love, and there was no love or light in what she had done.

Chapter 47

The night flight from Singapore to Bali landed on the tropical island to cheers and tears. In-flight internet service was both a blessing and a curse, and the reports of jets exploding and people falling from the skies had filled the aircraft with infectious fear. Terrorism was now an affliction of the entire world, and the emotions it generated encompassed all of humanity. Naturally the President of the United States condemned the violence and expressed his condolences to all of the victims' families, but deep down inside, he feared the attacks would increase the probability of retribution from the Montana. Everything was speeding up, and the pressure to interdict the remaining launch codes became even more pressing when he learned there were only two agents on station in Bali at this critical time, one of them not even an American.

Commissioner Fenwick and Lieutenant Olkowski timed their entrance into the main airport arrival building in Bali just as the passengers arrived from Singapore. They had both heard about the Middle East terrorist attack from the pilot of their own small jet, and they could still see the effect of it on the passengers as they gathered their bags and proceeded towards the customs gates.

As previously discussed, the men went their separate ways inside the terminal, casually checking out the passengers as they carried their own bags through the crowd. There were over two hundred people on the flight, mostly tourists and local businesspeople, but Olkowski quickly spotted a young man grabbing a surfboard from the baggage carousel. He didn't have Randall Roberts long blond hair or surfer dude appearance, but the surfboard bag was the same as the one in Randall's picture, and Olkowski quickly realized he'd found the second carrier.

'Got R. Short black hair. Carrying board in same bag as picture. Moving behind him.'

Fenwick read Olkowski's text and saw him casually join the "new" Randall in one of the customs lines. But as he observed them, he became aware of someone else doing the same thing, and quickly averted his eyes, recognizing the Slavic features and thick, muscular, frame of the first carrier - Moshi Ilyche - from the Sydney Station. Fenwick's first instinct was to send a text back to Olkowski, but he feared that would be a warning sign to the man he now knew was a professional, and he quickly joined another customs line, hoping to beat him and Randall outside.

Olkowski's decision to bring his surfboard now proved to be a good idea when Randall turned and saw him waiting in line behind him.

"Where you going?"

"Uluwatu. You been here before?"

"No, first time. Looks good in the promos."

"Yeah. Where you from?"

"West Coast. You?"

"Australia."

"You don't sound like an Aussie."

"Grew up in San Diego. Mother's from there."

"All right, well maybe I'll see you around." He moved on to the next customs officer and Olkowski felt a strong urge to turn and find Fenwick, but he had been cautioned not to do that, which proved to be good advice when the customs agent opened a camera bag Randall was carrying and for a moment revealed what appeared to be a hard drive just like the one Fenwick had shown him on the jet. It was like hitting the jackpot first time out, but before he could send another text, the next customs agent waved him forward, checking his bags and passport. It was a slow process, and before he was even close to finishing, Randall headed for the exit. He was getting away, and Olkowski became concerned until he saw Fenwick following him outside.

Bali is a beautiful, tropical island, a compressed idyllic world of green, terraced mountains, verdant valleys, pristine beaches, and the ubiquitous art of a people and religion that find beauty and grace in everything that surrounds them. But none of that was visible to Fenwick when he exited the airport into a deluge of rain, and heard Randall tell a taxi driver to take him to the Tandjung Sari.

Realizing time was of the essence, Fenwick quickly flagged down his own cab and surprised the driver with his rudimentary knowledge of the language, directing him to pull down the busy street and park where he could look back and see the airport. He knew that the first carrier would be looking for signs of anyone watching him or Randall, and quickly texted Olkowski a warning. *'First carrier watching U!! I'll follow him. R already in taxi to Tandjung Sari. U follow him.'* He could see Olkowski reading the message as he left the airport in a taxi, watched by the first carrier who paused beneath the airport awning, looking out through the rain at everything around him.

Fenwick could now see his adversary clearly for the first time. He did have Slavic features and a muscular frame, but he could now also see his professionalism as he surveyed everything around him. It was as if he could sense Fenwick's presence, and the Commissioner slid down in his seat as the man grabbed a taxi and drove past him.

Once again, it was a cat and mouse game between professionals, which became more complicated when Fenwick began to follow the first carrier and received another text from Olkowski. *'Saw hard drive in R's camera bag. Will try to grab it at hotel.'*

Fenwick immediately became concerned by the news and Olkowski's plan to grab the drive. It all seemed too easy. Would the first carrier let an apparent novice like Randall keep hold of the codes after he had successfully carried them through customs? It just didn't make sense, unless they weren't really the codes. Maybe the carrier had a second set of his own this time. The game was on, and he wondered what he should do as the first carrier's taxi turned down a road in a different direction than the Tandjung Sari.

"He's going to the coast," said the driver. "You want to follow?"

Fenwick was at the crossroads; he had to make a decision. And the only way to cover both possibilities was to play both hands. "Yes, but stay back at least four cars."

As the driver turned the corner continuing their discreet pursuit, Fenwick called Olkowski, knowing he was now alone.

"You still in the taxi?"

"Yeah. And you?"

"Following the first carrier. He's heading to the south coast, so you're on your own."

"Did you get my text?"

"Yes. Are you absolutely sure about what you saw?"

"Looked exactly like the picture. I couldn't read the model number, but it looked the same. You think it could be a fake?"

"I think it's a possibility," said Fenwick, "That's why I'm sticking with this guy. But it could also be the real thing, so if you can grab it, grab it."

Fenwick was feeling the pressure; he sensed he was being played, but with both carriers now on the island, the reality of the sub arriving there increased exponentially, and Fenwick sent a text to McCracken and Charlotte Ramsey explaining everything, including the specific area he was presently driving towards.

Chapter 48

Back at the Nimitz-MacArthur Command Center, Admiral McCracken was playing his own convoluted game of hide-and-seek. The terrorist attack on four Western jets in the Middle East had once again stirred the political hornet's nest in Washington, and the pressure to stop the Montana had escalated to near hysteria.

With secret calls and directives from the president and Admiral Stossel, McCracken started preparing for an attack on the Montana and made a classified special access call (SAP) to the pilot of the nearest P8-A, facilitated by Stossel. The P8-A, which was presently patrolling the northwest coast of Australia still searching for the missing Montana, was ironically, piloted by Captain Anik, the Eskimo lieutenant that had found the Russian sub off the Hawaiian coast.

"Lieutenant Anik?"

"Yes, sir."

"I'm reading you a directive presently en route to you via SCI (Sensitive Compartmented Information). This is a black ops directive covering all personnel presently on your aircraft. I'm speaking to you on direct orders from the President of the United States and Admiral Stossel, verified on your CEOI. We have reason to believe that the mutinous USS Montana is presently en route to the coastal waters of southern Bali, Indonesia. Coordinates included. You are to proceed to this area immediately. Initiate surveillance with sonar buoys and destroy any submarine in that location. There is no time to notify the

Indonesian military of this mission, so you will be flying black ops and will ignore the international twelve-mile limits agreement. Do you understand the orders as given, Lieutenant?"

"Yes, sir."

"Do you have any questions?"

"Yes, sir. Attacking any vessel without positive identification is against all rules, sir."

"Those orders have been preempted by presidential decree, Lieutenant. The president is now operating under the War Powers Act. You are not, and I repeat, NOT to communicate any of this directive to anyone until this mission is completed. All communications will be restricted to this classified SCI channel provided by Admiral Stossel out of Washington, D.C. Do you understand, Lieutenant?"

"Yes, sir. I understand."

"You're well aware of the Montana's danger to world peace, Lieutenant, so be bold in your pursuit. The president and the nation are depending on you."

Lieutenant Anik had written down the orders given by the admiral, but destroying an unidentified sub even by presidential decree seemed a questionable act until he received the written orders, which included Landsat images showing all Indonesian submarines presently in their home bases.

Since the release of the Montana Memorandum, several of the P8-A's crew members had casually expressed their personal admiration for the mutinous crew, so after presenting the presidential black ops directive, Lieutenant Anik reminded his men of their sworn allegiance to the nation's Commander in Chief, President Jack Anderson.

Chapter 49

THE Tandjung Sari was one of the oldest and most beautiful hotels on the island of Bali. Classic Indonesian bungalows set in manicured tropical gardens surrounded an exquisite central lobby, restaurant, and swimming pool facility.

Randall Roberts had already checked into the hotel and was driving through the rain in an electric cart to his bungalow with a porter when Olkowski arrived in his taxi and saw him. It was a fortuitous sighting, and he quickly spoke to his driver.

"Stop here for a minute!"

The driver stopped in the rain, which proved to be good cover as Olkowski watched Randall check in to his bungalow and tip his porter. He was about fifty yards away, and the lieutenant wondered what he should do. If it really was the hard drive Randall was carrying, he certainly wouldn't leave it unattended, so the only way to get it, other than a fortuitous distraction, would require a physical confrontation. It had been almost two decades since Olkowski's combat training, and he wondered if he still had the mental fortitude and physical ability to conduct such an action. Randall Roberts was also ex-military, and what were his skills? He was obviously still fit, but smaller in stature, a fact that gave Olkowski some measure of encouragement.

Okay, it was time for action. There was no reason to check into his own room if he was going to get the drive and leave, so he gave the taxi driver four hundred dollars in cash and told him to park down the driveway and wait for him with his bags. It was hard to make the transition from desk job to combatant, particularly in such a pastoral setting, but Admiral McCracken had lectured him on the importance of his mission, which could potentially involve saving millions of lives.

As the taxi drove down the driveway and parked in the shadows, Olkowski took a deep breath and approached Randall's bungalow. Lightning flashed across the sky, followed by rumbling thunder. In just a few moments, Olkowski was drenched to the skin as he climbed onto a private balcony and watched his adversary through a partially open curtain. The bungalow had a step down living room with a large bedroom and bathroom beyond it. Randall had already opened his suitcase and camera bag on the bed and poured himself a drink from an in-house bar, sipping it as he slipped out of his sandals and walked into the bathroom.

Olkowski could only see him partially now, but he did hear the shower turn on, and knew it was an opportunity. The sliding glass doors leading from the balcony into the bungalow's living room were locked, but he quickly grabbed a metal spatula hanging next to a grill, snapped off the handle and used it to pry open the latch, opening one of the glass doors. The water was still running in the bathroom, but the noise of the rain outside was even louder, and he quickly closed the door and entered the bedroom, peering into the camera bag, which no longer contained the drive. '*Where the hell was it?*' Olkowski searched the other suitcase and peered under the bed and pillows. He knew he had only so much time, but where could he have put it? He went back to the living room, looking under the couch and its pillows, then stood on a chair, checking the top of a media cabinet. Time was running out, and he returned to the bedroom looking into a closet with an empty, unlocked safe inside.

His heart began to beat faster then he saw a clue. A picture hanging on the wall next to the bed was slightly askew, and when he pulled it away from the wall and peered behind it, the hard drive fell out, clattering onto the bedside table before sliding behind it. Olkowski cursed and dropped to his knees, reaching for the hard drive when the shower suddenly switched off, freezing him in place. He was partially hidden by the bed and quickly flattened out beneath it as he saw Randall's wet feet appear in the bathroom doorway.

At first Randall wasn't sure if he'd heard something or not, but when he walked across the bedroom, wrapping a towel around his waist, he saw Olkowski's wet footprints on the floor by the sliding door. There was someone there, and he grabbed a knife from the bar, peered behind the couch, then followed the wet footprints back into the bedroom where he saw the toes of a pair of deck shoes protruding from beneath the bedroom curtains. Moving like a stalking cat, the knife now poised deadly in his hand, Randall reached out and pulled back the curtain, only to be hit from behind by Olkowski smashing the bedside lamp into his head.

But the surfer didn't go down. He just grabbed his head and howled, "What the fuck?!"

It was a surprising reaction. But before he could recover, Olkowski hit him again, and knocked him out cold. It was a violent attack, and the lieutenant quickly checked Randall's pulse then tied him up and gagged him with lamp cords. But when he retrieved his shoes and the hard drive, someone knocked at the door.

"Shit!" Olkowski knew he was trapped, and quickly ran out the sliding window, as a hotel maid let herself into the room with a complimentary tray of food.

At first the maid was confused by the open window, then she saw Randall rising up from the bed, covered in blood, and screamed.

By the time the maid had released Randall, Olkowski was already back in his taxi, dialing Fenwick on his phone.

"I've got the package. Already on my way to the airport."

Fenwick was, to say the least, surprised. "And what about Randall?"

"I knocked him out and tied him up. He was waking up when I left."

"Did he have anything else with him?"

"Not that I could find, but I did keep his phone."

"Throw it out the window!" said Fenwick. "They can trace you with it."

"What if it's got something important on it?"

"It doesn't matter! Get rid of it!!"

"Okay, it's gone," said Olkowski, obeying his command.

"You did good, mate. When you're safely in the air, call McCracken and Charlotte Ramsey and let them know you're clear with the package."

"And what about you?"

"I'm still following this guy and looking for the sub." He switched off his phone; now even more concerned that Randall was just a decoy. So who was the man he was following? Could he be the same? If he was the professional he suspected, why hadn't he initiated any procedure to mislead anyone that might be following him? Maybe there was a third carrier?

Moshi Ilyche was watching Fenwick's distant car through the back window of the taxi when Randall called him, agitated.

"They knocked me out and took the package. Should I call the police?"

"No," said Moshi, surprisingly unperturbed. "Just let it go. You did your job. Enjoy your holiday."

"And what about the people here?"

"Tell them you don't want to press charges, and they'll be fine. Did you ever tell anyone back in the States you were coming to Bali?"

"No! No one!"

"And you didn't mention it on your phone or write it down anywhere?"

"No! The only thing I wrote down was the name of the hotel, and I took that with me."

"And where did you write it?"

"On a pad by the phone. Is that a problem?"

"No, you did great. Enjoy your surfing."

"And what about you?"

"It doesn't matter. You never met me."

Moshi switched off his phone, knowing that once again it was the FBI he was dealing with. They had read the Bali hotel's name imprinted on Randall's notepad. But this time, they were too late. They didn't figure it out until after Randall had arrived in Singapore, and by that time Moshi was ready for them. In fact, he was pleasantly surprised by how quickly they had betrayed their presence on the island by taking the Randall bait. But who was the person following him now? Another agent? How could he have possibly ID'd him? Not even Randall or Staley Combs knew his true identity. Obviously, the Americans now presumed the Montana would follow the codes to Bali, but so far his contact in Hawaii had not reported any movement in that direction, so what was going on?

Still contemplating all the possibilities, and still aware that he was being watched, Moshi checked into a hotel perched on a cliff looking out at the spectacular southern coastline. It was now 10 pm local time, and as the porter took his bags to his room, he ordered a Scotch in the quiet bar restaurant and sent an encrypted message on his phone. *'Everything as expected here. Call J at 4 am, confirm.'*

Almost immediately he received a reply. *'Waiting in place. Raining heavy. Hope everything goes as planned. Miss you.'*

Moshi smiled at the message and wiped it from his screen. It was getting late, and he took a sip of his drink, looking up at a television silently showing the images of the crash sites of the Middle East jet bombings.

Moshi shook his head. Nothing had changed; the war with militant Islam continued unabated. But there was a new counter-story brewing. Images of the nuclear missile sub Montana and its threatening memorandum now ran opposite the burning planes.

"Can I buy you another drink?"

Moshi turned and saw Fenwick standing next to him. It was something he had half expected, and he smiled, recognizing the man from the Bali airport.

"Sure, take a seat."

Fenwick sat and indicated Moshi's drink to the bartender.

"Two more of the same, mate."

"You're an Aussie."

"Yeah, born and raised. And you?"

"Russian. From Ukraine."

"That sounds like a good place to be from." The drinks arrived, and Fenwick held up his glass. "Here's to a better world."

"Sounds good to me." They tipped glasses and Moshi smiled. "So you've been following me."

Fenwick hid his surprise. "Yeah, trying to. Deputy Commissioner Fenwick, Australian Federal Police. And you?"

"Private contractor."

"Working for…?"

"Unemployed right now. And you?"

Fenwick smiled. "Presently working for the Americans. They invited me here after they ID'd your second carrier."

Moshi didn't react to his statement, but it all made sense now. The commissioner had made him in Australia and followed him there.

"So you're wearing a wire?"

"No. And it wouldn't matter anyway. We're in a neutral country. It's just you and me, mate."

He ordered another drink, now speaking to the bartender fluently in the local language.

"You've been here before?"

"Yes, I was here for several months after the Jemaah Islamiyah terrorist bombings, picking up the pieces of my fellow Aussies. Eighty-eighty of them, mostly kids, just like they're doing up there now." He indicated the television screen, depicting a similar scene. He was obviously affected by it, and drained his second drink. "You want another?"

"Sure. I don't have to drive home. So what are your American friends expecting you to do here?"

"Find their launch codes."

"And you think talking to me can help you with that?"

Fenwick grinned. "Yeah, you want to sell them to me? I figure they're worth at least half a billion right now!"

"The sub's worth twice that, and that's without its weapons."

"Yeah, but that sub's going to cause you all sorts of trouble, mate. You really think you can change these people?" He indicated the burning crash zone playing on the TV. "They've been killing us and each other in the name of Allah for over 1,400 years, and they haven't figured it out yet!"

"I don't think the idea is to change them." It was an ominous statement and Fenwick shook his head.

"You're just going to mess up the whole world if you do that, and I sympathize with your cause. What we really need is containment. Keep them out of our part of the world, and we stay out of theirs."

"Unfortunately, they believe it's their religious destiny to rule the whole world."

"It's just a dream, a bunch of militant old imams trying to hold onto past glories. And every day they do it, they fall further behind the rest of the world. So why don't you let me be your new contractor and make you a rich man?"

Moshi smiled and finished his drink. "I'll think about it."

"You're just playing for time, mate, and time's running out. This can still be a good outcome for you."

"I think time ran out a long time ago."

"It's not going to make you feel good, mate. Revenge'll eat you up."

"So did you forgive the guys that blew up all your friends?"

It was a provocative question and Fenwick hesitated. "Not exactly, but I'm working on it."

"Well, you'd better work on it harder, because it's never going to end until someone really puts a stop to it. Thanks for the drink." He walked away knowing that Fenwick could do nothing about it. But the Commissioner picked up his shot glass and called him back.

"You forgot your glass, mate. Someone could take your prints off it."

Moshi grinned. "Why don't you take care of it? We're all in the same boat, mate."

Fenwick opened his fingers and let the glass shatter on the floor.

After his meeting with Moshi, Fenwick knew there was a third carrier. Obviously, the first carrier would not have revealed himself if he still had the codes. But he didn't mention any of that in his report to Admiral McCracken and the FBI. He couldn't prove it, and he didn't believe it would change anything they were doing anyway. The meeting between the Montana and the second carrier Randall was set for the Tandjung Sari, then changed after the raid on Staley Comb's home. But by that time, the Montana would have been close to Bali, so the new meeting place would still have to be in that immediate area. So it was all in the hands of serendipity and the military now, and he chose to simply take credit for tracking down the apparent second set of codes and leave it at that. After all, the Americans had not been particularly gracious considering everything he had done for them.

Chapter 50

There is always one bird that heralds the dawn before all others. One bird that senses the light while all others still sleep. It was such a bird that led Moshi's wife, Gwen, through a tangle of trees to a flight of stone steps that descended a cliff to an isolated beach on the south coast of Java, less than one hundred miles west of Bali. Dressed in a traditional Indonesian batik skirt with a long-sleeved silk blouse covering her translucent English skin, she looked like a local girl in the first light.

Dawn was the time of her meeting, and as she reached the beach, a quiet voice called out her name from the surrounding trees.

"Gwen! Over here!"

Three men dressed in black appeared from the shadows, standing next to a motorized rubber dinghy. John Besson hadn't changed since the last time she saw him. He and his navigator, Jones, and engineer, Parker, were all clean-shaven and regimented in their behavior, indicating the discipline that still ruled their lives and the Montana.

"John, it's good to see you!" whispered Gwen as she gave Besson a hug, and he introduced his cohorts.

"This is Lieutenant Jones and Petty Officer Parker."

Gwen greeted each of the men and handed John a transparent Ziploc bag with a couple of notebooks, pencils, and erasers inside. It looked like a kid's homework assignment.

"The hard drive's inside the books in another bag. I thought that would be the best way to keep it dry."

"That's good, thank you," said John, taking the package and checking it. "Have you spoken to Moshi?"

"Yes. He's on the other island. He sends his love."

"Did he speak with Monique recently?"

"She's been invited to meet with the president."

Besson smiled. "Well, she'll be looking forward to that." A bird flew from the trees, disturbing them.

"Okay, it's getting light; we have to go. Thank you again for doing this." Gwen gave him another hug and bid them farewell. There was nothing more to say, and she watched them drag their dinghy back into the sea and quickly leave. It was still barely light, and in just a few moments, they vanished into the mist shrouded ocean where they were destined to spend the rest of their lives.

Chapter 51

CAPTAIN Anik's P8-A had approached the Indonesian archipelago at two in the morning and began deploying three foot long sonic detection buoys along the southern and southeastern coastlines of Bali. The Montana was almost six hundred feet long, with a vertical draft of over seventy feet, so Lieutenant Anik concentrated his efforts in the deeper waters between the twelve-mile nation limit and the Java Trench that followed the archipelago's southern flank all the way up to the northern tip of Sumatra.

The P8-A is part of the Navy's maritime patrol and reconnaissance force (MPRF) and has a crew of nine. Filled with electronics and the latest AW/APY-10 Raytheon high tech radar, the aircraft has five separate operational bays, each equipped with two 24" high-resolution display screens. Each bay is manned by naval flight officers and aviation warfare personnel monitoring the vast amount of information flowing through the system. In addition to its high altitude anti-submarine warfare weapon capability (HAAWC), the aircraft carries anti-ship Slammer missiles, sea mines, depth charges, Mark 54 torpedoes and more than 100 deployable sonobuoys for submarine detection.

The Boeing aircraft also has an extended flight capability, but by the time daylight began to approach, it was getting close to the time when Anik would have to return to Australia for refueling. It had been a long, unfruitful night working beneath Indonesian radar, but as he was making a last pass along the southwest tip of Bali, his chief radar officer, Franzetti, called out, "I got a contact! SB23, bearing two-seven-zero." His voice was like manna to Anik's ears, and he quickly joined the operator, who pointed to a blip on his screen.

"It was right here, lined up behind this surface craft."

"And what is that?"

"Steel hull, maybe a hundred feet. Could be a fishing boat or small ferry."

"How far out?"

Franzetti checked his computer. "Just over sixty three miles."

"You said this is SB23?"

"Last one in," said Franzetti, referring to the sonobuoy, "looks like it drifted to the west. Okay, there it is again." He pointed to a second blip on his radar screen.

"Looks big," said Anik.

"Single blade. Could be our boy. Bearing zero-nine-five, coming right at us."

"How far off the coast?"

"Just outside the twelve-mile exclusion zone."

"Let me see it on the EI," said Anik. The four hundred pound Raytheon radar system has an enhanced imaging (EI) setting that magnifies its ultra-high resolution images and gives its operators additional information.

"She's moving fast. Blade count over twenty-five. Almost thirty knots. Looks like she's closing on this surface vessel."

"And what's this?" said Anik, pointing to an almost invisible artifact on the screen.

"Something small, maybe a speedboat or something."

"Okay, let's check it out," said Anik calling back to his co-pilot, "three-seven-zero."

The copilot turned the aircraft to the new heading, repeating his order.

"This could be it," said Anik, "keep on it." He turned back to the cockpit and sat in his seat. "Okay, here we go. Alert One. Let's ready two 54s and prep a dozen DCs (depth charges). Good morning, America!" He was gung-ho, but it wasn't a sentiment shared by all of his crew.

"She's an American vessel, sir. Don't we need permission to attack her?"

"Not if it's the Montana," said Anik. It was a statement of fact, but you could sense the reticence in his voice, and after a moment's hesitation, he placed a cautionary call to Admiral McCracken.

CHAPTER 52

A LIGHT mist still hung over the calm morning sea as Captain Besson and his two men continued their journey back to their deep water GPS rendezvous with the Montana. The light was still low, but the captain felt a growing sense of vulnerability. He didn't know where it was coming from, but he could feel it in his gut, and he yelled above the noise of the outboard engine to his navigator.

"How much further?"

Jones checked his GPS. "Just under two miles. She should be coming up soon."

The captain turned to Parker at the helm. "Can this thing go any faster?"

"She's full out, sir."

The outboard engine was literally screaming across the flat ocean, but Besson began to hear something different beyond its noise.

"You hear that?"

The other men shook their heads. Besson turned to the east and heard the sound again. "Shut her down!!"

Parker shut down the outboard engine, and the deep mechanical rumble of a large approaching vessel filled the air.

"Sounds like it's coming right at us!" said Jones.

Suddenly, the bow of an Indonesian Coast Guard vessel loomed from the mist five hundred meters away. It was over one hundred feet long, with a bow-mounted BOFORS 40 mm cannon, and two additional 50-caliber M2 Browning machine guns mounted on its forward deck.

Besson cursed under his breath. "Coast Guard cutter!"

Parker looked defiant. "We can outrun her, sir!"

"Not with those guns!"

"So what do we do?"

"Are we still in the twelve mile exclusion zone?"

Jones checked his GPS. "Half mile outside of it."

"Okay, let me try talking to them."

The Coast Guard vessel pulled alongside and reversed its engines, filling the air with diesel fumes as it stopped next to them. There were at least fifteen uniformed men on the vessel, several standing by its deck guns. Besson waved up at the deck officer.

"Morning!"

"Morning," replied the officer, speaking with an accent. "What are you doing here?"

"US Navy. We're from a vessel south of here."

"You're in Indonesian waters."

Besson shook his head and held up their GPS reader. "Half a mile outside."

"Your instrument is incorrect."

"My instrument is accurate, sir."

The deck officer lifted his radio and spoke to the ship's captain, standing on the bridge. It was a lengthy conversation, but when it was over, the officer turned back to Besson, speaking more officiously.

"We are going to have to take you in. Pull around to the stern and throw us your line."

"For what reason?" demanded Besson.

"Captain's orders."

"Your captain is breaking international law. He has no jurisdiction here."

"He is the captain. You must do what he says and pull behind us."

Besson realized it was pointless to argue and turned to Parker with a knowing look.

"Okay, you heard the man. Full speed to stern."

Parker got the message and gunned his motor, racing directly away from the cutter's stern out of sight line from its bow-mounted guns. Everyone on the cutter began yelling and running to battle stations as their vessel re-engaged its engines and turned toward the fleeing dinghy.

"See if you can make that fog bank!" yelled Besson, indicating the surface mist from which the cutter had appeared.

Parker turned the dinghy toward the fog, bending over his engine for additional speed. But before they were halfway there, one of the cutter's Browning machine guns opened fire, ripping the water ahead of the dinghy. It was a warning shot, and Besson quickly got the message. "Shut it down! Shut it down!!"

But before Parker could even react, one of the .50 caliber slugs sliced through Besson's upper arm, almost knocking him out of the dinghy. Jones cursed and pulled him back into the vessel, blood already oozing from the wound. But Besson didn't feel any pain. All he could think about was his mission, and the fact that one stupid mistake on the launch codes was going to cost them everything.

But this time, the approaching cutter herself was forced to stop when the Montana suddenly rose from the sea next to the dinghy. She was like some monstrous, shimmering mantle of protective hope, 18,000 tons of tempered steel, glistening in the early light and on her towering wing, the sub's XO, Garcia, appeared speaking on a PA system.

"You're threatening a US Naval vessel in international waters. There are two five hundred pound M54 high explosive torpedoes locked onto your hull. If you don't retreat immediately, we will commence firing."

The Indonesian captain looked shocked by the sub's appearance and size and when Garcia's threat was translated for him, he realized he had no counter for the torpedoes and waved a submissive greeting to the XO, ordering his helmsman to retreat.

It was a small victory, but before Besson and his men were safely in the sub, Garcia received an urgent message from the CONN radar. *'Aircraft approaching three-seven-zero, 3 miles out. Radar locked on.'*

Garcia realized the danger immediately and yelled an order. "Full speed ahead! Take her down! Dive! Dive!!" He could now see Anik's P8-A approaching through his binoculars.

Besson heard the dive alarm and felt the sub shudder as it surged forward. The dinghy was still in the water, but survival took precedence, and he yelled to his men to let it go, and ran for the sub's rear hatch with the other sailors helping them onto the deck.

The Montana was picking up speed and diving fast when Besson entered the hull with his men and slammed the hatch shut. Battle station alarms were sounding throughout the sub as the captain ran forward, clutching his bloodied arm.

The Montana's control room was a confusion of officers attending multiple tasks, preparing for an attack as the sub continued her dive.

Garcia yelled above the fray. "Seal all compartments!" His words were repeated on the intercom.

"You know what it is?" asked Besson, joining him.

"P8-A. He's going to hit us with his Slammers."

Besson checked the sonar and saw the Coast Guard cutter retreating from their position. "Left rudder 30 degrees! Bearing two-seven-seven. Take us under the cutter!"

Garcia saw the blood dripping from his wounded arm. "Let's get the quack in here for the Captain!"

"I'm fine," said Besson.

"You're pumping out. You need a clamp on it!"

Less than a mile away, Captain Anik could now see the nuclear missile sub directly ahead, and spoke to Admiral McCracken on his radio.

"It's the Montana, sir. I can see her clearly. Do I have your permission to engage?"

McCracken was in the Hawaii command center, watching the P8-A's battle station cameras in real time as everyone around him adapted to the sudden discovery of the Montana. His decision to keep the planned attack secret had caught everyone off balance, including Acker and everyone in the NSC except for Stossel and the president.

"Permission granted," said McCracken, well aware that all the NSC members were now in the Situation Room watching and listening to the unfolding drama with the president.

Permission granted? The words echoed through Anik's head as he spoke to his chief weapons officer. "Arm left and right Slammers," he referred to two large anti-ship missiles hung beneath the P8's wings.

"Slammers armed; radar locked on, sir!"

But before the captain could give the order to fire, his copilot yelled a warning.

"She's going behind the cutter!"

Anik looked out the window and saw the Montana's wing sinking behind the Coast Guard ship. They were now sailing parallel to each other, and there was no way he could fire without jeopardizing the other vessel.

"Hold fire! Hold fire!! Wait till she clears the cutter!"

Everyone in Hawaii and the White House watched and listened to the ongoing drama in rapt silence. They all knew the ensuing attack would determine the future of the Montana and potentially the world.

For a moment, time seemed to stand still then suddenly the cutter veered away from the Montana, revealing the sub now almost totally submerged except for its towering wing. Time was running out, and Anik reacted quickly. "Target clear. Fire Slammers!"

But the weapons officer hesitated. "She's going down too fast, sir!

The missiles won't operate beneath the surface!"

"Fire anyway!" yelled Anik, frustrated.

"Weapons away!" The P8 shuddered as the Slammer missiles dropped from its wings and fired their propellants.

The Montana was now less than 400 meters from the P8-A, but by the time the two missiles reached the sub, she was totally submerged, and the weapons skipped off the sea's surface, flew through the air and exploded when they struck the water again.

The sudden missile attack and explosions stunned the captain and crew of the Indonesian cutter. But the conflict wasn't over; Captain Anik was not to be denied, and escalated his attack.

"Coming about! Ready depth charges! Setting eight-zero feet plus twenties."

The P-8A flew directly over the Coast Guard ship and began dropping a pattern of depth charges into the water beyond it. They were set to detonate at escalating depths and a series of muted explosions shook the sea, sending plumes of water billowing across the ocean.

One hundred and forty feet beneath the surface, the huge missile sub bucked and twisted violently as the depth charges exploded around her double-skinned hull. Captain Besson held onto the sonar operator's chair, checking his screen as a medic pinched off his severed artery with a clamp and taped it to his arm. But Besson was oblivious to his personal drama as the sub continued to shake and groan under the onslaught.

"Right rudder twenty degrees! Let's get back under that cutter!"

The helmsman repeated his order. "Rudder right twenty, coming to zero-seven-five!"

The chief sonar officer on the P8-A saw the Montana's change of direction.

"She's lining back up with the cutter, sir! Zero-seven-five."

Anik could feel the pressure of everyone watching him. "Let's get another SB in there and arm the 54s! Acquisition set five-zero feet plus!"

"What's going on?" said the president, lost in the battle.

"They're launching a sonobuoy for tracking and two torpedoes set for fifty feet and deeper to avoid the surface vessel."

"M54s loaded and armed!" announced the P8-A's chief weapons officer.

Anik turned his aircraft to the sub's heading. "Coming to zero-seven-five…fire at will!"

"Weapons away!" The two torpedoes fell from the P8-A's bomb bay and plunged into the sea 200 meters aft of the Coast Guard cutter. The Indonesian crew looked horrified as the torpedoes rushed toward them and disappeared under their vessel.

Two hundred feet beneath the surface, the Montana had survived the P8-A's depth charges, but the weapons officer now heard the ominous sound of the torpedoes hitting the water in his headphones.

"Two fish in water; one locked on!"

"Conn, Sonar. I've got 'em both, bearing two-one-zero, closing one thousand yards. Second fish still searching."

The M54 torpedoes have their own autonomous tracking systems, and the lead torpedo was now using its homing sonar to close in on the Montana.

"First fish closing, eight-five-zero yards, depression angle one-five-zero."

Besson called out orders in rapid succession. "Planes full down, rudder right thirty, initiate acoustical jamming!" The helmsman pushed the steering yoke full forward and turned the rudder, repeating the orders. Simultaneously, the weapons officer captured the M54's sonar pulse on a separate decoy system, distorted it, then returned it to the torpedo with a false reading. It was a complicated battle of sonar deceit, both weapon and sub employing computer programs to counter each other.

"Bottom eight-five-zero feet; closing fast, sir!"

"Hold steady!" said Besson, staying calm.

The first torpedo's sonar pulse quickened as it closed on the sub. The weapons officer could hear it picking up speed. "Torpedo range five hundred yards; impact twenty seconds."

The captain was diving for the bottom capture field, an area of confusing sonic echoes. "Deploy countermeasures. Fire off four!"

The weapons officer fired off four cans of gas, filling the sea with millions of bubbles, creating an ensonified zone, which reflected back the M54s sonar pulse in an attempt to create ghost targets and confuse the torpedo's tracking system. But it kept on coming. Time was running out and the weapons officer expressed his concern to Besson.

"Torpedo range one-five-zero. Seven seconds to impact!"

"Full back on planes!"

The helmsman pulled back on the steering yoke, lifting the sub's nose upward just before it hit the bottom. The entire crew could now hear the quickening pings of the approaching torpedo. It was almost to the sub then abruptly everything changed as it skimmed past the stern, creating a Doppler effect as its pinging sonar lengthened again then ended in an explosion. The torpedo had hit the bottom, rocking the Montana from stem to stern, creating enough noise to make the sonarman rip off his headphones.

"One down!" said the captain, still keeping his calm but definitely breathing easier. "Anything on the second fish?"

The weapons officer indicated no. "Too much interference from the explosion, sir."

"Sonar?"

"She's on the other side of the ensonified zone."

"Level off at three hundred; slow to five knots, bearing zero-zero-five." Everyone looked surprised by the new heading, which took them back towards the land.

"You're going into the shallows?" said Garcia, concerned.

"They won't expect it." The captain was getting dizzy and caught himself from falling.

"You need a transfusion, sir. You're going to have to lie down," the medic was getting emphatic, but Besson remained focused on his job.

"I'll do it when I'm finished."

The noise of the exploding torpedo was heard clearly on the P8A's sonobuoy and Franzetti excitedly announced the news.

"We got a hit! I don't hear the boomer anymore."

Anik quickly joined the sonar officer, still aware of everyone in Hawaii and the White House listening to them.

"Any break up noises?"

"No sir, but I don't hear the reactor or prop anymore."

"If it's a hit, there has to be break up noise. Where's the second fish?"

"Still circling for contact east of explosion zone."

"Let's get another SB in there, west side, three miles outside the disturbance zone. I need data, let's get on it!"

Admiral McCracken listened to the unfolding drama from the Hawaii Command Center. Anik had done everything by the book, but unfortunately Besson had read the same book, and the admiral could feel the Montana slipping away. What else could he do? He looked up and saw Acker watching him as they waited for the outcome. The bond between them was frayed, but they still had to work together, and

McCracken walked down to the vice admiral's station.

"What are your closest assets to the contact zone?"

"Two SSN-774s, one east of Diego Garcia, one southwest of Guam. Nothing in the immediate area."

"Okay, let's move the three remaining P8's into the new zone and get a couple of refuelers in there to keep them up."

"If he goes into the Sunda subduction, it'll be one hell of a job to get him out," said Acker. He was referring to the Java Trench, using its oceanographic name, which reminded McCracken of the vice admiral's original suggestion that it would be the perfect place to hide and release missiles aimed at the Middle East.

"I'll have a carrier fleet in there in twelve hours," said McCracken, "and every other ASW asset I can round up. That'll include the Brits, Aussies, and the Japanese."

He was being dramatic, hoping to drive Acker into revealing his contact with the Montana. But it was a long shot, and he wasn't holding his breath.

Captain Anik dropped his second sonobuoy west of the explosion zone, plus two others in the surrounding area, but there were no more contacts with the Montana. Time was running out, his fuel was low, and with two Indonesian jets scrambling to the area after a call from their Coast Guard cutter, Anik dropped the rest of his depth charges around the explosion zone, just in case the Montana was damaged but still sitting there, and retreated to Australia.

Everyone on the Montana could hear the exploding depth charges, but they were a long way from the shallows where the sub now sat on the bottom in 200 feet of water, everything shut down and silent. The captain had sent up a flotation wire, giving the radio man a clear image of the surface noise.

"Aircraft departing, sir."

"He's running out of fuel," said Besson, "She probably came in from Australia. We'll give her an hour to clear, then move out of here."

"You need to get a transfusion," said Garcia.

"On my way. Thanks for saving our asses."

"Part of the team, sir."

"Yeah, well it's a great team. You'll all be pleased to know we now have the codes to launch and will be fully operational as soon as Lieutenant Flynn plugs them into the system." The crew made a few jokes about Flynn as the captain left with the medic, but Garcia quickly brought everyone back to order.

"Okay guys, one hour's rest, and we're back at it."

CHAPTER 53

CHARLOTTE Ramsey was angry. Her FBI agents were responsible for retrieving the second set of codes and tracking the Montana to Bali, but she and her entire organization were now excluded from the conclusion of their investigation, which became a closed-door military operation.

It was a frustrating turn of events, and when she learned from Lieutenant Silver that a confrontation with the Montana was now in progress, she could hardly restrain herself, castigating Sid Bailey about men, their boys clubs, and their obliviousness to everything women do to save the world from the mess inflicted upon it by them. It was a diatribe that only ended when Matt Weston knocked on the door and peered inside.

"I'm sorry to disturb you, ma'am, but Doctor Goddard from the DOD needs to speak with you. He said it's urgent."

Charlotte had forgotten about the doctor, who had been sent to the US Naval Base in Guam to take charge of the second set of codes from Lieutenant Olkowski.

"Doctor Goddard, how are things going with you?"

"Not so good," said the doctor. "I just received the second set of codes from Bali, and they're fake."

"Fake?!" said Charlotte, glancing at Sid.

"Yes. All it has on it is a smiley face and the words, '*This time we win. Touché.*'"

Charlotte immediately realized the ramifications of the information. "Did you call anyone else about this?"

"Not yet," said Goddard, "they're all in an NSC meeting."

"And how about Admiral McCracken?"

"I've got a call in to him, but he hasn't called back yet."

"Okay, I'll try and get through to General Pierce. You keep after the admiral."

She hung up and turned to Sid, reenergized. "The second set of codes are fake."

"You've got to be kidding?!"

"No."

"Son of a bitch!"

"So what do I tell the president?"

"Tell him the truth, and pray they got the Montana."

The Director of National Intelligence, General Pierce, was in the Situation Room with the president and his entire National Security Council speaking with Admiral McCracken about the Montana when he received the call from Charlotte. It came at a frustrating time, but when she told him about the fake codes, he quickly realized the seriousness of the situation and interrupted the president.

"I've got Charlotte Ramsey on the phone, sir. She just informed me that the second set of launch codes retrieved in Bali are fake."

"Are you kidding me?" said the president.

"No, sir."

They had just come to a general consensus that the Montana had probably survived the Bali attack but still didn't have the codes, and now this?

"Can you put her on the screen?"

Pierce made a quick call, and Charlotte appeared on another screen next to McCracken.

"Are you absolutely sure about this new information, Charlotte?"

"Doctor Goddard from the DOD just called me from Guam and confirmed it, sir."

"So we can now assume the Montana has the second set of codes?"

"I don't know the answer to that, sir, but I do believe it's a strong possibility. We didn't find out about the second carrier before he arrived in Singapore, and after that, they appear to have brought in a third carrier."

"A third carrier?" snapped the president.

"Yes, sir."

"So how are we going to resolve this? Do they have the codes or not?"

"I think we have to assume they do, sir," said the Secretary of Defense.

"So they're now operational?"

"I think that's the only safe conclusion we can make, sir."

"And when will they be ready to launch?"

The Secretary looked at McCracken on the screen. "What do you think, Jay?"

"If they've got the codes, they could be in range of the entire Middle East in less than two days."

It was a chilling assessment, and the dread in the room was palpable.

"I understand you were involved with developing this submarine, Admiral?"

"Yes, sir."

"And you never anticipated anything like this happening?"

"We ran multiple scenarios of every possible weakness in the system, sir, but not this connection with the Chinese."

The president took a deep breath and looked at Stossel. "So what do we do now, David?"

"We hunt her down and destroy her, sir! It's just fifteen men against the world. They'll make another mistake and we'll get 'em…!"

"And if they don't?"

Marine General Mack Harding had an answer. "We show the men on that sub that we're finally going to do something to end all this terrorism, sir."

"And how do we do that?" questioned the president.

"We isolate them from the rest of us. We rule the seas. We rule the skies. We shut them out. We don't go to their countries, and they don't come to ours and if they continue to launch attacks, we shut off their trade as well."

"The rest of the world's not going to agree to that, Mack. They live off their oil. And what about the press? They're certainly going to hear about this!"

"It's already out there," said Charlotte. "Lieutenant Silver just picked it up on the internet."

"The internet?!"

"Yes, sir. We can post the feed if you wish."

"Put it up!" ordered the president.

Lieutenant Silver appeared on Charlotte's screen with the internet connection next to him.

"This just came up on our Asian feed." He indicated a low-resolution image, which was apparently shot on someone's smartphone. "This is an Indonesian Coast Guard vessel trying to arrest three men in a dinghy leaving the coast of Java, and if you look closely," he enlarged the image, "you can see this is John Besson, the captain of the Montana."

"You sure about that?" questioned the president.

"Yes, sir, we already ran a face recognition program on it."

"And then what happened?"

Silver restarted the internet feed. "It looks like the captain tried to get away, gets shot, then this happens." The Montana rises from the sea like a monolithic monster, shocking everyone with its graphic image.

"Who shot this?" questioned the president.

"Someone on the Indonesian Coast Guard vessel then one of our P-8's showed up." The shaky image of the P8-A firing its Slammer missiles appeared on the screen, followed by the weapons explosions then everything ended in chaos as the cameraperson dived for cover.

"And that's it?"

"The cameraman comes back later saying there were more bombs and explosions under the sea, then the aircraft went away."

"And did he say anything about Besson and his men and what they were doing there?"

"He just said they were Americans from the missing Montana."

"And Besson got shot?"

"Yes, sir. It definitely appears that way. We're trying to get more information now."

The president turned to McCracken. "Can they run that sub without the captain?"

"The XO will take over, sir."

"Let me see the bit with him getting shot again."

Silver replayed the image, and the president shook his head.

"Doesn't look too bad to me. What do you think, Tom?"

"He got on that boat pretty easy," said Pierce.

"So is there any good news?"

"Not right now, sir."

"Well, I can think of one thing - we don't need to spend billions on foreign intelligence anymore. We can just watch the fucking internet!"

CHAPTER 54

MONIQUE Besson woke up in a luxurious Washington hotel, courtesy of the US government. It was early morning, and she walked naked to the window and looked out at the capital, thinking of what she and her husband had done, what they were going to do, and all the reasons why. Since the Montana Memorandum, the whole world waited in expectation, some thrilled by the possibilities, others fearful. It would be the ultimate act of terrorism the world had ever known; the fracturing of a greater morality and consciousness that had avoided such a calamity since Hiroshima and Nagasaki, and Monique, like her jihadist opponents, didn't care. She was like the bomber of her sister's plane now, intent upon primal revenge for that carnage and a thousand other acts of horror committed against her people and her values.

It was a strange sense of emancipation, giving her life to a cause. And in that new state of heightened existence, she wanted to compress every pleasure, every exhilarating emotion into the time she had left, and her new lawyer, Sean Lariat, was becoming the recipient of all that unfettered lust and need.

"Good morning," he said, seeing her standing like Aphrodite at the window as he awoke. "You look like a Greek goddess."

"I am a goddess. The goddess of war and lust."

She slid the covers off him, and crawled like a cat over his naked form, lowering herself upon him. Sean shuddered under the spell of her warm, pressing presence and rose to the occasion.

Less than two miles away, the president's wife opened the curtains of the presidential bedroom and approached her sleeping husband with a tray and coffee.

"Hey, wake up! I got you some coffee."

The president's eyes flickered open, disoriented. "What time is it?"

"Eight o'clock. You've got a meeting with Mrs. Besson at nine."

"Right!" He sat up. "I feel like hell."

"What time did you come to bed?"

"Three a.m. I took a couple of sleeping pills."

"I see from the news they didn't get the Montana."

"That's the way it looks."

"And the codes?"

"We don't know. The second one we got back was fake."

"Well that doesn't sound good. What are you going to tell everyone?"

"The truth."

"That you don't know."

"That's right."

"But you do know," said Tat, fearing the worst.

"I didn't say that, not even to you. If I lie and say they don't have them, they'll probably launch a rocket to prove it, and if I tell everyone they do have them, the whole world's going to panic! Is Gary here?"

"No. You sent him to get Mrs. Besson, but General Pierce, Tony Russo, and Bob Gaines are already waiting for your daily briefing."

"Great. I'll need another two of these." Tatiana refilled his cup. "I look like hell, right?"

"I think you look cute. But I've got some more bad news."

"What?!"

"I checked out Mrs. Besson for you, and I think you'll find she's a little more than the average military wife." She handed him some notes. "She has a degree in international politics, a master's in world history, and she's been an advocate for women's rights since her college years, specializing in the rights of women in Third World countries and those living under religious subjugation."

"Like?"

"Women in Africa having their clitoris' cut-off, honor killings, women not allowed to go to school or divorce their abusive husbands when the men can dump them any time they wish. And the case in Mecca where a group of Muslim girls trapped in a burning school were left to die because they didn't have the appropriate dress to leave!"

"That's not even possible."

"It was reported on the BBC, so you'd better be on your toes!"

"I'll wear my points."

Tatiana smiled and gave him a kiss. "Just be your charming self and wear a flak jacket! If she's really going to blow up the world, she may just add you to the list."

Chapter 55

MONIQUE Besson and her lawyer were picked up at their hotel and escorted to the White House by the president's personal assistant, Gary Brockett. Sean was dressed in a blazer and jeans, Monique in a fitted skirt and flattering jacket, but she made no effort with her hair, wearing it in a simple ponytail, establishing her independent feminist credentials.

"So you're a personal assistant to the president?" asked Monique observing Gary in the car mirror.

"One of many, ma'am. How are you enjoying your stay in Washington?"

"I'm one of the many who would like to see it disbanded. Too much money and too much power in the hands of too few."

"Well I think you'll find the president agrees with you on that."

"And how about you? You work here."

"I'm just a pawn in the game, ma'am."

"Well, I guess that's what we all are. But I think it's about time to change all that." Sean reached out and touched her hand, cautioning her to watch her words. It was a moment not missed by Gary, and Monique grinned. "My lawyer thinks you're a spy, and I should watch what I say in front of you."

"I look like a spy?" said Gary, disarmingly.

"No, you look like a nice guy, but then again, that's the point, isn't it?"

Gary smiled, amused by her candor. "You really do have a bad opinion of Washington."

"Give me one good reason why I shouldn't?"

"It keeps all the bad people in one place."

Monique laughed. "I like that. You should run for office yourself."

The president sat in the Oval Office attending his daily intelligence briefing with the Secretary of Defense, Bob Gaines, the DNI, Tom Pierce, and his personal National Security Advisor, Tony Russo. The dominant issues were the Al Qaeda attack on four Western jets in the Middle East and the P8-A's attack on the missile sub Montana. As they spoke, the president ate a breakfast sandwich and flipped through a pile of national and international newspapers, checking the headlines.

Al Qaeda Strikes Again!

International Travel Threatened

US Plane Attacks Missing Sub

Montana Captain Shot!

Jihadists Rule The Air

"Do we have any idea how they took down these planes?"

"Explosive devices," said Pierce, "but we don't know how they planted them yet."

"So they can do it again?"

"Until we find out how, yes, sir. Everyone's working on it, including the Russians."

"This is going to play havoc with international travel."

"It already is. Flight cancellations are running over fifty percent, and new purchases are down almost eighty. They're trying to stop our international commerce, and in the last two days, we've picked up increasing chatter about a new attack on the homeland, including information from an ISIS informant who said they're preparing something big."

"So they don't give a damn about the Montana?"

"It doesn't appear that way," said Russo. "Most of the world still believes it's a ruse, including the North Koreans, who just fired off another test rocket. They're getting better at it everyday."

The President shook his head, frustrated. "So how are things going with the Montana, Bob?"

"We have two carrier task forces moving into the search area now, plus additional ASW elements from Australia, Japan, and the Brits. All countries with subs in the immediate area have agreed to remove their assets until this is over."

"Including the Chinese?"

"No one wants to lose a sub, sir."

"And how about Mrs. Besson? Have we figured out how she's communicating with her husband yet?"

"Not that I know of. I know Charlotte Ramsey and Admiral McCracken are still working on it."

"But you do believe the men on the sub are monitoring the news?"

"Yes, sir. We still use it for our own communications sometimes. They can watch it on the internet if they're in a service area."

The president checked his watch. "Okay, gentlemen, I have another meeting. Tom, would you stay behind for a minute please?"

The Secretary of Defense and Tony Russo left, and the president turned to his DNI. "Has Mrs. Besson tried to meet with the press yet?"

"No, you want me to make it happen?"

"Yeah, we might as well get on it. And you'd better make sure she has some security if she goes out in public. Anything new on the conspiracy theory?"

"Admiral McCracken believes it may involve one of his subordinates, Vice Admiral Acker. But the evidence so far is only circumstantial."

"And how about our own staff?"

"Nothing so far, but Acker is a close personal friend of General

Hayden's, and they do spend a lot of time on the phone together."

"Have you listened in on that?"

"Yes, sir. Nothing definitive yet."

"But there is something?"

"Their conversations seem a little stilted, in my opinion."

"Like?"

"Too controlled, devoid of opinion. We all go off about something with our friends, but there's none of that, and we all know Hayden's not someone to hold his tongue."

The president got the point. "Okay, well let's keep on that, and I'd like to review the circumstantial evidence against the vice admiral."

"Very good, sir. I'll get on that right now."

The general left, nodding a greeting to Gary Brockett as he arrived at the office.

"Is she here?" inquired the president.

"Yes, she is!"

"And how is she?"

"Charming, smart and a pain in the ass."

"And her lawyer?"

"Quiet and love struck."

The president looked surprised. "You think they're an item?"

"Yes, I do."

"Did she say anything about her husband being shot?"

"Nothing."

"Does she know?"

"Everyone else does."

"Well, maybe she doesn't care."

"Or she already knows he's okay."

"That's a good point," said the president. "Bring her in."

"You want me to stay with you?"

"No. But Tat did tell me to wear a flak jacket."

Gary led Monique into the Oval Office and introduced her to the president before leaving.

"Sit down, please," said the president, joining her in a sitting area separate from his desk. "Would you like some water or coffee or something?"

"No, I'm good, thank you." She looked around the elegant room. "So this is Ground Zero?"

"Ground Zero?" said the president, conjuring up images of a nuclear explosion.

"Where you run the country from."

"Well, I suspect there are a few Congressmen who would disagree with that." He became more personable. "Thank you for coming."

"Thank you for inviting me," said Monique. "Is this conversation being recorded?"

"Absolutely not. It's just you and me in a private meeting. So you must be feeling a lot of stress after everything that's happened?"

"Certainly no more than you are."

"You're right about that. The whole world's on edge."

"Well, it'll be interesting to see if it has any effect on the enemy."

"The enemy?"

"Militant Islam. I see they blew up four more jets yesterday."

"Unfortunately, yes."

"Well, maybe that's all going to change now."

"Do you really think you can threaten these people into changing their ways?"

"Personally, no. I suspect it'll require sending them all to their collective heavenly virgins."

"That's a little excessive, don't you think?" suggested the president, offended by her callousness.

"No," said Monique without hesitation. "I think that after fifty years of trying to impress the values of Western freedoms and inclusivity on the Muslim world, it's pretty obvious they prefer their own separate religious culture, including Sharia law and the dictate that all non-believers must submit to their beliefs or be eradicated."

"That's not the way all Muslims are, Monique, and you know that. The majority are peace-loving people."

Monique smiled. "Well, I find that hard to believe when over ninety percent of all conflicts on the planet today include Muslims killing Muslims, Muslims attacking their non-Muslim neighbors, or militant Muslims terrorizing Westerners who have generously invited them into their countries and given them better lives than they could ever get in their own religious theocracies."

"So if all that's true, do you really want to add more misery to it? Don't you think we should at least try to set a better example?"

"You mean turn the other cheek? Keep making more excuses for an archaic religion that wants to take us all back to the Dark Ages? I've been to Saudi Arabia; I've seen what it's like. Women so brainwashed and intimidated by men, they cover themselves up like they're ashamed of who they are."

"That's just their culture."

"That's right - a culture of misogynistic old men using religion to subjugate over half their population! Every successful country in the world today is a matriarchal society, where women have equal rights to men. But that's not the case in countries practicing Sharia law. Women are second-class citizens all in the name of religion. Did you know you're not even allowed to take a Bible into Saudi Arabia, while they build their mosques all over the world and spread their violent Wahhabi religion? They're the most hypocritical people on the planet." She was getting strident, and finally smiled when she saw the president's eyes glazing over. "Aren't you glad you invited me over?"

The president was surprised by her change of demeanor. "So you're saying this is all about a feminist cause?"

"No, that's just my stuff. My husband's memorandum explains his reasons."

"And you really think he wants to blow up the Middle East?"

"No. I think he just wants them to stop terrorizing our world so he doesn't have to terrorize theirs. It's their choice."

"Did you ever see pictures of Hiroshima and Nagasaki? All that horrendous destruction; survivors with the skin burned off their bodies?"

"No, but I saw my sister like that, and a row of children burned beyond recognition in the name of Allah."

The president took a deep breath. "I know you've been through a terrible time, Monique, and I sympathize with that, but it's not going to help the world killing millions of people for revenge. We have to be more tolerant than that, as individuals and as a nation."

"So here we go again!" snapped Monique. "Every time some militant Muslims kill Americans, the first thing our presidents do is go to a mosque, then lecture the whole nation on tolerance, and never say a damn thing about the religion that caused it! Why don't you lecture the Muslims?"

"It's not their religion, Monique; it's just a few militants that have perverted the teachings."

"It's not just a few men, Mr. President. It's the teachings of their leaders. Every week for forty years, the ayatollahs of Iran have led tens of thousands of their followers chanting, 'Death to America! Death to Israel!' And they're that nation's spiritual leaders, their chosen men of God! Can you imagine if the Pope did the same thing? The whole world would go crazy. And that's just the Shias! There are also millions of Wahhabi Sunnis who believe killing infidels, which includes you and me, is their religious duty!"

"I don't believe there are millions of people like that, Monique."

"Well, it sure as hell looks like it to the rest of the world! We have people coming here from every country on the planet, and the only ones trying to kill us are militant Muslims!"

The president was getting tired of it and said, "Well, I can see we're never going to agree on any of this, so...."

"...So what don't you agree with?" interrupted Monique. "Tell me one thing I've said that isn't true!"

"They're other countries, Monique. It's not my job to tell them how to live their lives." He was getting frustrated. "So let me get to the point of why I invited you here. As the president of the country, I'm offering your husband and his crew, and yourself if you're involved in this, full presidential pardons if you return the Montana and all of its weapons back to the Navy, and I'm going to give you forty-eight hours to make that decision and respond."

"So you want to let them off the hook?"

"No. I want to stop millions of people from being killed and a whole part of the planet from being destroyed for nothing more than hate."

"My husband and his men are not doing this for hate, Mr. President. They're doing it for love. For love of their country, love of its values, and love of its freedoms."

"Well, it's your choice now," said the president. "You have forty-eight hours to make a decision." He stood up and opened the door to Gary's office, ending the meeting. "Gary will give you a private number where you can reach him with your decision."

"Forty-eight hours is not a very long time."

"Considering the circumstances, I think it's long enough. Thank you for your time."

"Thank you for yours," said Monique, starting away.

But the president hadn't finished. "Does your husband believe in God?"

"Not anymore. They do it in the name of God; he's doing it because he no longer believes in God."

She left with Gary and the president poured himself a glass of water, calming himself. He had a whole country that needed rebuilding, but he spent ninety percent of his days dealing with militant Islam, the

Middle East, and now a new American terrorist group.

There was a knock at the door, and his wife peered into the room. "You okay?"

"Yeah, come in."

"So how did it go?"

"It was like being in a meeting with Gloria Steinem and Rush Limbaugh on steroids!"

Tatiana smiled. "Did you come to a resolution?"

"I offered her and all the officers on the sub presidential pardons if they surrender their vessel with all of its weapons intact."

"Wow, I didn't see that coming! That's going to drive a lot of people crazy."

"I don't care. I just want to get that sub back before something stupid happens. She's as fanatical as the people she wants to destroy."

"And if they don't do it?"

"They have to do it," said the president. "Positive thinking, right?"

CHAPTER 56

MONIQUE had Gary Brockett drop her and her lawyer two blocks from their hotel so they could walk back in privacy.

"So how was he?" asked Sean, watching the car leave.

"Typical politician looking for an easy way out."

"And what was that?"

"He wants to give all the men on the sub presidential pardons if they'll surrender with the sub."

"Well, that's good, isn't it?"

"Depends on how you see the future."

"So you don't think it's a good idea?"

"It doesn't matter what I think, Sean. It's what John and his men think."

"But the president wants you to tell them about it?"

"Yes."

"So he knows you're in touch with them?"

"It appears that way, yes."

Sean shook his head. "You're on dangerous ground with this, Moe. I'm telling you."

"He also said he'd give me a personal pardon if I needed it. Can he do that?"

"Article II, Section 2 of the Constitution. It gives him the right to pardon anyone he wants, but he can face a lot of criticism if he misuses it."

A crowd of reporters waiting in front of the hotel saw Monique approaching and quickly surrounded her and Sean with flashing cameras and a barrage of questions.

"Mrs. Besson, does your husband really want to blow up the Middle East?"

"Did you see the president?"

"Do they have the codes yet?"

"What do you think of your husband's memorandum?"

Monique seemed amused by the sea of humanity, but Sean quickly pushed her through the crowd, "Keep going! Get into the hotel!" He knocked aside a couple of overzealous cameramen, yelling, "Hey, knock it off! We're not doing interviews!" In just a moment, they were inside the sanctuary of the hotel where Monique seemed calm and amused by it all.

"How did they know we were here?"

"We're in Washington. Everyone knows everything." They headed for the elevators, passing the front desk where a clerk spoke to Sean.

"We have some messages for you, Mr. Lariat."

"I'll get them later."

"No, get them now," said Monique.

Sean acquiesced and collected his mail, looking at it as they entered an empty elevator.

"What does it say?"

"They want you to go on television."

"Who?"

"Looks like all the networks and cable channels! This one's offering you money for an exclusive interview."

"How much?" said Monique.

"It doesn't matter how much, Moe. You can't do it. You can't risk incriminating yourself."

"I have to do it, Sean," she lowered her voice. "That's the only way I can reach John right now."

Sean looked surprised. “He watches the news?”

“Of course he watches the news. The whole world’s watching the news! I have to tell him about the president’s offer.”

“So which channel do you want to go on?”

“Which one has the best ratings?”

“Whichever one does the interview. You want a male or female reporter?”

“How about we just have a press conference and I speak to everyone?”

“You’ll never get to say anything. Everyone’ll be interrupting and yelling.”

“Not if we set it up right. The president has them all the time.”

“He has a selected group, Moe!”

“Well, we’ll select ours as well!”

“And how about the foreign press?”

“I think we should include everyone.”

“And security?”

“Everyone gets searched before they come in, just like at the White House. And I’ll still have you and John and his submarine to protect me.” And there it was again; that subtle threat of unimaginable consequences, and Sean felt another chill run up his spine.

Chapter 57

CHARLOTTE Ramsey arrived at the Seattle control center early and started tidying up all the loose ends of her investigation into Monique Besson, Tommy Chang, and the two known code carriers. After conversations with Admiral McCracken, Sid Bailey, and Lieutenant Silver, it was obvious that their efforts to stop the launch codes from reaching the Montana had failed, even though the president had not yet announced that fact.

So what could she do? Sid had suggested following up on the first carrier in Australia, so after reviewing the video footage Fenwick had sent from Sydney station, including the brief image of the carrier looking up at the sky, she decided to process it through the newest face recognition software developed at the agency. It was infinitely more advanced than anything Fenwick had in Australia, and with the possibility that the carrier did have an East European accent and professional training, she thought it might be something worth pursuing.

Even though the agency had successfully tracked the Montana to Bali, the failure to interdict the second set of codes weighed heavy on everyone.

Charlotte was surprised to see Matt Weston and Sarah Singh approaching her office, looking enthusiastic about something.

"Can we speak with you for a minute?"

"Sure, come in, take a seat," said Charlotte, enjoying their youthful aura. "What happened?"

"We got a call yesterday from a man on Bainbridge Island who said he found blood in his boat and believed it had been used in a crime or something. So we took the ferry over and checked it out and just got the blood report back. It's Thomas Chang's. And what's even more interesting is that the boat and a large fuel tank in the boat house both have multiple fingerprints of Monique Besson on them."

"When did the man discover this?" questioned Charlotte, realizing the possibilities.

"He just came back from a vacation in Mexico yesterday," said Sarah. "And he also said he was a personal friend of Mrs. Besson, who works with his wife in a real estate company. He said Mrs. Besson had been out on the boat multiple times, but also noted she had never been near the fuel tank."

"Excellent work, guys!" Charlotte was pleased not only with their effort, but also with the possibility of being able to arrest Mrs. Besson. "What is the name of this man?"

"Jack Haber," said Matt. "Fortunately, he keeps a log of the hours he puts on the boat, which revealed that someone has put an additional six hours on it since he last took it out."

"How far would that take someone?"

"All the way to the Fairview Jetty, with plenty left over to go to Staley Combs' house and back to Bainbridge."

"So you think she got the codes from Chang and possibly killed him?"

"It would certainly answer a lot of questions," said Matt.

"And how about the girl in the car? Who killed her?"

"Either Chang or Mrs. Besson."

"Okay, we still have a search warrant for the Besson house, so why don't you see if you can find the bike outfit she was wearing when she left the house?"

"We already did that," said Matt, feeling a little uncomfortable.

"You already went there?"

"We had agents Siebert and Kelly check it out, and they found the bike leggings which also have traces of Chang's blood on them."

"Well that was enterprising of you," said Charlotte.

Sarah sensed they had overstepped their mark and tried to ameliorate their position. "We just tried to anticipate what you would need, ma'am."

"Okay," said Charlotte, letting it go. "Why don't you get with Sid, review the evidence, and if everything's okay, get a warrant for Mrs. Besson's arrest."

General Pierce was in another meeting with the president when Charlotte called and told him about the new evidence against Mrs. Besson. Murder was a serious accusation, and when Pierce mentioned it to the president, he quickly got on the phone.

"Charlotte, I don't want you issuing any arrest warrant for Mrs. Besson, and I want the whole investigation against her shut down until I tell you otherwise. I just offered her and her husband and all the mutineers presidential pardons if they surrender the sub, and I don't want anything interfering with that, you understand?"

It was a straightforward request, but Charlotte couldn't help her natural law-and-order response. "Yes, sir, but she did murder two people, and we can prove it!"

"I don't care if she murdered twenty fucking people!" erupted the president. "I'm trying to save millions! If you want to help resolve this issue, find out who the conspirators are. In the meantime, Mrs. Besson is the only connection I have with the Montana, and I want her case shut down without a leak! You understand?"

"Yes, sir, I understand."

Charlotte had retreated into her docile public service mode - into that state of being that all people in government and big businesses are conditioned to accept. It was an act of will made easy with practice, and she quickly informed Sid, Matt, and Sarah to drop the case and ask no more questions.

It had been a long, intense week for Charlotte, and after a brief conversation with Sid, she decided to fly back to Washington where the Montana issue was becoming an international crisis on a grander scale than the reach of her own agency. If there were any more surprises, she wanted to be there personally for the president and more importantly, she wanted to keep an eye on the murderess, Monique Besson.

Chapter 58

SEAN Lariat was a good organizer, and by late afternoon, he had arranged for a press conference in a small banquet room at the hotel where he was staying with Monique. Over thirty reporters from US news outlets and members of the foreign press were invited, all brimming with expectation. At first, it seemed like it was going to be an expensive undertaking with all of the required security, but after a call by Monique to her new best friend, Gary Brockett, the White House agreed to provide metal detectors and private security officers for the event.

For Monique, the whole affair was a grand coming out ceremony - a chance to be center stage and watched by the entire world, including her husband. Gary Brockett was invited and joined the crowd of reporters and cameramen gathered in the small room. He was the only government official present and took pleasure in his anonymity in the distracted crowd.

At precisely six pm, Sean checked his watch, whispered to Monique, "Be careful with your words," then stepped up to the mic on a dais and faced the world.

"Ladies and gentlemen, may I have your attention please! My name is Sean Lariat; I'm Mrs. Besson's personal lawyer. As you all know, this is a private press conference, and each of you has been given a number, which is now inside this bowl," he indicated a transparent container next to the dais. "For fairness in the proceedings, Mrs. Besson will take one number at a time, and the person it represents will ask their questions, which will be limited to two per person. We have a lot of people here, so please do not exceed your allotted time. With that understood, may I introduce you to Mrs. Monique Besson."

Monique stepped up to the dais, placed the picture of her and her sister on top of it, adjusted the mic then faced the cameras. She was now wearing a simple, flattering skirt and blouse that made her look young and vulnerable.

"Thank you all for coming. As you know, my husband is one of the fifteen officers that have taken control of the nuclear missile submarine Montana. So before I start answering your questions, I'd like to take this moment to speak directly to my husband, John, and his crew, who I hope are watching this news conference. This morning, I had a private meeting with the President of the United States, who has offered to give all of you presidential pardons if you will surrender your vessel back to the Navy with all of its weapons intact. This offer lasts for 48-hours, which will give you time to make your decision and notify your commanding officer. The president said this is a one-time offer and hopes you will respond to it positively. Okay, now that's out of the way, I'll take the first number and question." She lifted a slip of paper from the glass bowl. "Number fifteen."

A female reporter stood up taking a floor mic from a sound technician. "How do you think your husband is going to respond to the president's offer?"

"I'd like to know the answer to that myself," said Monique, "but so far, I have no idea!"

"So you know nothing about what your husband is thinking or doing, even though you live with him, and he's the instigator of this mutiny?"

"My husband spends six months of the year under the sea with his men, which is more time than I get to spend with him. So the answer to your question is 'No, I don't know.'" She drew another number from the bowl as Charlotte Ramsey entered the back of the room and stood watching her. She was a menacing presence, but Monique was not disturbed by her cold stare. She had the whole world as her audience now, and there was nothing the FBI could do about it.

"Number seven."

A Muslim woman wearing a hijab took the mic. She was intense and focused. "I understand your sister was reputedly killed by Islamic terrorists, and…."

Monique cut her off. "Not 'reputedly', ma'am. The man that murdered my sister and killed over one thousand people, including women and children, took great pleasure in telling the world that he did it in the name of Allah."

"So is that the reason your husband is doing all of this?"

"I'm sure that could be part of it, but his memorandum lists a lot more reasons than that! As he said, over ninety percent of all conflicts on the planet today involve militant Muslims."

"And how about Israel and its part in all of this? What do you say to all the Palestinian people who have had their lands overrun by Jews?"

"Get used to it! In the time six million Jews have immigrated to Israel, tens of millions of Muslims have come to live in the West. In fact, the West has been infinitely more generous and accepting of Muslims coming to their countries than any Muslim country has been to either Jews or Christians. It's Muslims that are systematically murdering, beheading, and eliminating Jews and Christians and any other non-Muslim people from Middle Eastern lands where they have lived for centuries. And they're doing it in the name of your religion!"

"So you think this justifies killing millions of people?"

Sean interrupted her. "You've already asked three questions ma'am."

"It's okay," said Monique. "I think killing any people is a terrible thing, but the ultimate decision isn't my husband's anymore; it's in the hands of militant Islamists. If they want to continue their war of terror against non-Muslims around the world, they now know the consequences."

"It is the West that has caused all of these problems - their colonization and constant meddling in the Middle East."

"If I remember my history ma'am, Muslims have had their fair share of invading and colonizing other people's lands. At least you got something back from the West."

"And what was that? Your wonderful social values? A country that puts more people in prison than any other country on earth?"

"No. You got the greatest handout in history. What did you do to improve the world in the last thousand years? Everything that makes your life better comes from the West! The medicines that keep your children and families alive, electricity, phones, computers, televisions, refrigerators, cars, planes, weather satellites, the internet...what did you discover to make the world a better place? It was even Westerners that invented the internal combustion engine that gave your oil value then showed you how to find it and get it out of the ground. And now you want to destroy those very same people, and you know why? Because you can't compete with them! Because you have an archaic misogynistic religion that keeps you living in the Dark Ages! I've been to Saudi Arabia. I've seen how the richest Muslim nation in the world treats its women. And you're one of them! Why don't you stand up and defend your rights in your own country? Well I'll tell you why! Because they'll kill you if you do!"

Sean could feel the tension and interceded. "Okay, let's move on to the next question, please."

"Number twenty," said Monique, still fuming.

A famous liberal cable pundit took the mic. He was as passionate and self -aggrandizing as Monique and the Muslim reporter.

"Don't you see how completely mad all of this is? Only crazy people would think about using nuclear weapons! Now you're talking about it like it's some sort of game of 'Gotcha!' If you do this, you'll go down in history as the most despised people that ever lived. You're an embarrassment to the human race!"

"And your question is?" said Monique, cool as a cucumber.

"The question is, WHY?? Why would you do something like this?"

"Because we can and because they will if they get the chance. They do it in the name of God and for a future in heaven. They don't care about this world, and they don't give a damn about your values."

"And who are THEY?" said the pundit. "Who are you talking about!"

"You want an example? How about Boko Haram strapping bombs onto 12-year-old girls and sending them into marketplaces to kill civilians in the name of Mohammed. So far they've killed over 20,000 people. I'm surprised you don't talk about that considering the fact that you spend every day of your life pontificating about it on your television program. But of course you never use the words 'militant Islam', you just dance around it like you're doing now."

"You're a cancer on the world!" retorted the pundit, waving his finger defiantly.

"No, militant Islam is the cancer, and people like you making excuses for them. Every other religion and political group on the planet manages to get along except for the people you're defending."

She took the next slip of paper. "Number nineteen."

Another male reporter took the mic. "Many people believe this whole thing with the Montana is just a ploy by the US government to stop any more attacks by militants. What's your opinion about that and did the president say anything about it in your meeting?"

"No, he didn't mention it. But if it is just a ploy, I'll be the first person to celebrate that fact."

"But you don't believe that's the case?"

"No. The military has fought three questionable wars in Vietnam, Afghanistan, and Iraq and never questioned their political leaders, so

I doubt they're going to start doing it now."

"Then you believe this is your husband's personal war?"

Sean gave her a cautionary glance, "I don't know the answer to that."

As the questions and answers took place, Charlotte surveyed the room. Every person present appeared to have a legitimate reason to be there, except for one middle-aged woman sitting near the front. At first Charlotte couldn't see the woman's face, but when she looked back at the next reporter asking a question, she realized she had seen her before, but she couldn't remember where. It had to be someone she'd seen recently, and she suddenly had an epiphany. *Photographs!* She'd seen the face in a photograph and quickly flipped through her iPhone, finding the woman's image on a picture she had photographed in Monique's house. She was with a man in front of the Houses of Parliament posing with the Bessons, and Charlotte remembered something Monique had said. She'd gone to London and met the security chief of the airline her sister worked for...Jewish name...*Mo, Mo, Moshi...Moshi Ilyche.* It was a Russian name, and Fenwick had said the first carrier had an East European accent. Charlotte quickly checked her emails for any response from her Face Recognition Department on the Australian carrier, and there he was; an almost perfect facsimile of the man in the Sydney station video.

Charlotte quickly exited the conference room into the hotel lobby and called Sid.

"I got the first carrier! His name's Moshi Ilyche. Worked as Head of Security for Air West in London when Besson's sister was killed. His wife's sitting right here in the press conference. You watching it?"

"Yes, we are," said Sid, observing a television in his office with Lieutenant Silver. "What's she doing there?"

"No idea. Maybe her husband's here, but I bet she's the third carrier."

"Is he still with the airline?"

"No, he resigned after the attack. I'll get someone to follow her when she leaves. So what do you think of the press conference?"

"Never seen anything like it! Does the president know she probably killed two people?"

"Yes, he does."

"So does she get a pardon as well?"

"I don't know. I'm waiting to find out."

As she was speaking, the soundman appeared from the conference room, spoke briefly to the two guards at the door, then retrieved another mic in its case from a cart parked in a side hallway attended by another technician. It all seemed natural, but as the soundman returned to the conference room, the second technician quickly retreated from the building. *What was that all about*? Charlotte felt her instincts come alive and quickly got off the phone, approaching the door guards, flashing her badge.

"What did the sound guy want?"

"New mic."

"Did you check it?"

"Yes, it was in a box."

"And did you check the box?"

As the guard hesitated with his answer, Monique finished answering another question in the conference room and was interrupted by the soundman. "I need to change your mic; I'm sorry. It's giving a bad feed. Just take a second."

Monique let him replace the mic, which he then tested. "Testing… one, two, three…can you hear me?"

Someone in the room said, "Yes."

"Okay, that's good. I just wanted to say God is great, and his warriors are everywhere! Allah Akbar!!" He pulled a small, snub-nosed revolver from the mic box and shot Monique in the chest – once, twice, three times.

Everyone dived to the floor as Charlotte returned to the room pulling her own pistol. "Put down the gun!"

The soundman spun around, shooting at Charlotte, hitting her in the arm before she popped three bullets into his brain and sent him to Allah. The noise of firing guns and screaming people echoed through the hotel. The door guards rushed in, wielding their weapons as people crawled away from the violence in terror. Gary Brockett was one of the first to Monique, now lying on the floor, drenched in blood with Sean pumping her chest, trying to resuscitate her.

"She's not breathing!"

"Blow into her mouth!" said Gary, calling for help on his phone.

A cameraman swooped in for a close shot of Monique, then panned down to the picture of her and her sister lying on the floor in a pool of blood.

"Get out of here!" yelled Gary, pushing him away.

Two miles away the president's wife hurried into the open door of the Oval Office where her husband and several of his national security advisors stood watching the chaos of the shooting on television.

"What happened?" said Tatiana to the president's secretary, Betty.

"Someone just shot Mrs. Besson!"

"Oh, my God!"

The president turned to General Pierce, furious. "Didn't I tell you to put guards with her?"

"They were there, sir!"

"Well what the hell were they doing?!"

A phone rang and Betty held it out to the president, "It's Gary, he's at the hotel."

The president grabbed the phone, concerned. "You okay?"

Gary had moved back from Mrs. Besson as the medics arrived. "I'm good, but Monique Besson's dead."

"You sure about that?"

"Looking right at her. Charlotte Ramsey got shot as well."

"What was she doing there?"

"I don't know, but she was the one that killed the shooter."

"Is she okay?"

"They're attending to her now. She's talking on her phone, so I guess she's okay. Could you see it on the TV?"

"Yes, the whole world saw it, and that probably includes her husband!"

"So what are you going to do?"

"I don't know what I'm gonna do! I just lost my only contact with a bunch of people that are probably going to blow up the whole fucking world! Just check on Charlotte and come back here." He hung up the phone and turned to the others. "Mrs. Besson's dead, and Charlotte Ramsey was shot as well. She's the one that killed the shooter." He turned to the Secretary of Defense and Tony Russo. "You need to call an NSC meeting and see what sort of response we can come up with if they launch on the Middle East and can everyone get out of here so I can have a private conversation?" He was angry, and everyone left in a hurry except for General Pierce who he told to stay behind.

"I read Admiral McCracken's report on Acker, and it's pretty incriminating. Did you read it?"

"Several times."

"And what do you think?"

"I think he's involved, but we've been holding out, hoping he may lead us to some others."

The president shook his head, frustrated. "He knows he's being watched, Tom! This is just a waste of time. I want him arrested and forced to tell us what the hell's going on! I need to communicate with that sub, now!"

"He's not going to tell us anything we need to know, sir."

"And you already know that??"

"It's just the way it is. He won't betray his men, and they won't betray him."

"The corps before anyone?"

"That's what I believe."

"That's what you believe?" asked the president confrontationally.

"No, that's what I believe he will do, sir," said Pierce, correcting himself.

"Well, I'm the Commander in Chief of all US forces in the whole fucking world, and I'm ordering you to arrest Vice Admiral Acker now, and bring him here so I can confront the son of a bitch! Can you do that?"

"Yes, sir. I'll get right on it."

He started away and the president called after him. "And forget about your code of honor, Tom. I've got one more day before that sub goes operational, and I want her stopped!"

Chapter 59

Gary Brockett saw Charlotte Ramsey leaving the bloody conference room into the hotel lobby, which was already a sea of cops and shaken reporters calling their networks around the world. She was being followed by a medic, insisting she should be in a wheelchair.

"I walked in here, and I'm walking out!"

"You could go into shock, ma'am. I'm not supposed to let you go like this!"

"I've been shot before; don't worry about it." She was distracted looking for Moshi's wife Gwen when Gary approached her.

"Charlotte – Gary Brockett. I just spoke to the president, and he asked me to check and see how you're doing?"

"I'm fine. Bullet went between the radius and ulna."

She finally saw Gwen exiting the hotel and followed after her.

"Do you have a car?"

"Right here," Gary indicated his sedan parked next to the hotel entrance with its privileged government license plate.

"Can you give me a ride?"

"Sure. You want to go to the hospital?"

"In a minute." She slid into Gary's sedan, watching Gwen get into a taxi on the street. "You see that lady over there…getting into the taxi?"

"Yes."

"You need to follow her. LET'S GO!"

Gary was surprised by her decisiveness, and quickly pulled away from the hotel, following the cab down the busy street. "Who is she?"

"Possible Montana conspirator. Hopefully, she'll lead us to her husband." As she was speaking she dialed FBI headquarters and spoke to an associate. "Paul!"

"Charlotte? I thought you were in Seattle?"

"Just got off the plane. I need some backup following a lead. City Taxi, moving south on Georgia Avenue. I'm in a black government sedan three vehicles back, license number…?" She turned to Gary.

"WH 267."

"WH 267. Its just surveillance. I don't want the locals involved."

"Aerial surveillance on its way. I'll get some manpower into the area now."

Charlotte hung up and pulled out her pistol, popping out its cartridge, checking its remaining load before returning it to its holster.

"You think these people are dangerous?"

"Anyone losing their freedom usually is. Do you have anything in here for pain?"

"I've got some Scotch," said Gary, pulling a flask from his inside jacket pocket.

"That's it?"

"It's good Scotch."

Charlotte took a swig and caught her breath. "Wow, that's strong!"

"Presidential stand-by."

Charlotte took another slug as the taxi they were following pulled to the curb in front of a shopping arcade. Gary cursed and went for his brakes, but Charlotte intervened.

"Don't stop! Keep going. Turn right at the next corner." She watched Gwen exit the taxi and start into the arcade as Gary turned the corner and stopped in the red zone. "Okay she's going into the arcade. Leave the car here and go around back; make sure she doesn't come out the other side. This is her husband, and my number." She gave him a card and showed him a picture of Moshi on her iPhone. "Call me if you see either of them." She left and Gary was on his own, hurrying up the side street to the next corner. He was already breathing hard when he turned onto the next street and came face to face with Gwen and her husband Moshi, passing him in the opposite direction. Fortunately they didn't know who he was, and Gary could hear Moshi talking on his phone as they passed.

"...Okay, I can see you now. Just hold it out."

Gary looked back and saw Moshi taking an envelope from a man in a passing car. It all happened so fast all he could see of the driver was his arm as he continued away. He was wearing a dark blue sweat suit and had one of those narrow band heart monitors on his wrist. Excited by his discovery, Gary quickly grabbed Charlotte's card and dialed her number as he followed the fast moving couple down the busy street.

"Hello? Charlotte?"

"Charlotte who?" said a stranger.

Gary realized he had misdialed, and tried again as Moshi and Gwen started down some steps into the city subway.

"Charlotte?"

"Did you see her?" asked Charlotte, answering his call.

"She's with her husband, and he just took an envelope from a man passing in a car!"

"Did you get the license number?"

"No. They're going into the subway now!"

"What street?"

"Shaw Howard Metro. 8th and S. I'm following them down." He ran down the steps trying to keep up with the fit couple, but the turnstile stopped him in his tracks. It took him a moment to realize he needed to pay, but couldn't figure it out. Moshi and Gwen had already reached the station platform below, so he cursed and climbed over the turnstile, huffing and puffing.

"You okay?" said Charlotte running towards him.

"I'm going down to the platform now! They're getting on a train!"

"Which track?"

"I don't know! I've never been down here before!"

"Read the sign!"

"Seven! They're on the train!"

"Okay, keep with them! I'm coming down the stairs!"

A bell sounded, indicating the train was leaving. Gary couldn't wait any longer, and stepped onto a carriage two cars back from Moshi and Gwen. "Okay, I'm on the train. Now what do I do...Charlotte? Charlotte are you there?" His phone had cut off. The train pulled out of the station, and he sat down trying to redial when a large, meaty hand removed the phone from his fingers.

"It won't work down here." Gary looked up and saw Moshi Ilyche sit next to him. He was large and menacing, and Gary's blood pressure shot through the roof. He was having a panic attack, and turned bright red trying to catch his breath. Even Moshi became concerned. "You okay?"

Gary nodded, pulling out a bottle of pills, swallowing two of them. "Angina."

"Well, you need to calm down."

"That's what I'm trying to do!" His phone began to play The William Tell Overture, and Moshi answered it.

"Hello?"

"Who's this?" said Charlotte, arriving on the empty platform.

"A good Samaritan. Your friend's having heart problems, so I'm trying to calm him down."

"Can I speak to him please?"

"No. But you can tell your president there's going to be retaliation for the four downed Western jets and what just happened to Mrs. Besson."

"What are you talking about?"

"You know exactly what I'm talking about. You just haven't

adjusted to the new reality yet." He switched off the phone and turned to Gary as the train stopped at another station.

"Go and get some help. And lose some weight."

Gary stood up. "Can I have my phone back, please?"

Moshi finally lost his patience "No, just get out of here."

Gary retreated from the train and watched the Russian and his wife disappear down the station tunnel.

Chapter 60

ADMIRAL McCracken spent his entire day in the Hawaii command center deploying two carrier strike groups (CSGs) into the Sunda Subduction Zone, better known as the Java Trench. With additional assets from Britain, Australia, and Japan, there were now over one hundred and thirty aircraft and thirty-seven ships searching the area for the elusive Montana. But the admiral was still uncertain. Acker had originally suggested the subduction zone as the perfect place to launch an attack on the Middle East, and the question was would he have mentioned that if they were really going to use that area?

There was also the further consideration of Captain Besson and his reaction to the P8A's attack. What would he do? He was not given command of an *Ohio*-class submarine because he was predictable. In fact, unpredictability was his greatest asset. So the admiral tried to put himself into the mind of the Montana's commander. He would obviously anticipate the flotilla of anti-submarine assets arrayed against him, so how else could he proceed to the Middle East launch zone?

He could sail west into an area north of the Chagos Islands, but that could put him in jeopardy from other Naval assets approaching from the Atlantic command and the American/British base in Diego Garcia. Or he could sail north between Java and Bali and proceed west to the Sunda Strait, a narrow channel between Java and Sumatra, leading back into the subduction zone north of McCracken's present deployment.

It would be a hazardous journey taking the huge Montana through the shallow Java Sea and the narrow Sunda channel, but it was possible. Possible enough for McCracken to secretly re-direct Commander Harry Hamasaki and his *Virginia*-class nuclear attack submarine, presently deployed in the Nimitz battle group into the channel to lay in wait for Besson's possible appearance.

Destroying the Montana was now an obsession with McCracken, a need made even more imperative when he saw Mrs. Besson assassinated on television, and received a call from General Pierce informing him that the ODNI (Office of the Director of National Intelligence) had cracked the encryption on Staley Combs' phone. With the code broken, it didn't take long to trace the sushi chef's number in the system, and verify he had exchanged several text messages with the veteran, including times and coordinates coinciding exactly with the Montana's appearance in Fiji and its deployment to the coast of Australia. It was devastating evidence, and McCracken felt relieved that today was Acker's day off in the rotation.

"So what do you want to do?" questioned the admiral, now sitting in his office, speaking with General Pierce on a secure line. "We're obviously going to have to tell Stossel and everyone else about this."

"Not necessarily," said Pierce. "I think we should try and keep this conspiracy thing secret and come up with some other way to deal with it. The whole world already believes our government's involved, so something like this could easily destroy all of our careers, including the president's."

"Did you tell him that?"

"I tried to, but the only thing he can think about right now is stopping the Montana. This could be a big embarrassment for the service, Jay. You know as well as I do, there's no way we're going to keep all this secret once it starts. There's going to be Senate hearings, independent investigations, subpoenas, court martials, and they're already talking about more oversight."

"So how do you want to handle it?"

The general paused for a moment then said, "I think we need to take care of it in-house. You've got a good man in Darden; he's old school, and he'll understand. His father's a good friend of mine."

"And what's the president going to say about that?"

"He doesn't need to know all the details. He's already buried in problems; at least we'll be taking this off his plate. I know it's difficult to do, Jay, but Don Acker's a traitor. He's threatening everything we believe in."

Admiral McCracken had known Acker for over thirty years. Their wives had been best friends; they vacationed together, worked together, shared personal concerns, and problems together, and now it was all going to end in a terrible way.

Lieutenant Darden had already heard about the encryption breakthrough when he picked up McCracken, believing they were going to arrest the vice admiral. At first, the lieutenant wanted to take an extra man with them, but when McCracken suggested there was another way to deal with it, another way that was better for the Navy, better for the country, better for Acker and even the presidency, the lieutenant quickly understood and concurred. Like General Pierce had said, the lieutenant was old school.

"When we get out there, wait in front," said McCracken. "It'll set a parameter, and he'll understand that."

"And what about his wife?"

"Tuesday night's usually girl's night out, so hopefully she'll be out doing that."

Vice Admiral Acker lived in Officer Country, similar to McCracken, but without the spectacular view. It was not the admiral's usual behavior to drop by his friend's house uninvited, but he took a deep breath and rang the doorbell anyway.

Vice Admiral Acker was surprised and apparently pleased to see his commanding officer.

"Jay! What are you doing here? Everything okay?"

"I wondered if I could come in and have a chat?"

"Sure, come in!" said the vice admiral, noting Lieutenant Darden waiting stoically outside as he closed the door.

McCracken entered the pleasantly decorated house and came face-to-face with Acker's wife, Jenny. She was all dressed up and heading for the door herself.

"Jay! How nice to see you!" She gave him an affectionate kiss on the cheek. "He never told me you were coming."

"I just stopped by and surprised him."

"How nice. You can keep him company while I'm out with the girls."

"Where's the meeting tonight?"

"Joan Batista's. We're raising money for the vets."

"Well that's good."

"Yes it is. Next time you're dropping by let me know, and I'll cook your favorite bouillabaisse."

"Sounds good!" said McCracken. "I'll see you later."

"Okay, I'll be back by eleven. You boys have a good time." She gave them both pecks on the cheek and left.

"Come into the living room," said Acker. "You want a drink or something?"

"Sure," said the admiral, sitting on the sofa.

"Usual?"

"Yep."

The vice admiral poured two shots of whiskey and handed him

one, "To us and the hell with everyone else!" He sat, and they both sipped their drinks. "So they didn't get her," said Acker referring to the Montana.

"Nope, looks like she got away clean, and they now have the codes."

"Well that's not good."

"No, it's not."

"So you went around everyone on this new sighting."

"Yeah. The president thinks there's a conspiracy and didn't want the second code carrier tipped off like the first."

"Is that what happened?"

"Yes, it is. Which brings me back to our earlier conversations, Don. Your personal involvement with the Montana's crew, the use of the code name Touché, your inexplicable knowledge of the Russian sub's presence, the use of your exact words in Besson's Memorandum, and now two additional things."

"Which are?" asked the vice admiral quizzically.

"Your daughter's involvement with oil futures..."

"Wow, you've really been looking into things."

"...and your involvement with a sushi chef who provides you with a private phone to send secret, encrypted messages. Messages that discussed the Montana's exact coordinates in Fiji and Australia."

"That's pretty incriminating," agreed the vice admiral, realizing the game was over.

"Yes it is. So unless you've got one hell of an answer for all of this, we're standing on the precipice."

"So what do you want to do, Jay? I guess it's your call."

"We always talked about a day like this, Don. One of those days when you have to do the right thing, the honorable thing, and now it's that day, and it's your decision to make."

"It was all done for good reasons, Jay. You can't let piss ant little terrorists rule the world in the name of political correctness. It's a waste of manpower, a waste of money, and a waste of good American lives.

They believe God's on their side; I know He's on ours or He wouldn't have given us the means to end this."

"It wasn't your decision to make, Don. You know the rules; you know the system. And you know God wouldn't condone something like this anyway. So why don't you tell me how to reach those boys and put an end to all of this?"

"It's too late for that. They're already strapped into their suicide vests."

"And now you're going to destroy the world?"

"We're just going to shake it up a little. Sort out the boys from the men. Put these little fuckers in their place. I'm sorry I put you through this, Jay. I'll need five minutes." He finished his drink and left into the bedroom side of the house. It was the last time McCracken would see his old friend alive, and he poured himself another drink. He was running on automatic pilot now, falling back on the military conditioning of honor and order to hold himself together. Every passing second now felt like an eternity, and he stepped out into the back garden breathing in the night air.

Jenny Acker was already a mile from the house when she received her husband's call and smiled. "What did you lose now?"

"You need to come home."

"What is it?" asked Jenny, sensing the resignation in his voice.

"Just come back, okay?"

He hung up, and Jen realized the world, as she knew it, was coming to an end. She had listened to her husband's diatribes about politicians, political correctness, and the Middle East for years, and knew it was all coming back to haunt them now. She was a good wife, a loyal wife, and loved her husband beyond all reason, which in the end, was a bad thing because she never confronted him about his obsessions. Not because she didn't have her doubts, but because everything he said seemed to come true. The world really was becoming a nasty place to live. A perpetual war of words and hate and religious disagreements. Everything on the news was death and destruction, so Jenny lived in her own little world, being the perfect wife, the happy, harmonious partner that only accepted joy into her world, and now all that was ending.

It was the last moments of a man's life, and with McCracken sitting in the back garden and Darden waiting in front, the vice admiral dressed in his perfectly pressed white uniform, replete with stripes and medals, then lifted his braided cap from the dresser and placed it on his head. He looked immaculate - the perfect officer in his perfect dress, and he observed himself in the mirror for the last time. It hadn't been a bad life. Unlike many of his comrades, he'd been lucky in battle, lucky in love, lucky in all that he'd done, and the only regret he had was leaving his Jenny. She had been the perfect partner, the perfect mate, and he hoped she would understand he was ultimately a soldier, and the Montana was his final sacrifice for his country.

With white-gloved hands, he retrieved a military pistol hidden in a drawer, checked its load, then stepped into the shower, closed the door, and shot himself in the temple.

The noise of the exploding gunshot shook the house, and echoed across the surrounding hills, heralding the demise of yet another victim of a war that had gone on too long.

Lieutenant Darden took a long drag on his cigarette then extinguished it deliberately beneath his foot. On the other side of the house, Admiral McCracken sat unmoving. He was frozen in place, drained of all feelings and reason. Death in battle was one thing; death as a willful act of honor was something else. But honor was an integral part of a soldier's life, and after a moment, the admiral finished his drink and walked into the master bathroom, where he observed his now-deceased comrade. McCracken had seen men killed in battle, but the grotesquely disfigured face and blood drenched image of his friend slumped in the glass shower seemed to mock everything he ever was. It was as if God in His wrath had destroyed one of His creations in a fit of destructive rage.

Lieutenant Darden was waiting at the front door when McCracken opened it and let him inside.

"He's in the shower. See if you can cover him up. His wife's on her way here." The lieutenant left into the bathroom as the admiral stepped outside and called 9-1-1.

"I need an ambulance at 5 Alakea Street."

"And the reason for the emergency, sir?"

"A man just killed himself."

"And you're sure he's dead?"

"Absolutely sure."

"And your name is, sir?"

"McCracken, James McCracken."

As he switched off the phone, he saw Jen's car returning down the driveway and stepped forward to meet her.

"What happened, Jay? What's he so upset about?"

"He just shot himself, Jenny."

"What are you talking about? I just spoke to him! What did you do to him??" She started for the house, but McCracken grabbed her arm.

"You don't want to go in there, Jen."

"I don't care! I'm going to be with my husband; let me go!"

She was emphatic, and pulled away, heading for the house. McCracken felt trapped and called out for Lieutenant Darden who appeared in the doorway, blocking the entrance.

"You think you can stop me going in my own house?"

"I beg you not to do this Jenny. You don't need to go through this."

Jen could feel the depth of his concern and finally relented.

"What did you say to him? What did you do to make him do this?"

"It doesn't matter any more."

"It matters to me. It's about the Montana, right?" The admiral didn't want to answer her. "Tell me! I need to know!"

"Yes, it's about the Montana. He broke all the rules, Jen. He turned on his own country."

Jenny shook her head, despondent. "I should have told him to stop it! I should have made him stop it! It's not good to hate like that. And now he's gone and all those boys are out there."

"You don't have to think about it anymore, Jenny. I'll make sure you're taken care of. Life will go on."

"You made him kill himself."

"No, he made that decision himself. It was the only honorable choice he had left."

Jen started to cry, and he held her in his arms.

"He was a good person, Jay. He just wanted to stop all of this madness."

Chapter 61

The clock chimed eleven, and the president was still in the Oval Office going over a speech he was supposed to give at the United Nations the following day. His speechwriter, the usually effervescent Maggie Malone, and her assistant Farah Saab, a specialist in Middle Eastern affairs, both looked tired. Only the president's National Security Advisor, Tony Russo, still looked fresh and focused in his immaculate three-piece Italian suit.

"...I like McCracken's list of ships and aircraft deployed to the sighting area," said the president, "but I don't want to just talk about the Montana, I want to address the whole issue of state-sponsored terrorism. They're all whining about our terrorists; I want to talk about theirs!"

"I think that's good," agreed Maggie, "but are you sure you want to go into this whole issue of a Muslim reformation?"

"Yes! We've danced around it too long. Christianity had its reformation, or there wouldn't be any Muslims living in the West right now! They need to clean up their act like everyone else! Join the 21st century and stop teaching all this jihadist nonsense! Is there a reason you're against that?"

"It's just that every Middle East advisor I've spoken to believes it'll create even more conflict between us and the Muslim world."

"We're already in conflict with them," said the president, "and so is the rest of the world! Can you imagine if the Pope started telling two billion Catholics and Christians to wage war against Muslims? It's time to face the facts, guys. If I'm going to make apologies for our terrorists, they can start making apologies for theirs and do something about it…you don't agree, Farah?"

"I think it's the right thing to do, sir. But I don't think it's the right time. I'm a Muslim myself, and I think it'll just become another reason to hate America."

"So once again we have to sacrifice our needs and values and adjust to theirs."

"It's just my opinion, sir. But people are very sensitive about this."

"Yeah well, most Americans are pretty sensitive about it as well. What do you think, Tony?"

"I think you should do it. We're all going to have to deal with it sooner or later."

"Okay," said the president sounding tired. "Let's reconvene on this in the morning. But like I said, the most important thing about this speech is not the United Nations. It's reaching out to the Montana and letting those boys know my offer for amnesty is still available."

Russo and the girls left as Tatiana joined her husband. "Did you hear about Gary?"

"No, what happened?"

"He's in the hospital with Charlotte Ramsey. They think he may have had a heart attack!"

"Are you kidding me?!"

"No, I've been trying to call him, but he's not answering."

The president called his secretary. "Have you heard anything from Gary?"

"He just walked in with Charlotte Ramsey."

"He's here?" asked the president surprised.

"Yes, sir."

"Okay, send them in!" Tat looked as surprised as the president when Gary walked in with the FBI Director, who was now wearing a brace over her bandaged arm. "I thought you guys were in the hospital?"

"We were, but they kicked us out," said Gary.

"And how are you doing, Charlotte? I understand you saved a lot of lives with your quick reaction."

"I'm good, sir."

"Bullet went right through her arm, and she didn't even say anything," said Gary.

"That's because he gave me some Scotch!"

The president grinned to his wife. "I told you it was medicinal! And how you doing, buddy? I heard you had a bit of a scare?"

"Yeah, too much stress and too many doughnuts."

"It's all my fault," said Charlotte. "I commandeered his car and had him follow two people I was tracking, and he had a confrontation."

"A confrontation?" said Tatiana.

"Yeah, I had to tackle the guy to the ground and disarm him."

"Are you kidding?"

"Yes, I'm kidding! I had a panic attack, and they took my phone off me!"

"Who were these people?" asked the president turning to Charlotte.

"Moshi Ilyche and his wife. They were personal friends of the Bessons. He was the first code carrier in Australia, and I believe his wife was the third who finally got through to the Montana in Java. Unfortunately, they both got away, but not before Gary saw Ilyche receive an envelope from a man in a car that we just traced back here to the White House."

"Whose car?" said the president surprised by the implications.

Gary glanced at the door and lowered his voice, "General Pierce."

The president felt a sinking feeling in his stomach. "Are you sure about that?"

"I didn't see his face, but he was wearing a dark blue jogging suit and one of those health-monitoring bracelets I've seen him wearing before."

"Have you told anyone else about this?"

"No, we just found out," said Charlotte. "He checked the car out two hours ago and just returned it."

The president called his secretary, "Do you know if General Pierce is in the building?"

"He just came in, sir. Said he was coming up see you."

"Okay, send him in when he gets here." He turned to the others, "He's coming up to see me now; why don't you guys wait upstairs and let me handle this with Charlotte?"

Gary quickly left with Tatiana, and the president turned to Charlotte. "So, how do you think we should do this?"

"It's just Gary's word against the general's, so it's going to be hard to make a case unless we can find additional evidence."

"I don't have time for that. It's less than 24 hours before the Montana's in range of the Middle East. I need to get to the bottom of this now!"

"It's your call, sir. But I don't think he's going to tell you anything without more evidence against him."

There was a knock at the door, and General Pierce entered wearing a dark blue jogging suit with a distinctive health-monitoring bracelet on his wrist. He was surprised to see the FBI director.

"Charlotte, I thought you'd been shot?"

"Just a light wound."

"Well, that's good to hear."

"She's going to be a national hero," said the president, discreetly observing the bracelet on the DNI's wrist. "Do you need to see me privately?"

"No sir. But it's not good news. I just received a call from Admiral McCracken telling me that Vice Admiral Acker shot himself."

"When did this happen?" inquired the president barely hiding his frustration.

"About an hour ago. The admiral went to pick him up with an

arresting officer, and he said it happened so fast there was nothing they could do to stop it."

"And he just happened to have a loaded weapon available to him when this happened?"

"I don't know the details, sir. He just said there was no time to react."

"So in the last three hours, we've lost the only two people that could possibly put us in contact with the Montana?"

"I'm afraid so, sir. But we do now have the names of the two missing code carriers."

"And who are they?" snapped the president, catching the surprise in Charlotte's eyes.

"They're a husband and wife team from England; Moshi and Gwyneth Ilyche." He checked the name on his phone then realized the information had come from Charlotte's office and tried to recover. "… You know all about this, Charlotte."

Charlotte was stunned by his statement; she had only just discovered those facts herself and realized the Director of National Intelligence was spying on her special FBI unit.

"Yes, but I just got that information, and I'm surprised you already have it."

"Well, I don't know exactly where it came from. It's just one of a thousand bytes of information coming into our office every minute of every day; even I have trouble keeping up with it."

The president knew the DNI was probably spying on the FBI. He had all the tools to spy on anyone he wished, tools the president himself had unlawfully used for his own reasons when it suited him, and he quickly changed the subject.

"So this is potentially another contact with the Montana, Charlotte?"

"Yes, sir. We've already released their profiles to INTERPOL, and they'll be on every television station around the world by tomorrow morning."

"You think they were working with Acker?"

"I think it's a good possibility."

"And you, Tom?"

"I agree. Acker was one of the few people in a position to warn the mutineers we were closing in on their code carriers."

"Okay, well I guess there's nothing else we can do about this tonight, Tom. I'll see you in the morning."

"Very good, sir. Have a good night."

The general started to leave, but the president called after him. "What is that thing you wear on your wrist, Tom?"

"Health monitor. I wear it when I go jogging. It keeps track of how many steps I take, heart rate, and even my blood pressure."

"So what is your blood pressure right now?"

The DNI checked his wristband and smiled. "117/72. Always comes down after exercise."

He left and the president checked the door before turning back to Charlotte.

"So, what do you think?"

"I think he's one of them, and he's definitely spying on my agency."

"Then why did he bring up the carriers if he knew they were your suspects?"

"He made a mistake. He was grandstanding and forgot where the information came from."

"You think he's listening to our conversations?"

"I don't know, but I bet he's wondering why you let him go and kept me here."

"I thought I'd put a little pressure on him." He smiled and Charlotte reciprocated.

"Do you want to share this information with anyone else?"

"I don't trust anyone else. I don't trust the military after what happened with McCracken and Acker, and as far as I'm concerned, the whole DNI's suspect."

"How about the Secretary of Defense?"

"Even if he knew it was a conspiracy, he'd cover it up. And he also recommended Pierce for his job in the first place."

"Can you give me until tomorrow to check him out?"

"I'll give you until after my UN meeting. But you'd better be careful. If these people are willing to kill millions to get what they want, they probably won't stop at you or me. Here's Gary's personal number. It's in his mother's name and hopefully not being monitored."

Chapter 62

THE conspiracy was alive, and the president could literally feel its presence as he lay down to sleep with his wife. It was in the Oval Office, in the Situation Room, in the military and probably festering in the Secret Service assigned to protect his life.

General Pierce had been his closest confidant and advisor; the one man who knew all of the nation's secrets, including the president's personal strengths and peccadilloes. There was no one better placed to organize and administer a military coup than the Director of National Intelligence. He was the keeper of the nation's secrets. The king maker with the power and knowledge to destroy anyone he wished. Darwin's Law of Natural Selection was now running amok in the nation's capitol, where the pursuit of unbridled power had replaced the virtues of public service and the evolved principles that had inspired the nation's original founders.

Tatiana could feel the distressing thoughts coursing through her husband's mind. "You going to be okay?"

"I'm beginning to wonder. Everything I do is being watched, and now the man that knows every secret in our government is the potential leader of this mutiny."

"So why don't you have him arrested?"

"I don't have enough evidence. And I don't know who his accomplices are and besides all of that, Gary told me the man on the train told Charlotte there would be retaliation for what happened to

Mrs. Besson and the four downed jets, and she didn't even mention it to me."

"She was probably distracted, Jack! She'd just been shot! You're getting paranoid!"

"Yeah, it's a form of self-defense!"

"So is sleep. You need to put it out of your mind until tomorrow."

"You mean pretend it's not happening?"

"We all have to sleep, Jack."

"They still don't know how they brought down those four jets, so it could all happen again."

"So why are they still letting people fly??"

"You can't shut down the world. Then they really *have* won. I just hope there are no more attacks before I can reach those boys on the sub."

Chapter 63

HALFWAY around the world Captain Besson stood in the Montana's control center looking over the shoulder of the sub's navigator, tracking the shallow undulating Java seabed on a geographic display with a geo-plot overlay. They were approaching the eastern edge of the Sunda Strait, the fifteen-mile wide channel separating the islands of Java and Sumatra and leading back to the deeper waters of the Indian Ocean and the Sunda Subduction Zone.

Dotted with small islands, abandoned oil derricks and subject to heavy tidal surges, the channel was a dangerous place for all large shipping, including the massive missile sub which was forced perilously close to the surface by the constantly shifting sandbars. It was also a difficult place for the sub's sonar officers, with its multiple convection zones created by the warm waters of the Java Sea, mixing with the colder, deeper waters of the Indian Ocean.

With his wounded arm in a sling and fighting off the effects of pain medicine, Besson knew he was approaching a high-risk zone. It was the perfect place for Admiral McCracken to set a trap, and his XO Garcia shared his concerns. "You think he's waiting for us?"

"I think it's a long shot, but with Acker out of the game, I'm not going to take any chances. The old man's going to try every trick in his book - how we doing on the ferry?"

"Five minutes out. Just cleared the point." The captain turned to his navigator. "We still lined up with the ferry, Mason?"

"Directly in line, sir."

"Okay hold course. Slow turns to eight knots." The helmsman relayed the message to the engine room, and the sub slowed. Besson was living on his instincts now, and he turned to his XO. "Let's load three fish - 2, 3, and 5 - and put a MOSS in 6."

Garcia relayed the order to the weapons officers manning the torpedo tubes at the stern of the sub. Everything was automated, and three MK-48 torpedoes were quickly loaded with a MOSS into the tubes.

The MOSS was a mobile submarine simulator, a decoy torpedo that simulated the Montana's sonar profile. Garcia, like everyone else, was now in charge of multiple procedures, and after checking that the weapons were armed and loaded, he turned back to his CO. "Fish loaded, sir. You want ceilings on the 48s?"

"Twenty feet," said the captain, setting the torpedoes detonators to trigger only below that depth to protect civilian shipping.

It had been a long twenty-four hours, and Besson could feel the tension building as he double-checked the local maps. A mistake now would be catastrophic.

"You think he'll bring in more P8s?" queried Garcia.

"We'll be through the strait before they get here."

The crew of the Montana, including Besson and his XO, were now down to fifteen officers all performing multiple tasks. They had been practicing their new responsibilities since escaping Hawaii, but unlike other notorious mutineers of history, the officers of the Montana still maintained the rigorous discipline and naval procedures necessary to run a vessel as large and complicated as the *Ohio*-class submarine. They were like a super crew, every man united in their cause to destroy militant Islam and the threat it represented to their values, their freedoms, and their way of life. They were also new terrorists in the world motivated by the same all-consuming rage and righteousness that motivated Mohammed's jihadist warriors.

Less than two miles beyond the Sunda Strait in the Indian Ocean, another crew of dedicated warriors manned Captain Hamasaki's SSN-774 fast attack *Virginia*-class submarine. But these men still served the President of the United States and the presumed will of the American people.

Almost as silent as the *Ohio*-class missile subs, the SSN-774 was the Navy's fastest and most agile hunter/killer submarine, and once again Captain Hamasaki was set to confront his archrival, Commander John Besson.

It was a second chance at redemption for Hamasaki, who presently had all of the advantages of surprise as he lay in wait, drifting invisible through the dense convection zones beyond the western edge of the Strait. But waiting itself had its own disadvantages, and with the passage of time, the crew's concentration and acuity slowly diminished. The men had been on station guarding the Strait for over ten hours when an alarm suddenly went off in Sonar.

Startled by the noise, Sonarman Wallace looked up at his screen and yelled a warning, "Full rise on shearwaters! Object in water!"

Everyone on the sub leapt to their stations as the helmsman pulled back on his yoke, lifting the nose of the sub acutely. "Conn, Helm, full rise on shearwaters."

"What is it?!" said Hamasaki, rushing to Wallace's station.

"Debris in the water, sir. Looks like the remains of an oil derrick."

Something slammed into the sub's hull, grating down its length, metal on metal. It was a jarring, life-threatening sound and everyone stood frozen in place until it ended abruptly.

"Check all stations!" yelled the captain.

The order rippled through the sub. Crewmen ran checking every section of the vessel, but there was no apparent breach and the XO finally called all clear. "Shearwaters, prop, towed sonar; all functioning, sir."

It was good news, and Hamasaki resumed the hunt. "Level

shearwaters at one-five-zero."

The Conn Tower repeated his command, leveling the sub at its new designation. Everyone could feel the captain's frustration at the collision, but instead of confronting Sonarman Wallace, he directed his ire at the entire crew.

"Captain Besson is one of the best submariners in the U.S. Navy. He'll be looking for any mistakes he can exploit to destroy you. Before taking command of the Montana, he ran a 774 just like this one. If you underestimate him, it will cost you your lives." His words hung in the air threateningly until Sonarman Wallace picked up the approaching channel ferry on his screen.

"Conn, Sonar, large surface craft bearing one-six-five." Hamaskai peered over the man's shoulder observing the slow moving blip created by the rotating sonar arm.

"Ferry returning to Merak, sir."

It was a regular three-hour service from Sumatra to Java, and Hamasaki was well aware that such an occurrence presented opportunities for someone like Besson. "Keep an eye on it. It could be used as a distraction…what are these clusters?" He indicated another group of ghosting images now appearing on the sonar screen.

"Fishing boats sir. There must be a run in the area."

Hamasaki was well aware that overestimating his rival could be just as dangerous as underestimating him, and he took a deep breath, steadying his nerves. Anxiety was the enemy of concise thinking, and concise thinking was exactly what he needed.

Captain Setya Laksono, Commander of the Merak Channel Ferry knew the waters of the Sunda Strait better than any man alive. He had grown up as a fisherman in the area, his father was a previous captain of the ferry, and he lived and breathed the shifting currents and constantly drifting shoals of the channel. But as much as instinct played a part in the captain's seamanship, he was also a disciplined sailor who stuck to procedures, plying the exact same course through the strait on a daily basis. He was the sort of sailor Besson admired, a man in harmony with the sea around him, and he felt no trepidation in placing his own destiny in the man's hands. In fact, Besson felt like he knew the captain personally after reading his impressive bio on the internet.

"Ferry 1000 yards - closing at twenty knots," said Sonar.

Besson observed the approaching vessel on the sonar screen. "Same heading?"

"Aspect change seven degrees west of ours, sir."

The sound of the ferry's approaching props and engines could now be heard in the Montana. It was time for action, and Besson began his game. "Increase turns to twenty knots - seven degrees left to one-seven-zero degrees."

The Conn Tower and engine room repeated his command, and the sub picked up speed, slowly turning to the exact bearing of the channel ferry.

"Eighteen feet up on shearwater planes," continued Besson. "Steady at twenty-five feet."

The massive sub rose up beneath the fast moving ferry, shadowing her into the strait just twenty feet beneath her racing hull and aqua foils. It was a strange and dangerous place to be, and the crew could literally hear Balinese music from the ferry's speaker system.

Sonarman Wallace took a one-minute bathroom break to nurse his wounds after the oil derrick fiasco. He was one of the best sonar men in the *Virginia*-class fleet and hated sullying his reputation. Interpreting the multitudinous sounds of the undersea world was his specialty, the source of his own personal pride and celebrity. So when he returned to his station and heard a ghosting abnormality ushering from the ferry's sonar, he quickly turned his focus back to his work. The noise was like something he had heard before, something from the distant past: the Naval Academy, ship on ship distortions, a long shot lesson on what could happen if two vessels appeared stacked upon each other, and he suddenly knew what it was.

"Conn, Sonar sir, I'm getting a ghosting image from the ferry." Hamasaki joined him at the screen, listening in on the seaman's earphones.

"Did you check it on the HP?"

"Yes, sir. Said it was a 350 foot vessel riding on hydrofoils, but I think it's more than that."

Hamasaki looked surprised. "You think it's wrong?"

"Yes, sir. The further east she moves from our position the longer this spacing becomes." He pointed to a graph recording the sonar imaging. "Front on it looks the same. The more side we see, the longer it gets. It's extending beyond the vessel."

Hamasaki got the point and called back to the Conn Tower. "Thirty degrees right, come to zero-nine-zero." The helmsman turned the steerage, moving the sub back toward the ferry's bow, and sure enough, the sonar imaging on the graph shortened.

"There it goes, sir." Wallace pointed to the changing image.

Hamasaki looked concerned and called over his XO, "Looks like another vessel riding under the ferry." He showed him the discrepancy in the two positional reads.

"You gotta be kidding!" said the XO. "You think it's the Montana?"

"I think it's a possibility. But he's going to have to pull out before the harbor, so let's get ready. Load four 48s. One, two, five and six. Slow turns to fifteen knots. We'll get him broadside." The orders went out. Torpedoes were loaded into launch tubes; everyone was now running on adrenaline.

They were about to ambush the Montana, but Hamasaki still had his reservations. Could it be this easy? But then again, it wasn't that easy. Only the best sonarman in the Navy would have picked up that ghosting anomaly, and the captain moved from frustration with his sonarman to outright anointment of his skills when the ghosting image of the Montana suddenly drifted back from the ferry and set a separate course.

"There she goes," said Wallace, pointing to the new separate image of the Montana on his screen. "Heading two-seven-zero; twenty knots; descending through one- zero-five… acquisition range one thousand yards."

Hamasaki stayed calm, but beneath it all, he knew he'd remember this moment for the rest of his life. His submarine was still riding the convection zones, invisible to the Montana, and with every advantage in hand, the captain prepared to launch his torpedoes.

"Acquisition two-seven-zero; nine hundred yards. Flood two and six."

The weapons officer flooded the torpedo tubes. "Torpedo tubes two and six ready and loaded. Acquisition two-seven-zero; nine hundred yards."

The rush of water into the torpedo tubes made a distinctive sound, which was quickly picked up by the Montana's sonar operator.

"Torpedo tubes flooding. One-five-zero."

"I've got him," said the Montana's weapons officer, finally picking up the *Virginia*-class sub's image ghosting through the convection zone.

Besson breathed a sigh of relief. He had fired off his MOSS torpedo simulating his separation from the ferry and waited for a response. But as time passed, the ferry approached its harbor, and the seafloor rapidly rose up beneath his sub. It seemed an interminable wait. But his gambit finally paid off when the *Virginia*-class sub revealed her position and fired its torpedoes at the Montana's MOSS. It was a brilliantly executed deceit, and Besson quickly prepared his counterattack.

"Right fifty degrees, down on shearwaters two-zero-zero." The helmsman turned the helm right and pushed the yoke forward, obeying the order.

Sonarman Wallace was still basking in the glory of discovering the Montana when he picked up the sound of Besson's sub flooding its torpedo tubes. At first, he thought it was an echo, an artifact of his own sub's launch procedure. But when it was quickly followed by the unmistakable sound of a torpedo being launched in his direction, he finally saw the real Montana separating from the ferry and realized the enormity of the error he and the captain had made. In their exuberance at finding the Montana, they had not even considered the possibility that Besson had set them up and launched a MOSS.

It was a life threatening revelation, and Hamasaki could read the horror in his sonarman's voice. "Fish in water, sir. Bearing two-four-zero!"

The sub's weapon's officer picked up the same information. "It's coming right at us sir, five hundred feet and closing!"

Hamasaki heard the incoming torpedo's acquisition sonar start pinging off his hull, and tried to take evasive action. But he had made an irreversible mistake, and the last thing he ever heard was his XO yelling, "SECURE ALL HATCHES!" followed by an explosion and a wall of water that crushed every molecule of air out of his being until he ceased to exist.

Captain Besson knew he'd destroyed the *Virginia*-class sub when he heard it breaking up on his sonarman's phones; the core of the reactor rupturing, the violent hiss of water as it hit the radioactive rods. It was a sound he'd only heard in simulations, and he quickly turned back to the business at hand, redirecting his nuclear missile sub back on its crusade to the Middle East. They had just killed 126 U.S. Navy men, and even though it was an act of self-defense, Besson couldn't bear to think about it anymore. Collateral damage was the curse of all contemporary warfare. At least, that was the excuse he made for himself.

After the disappearance of Hamasaki's sub, Admiral McCracken swept the Sunda Strait with aircraft and shallow draft ships, which found an oil slick in the Indian Ocean just west of the Strait with debris from Hamasaki's sub. It was enough evidence for McCracken to come to the conclusion that the *Virginia*-class sub had been destroyed in a confrontation with the Montana. There was, of course, the possibility that the Montana had also been damaged or even destroyed in the same confrontation. But when a P8-A aircraft patrolling the edge of the Java Trench north of the Sunda Strait made fleeting contact with a large submarine bearing the signature of an American *Ohio*-class sub, it became evident that the Montana was still alive.

It was depressing news, and Admiral McCracken informed his senior officer Stossel of the loss. The submarine he had built to protect the free world was now threatening the world it had been designed to protect, and for the first time in his life, the admiral understood the pacifists and anti-nuclear activists who had warned of the potential nuclear holocaust now facing the world. What kind of defense was designed annihilation anyway? What Faustian mind could have created such an idea?

There were no good wars, the admiral had been told by a professor at Annapolis, but winning was at least a consolation for the stupidity of it all. And ironically, as he redirected his assets to defend the people of the Middle East against a weapon of his own making, he questioned his allegiance to the cause. It was, after all, the violent militant religiosity of the Middle East that was responsible for the deadly doppelganger they had created in the new American terrorists.

CHAPTER 64

BANDER El Hashem and Mohammed Al Zahrani were students attending Berkeley University in sunny California. It was a popular destination for many of the thousands of Saudi students studying in the United States, and the university took great care in attending to the needs of its rich Middle Eastern students and their government's generous endowments and grants for the advancement of their preferred Islamic studies.

University life was a wild and emancipating experience for men living beyond the restrictions of the Islamic fundamentalist state, where the police for 'The Promotion of Virtue and Prevention of Vice' kept the sexes apart, and the women permanently covered from head to toe. But ingrained in both of the men were the jihadist teachings of Wahhabi Islam. And as they flaunted their wealth and indulged the promiscuity of Western life, they joined forces with five other Wahhabi Islamists and plotted an attack on the people and the nation they secretly abhorred.

Bander, the leader, was in his third year at the university, and like his hero Osama bin Ladin, he wanted nothing more than to inflict death and destruction on the Great Satan, America; death and destruction for its support of Israel, for its war on Islam in the name of democracy, pluralism, and equal rights for all, including women.

Wahhabism is an indoctrinal faith of pious hate planted in its adherents during childhood, then fixed in place by endless tales of heavenly glory and jihadist victories, which gave Bander's unproductive life a sense of purpose and virtue in an evolving world that contradicted everything he was trained to believe.

Every morning, Bander would rise at dawn, pray at sunrise, then spend his most productive hours conceiving and plotting the intricate means of his attack on America. It had to be something big; it had to be something spectacular to raise the money and support he'd need to achieve his glory, and under the divine guidance of Allah, his mind miraculously provided him with the perfect concept.

Money was the root of evil, according to Mohammed, but Bander found no problem in raising ten million dollars for his glorious new plan of jihadist mayhem. Ten million dollars from decadent Middle Eastern princes and a friend from ISIS to pay a group of international hackers, working surreptitiously out of Ukraine, to join him and his six Saudi brothers in an attack on America.

For the past week, Bander and his followers had watched with growing interest the mutiny on the Montana and the memorandum issued by its fifteen officers. But like most everyone else in the world, they considered it a ploy by the U.S. government to dissuade any future Islamist attacks on their nation, and certainly not something they would ever really do. Nothing had happened after Al Qaeda's recent attack on four Western jets or the jihadist assassination of Monique Besson. Americans were too politically correct and morally bound to initiate such an overt act, which left Bander and his men relishing the very idea of flaunting their own willingness to die for their God-inspired cause.

It was late autumn, and the drought-ridden hills of Southern California were burned to a crisp. It hadn't rained in over six months, and as the land shimmered under the unrelenting sun, Bander and his six jihadist warriors drove into the outskirts of Los Angeles on seven separate motorcycles. During the previous three months, they had ridden together, perfecting their plan, which was now coming to fruition on this perfect one-hundred-degree day, with blistering Santa Ana winds sweeping in from the Mojave Desert. It was like being back home in the summer cauldron of Riyadh, and Bander considered it yet another sign and blessing from Allah for the destruction he was about to inflict upon his enemy.

In one hour, it would be the hottest, windiest time of the day and with everything in place, Bander sent an encrypted text to his professional hackers in Ukraine to initiate their pre-planned attack on the electric grid of Southern California. It had never happened before; experts had warned of the possibility, but few had imagined the culprits would be Islamic terrorists.

Spread out along the base of the Santa Monica Mountains, from Ventura County all the way to Griffith Park, less than two miles from downtown Los Angeles, Bander and his jihadist warriors started their motorcycles, ready for war. They were trained like machines, dedicated like Marines, and filled with uplifting joy at the prospect of fulfilling their jihadist dreams and destinies. Today was the chosen day, and with a little luck they would even survive their mission and retell the glory of their exploits, inspiring yet another generation of jihadists.

With over five million air conditioners cooling the homes and schools and businesses of Southern California, the stress on the electric power grid was considerable. So when the first transformers began to shut down, the power companies believed it was a local event, the stress of yet another blistering day. But when the entire system quickly ceased to operate, they knew it was something more cataclysmic, a sophisticated hacking attack they could not control.

Traffic lights stopped working, all communications ceased, people on life support systems struggled to breathe, and everywhere police officers and firemen rushed to help the needy. And in that sea of chaos and distraction, Bander and his fellow jihadists rode their motorcycles through the gridlock, around the accidents, and started dropping incendiary devices along the tinder-dry hillsides of the Santa Monica Mountains from Thousand Oaks to Griffith Park.

One uncontrolled fire on a day with gusting sixty-mile-an-hour Santa Ana winds would be a disaster for the city - but with over one hundred blazes being set within an hour, the entire mountain range was quickly engulfed in flames. People trying to flee their homes and the ensuing inferno created even more pandemonium. Thousands of citizens abandoned their cars on gridlocked freeways and roads, trying to outrun the unrelenting flames, which reached the coastline in less than two hours, leaving hundreds of thousands of people engulfed in a firestorm that looked like the surface of the sun.

People swam out into the sea trying to breathe, trying to comprehend, trying to survive. Even some of Bander's own men became victims of the chaos they had created, as other citizens stole their motorcycles in a desperate effort to escape the all-consuming fire. It was a disaster of biblical proportions - a man-made holocaust. Bander, overcome with the splendor of his victory, fell to his knees facing the east and praised the Lord Mohammed for his wisdom, his goodness, and for destroying all those who failed to recognize the virtue and glory of his holy being.

Chapter 65

THE president was at the United Nations giving his speech about the escalating dangers of terrorism when the first news of the disaster in Los Angeles reached New York. iPhones began to flash, aides to ambassadors whispered details of the attack in a hundred different languages, and in just a few moments, even the president felt compelled to end his speech and retreat to the White House, where he issued a National State of Emergency to deal with the crisis.

In today's world, news travels fast, and in less than an hour, the terrorist organization ISIS was claiming responsibility for the attack and its ensuing firestorm. Aerial photographs and pictures from the space station confirmed the extent of the disaster, and it quickly became apparent that as many as 100,000 people may have perished in the conflagration that would cost tens of billions of dollars to restore.

At first, the president wanted to fly directly to California and lend his personal presence to the rescue, but with all infrastructure destroyed in the immediate crisis area, he decided to stay in Washington and work from the White House. In a strange twist of geography, California was isolated from the rest of the country by the great western deserts, but within hours the nation was mobilized, and waves of aircraft, military and otherwise, started landing in the surrounding surviving cities, bringing in supplies and help, and removing the severely injured.

With ISIS and Bander's surviving jihadist warriors claiming responsibility for the attack, militant Muslims around the world began to celebrate in the streets, while those less inspired by radicalism still smiled discreetly, rejoicing in the success and glory of their God-inspired jihadist warriors. The victory was, after all, yet another step in their religion's prophesied destiny of world domination.

But as the victors celebrated and the fires burned across the Santa Monica Mountains, the potential threat of a nuclear attack on the Middle East by the Montana mutineers grew exponentially. Stock markets crashed around the world. Oil futures soared. And with the nation enraged and people around the world living in fear, the president found himself in the unsavory position of trying to calm the anger of his own people, admonishing militant Islam for its deplorable attack, and beseeching the Montana mutineers not to respond to the violence.

"Over 100,000 Americans died today in a manmade firestorm of catastrophic proportions," said the president to a waiting world. "That's more than all the American men and women killed in the wars of Korea, Vietnam, Iraq, and Afghanistan combined. All in the name of jihad. All in the name of a religious point of view that not even most Muslims reputedly believe in. But terrorists do not live in a vacuum; they need financial support, places to hide, and help in their attacks, all of which is provided by the Muslim diaspora. And now America has its own terrorist organization that threatens the Muslim world. Many people believe the Montana mutiny is a contrivance of our government, an attempt to spread fear into the jihadist world and force them to stop their attacks. But I can assure you that is not the case. This threat is *real,* and I'd like to take this moment to implore the mutinous crew on the Montana not to respond to this reckless attack on America. Something has to be done to stop this never-ending escalation of violence, and I implore Captain Besson and his men to take the first step in bringing a new peace to the world. Both Christianity and Islam teach forgiveness and love as their founding principles, and I beseech every one of you to consider the consequences of continuing this violence that is now consuming us all."

It was a difficult speech for the president to make, particularly considering the fact that his all-consuming emotions were now rage and revenge, the same sentiments shared by the Montana's mutineers. But he was the designated Leader of the Free World. The moral, responsible president of the richest and most powerful country on Earth, and there was ultimately nothing he could do to change anything that wasn't politically incorrect.

Islamic terrorism was an amorphous enemy, a militant religious ideology lurking in Muslim societies around the world, where power-centric imams manipulate their selectively educated followers into a state of perpetual God-inspired war. Religious martyrdom had become the preferred weapon of militant Islamists, who convince their acolytes that dying for their cause would give them never ending heavenly bliss with just the push of a button. It was the perfect job for someone too lazy and self-deluded to get a real job, create a real life, or even have a personal relationship with whatever gods may be.

Still seething at the position in which he found himself, the president returned to the Oval Office to prepare for a National Security Council meeting about the ever-escalating crisis.

"Nice speech," said Gary peering into the office.

"Platitudes. That's all I've got left." He heard something beyond the window. "What's going on out there?"

"Demonstrators. They want us to use the Montana."

"You've got to be kidding."

"There's just a few now, but there's probably going to be a lot more coming." He lowered his voice. "Charlotte wants to see you before the NSC meeting. She's in my office."

"Bring her in. Everyone's already at the meeting."

Gary ushered Charlotte into the Oval Office and discreetly left. The FBI Director had been up all night, but that was not evident from the way she looked.

"So, how did you do?" asked the president switching his mindset from the California fires to her investigation of Pierce.

"Good," said Charlotte placing a pile of papers on his desk. "These are all calls General Pierce made on his private line at ODNI."

"How did you get this?" inquired the president, surprised.

"He hacked us, we hacked him."

"I thought they had their own proprietary encryption system?"

"They do. But what he said is less important than the numbers he communicated with." She pointed to the sheets. "Pierce made over twenty encrypted calls to Vice Admiral Acker before he shot himself, then multiple calls to a number in Sydney, Australia, and to the same number in Bali after that."

"The same person?"

"Yes, Moshi Ilyche, the first carrier; and he's still having conversations with him, including one last night, part of which Gary overheard, when he saw Ilyche hand a note to Pierce in his car. A car that we have now definitely established as Pierce's."

"But Pierce was one of the first to turn Acker in."

"He knew he was going down, so he moved on. The art of sedition; they write books about it."

"And the rest of these?" asked the president flipping through the remaining pages.

"We're still going through them."

"So you think he's running the whole thing?"

"I think it's a possibility," said Charlotte. "But he could still have other people over him."

"So what do we do?"

"Well, there's certainly enough evidence here to put him with at least two of the known conspirators."

"Is that enough to arrest him?"

"At least enough to force his resignation."

"And you're absolutely sure about this?"

"Yes."

The president took a deep breath, "So, do we confront him now or after the NSC meeting?"

"That's up to you, sir."

The president checked his watch, "Okay, well we better get down there. Why don't you go ahead, and I'll follow you."

"He may already know we've hacked him," said Charlotte.

"I already figured that."

Charlotte left and the president gathered up her papers and handed them to Gary in his adjacent office. "Put these in a safe place."

"How safe?"

"Very safe. Take them home with you." He started to leave, then turned back. "You know what, give them to me. I might as well face the truth now."

"There'll be a lot of warmongers down there today."

"Yeah, and I'll be one of them."

"Well, remember what happened to George Bush. He got talked into a war that cost trillions of dollars, killed more of our boys than 9/11, and didn't fix anything."

"You think I don't think about that everyday?"

Chapter 66

The president entered the Situation Room just moments after Charlotte, a coincidence not missed by General Pierce.

A strange collective rage simmered beneath the surface of the gathered NSC members as news footage of the California firestorm, and celebrating jihadists, played on the room's video monitors.

"All right, everyone, let's sit and get on with this, and can someone switch off those screens?" He turned to Pierce. "Is there anything new on the people who did this?"

"Students from Berkeley. Four Saudis, one Kuwaiti, the rest from the Emirates. All Sunni-Wahhabis."

"And the hackers?"

"Professionals working out of Ukraine. We've already picked up two of them. Said they were paid from banks in the Middle East."

"And how about the Montana, anything new on that?"

"I believe David has something," said the Secretary of Defense.

Admiral Stossel checked his notes and addressed the president. "Less than six hours ago, one of our *Virginia*-class attack subs made contact with the Montana and is believed to have been destroyed in that confrontation."

"They sank one of our ships?" exclaimed the president.

"Yes, sir. It appears that way."

"So they have no intention of accepting my offer of amnesty?"

"I don't know the answer to that, sir. Maybe they didn't hear about the offer, or maybe they were defending themselves?"

"So where are they now?"

"We believe they're still in the Sunda Subduction Zone, continuing north along the coast of Sumatra," said the Secretary of Defense.

The president took a deep breath. "So how are we going to respond to this attack on California? There has to be something we haven't tried yet."

A strange silence fell over the room, everyone aware of the one sure way to stop it all - the nation's first unbridled, politically incorrect terrorist organization.

"Maybe it's not something we have to do anymore," said the Secretary of Defense. "Maybe it's just something we don't have to get involved with."

"What are you saying Bob; that we start condoning the Montana?"

"I'm just considering the facts in light of what happened today, sir. As you said, this has all gone on too long."

"Launching nuclear weapons to solve this is not going to happen on my watch, I can tell you that now."

"Then why do we have them?" asked Mack Hayden, Head of the Joint Chiefs.

"Deterrence, Mack. Something you're well aware of. You want to launch a nuclear weapon just to prove we have one?"

"I think someone has already come to that conclusion, sir."

The president could literally feel the consensus building against him. The toll of radical Islam had finally reached a tipping point, and the consensus for tolerance and peace was being replaced by a new political expediency.

"So what do you think, Tom?" The president turned to General Pierce, barely disguising his disdain. "You think we should step back and let the Montana become the arbiter of our foreign policy? Fifteen young men on a submarine…or is it more than that? How many people do you think are really involved in this conspiracy?"

It was a provocative question, and Charlotte glanced around the room waiting for Pierce's response.

"As of today, I don't think who did this is the issue anymore," said Pierce, strangely unruffled. "The only important thing now is what the world believes, and the idea that this is a purely independent terrorist uprising involving fifteen misled young men is a scenario that best protects the nation's credibility and your credibility as well, sir. If that scenario is undermined, there will be international tribunals set up to try you and everyone else in your government involved in this."

Charlotte finally stepped into the fray. "Those tribunals would have absolutely no jurisdiction in this country, General, and you know that."

"That's true Charlotte, but an international warrant for the arrest of any of us is not something to be taken lightly. Germany is still paying reparations for their misconduct in World War II. So we'd be facing the same problem if people can prove our government's involvement in any of this. But if the Montana's crew did initiate an attack on the Middle East as a pure act of terrorism, what could the world say? We all know that terrorists can get away with anything." He was flirting with sedition, and the Secretary of Defense hurried to cover him.

"I think what Tom is saying, sir, is that considering what happened today, a witch hunt of our military's involvement would be counterproductive. This endless war is costing the nation too much money, too many lives, and too much time that should be spent on more productive things."

"He's right," agreed Mack Hayden. "It's time someone taught these people a lesson they won't forget."

"And you really think they won't respond to that?" asked the president. "There'll be even more attacks."

"Attacks by who, sir? When that submarine's finished with them, there won't be any of them left."

"So what are you saying, Mack? That annihilating the Middle East is acceptable to you?"

"I'm a marine, sir. Annihilation is my business. And with all due respect, if you really want to end this once and for all, you'll have to make it your business as well."

"Is that some sort of threat? Because if it is, you're stepping on thin ice."

"No, sir, it's just a reality check for everyone here. We just lost over 100,000 of our citizens in California, and like Bob said, it's time to put an end to it."

"You mean, let someone else put an end to it?" The president was at the cross roads and reached out, fingering Charlotte's incriminating papers stacked on the table in front of him. It was a moment not missed by the Director of the FBI or Pierce, who both knew what was in those papers.

What should he do? Maybe unrestrained terrorism was the only way to fight terrorism.

Maybe the mutineers knew more of life and people than he did. But then again, where would it all end; had anyone even considered that? "So what happens after they've blown up the Middle East, Bob? Do they tell Congress what to do next? How about the Presidency or the Joint Chiefs of Staff?"

The Secretary of Defense was ready with his response. "Like you said in your speech, sir, all terrorists have their backers, or they cease to exist. I think it's quite obvious that the backers of the Montana, whoever they are, have only one thing in mind, and that's ending Islamic terrorism."

"With terrorism?"

"With whatever it takes, sir."

"So what you're advocating is that I sit back and let the Montana take care of this?"

"No sir, I'm advocating that we continue trying to destroy the Montana, but if we fail and the Montana succeeds, we've at least covered our asses."

"So, how much longer before the Montana's in range of the Middle East?"

"Just a few hours."

"Well, regardless of your dreams of a quick solution to all of this, gentlemen, I still expect that sub to be stopped, and I expect it to be stopped now. So let's get on with the jobs you were hired for and keep me informed." He grabbed his papers and left the room, barely hiding his rage.

The president's wife and Gary Brockett were in the White House residential quarters watching the disturbing international news when the president joined them, still flushed with frustration.

"What happened?" inquired Tat.

"They want to let the Montana blow up the Middle East. Just like everyone else in the country." He poured himself a double Scotch.

"You sure you want to do that right now?" asked Tat concerned.

"Yes, I'm sure! They should all be fucking court marshaled!" He slammed his glass into the sink, shattering it.

"Well, if they are siding with the enemy, why don't you do it?"

"Because if I do anything that exposes anyone in our government's involvement in any of this, my entire administration will be held responsible."

"So why don't you just fire them all?" suggested Gary. "People get fired all the time for incompetence. It doesn't mean to say you or they are involved in the mutiny. At least that way, you'll get rid of them."

"They'll just be replaced with more conspirators, Gary. There's no way to know who's in this and who isn't anymore! And besides that, they can set me up anytime they want."

"Set you up how?" questioned Tat.

"Perception. All they have to do is say that I knew about this."

Gary's phone rang and he answered it. "It's Charlotte; she says she has some important information she'd like to give you in person."

"Send her up."

Gary passed on the information to Charlotte and hung up. "You want us to leave you on your own?"

"No! At this point, you're the only advisors I have that I can trust."

An aide let Charlotte into the president's private quarters, and Gary quickly led her to the president and his wife.

"What did you think of that fiasco?" asked the president referring to the NSC meeting.

"I think General Pierce found out he'd been hacked and came up with a surprisingly clever defense: take him down and he'll take everyone with him."

"Yeah, and there's nothing I can do about it."

"Well, if you stop the Montana, you can do anything you want," said Charlotte.

"And you know how to do that?"

"We just found Moshi Ilyche, and he said he'd arrange for you to speak with John Besson if you give him and his wife presidential pardons and immunity for his help."

"Where is he?"

"Just got off a plane in Israel. The problem is if you don't take the deal, it'll be a long wait to get him extradited. The Israelis are tough on protecting their own people."

"So how would we do it?"

"He said he'll make the call the moment he receives your pardons."

"Can he really do that?"

"I don't know, but I don't see any other choice right now."

"Okay, let's do it. But he and his wife will have to sign affidavits of secrecy about this whole thing."

“Very good, sir. I’ll draft an agreement with the Attorney General and get you in contact with Besson as soon as I can.” She left and the president looked a little happier.

“Best person I have in the whole government.”

“She’s a woman,” said Tatiana with a grin.

“So what are you going to say to Besson if you get to him?” Gary asked.

The president looked bemused. “I don’t know.”

CHAPTER 67

LIKE some unstoppable harbinger of death, the massive nuclear missile sub Montana moved silently closer to the Middle East, three hundred feet beneath the surface of the Indian Ocean. Inside the black-hulled vessel, John Besson sat in his small captain's cabin watching his wife's press conference, recently downloaded onto a computer. She was combative and convincing in setting forth all the reasons why her husband and his men had taken over their missile sub. It was everything they had discussed prior to the mutiny, all of the issues stated in their memorandum, clarified in her answers to the predictable press...and then she was assassinated. The image was grotesque, and Besson played it over and over again, his expression never changing.

They all knew they were going to die. It had all been anticipated, and Besson turned to other images of jihadist carnage: the collapsing Twin Towers, his sister-in-law's jet slamming into a Colorado field, California burning, and then the most egregious image of all in his mind, twenty-one Egyptian Coptic Christian men dressed mockingly in orange jump suits, forced to kneel on a Mediterranean beach, where Sunni ISIS fanatics grotesquely hacked off their heads in front of the whole world. It was an affront against humanity, perpetrated in the name of Allah, and Besson allowed the bloody images to seep into his brain, destroying all possible moral reasoning that might dissuade him from the ultimate revenge he was about to administer to the world of jihad.

There was a quiet knock at the door, and Besson called out, "Come in." Garcia, his XO, peered into the room. "Everyone's ready, sir."

"Okay, I'll be right there." The Captain took one last look at the grotesque beheadings on his computer then left on his own mission of revenge and annihilation.

All fourteen of the Montana's mutineers, including Garcia, were gathered in the sub's control room or listening on the intercom. They were all clean-shaven, still dressed in appropriate uniforms, and stood respectfully as their commander entered the room.

"At ease gentlemen, as you all know, today is good luck Friday, the day we initiate our own war against militant Islam. You've all seen the president's offer of amnesty, the Pope's plea for forgiveness, California burning, and all the other acts of terrorism inflicted on the free world in the name of jihad. So this is the last time for anyone who has any doubts about our mission to state your grievance."

"...and get off the boat," said Garcia, which elicited laughter from everyone, including the Captain.

"Very well, gentlemen. With no regrets, we will launch our first weapon in exactly," he checked his watch, "fifteen minutes from now. Slow turns to five knots, twelve degrees up on shearwater planes; proceed to launch depth. Mr. Flynn, prepare your first weapon for its preselected targets."

"Aye, aye, sir." Lieutenant Flynn, the weapons officer who had replaced Lieutenant Chang, left with another officer as the helmsman pulled back on the helm, starting the deadly missile sub up to its prescribed launch depth.

"U.H.F message from 'M', sir. Needs to speak with you urgently."

The radio operator handed the printed message to Besson, who confirmed its authenticity from a series of coded numbers. "What the hell does he want?"

"That's all that came in, sir."

"Okay, send up the buoy."

"Aye, aye, sir."

The radio operator initiated a series of procedures that released a towed radio buoy up to the sea's surface, positioning an omnidirectional antenna that connected the Montana to Moshi Ilyche through a series of untraceable satellite and internet connections.

"Allah Akbar," said Moshi, speaking into his iPhone, sitting in a hotel room, watched by two Mossad officers.

"'M', how you doing buddy?"

"Not my best day, but I'm back in Israel, and President Anderson wants to speak with you."

"So you're getting out?"

"They've got pictures of me and Gwen everywhere in the world, John. There's nothing else I can do."

"So you made your deal?"

"Yes, I did."

"And it's signed?"

"Yes, it is."

"Okay, good luck to you my friend, thank you for everything. You can put him on the line."

The president was in the Oval Office with Charlotte Ramsey, Admiral Stossel, Tony Russo, and his personal assistant, Gary Brockett. They were a select group of trusted friends, and the tension in the room was palpable. This was the last chance to interdict the Montana, and everyone knew it.

Admiral Stossel handed the president a typed sheet. "These are the procedures he should use to end hostilities and surrender his vessel. Admiral McCracken is standing by to speak with him personally from

PACOM if he has any questions."

Russo gave him another sheet. "And this is your list of why they shouldn't do it."

"Anything else?" asked the president.

"He may ask you for an opportunity to speak publicly," said Charlotte. "So you should have a response for that."

"I'll let him do it."

"And how about amnesty for any of the others?"

"That'll have to be negotiated." The president wasn't ready to let anyone else off the hook.

There was a knock at the door, and the president's secretary peered into the room. "They're ready on the phone now, sir. You want to take it at your desk?"

"Yeah, that'll be fine. Okay, everyone, keep your fingers crossed. Charlotte, I'd like you to stay behind in case I need a female voice." He sat at his desk and lifted the phone as everyone but Charlotte left. "Hello, this is President Anderson."

Moshi spoke first from his guarded hotel room. "This is Moshi Ilyche, sir. John Besson is on the line with me."

"John, I hope I can call you that."

"That's fine," said Besson.

"So we find ourselves in a predicament here. I understand all the reasons you and your men have done what you've done, and although I don't agree with your methods, I can certainly empathize with the reasons, particularly after the murder of your wife, for which I offer you my condolences."

"She was killed for exercising her First Amendment rights. Not something Islam encourages."

"Well, it's a tragedy whatever the reason, and what I'm trying to do here is prevent anyone else from losing their lives over this. As you probably know, I'm not a professional politician, John, and like you, I want to try and make the world a better place, but I don't think the methods you and your men are pursuing will solve the problem."

"So what are you going to do to end it, Mr. President? Another ground war? Another trillion dollars on measured responses? More spying on our citizens? More embarrassing excuses for what they keep doing in the name of God?"

"We're winning the war, John. ISIS is in retreat everywhere."

"And when they're gone, there'll just be another group to replace them. We've been dealing with this for over a quarter of a century, and it keeps getting worse. You're not dealing with a country, Mr. President; you're dealing with a religious order that wants to force its values on the world, because they ultimately believe it's preordained."

"So you're doing this because of their religion?"

"No. We're not interested in their religion; we're not interested in their Sharia law; we're not interested in their caliphate or their misogyny. They can do whatever they want in their own countries. We're just interested in ending their war of terror against us."

"And you think blowing up the Middle East is going to do that?"

"They chose the war, Mr. President; we're going to end it. The problem is you keep applying western values to people that don't think like us. They think kindness is a weakness. They're on a religious quest where lying and dying to achieve that end is encouraged by Muhammad himself."

"They just want to worship God in their own way, John. You're going to destabilize the whole world to punish a few people?"

"It's not just a few people, and the world is already destabilized. Every country has had to deal with the problem of militant Islam and the Middle East for decades. They're a drag on the whole world."

"And what about international treaties that have kept us safe from nuclear war for seventy years – are you just going to ignore those as well?"

"We're terrorists, Mr. President. We don't give a damn about rules and treaties. We're exactly like militant Islam, and our mission is to destroy their culture, their religion, and their economies, just like they want to destroy ours. The only difference is we have 176 nuclear weapons with which to do it."

The noise of a claxon became audible on the phone. "You hear that?"

"What is it?"

"It's the launch warning. Just twelve more minutes to a new world, Mr. President. You should celebrate the occasion and thank God for your new American terrorist organization."

"My God would never condone such a thing."

"Precisely the point. Their God does." He hung up the phone, and the president sat in silent dread.

"He hung up?" questioned Charlotte.

"Yes."

"You want me to try to get him back?"

"No. He said he's launching now. Did you speak with his friend, Ilyche?"

"Briefly."

"And what did he say?"

"He said it all started with an imam in London who encouraged his jihadist followers to bomb the plane flown by his sister-in-law."

"And where is that imam now?"

"He's moved back to the Middle East."

"Well, I guess he's going to pay for his sins." He opened the door to his office, drained of hope, and addressed the others waiting outside. "He said he's launching in twelve minutes, and nothing's going to stop him."

Everyone looked incredulous.

"And you couldn't talk him out of it?" questioned Gary.

"No. What time is it in the Middle East now?"

Russo checked his phone. "Just coming up on six a.m., sir."

"So what do we do? Do we tell them what's going to happen, give them a warning?"

"I don't think you should do anything," said Stossel. "They haven't launched yet, and if they do, there's nothing they can do to survive what's coming anyway."

"And what about our own people?"

"We've been pulling them out, discreetly, for the last few days."

"And the ones still there?"

"It's too late, sir. And if we say anything before it happens, it'll look like we're part of it. I'll get everyone back into the Situation Room."

He left with Charlotte and Tony Russo.

"You want me to do anything?" asked Gary.

"Just tell Tat what's happening, and stay with her."

The president saw General Pierce entering his office down the corridor with an aide and quickly joined him, addressing the aide.

"Can you leave us, please?"

"Yes, sir." The man left and the president confronted Pierce.

"You need to stop that sub now, Tom. I know you're involved, and you need to stop it. If you don't, I'm going to have you arrested and court martialed."

"If I go down, Mr. President, so will you and your whole administration. So what would be the point? There's nothing you can do to stop this now, so you might as well get used to it and turn it to your advantage. And for the record, I'm not one of them. The boys on the sub did this on their own. I just became a sympathizer like a lot of other frustrated people."

The president's secretary appeared in the doorway, addressing her boss. "A fishing boat just sighted what appears to be the Montana, and Admiral Stossel is requesting you in the Situation Room."

"Okay, on my way." He turned to Pierce. "You coming, or do you already know what's going to happen?"

"I'm coming," said Pierce, following the president into the elevator connecting the underground Situation Room to the rest of the White

House.

"You're a traitor to the world and everything that lives in it," said the president as the elevator doors closed.

"You know the reason why they're doing this?" questioned Pierce, unmoved by his statement. "To make it possible for you to achieve all the things you said you were going to do for the country. We all believe in you, and that's why we voted for you. But this endless war of jihad is eating up all the money and energy needed to achieve it. And all you do is keep talking about measured responses."

"So you're going to take the law into your own hands?"

"There are no laws of engagement with terrorists. That's why you can't end this. The only thing they will respond to is the same terror they're inflicting on us."

"So you're going to become just like them?"

"You're in a war without end, Mr. President. How are you going to respond to what happened in California today?" The president hesitated. "Well, I'll tell you. There will be no more measured responses, and that includes the North Koreans. We're now in the business of annihilation, like Mack Hayden said. We've had enough of this, so we're going to end it, and you need to deal with that for the sake of your country and for everything that makes our way of life better than theirs."

But the president had had enough, and exercised his ultimate prerogative.

"I'll expect your resignation immediately."

"The trouble with that, Mr. President, is that I'm the only intermediary you have left with the boys on that sub, so you should think about that before you make your final decision."

"I've already thought about it, and you're out."

"You didn't think, you just reacted to your emotions, and even you know better than that."

The president felt like he was living in some alternate universe. This couldn't really be happening. Eight nuclear weapons about to be launched at the Middle East, and he was responsible for it. They were his weapons, his submarine, and he could do nothing to stop it. He'd come into office hoping to rebuild the nation, but like multiple presidents before him, the problems of the Middle East and their endless tribal and religious wars had sucked up all of his energy. Now he was about to face the greatest crisis of all: a new, homegrown terrorist organization with enough firepower to literally destroy anyone they wished, including the presidency.

CHAPTER 68

THE entire NSC had reconvened in the Situation Room when the president and Pierce arrived. Everyone was preoccupied with a video screen, where five fishermen on a boat were trying to grab the Montana's radio buoy. The apparatus looked like a large, black World War II bomb with hydrodynamic smooth edges and a single fin on the underside of its tail. Over four feet long, the buoy skimmed under the waves, towed by a cable attached to the Montana, invisible beneath it. The shaky image was being filmed by one of the fishermen on his smartphone and relayed to his friends on the internet using FaceTime.

"What are they doing?" queried the president.

"It's the Montana's radio buoy," said Stossel. "It's being towed on a cable, and it looks like they're trying to grab it."

"Who are they?"

"Local fishermen. The FaceTime feed's coming from a Sri Lankan phone; they're somewhere off the southern coast of the island."

"Do we have any assets in that area?"

"One Aegis cruiser, the USS Lake Erie. She's at least five hours away," said Stossel. "Admiral McCracken is deploying her to the area now." He looked back at the video screen. "I'm surprised they haven't pulled in that beacon."

One hundred and eighty feet beneath the Sri Lankan fishermen, the crew of the Montana continued their launch countdown.

"Nine minutes to launch," said Garcia, sitting at the weapons control console. "Commence missile pressurization." He was running down a checklist, speaking in a calm, modulated voice.

"Pressurization initiated – all systems now on line," responded the Chief Weapons Officer Flynn, now standing with Besson and his second officer at a computer terminal in the cavernous missile silo. The hiss of compressed nitrogen filling the rocket's shell emanated from the weapon's launch tube. The inert gas would protect the missile's interior from water seepage as it exited the sea.

Besson and his men looked small and insignificant surrounded by the towering missile tubes, but with the new Chinese launch system now operational, the captain and Lieutenant Flynn had control of a weapon with as much explosive power as all of the bombs dropped on Europe during World War II, a conflict that killed over 70 million people.

Checking the launch readout on the computer terminal, Besson turned to Flynn. "Excellent work, Lieutenant. You're all set. I'll be in the CONN." He left the two officers as Garcia continued the countdown.

"Eight minutes to launch. Flood tube one."

Lieutenant Flynn initiated the order. "Tube one flooding." Rushing water could be heard filling the massive launch tube.

Besson joined Garcia in the weapons control room. "How we doing?"

"Everything's good. Tube filling. Spinning up missile now." He was referring to the rocket's inertial navigation system. "Launch hatch opening in twenty seconds."

As the massive missile sub slowed for its launch, one of the Sri Lankan fishermen snagged the radio beacon's cable with a gaffe and pulled it to the stern of the fishing boat. He was like a kid catching a giant fish. But when the beacon's cable reached the stern it snagged the boat's propeller, entangled its spinning drive shaft then ripped the entire apparatus from the boat's hull. It was a disastrous event, stopping the boat dead in the ocean as water gushed into its torn stern.

Fearful of sinking, the fishermen tried to stem the flood of water as the entire radio buoy was dragged beneath the sea by the weight of the fishing boat's propeller and drive shaft. In just seconds, the entire apparatus slammed into the stern of the Montana and its massive propeller. It was like something hitting a blender; the large float slamming multiple times into the spinning blades of the sub.

Garcia looked up, startled by the noise. "What the hell is that?"

"Shut it down!" yelled Besson, "Something hit the prop!" The helmsman quickly disengaged the propeller.

Distracted by the launch and his additional responsibilities, the radioman suddenly realized he had left the radio beacon on the surface and tried unsuccessfully to wind it in.

"It could be the radio beacon, sir. I forgot to bring it in! It could have snagged something on the surface."

Besson was furious but contained his rage, quickly trying to counter the problem. "Let me see the wing camera."

The sub's engineer, Parker, switched on a fiber optic camera on the sub's wing, revealing its multiple launch tubes and the stern of the vessel. It was there to observe missile launches, but the radio buoy's cable could be clearly seen, dragged taut over the stern of the sub.

"There it is," said Parker, pointing to the screen. "Looks like it's caught on the prop."

"Let's try and reverse it," said Besson. "Slow turn."

The helmsman repeated the captain's order, and the propeller slowly turned in the opposite direction, followed by a loud clunking sound.

"It's not going to work," said the captain. "Shut it down!!"

The prop stopped and the sound abated. "There's something

tangled on it. We're going to have to take her up."

The sonarman finally saw the fishing boat on his screen and turned white. He'd failed to notice it with all the launch activity.

"There's a small vessel on the surface, sir. It's hardly registering."

"What kind of vessel?!"

"Wooden boat by the looks of it."

Besson cursed as his XO added to his problems. "Do we continue the launch, sir?"

"NO! We'll be a sitting duck if we reveal our position now! Put it on hold!"

The control room weapons officer spoke up, alarmed. "We've already flooded the tube, sir. Pressurization will only last seven minutes."

"Repressurize it!" yelled Besson, sending the officer rushing to the sub's silo as he turned back to the sonarman. "Anything else in the area?"

"No, sir. It's all clear."

"Okay, let's take her up. Flood ballasts one and two, and let's get some small arms up here." He turned to Parker. "Get a couple of breathers and some tools. We're going to have to cut loose whatever it is. And remember, the entire world is looking for us, so we'll have no more than fifteen minutes before they see us on a NOSS and send in a missile."

Ninety feet above the rising Montana, the fishermen were still trying to plug the hole in their boat's hull, now inundated with water. They stuffed canvas into the hole, and tried to bail out the water with plastic bowls but to no avail.

Halfway around the world, the president and his NSC advisors were still watching the drama through the fisherman's FaceTime connection, but the phone was now sitting stationary on the boat's bridge as its operator sent out a mayday message on the radio. Speaking in Sinhalese, then repeating himself in broken English, he gave out the sinking boat's GPS coordinates, his voice reflecting his growing fear.

"What were those numbers?" queried Stossel, writing on a pad in the Situation Room.

Pierce repeated the coordinates, which Stossel passed on to Admiral McCracken on an open line to PACOM in Hawaii.

"Looks like they're going down," said the president. "You think the sub's still there?"

"I don't know, but at least we have a fix on her now."

Suddenly the fishermen turned their attention beyond the bow of their boat. There was something there that gave them hope, and they started waving and yelling towards it.

"Looks like they've seen another vessel," said Stossel.

In the ensuing excitement, the camera phone was retrieved by its owner and re-directed to the bow of the sinking fishing boat, where the Montana could be seen, breaching the surface 150 yards away.

"It's the Montana!" exclaimed Stossel, both pleased and surprised by the sub's appearance.

CHAPTER 69

AT the Nimitz-MacArthur Control Center in Hawaii, Admiral McCracken sat with Fleet Master Pete Yannis in front of the room's giant digital screen, where one of the Navy's NOSS satellites was already zooming in on the fishing boat's coordinates, and newly confirmed location of the Montana.

"There she is!" exclaimed Yannis, pointing to the sub taking shape on the video display. "Doesn't look like she's moving."

McCracken walked closer to the screen where the Montana was now clearly visible. "Must be something wrong with her. How far is she from the Erie?"

Yannis deferred to one of his staff officers. "Two hundred and thirty eight miles, sir. Should be there in just over five hours."

"Too long!" said McCracken. "Let's see if we can take her out with a SM-6."

The SM-6 was a surface-to-surface, over the horizon, anti-ship weapon, and the admiral quickly explained his plan to Stossel on the open line to the Situation Room.

It was good news, and Stossel passed it on to the president. "They've got her on the satellite now, so they're going to try and take her out with a missile."

"How long will that take?" queried the president, feeling a glimmer of hope.

Stossel conferred with McCracken. "Less than fifteen minutes, sir."

Two hundred and fifty miles south of the Montana, the captain of the Aegis missile cruiser Lake Erie, stood next to his chief weapons officer as he input the Montana's coordinates into an SM-6 missile, already waiting to be launched. Everything was double-checked, then cleared for firing. A launch klaxon echoed across the ship. The order to "Fire Missile" was given, then in a roar of billowing flames and smoke, the large rocket lifted from the ship's deck, on its mission to save the Middle East and rescue America's reputation as a reliable, politically correct nation.

With water still cascading from the Montana's main deck, Besson opened the hatch on the sub's towering wing and climbed out onto the bridge. He was accompanied by the sub's warrant officer, McKenzie, clutching an M16 automatic rifle and extra clips.

From the bridge, Besson could clearly see the five fishermen now abandoning their sinking boat in a small, motorized skiff they had been towing behind their vessel. It was another problem to deal with, and Besson spoke to McKenzie as the skiff turned toward the Montana.

"Don't let them come too close. And tell Jones to bring up some water and food for them."

Forty feet beneath the sub's wing, Parker and three other officers appeared from the rear hatch and ran down the long deck toward the sub's stern. They were carrying diving equipment, assorted tools, and a rope to clear the sub's prop. Two of the officers also had Beretta M9 pistols strapped to their waists.

Time was of the essence, and as Besson scanned the surrounding horizon with binoculars, Parker and another officer reached the stern and jumped into the sea, wearing masks and small, underwater breathers.

The ocean was clear, and the divers could easily see the radio buoy and the fishing boat's propeller and drive shaft tangled around the sub's huge prop by the buoy's cable.

Bursting back to the surface, Parker quickly explained the situation to Besson through a head set held out to him by an officer on the deck.

"Any damage to the prop?" queried the captain.

"Nothing I can see," said Parker, already breathing heavily.

"Okay, see if you can get it off. You've got ten minutes."

Parker dived back under the sea, as the fishermen's skiff approached the sub. Besson could now see the young fisherman with his phone filming everything and looked frustrated.

"Warn them off. I don't want them any closer."

McKenzie called out to the fishermen on the sub's PA system. "Do not come any closer! We are getting you food and water."

The fishing boat paused, and its captain yelled out in broken English, "You owe us money for the boat! And you need to take us back to land!"

"What did he say?" asked Besson, speaking with the deck officer on his headset.

"He said we owe him money for his boat, and he wants us to take them back to land, sir."

Besson spoke to Garcia in the sub's Conn. "Get ten grand out of the safe and give it to Jones with the food." He switched back to the deck officer. "Tell him we're getting him some money and to stay where he is."

Fifteen feet beneath the sub's stern, Parker and his assistant unraveled the fishing boat's prop and drive shaft from the missile sub's propeller. It was arduous work, and streams of bubbles flowed from their breathing apparatus as they raced against time.

The president and his NSC staff, plus McCracken and his PACOM crew in Hawaii, were still watching the Montana and its unfolding drama on the fisherman's phone feed. The image was shaky and amateurish, including selfie shots of the operator, excitedly narrating what he was seeing in his Sinhalese dialect. The fishermen had now realized the submarine was the Montana, and speculated about the possibility of receiving a reward for finding it.

"They already know it's the Montana," said the president.

"Well, if they get any closer, that missile's going to take them out with it!" Stossel said, checking his watch, feeling the pressure.

"How much longer?"

"Six minutes, sir. Looks like they've got something on the prop and are trying to get it off."

"How accurate is that missile?"

"Almost one hundred percent with the satellite."

The video feed from the fisherman's phone began to break up.

"The battery's running out," said Pierce.

The president hissed a curse, revealing the intensity of his frustration. "Can't we see it on the satellite feed?"

"Let me see what I can get," said Stossel.

McCracken had the satellite feed patched through to the White House in less than one minute. It was a high-resolution video feed from space, clearly showing the Montana. But without sound and color, it lacked the immediacy and clarity of the fisherman's camera.

This was probably going to be McCracken's last chance to destroy the Montana, and by now he was looking forward to achieving that end. His ambivalent feelings about the sub's survival were now playing havoc with his conscience, and he looked forward to ending the whole episode. Just another six minutes and it would all be over.

Traveling at over 2,000 feet per second, the Lake Erie SM-6

surface-to-surface missile was already closing rapidly on the Montana. Time was running out, and Besson checked his watch. It had been over twelve minutes since they had surfaced, and he could literally feel the missile bearing down on him.

Everything was taking too long. He looked down at Lieutenant Jones, the ship's navigator and one of the deck officers transferring several containers of food and water to the fishermen. But it was not the supplies that interested the Sri Lankans; it was the cash, given to them by the lieutenant.

"How many dollars?" demanded the captain, trying to count the money.

"Ten thousand," said Jones, expecting a smile, but receiving a rebuke.

"Ten thousand is not enough. My boat is worth fifty thousand!"

"Well, that's all we have," countered Jones.

"No! I will not accept it! It is nothing! It is an insult!" He tried to give the money back.

"What's going on?" shouted Besson from the bridge.

"He wants more money!" said Jones.

"Tell him to send a bill to the US Embassy for the rest!"

"They will not pay anything!" yelled the irate fisherman, now looking at Besson. "You are the Montana! You must give me the rest now, or I will tell the whole world where you are hiding!"

Besson couldn't believe his whole odyssey to rid the world of militant Islam had come down to haggling about the price of a boat with a third world fisherman.

"They already know we're here!" countered Besson. "There's already a rocket on its way. And if you don't leave now, it will destroy you as well!"

"If that were the truth, you would not still be staying here!" replied the fisherman. "We will not leave until you pay us!"

Besson had had enough and turned to McKenzie. "Put a round in his gunnel."

McKenzie opened fire with his automatic M16 rifle, blowing holes into the skiff above its water line. The noise of exploding bullets and splintering wood quickly sent the fishermen retreating in their skiff.

Fifteen feet beneath the Montana's stern, Parker and his partner could hear the muted gunshots. They had already cleared the sub's prop of the buoy and the fishing boat's propeller and drive shaft, but the cable was still wrapped tightly around the main bearing. It was not something they could move by hand, and Parker signaled upwards to his partner and rose to the surface, yelling to the deck officer.

"We can't pull the cable off the drive shaft! Try turning it in reverse three times."

The message was passed on to the sub's command center, and the giant propeller slowly turned, unraveling the last of the cable. It was an answer to prayer, and Parker yelled with delight. "That's it! She's all clear!"

Even Besson looked relieved and yelled back to the men. "Okay, get them out of the water! I'm taking her down!"

The moment Parker and his partner were pulled on board Besson sent a message to control. "Helm ahead flank speed! Prepare to dive!" It was the order he'd been waiting to give, and the sub surged forward under the force of its giant propeller.

Fleet Master Yannis was the first to see the Montana moving on the Pacific Command's satellite feed. "Target moving – bearing two-seven-zero!"

McCracken turned to the weapons officer monitoring the SM-6's telemetry. "How long before impact?"

"Ninety seconds, sir."

“She’s already going flank speed,” said McCracken.

The president and his NSC staff could also see the Montana’s movement, and the president expressed his concern to Stossel. “Will that missile be able to follow her?”

“Yes, sir. The SM-6 has its own independent tracking system,” said Stossel. “It’ll override the original coordinates.”

“Sixty seconds to contact,” said Yannis, continuing the countdown.

The president and his staff turned their attention back to the video screen showing the Montana, now leaving a wake as it picked up speed.

“She’s going down!” said Stossel.

“How long will that take?”

“Less than a minute, sir.”

McCracken shook his head. “It’s not going to get there in time.”

The fleet master could feel his growing concern. “Thirty seconds to impact, sir.”

It was a race of good against evil – the Navy’s latest surface-to-surface weapon against a doomsday submarine with the potential to destroy the world.

“Twenty seconds to impact!”

McCracken walked closer to the screen. It was the slowest countdown in history, and he weighed all the details he had put into the Montana’s survivability, including her speed and ability to dive rapidly. Would she make it, or would the massive warhead of the SM-6 win the day?

“Ten seconds to impact! Nine…eight…seven….” As the fleet master continued his count down, the president prayed for the sub’s annihilation, while others in the room hoped for a different outcome. It was like the divide in the nation, those still clinging to hope and political correctness and those that had given up on the cause.

The dive klaxon was still echoing through the Montana as her crew maximized the sub's speed, pushing its abilities to the limit.

Besson was now running on instinct. All the lessons and simulations of his diligent, competitive career rushed through his mind at once. It was the last moment, and as the main deck of the sub dipped beneath the surface, Besson yelled, "Left full rudder, ninety degrees!"

The quick turn slowed the sub, but it also required the incoming missile to realign its trajectory. And that small adjustment, that last instinctual change of direction and speed, sent the Lake Erie's SM-6 missile slamming into the ocean eighty feet in front of the sub and off to her starboard side.

It was a miraculous miss, but the concussion of the exploding missile blew the 560-foot long Montana onto her side, her propeller spinning free in the air before she finally settled back into the water and continued her pre-set dive. The double-hulled sub held together under the onslaught, but inside the massive vessel, the concussion ruptured pipes and ripped electrical systems from the walls, showering the control room with water, steam, and flying sparks.

Several of the crew suffered concussions, cuts, and bruises, and Garcia yelled above the noise, doing a quick head count and status report.

"All crew members and all systems still operational, sir!"

The captain was relieved, but there was now another pressing concern presented by the weapons officer.

"We're still on hold for the launch, sir. You want to abort and use another missile later?"

"NO! I want to finish it NOW."

Chapter 70

THE bright flash of the exploding SM-6 missile momentarily obliterated the satellite's video feed to the president and his advisors, in both the Situation Room and Hawaii. But when the image returned, the Montana was no longer there.

"What the hell happened?" said the president. "Did we get her or not?"

Stossel didn't know the answer, and deferred to McCracken. "Any evidence of a hit on your end, Jay?"

"Nothing I can see, but I'm not sure you'd see an oil slick or debris on this system."

"So how are we going to resolve this?" continued the president. "The whole world's waiting for an answer!" He caught Pierce observing him, waiting for the same information, but with a preferred, alternate ending.

"We'll have the Lake Erie there in less than five hours," said McCracken. "In the meantime, ODNI is trying to reach the fishermen directly on their phone. Hopefully, they have extra batteries."

"We have them on the line now, sir," stated a signals officer in the control center.

"Can you patch it through to the Situation Room?" queried McCracken.

"Yes, sir. Open line going through now. He's still using FaceTime. Image looks good."

"You want to conduct the interview on your side," questioned McCracken "or leave it to us?"

"I'll do it!" said the president impatiently, as the fisherman's image appeared on the screen in front of him.

"Hello? Is anyone there? Hello? To who am I speaking?"

"You are speaking to the President of the United States, sir."

"Well, this is good to hear because you owe me $40,000 for my boat which your submarine just sank, plus another $2,000 for my little boat that they have just shot holes into! You see this, and this here?" He revealed the damage with his phone's camera.

Like Captain Besson, the president couldn't believe he was now being hustled by a fisherman from Sri Lanka while the world waited to know its fate.

"What is your name, sir?"

"My name is Tharindu Madugalle."

"Well, I'm sure we can arrange to take care of all your problems, Mr. Madugalle, but the most important issue facing everyone right now is what happened to the submarine?"

"That may be important to you, Mr. President, but the $42,000 you owe for the boats is even more important to us!"

The president shook his head, incredulous. "Well, considering the fact that you're in a boat, in the middle of the ocean, how do you expect me to do that?"

"It is very simple, sir. I will give you my bank account number and you will wire the money directly into that account, which my wife will be very happy to confirm." He paused as a loud, roaring sound echoed through the phone, followed by the excited voices of his fellow fisherman. "Oh my goodness! Oh my God, they are crazy people! They have just sent up a rocket of their own! It could have killed every one of us!"

"What kind of rocket?" asked the president, fearing the worst.

"A very big one! It came out of the water. But I will not give you any more information until I have received my money! So, let me get that account number and call you back."

The moment he mentioned a rocket, Stossel was on the phone with McCracken, who was already receiving the same information from the nation's early warning satellite system.

"We've already got it on the DSP. Same coordinates, bearing two-seven-zero. It's heading directly toward the Middle East." You could hear the gravity in McCracken's voice.

"Is there any chance we can shoot it down?" asked the president.

The Secretary of Defense shook his head. "We don't have any ABMs (anti-ballistic missiles) in that area, sir. Only the Israelis have them, but I can't imagine them trying to save people dedicated to destroying them."

"So there's no way to stop this?"

"No, sir. It's too late." The secretary's words echoed through the president's mind like a death sentence to his sanity. He felt like he was being engulfed in a great darkness.

"We have to let them know what's happening. I don't care about culpability anymore. I have to tell them!" He stood up, everyone sharing the depth of his concern.

"It's not going to make a difference anyway," said Mack Hayden. "The Russians just picked up the launch and are going to DEFCON-2."

"For what reason?" asked the president.

"They don't know where that rocket's going, sir. It's just standard procedure. They posture up; we do the same. We need to get you up on Air Force One now, sir. You can make any statements from there."

"I'm not running away from this."

"It's national protocol, sir."

"I don't give a damn." He turned to his advisor, Russo. "Get a camera crew up to my office now. I'll write my own statement. How long do I have?"

"Less than twenty minutes, sir."

But as the president started for the door, a familiar singsong voice brought him back to another reality. "Okay, Mr. President, I have my bank number and address now. It is 'Mr. Tharindu Madugalle and the bank is…"

"Can someone shut that off?" snapped the Secretary of Defense, frustrated.

"No, take down his information and pay him!" ordered the president. "It may be the last good thing I ever do!" He left the room, and General Pierce couldn't help but respond.

"He's going to panic the entire Middle East."

"Isn't that what you wanted?" asked Charlotte, not hiding her disdain. "Spread a little terror of your own?"

"No, Charlotte, I just want them to stop attacking us. I lost my only son and my wife in California today, along with a lot of other innocent people. It's time to put an end to this."

Chapter 71

Gary Brockett and the president's wife continued their vigil of the news from the residential quarters of the White House. There was more graphic coverage of the inferno in California, people's reactions around the world, the growing fear of a response from the Montana, and endless speculation about the mutineers true motivations, and the possibility of a government conspiracy.

It was an escalating crisis made even worse when a breaking news report from the Kremlin announced the launch of a submarine-based intercontinental ballistic missile (ICBM) in the direction of the Middle East. Tatiana stood up, trying to comprehend the madness of it all.

"Oh, my God, this can't really be happening!"

"I don't think they'd say it if it wasn't," said Gary.

"How could they do this? They're completely mad..." But before she could finish her sentence, the television announcer interrupted with more breaking news.

"We are interrupting this broadcast with an urgent message from the President of the United States."

Tatiana watched in horror as her husband appeared on the television screen, speaking from the Oval Office.

"Fellow citizens of the world, I have just been informed by the Secretary of Defense that the mutinous crew of the missile submarine Montana has launched a Polaris intercontinental nuclear weapon in the direction of the Middle East. As yet, we don't know where the missile's multiple warheads are directed, but we're urging all people in the threatened region to take shelter underground immediately."

The shockwaves of the president's announcement echoed around the world. In just minutes, millions of people in the Middle East took to the streets, trying to flee the major cities. It was like some biblical Armageddon. Chaos ruled. People fought each other to get into basements and underground parking lots. Children were separated from their mothers, families turned on each other; cars and aircraft fleeing the threatened areas collided on roads and runways. There was no compassion left, even rescue workers ran from the infirmed and injured to save their own lives.

If terror was the intent of the Montana's mutineers, they had achieved their goal on a scale never before seen. It was a disaster shared by the entire world, but it was only the beginning. The intercontinental ballistic missile had not yet delivered its eight 100-megaton nuclear weapons, each one thirty times bigger than the bomb that devastated Hiroshima and killed over 130,000 human souls.

After finishing his statement in the Oval Office, the president returned to the Situation Room, calling his wife on the way.

"You okay?"

"Yes. How are you?" asked Tatiana, hardly containing her emotions.

"I'm going back to the Situation Room."

"Do you know how long before it happens?"

"We don't know yet, but it's soon. You'll probably see it on TV before I do. Is Gary still with you?"

"Yes."

"Okay, I'll speak to you later."

A foreboding silence hung over the Situation Room. No one wanted to contemplate what was about to happen. Images of the chaos descending on the Middle East played silently on multiple screens, but everyone focused their attention on one single video showing the early warning satellite's view of the Montana's Trident missile. Even though the rocket was traveling at an incredible rate of speed, it seemed to move slowly against the backdrop of the vast, encroaching Middle Eastern deserts.

It was a place the president had spent a lot of time making documentary films. He'd been to Yemen, filming its perpetual tribal and religious wars. He had ridden into Baghdad with George Bush's victorious army, then documented the country's dissolution into unrelenting Sunni/Shia conflicts. He'd spent time in Afghanistan and Saudi Arabia, where Islamic fundamentalism had bizarrely regressed its citizens into a world that mockingly resembled the Dark Ages. And last, but not least, he'd visited Israel and Jerusalem, where the three great monotheistic religions, Judaism, Christianity, and Islam, had blossomed into being over 2,000 years ago. It was a miraculous place, permanently scarred by the adherents of those great religions, who, after all that time were still fighting and killing each other in the names of their perfect, compassionate, all-loving gods.

The video images surrounding the president in the Situation Room now bore witness to the culmination of all that rage, and the madness it was about to inflict on all of its participants.

"Any indication yet?" asked the Secretary of Defense, speaking to someone on the intercom.

"Nothing yet, sir," replied a tracking officer, visible on a screen in the massive National Military Command Center (NMCC), situated in the D-ring next to the Pentagon.

The president turned his attention back to the ICBM feed. "They should have put a self-destruct mechanism into that thing."

"It was discussed by multiple administrations," said the Secretary of Defense, "but there was no way to guarantee that system wouldn't be compromised, so it was eliminated."

"Is there any way to tell where it's going by its trajectory?" inquired Charlotte, preferring conversation to the pervading silence.

"Looks like it's approaching the Arab Emirates right now," said the president.

Traveling at over 20,000 feet per second, 13,600 miles an hour, the Trident missile streaked through the stratosphere, guided by the stars. The astro-inertial guidance system controlled the rocket's velocity and direction, preparing to deploy its multiple, independent re-entry vehicles for their separation and ultimate descent to eight pre-selected targets.

Time was running out for the millions huddled in fear, waiting to see if they were going to live or die. The rocket was a technological miracle. Designed by so-called civilized nations and men for just one purpose: annihilation. The president wondered what madness man had created for his future? He observed Pierce, now aware of the general's lost family, and contemplated if there really was such a thing as karma with its joyous gifts and devastating retributions.

"Missile deploying weapons now," announced the NMCC tracking officer, observing the downrange/crossrange dispersion of the missile's weapons on his large viewing screen. It was as if he were playing a computer game, his voice devoid of emotion.

The nation had created perfect, desensitized human machines to protect itself, thought the president. And for the first time, he began to realize the true indoctrinated nature of Besson and his mutinous crew. They were living in a future where emotions were replaced by the clarity of procedures and the precision of machines.

"Can you ID where they're tracking now?" asked the Secretary of Defense.

"Three MIRV's north towards Iran, two on separate trajectories for the Gulf States, and three heading directly towards Saudi Arabia, sir."

"Any specific targets?" queried the president, now observing the eight nuclear weapons descending like angels of death toward their earthbound destinations.

"Yes, sir. The overlays are indicating principal oil production zones in all four countries."

The president felt a slight easing of his fears. "Any of them near major cities?"

"No, sir. All under-populated areas."

It was better news than expected, and the president looked back at Pierce, realizing the general had known the targets all along. Then the bright flashes of eight separate detonations appeared on the satellite feed. It was no different than a video game, each target's coordinates, calmly identified by the tracking officer, along with their Arabic and Farsi geographic names.

"Looks like they're destroying all the major oil fields," said the Secretary of Defense.

"How many people live in those areas?" inquired the president, relieved and disgusted at the same time.

"We won't have that information for a while, sir. But every unprotected person within seventeen miles of each detonation will be eliminated, plus all above ground structures within ten miles."

"And how about radiation?"

"That will go on for months, sir."

Chapter 72

Within minutes of the nuclear detonations, stock markets collapsed around the world, as people everywhere watched the horror of it all on their televisions. At first, it was all madness and disarray. The planet had been wounded and everyone could feel its pain. Images of the dead, billowing mushroom clouds, and endless smoldering devastation gave a glimpse into the future, where even the earth itself could now be destroyed in the name of revenge, religious fanaticism, cultural differences, and historical hatreds.

But it did nothing to lessen the anger that had caused the original problem.

"We're getting multiple reports of embassies and American businesses being attacked around the world," said General Mack Hayden, handing the president a transcript as images of the attacks began to fill the room's multiple screens.

Even non-radical Muslims were now expressing their desire for revenge. The rage was palpable. Pakistan threatened a response with its own nuclear arsenal. The world had descended into madness, and the president turned on Pierce and his Secretary of Defense, unleashing his own rage.

"I told you this would happen! You've turned a religious war into a fucking world war!"

"It'll be short-lived," said Pierce, surprisingly calm.

"The whole world's turning against us, and you think it's short-lived?"

"The whole world still has to face the fact that this is a terrorist act against terrorism, sir. And as much as they want to blame America, they're still going to have to deal with the Montana."

"They believe we *are* the Montana!"

"It doesn't matter what they believe!" countered Pierce, as forcefully as the president. "Only the facts on the ground stand, and the facts are clear. The Montana dictates the future!"

"So what about this – and this – and this!!" exclaimed the president pointing to the anti-American violence invading the surrounding screens.

"Its just hysteria. In the end, they still have to face the fact that Islamic terrorism will no longer be tolerated, and will carry a price they cannot absorb."

Suddenly, over the images of anti-American mayhem, the superimposed face of John Besson appeared on the screen, his stoic features dominating the chaos he had created.

"Turn up the sound!" said the president, as the mutineer began to speak in his calm, modulated voice.

"My name is John Besson, commander of the nuclear submarine Montana. You were warned in our memorandum that any more terrorist attacks on the non-Muslim world would be met with our own response, and now, that declaration has been demonstrated. This time we limited our attack to the source of your wealth and self-sufficiency. Next time, we will go after your families, your cities, and your radical religious leaders, who have fomented this war in the name of Allah. So once again, the decision is in your hands. But if you still have that uncontrollable urge to wage jihad against the rest of the world, go ahead and make my day. I'll look forward to responding."

His words sent a chill around the world. There was no doubt left in anyone's mind that he meant what he said. You could even see his words affecting the rioters on the video screens as they heard his words and began to lose their resolve. In just one attack, John Besson had established himself as the final arbiter of what would now be tolerated on the planet, and every politician around the world, including the American president, militant Islamists, and North Korea, took note.

For the president it was like a nightmare that had come to life and destroyed his very soul. He had come into the White House filled with hope and grand dreams of a better world and now faced nuclear annihilation. He needed to get away; he needed to think, he needed to breathe, and he left the Situation Room without saying another word. People in the corridors of the White House acknowledged him, but he made no effort to respond.

What should he do? Margaret Thatcher had said to George Bush after 9/11, *This is no time to go wobbly*, which was the perfect description of how he now felt.

Tatiana was waiting for her husband at the door of the Oval Office when she saw him approaching down the corridor. She could see the weight of it all on his shoulders and the fermenting anger in his eyes.

"You okay?"

The president shook his head and entered his office, closing the door behind his wife. "They blew up all the oil fields. We don't know how many are dead yet." He walked to his desk and took a sip of water, trying to contain his feelings. "Now we're going to face the wrath of the world. And what's even worse, that sub is still out there!"

"They'll get them in the end," said Tat, trying to be positive.

"I'm not so sure about that."

The red phone in the room suddenly rang, shrill and demanding. It was the Russian President, standing at the window of his own office in Moscow, and the president answered him.

"Vladimir?"

"I underestimated you, my friend. What a brilliant idea! You even sank one of your subs to make it all seem real!"

"I know you don't want to believe this," said the president, "but we didn't do that. They did it on their own."

The Russian smiled. "Well, however it happened, we should both congratulate them. The militants are in retreat, and the price of oil is back over $120 a barrel, which makes us both, once again, the richest countries in the world. But I want to remind you, Jack, if those boys turn that sub against my country, I will hold you and America responsible and act accordingly."

"And as I have already told you, Vlad, I have no control over those people. They're renegades, so I will respond to any attack on my country with the same vigor."

"Well, at least we understand each other," said the Russian President, undeterred in his optimism. "In the meantime, I'm going to enjoy the bounty you have bestowed upon us. Dosvidanya."

The president hung up, and took a deep breath.

"What did he say?" inquired Tatiana.

"He still thinks we're in control of the Montana. And so does most of the world."

"So what are you going to do?"

"I'm trying to figure that out. Is Gary here?"

"In his room."

"Tell him to come in."

Tatiana brought Gary into the office, and the president greeted him.

"How you doing, buddy?"

"Shitty. So I won't even ask how you are!"

"Sit down," said the president, addressing them both. "So here's the predicament or at least one of the many. General Pierce is involved with the men on the Montana, and Charlotte Ramsey now has evidence to prove it. So do I have him arrested or keep him around and try to use him to control the Montana."

"You're talking about keeping him as your DNI?" said Tat, incredulous. "Working with him every day?!"

"You know what they say, keep your friends close, and your enemies closer. At least, that way I'd know what he's doing."

"God, you're going to get dragged into this whole thing yourself now! That's not who you are, Jack!"

"I'm running a country, Tat! I can't afford to make a mistake here! We still don't know how many people are involved in this, and until Besson appeared on the internet, they were burning down our embassies and threatening retribution around the world!"

"And he stopped all of that?" questioned Gary, skeptically.

"Damn right he did! Who wants to go to war with someone you can't see, can't find, and has already demonstrated his willingness and ability to destroy anyone on this planet. I know I don't!"

"So now you want to join him?" asked Tat.

"No. I don't want to do any of this. But considering everything that's happened, maybe it's not such a bad fucking idea."

Tatiana and Gary couldn't believe what he was saying.

"So we're going to become a terrorist nation now?"

"We live in a terrorist world, Gary. Right now the North Koreans are building ICBMs that can reach America, and with the Russians and Chinese giving them cover, there's nothing I can do to stop that. But the Montana can."

"And you don't think that's getting a little crazy?"

"I can't change what's already happened, Gary, and I can't leave another 160 nuclear weapons in the hands of a madman with absolutely no control or contact with him."

The phone rang, and the president answered it. "Yes, Bet?"

"Charlotte Ramsey's here and wondered if she could speak with you for a moment?"

"Send her in."

Charlotte peered into the room. "I know this is the last thing you want to deal with right now, but do you want me to go ahead and have Pierce arrested?"

The president hesitated. It was a seminal moment, and everyone knew it.

"No, I have more pressing things to deal with now."

"So, you want to drop the whole investigation?" asked Charlotte, barely hiding her frustration.

"For the time being, yes."

"Very well, sir. If you change your mind, let me know." As she was speaking, General Pierce appeared in the doorway behind her. For a moment, the two antagonists faced each other then Charlotte left.

"You need to see me, Tom?"

"I just wanted to let you know the Russians just backed down to DEFCON 5. General Hayden's keeping ours at 3 for the next twenty-four hours, just in case there's a response to the bombing."

"Very good. Thank you."

Pierce left and Tatiana turned back to her husband. "I think you just lost a loyal friend, dismissing Charlotte like that."

"I don't have friends anymore," said the president. "Even you guys are against what I need to do now."

"So you're going to join them? Join the enemy?"

"I'm going to do what is best for the country. And if that requires redefining the word 'enemy', I'm going to consider it."

"That's such bullshit!" said his wife, disgusted. "They just killed hundreds of thousands of people! And you're going to condone it?"

"As I already said, I'm going to do what is best for the country."

It was all too much for Tatiana, who stood up. "Well, I'll leave the politics to you guys from now on. I'll see you later."

She left, and the President turned to Gary. "What the hell does she want me to do?"

"She just wants you to be like you used to be."

"And how was that?"

Gary grinned. "A pure and beautiful soul."

"You can't do this job and remain pure. Sometimes, you just gotta do what you gotta do."

"So, what are you going to do?"

"Whatever it takes to win."

Chapter 73

THREE months later, a strange *pax en terra* settled over the world. The kings and princes and theocratic leaders of the Middle East Gulf States were bankrupt, and without oil money, they could no longer finance their endless wars of jihad against the West and the rest of the world at large. But even more importantly, there was no longer any public support for a conflict that had created a new terrorism that was even more hideous and deadly than the one they had unleashed themselves.

The Ayatollah Khomeini had never seen a Clint Eastwood movie and was confused by Besson's words, '*So go ahead and make my day*'. But after conferring with one of his younger acolytes, he quickly got the point. The Montana terrorists were unconscionable, cold-blooded killers, just like the men he used to wage his own undeclared wars, and he quickly came to the conclusion that terrorism was no longer a viable means of nation building. It was a big decision for the spiritual leader to accept and he retreated back to his Koran and the Suras that had encouraged his war of hate in the first place, pondering the question: if Allah really was the only true and almighty god, why were people of other faiths and beliefs doing better than his people?

There were also some unexpected consequences to the Montana's nuclear attack. The North Koreans decided to abandon their nuclear weapon program and America finally withdrew all of its forces from the Middle East. And in that new, uncontested Islamic world, Sunni fundamentalism once again flourished. Without the corrupting influence of oil money, all the temptations of western culture evaporated, giving the imams exactly what they had always wanted: a simple, pious state where Sharia law ruled, women accepted their diminished status, and the ancient words of the great prophet Mohammed once again ruled the land.

As for the Montana, there were occasional sightings and videos of the submarine around the world. Its officers were photographed frolicking on isolated tropical islands. Crewmembers were reputedly seen in casinos and nightclubs, but there were no more statements from Besson. He was a man of few words, and everyone on the planet, including the president, felt relieved not to hear from him.

Love of money is the root of all evil, say the sages, but it can also be the harbinger of better times. And with America's oil and gas industries once again booming, and its defense and Homeland Security requirements rapidly shrinking, the economy grew by leaps and bounds. The president made a new energy deal with China that helped balance the nation's trade deficit, and with the national debt declining, the president finally got his flat tax bill through Congress and put the IRS in charge of stopping theft against the nation's institutions. He also got US companies to repatriate trillions of dollars kept offshore with a new retroactive business tax that was compatible with other countries.

The fortunes of the nation were once again on the rise, and Jack Anderson was its celebrated champion. But Jack knew the real cause of his success and popularity was fifteen men on a submarine who had broken all of the laws of the nation, killed over a quarter of a million people, and were still imposing their will on the planet with their continuing, lurking presence.

It was a complicated new world for the president, accommodating

General Pierce still working as his DNI, and moving the nation forward. But as the country's fortunes soared, things became easier. Guilt and introspection about everything that had happened faded, and the president became the very essence of his new circumstances, a man of compromise, diminished morals, and immense success.

So one day when Gary Brockett called the president and said Charlotte Ramsey was in his office and wanted to see him on a private matter, the president's new persona was put to the test.

"What does she want?"

"She said it's for your ears only."

"Okay, send her in."

The president dismissed Pierce and his national security advisors, who had just finished their morning briefing and greeted the FBI chief graciously.

"Charlotte, long time, no see. I understand you've been getting after the hackers."

"Yes, sir, we're finally getting it figured out."

"So, what have you got for me?"

Charlotte placed an iPad in front of him. "These are all the different recordings of the Montana and her mutineers shot around the world since the bombings."

"And?" questioned the president, unimpressed by the images.

"They were all shot on the same day, and on the same iPhone. Plus, I also have these additional pictures of the Montana's periscope entering the Strait of Juan de Fuca. They were shot at night by a fisherman and given to his son who happens to work for me."

The president looked confused. "So what does it all mean?"

"I think the Montana is back at its base in Kitsap, Washington. And all these videos and pictures were created to give the impression that she's still out there, threatening the world."

"So who else knows about this?"

"Just my assistant and his father who shot the periscope pictures."

"And you're absolutely sure it's the Montana?"

"Admiral McCracken confirmed it himself."

"And did you tell him where it was shot?"

"No, I just said it came from an unconfirmed source."

The president took a deep breath. He was cornered and frustrated, and decided to confront the issue head-on. "You're a smart lady, Charlotte, smart enough to know why they did all this. So, why are you still pursuing it after I asked you not to?"

"Justice, sir."

"My wife said you'd do something like this after I shut you down."

"So why did you do it?"

"Because the needs of the nation transcended your personal needs. You wanted to get rid of Pierce; I needed him for my own reasons. Reasons for which you are well aware."

"General Pierce and his friends killed over a quarter of a million people, sir."

"And they ended the war, Charlotte. Made the country rich again. Put millions of people back to work. Gave everyone a new future, and you want to take all that away? This is the only way I could resolve this. You were there; you saw how it went down. But I don't think you're really that stupid. So what do you *really* want? You want to be a senator? I can arrange that. You want to be the next Secretary of State? I could probably make that happen."

Charlotte smiled. "So this is the new world we're living in?"

"It's the future, Charlotte. You should join it, not fight it."

"And Besson?"

"Decommissioned with his submarine and living in the witness protection program, where he's still available for more videos. The country's on a roll, Charlotte. You should reap the benefits. Take the ride and forget about all this justice nonsense. It's too late for that."

It was a lot to take in, and Charlotte hesitated. "I'll need a little time to think about it."

"I'm out of town for the weekend, so why don't you come and see me on Monday, and we'll work something out."

"Okay, I'll do that. Thank you for your time." She started to leave, and the president called her back.

"You know you can't discuss this with anyone, Charlotte."

"I understand."

The president smiled. "It's good seeing you again."

"You too, sir."

Charlotte left, and the president buzzed his secretary. "Tell Pierce to come back." He took a couple of pills and walked to the window, watching Charlotte getting into her car. Pierce joined him, observing the same view.

"Did she figure it out?"

"Yeah."

"You think she'll keep it secret?"

The president shook his head, disappointed. "I don't think we can risk it. There's also two other people involved: her personal assistant and his father, a fisherman. They figured out all the Montana videos were shot on just one fucking camera!" You could sense the new, practical, cold-blooded Jack in his words.

"I'm sorry about that, sir. I'll take care of it."

They were interrupted by the president's wife, knocking on the door, peering inside. She was dressed in a coat and holding a young, Labrador dog on a leash.

"Jack, are you ready?"

"Yep! Ready and waiting. Let me get my phone." He turned back to his desk, speaking to Pierce. "We're going to Camp David for the weekend. They're culling out some deer, so I'm going to try my hand at shooting."

"Well, be careful the dog doesn't run off when you do it."

"They're already inseparable," said Tatiana. "Do you have a dog?"

"No."

"Well, you should get one. We all need a friend we can trust."

"Okay, let's go!" said the president. "See you Monday, Tom." He took the dog's leash and they left.

Pierce turned back to the window and saw Charlotte driving away. It was a perfect, sunny morning, and the general pushed the talk button on a small radio clipped to his lapel and uttered just two words, "Second option."

Charlotte Ramsey looked back at the White House receding into the distance. She was being driven by her new personal assistant, Matt Weston, who observed her in his rearview mirror, removing a miniature camera hidden in the curls of her hair. It was a new technology, and she plugged it into her cell phone, revealing a perfectly clear image of the president speaking with her in the Oval Office.

"Did you get it?" asked Matt.

"Picture and sound," said Charlotte, displaying her phone. "Network quality; time to bring back some justice."

Her words suddenly felt strangely transcendent, like she was seeing the world from a totally different perspective. Then she realized she was flying through the air, headless, blown to pieces with her assistant, by a bomb that General Pierce could clearly see from the window of the White House.

But the general wasn't feeling transcendent; he was feeling triumphant, celebrating the fact that he was once again the uncontested keeper of the nation's secrets, with all the power and influence that embodied.

Turning back into the Oval Office, the Director of National Intelligence circled the president's desk, and sat imperiously in his chair. It was a perfect fit, and he looked out contentedly at his surroundings. He was at the center of the world, the heart of Western democracy, and the bastion of a new, global terrorist organization. *Touché.*

MANKIND

We dream of gods and celestial beings
We live on hope when there is none
We are the bravest creatures the earth has fostered
Because we know time reaps its harvest, no matter what is done.

Only love is the sign of something grander
Only love lingers after all else has gone
So let's fill our hearts with love, and linger
In that place where God should have been, but is gone.

- *SR*

About the Author

Stewart Raffill grew up on a farm in England and emigrated to America when he was eighteen where he began a business training wild animals for the motion picture industry. Working with many celebrated writers, directors, and actors in Hollywood, Mr. Raffill began writing and directing his own feature films which have taken him on multiple adventures around the world. His globe-spanning career has provided him with unique insights into the politics, cultures, and diverse characteristics of many communities some of which are integrated into his first novel, *Rage*.

ABOUT THE TYPE

THE BankGothic (Medium and Light) typefaces used throughout this book were designed by Morris Fuller Benton for the ATF (American Type Founders) foundry in 1930. These fonts are used for the Chapter Numbering and Incipits, throughout the book. The Minion Pro typeface used in this book was designed by Robert Slimbach. It is used as the main body/narrative font. The BankGothic is licensed via Myfonts.com. This license is included as part of the content.opf (metadata) for the ebook version. The MinionPro typeface is used under an Adobe License. All fonts used in this book and the digital editions of this book are properly licensed and subject to all applicable copyright and software laws.

All fonts used in this book have been subset in the digital edition(s) to disable any ability by any third parties to reuse any of the fonts used in this book.

CPSIA information can be obtained
at www.ICGtesting.com
Printed in the USA
LVOW08*1439260417
532270LV00005B/33/P

9 780998 587318